KU-573-018

Lynda La Plante

TASTE OF BLOOD

ZAFFRE

First published in the UK in 2023
This edition published in 2024 by
ZAFFRE
An imprint of Zaffre Publishing Group
A Bonnier Books UK company
4th Floor, Victoria House, Bloomsbury Square, London, WC1B 4DA
Owned by Bonnier Books
Sveavägen 56, Stockholm, Sweden

A CIP catalogue record for this book is
available from the British Library.

ISBN: 978-1-80418-153-9

Also available as an ebook and an audiobook

1 3 5 7 9 10 8 6 4 2

Typeset by IDSUK (Data Connection) Ltd
Printed and bound in Great Britain by Clays Ltd, Elcograf S.p.A.

Zaffre is an imprint of Zaffre Publishing Group
A Bonnier Books UK company
www.bonnierbooks.co.uk

TASTE OF BLOOD

Lynda La Plante was born in Liverpool. She trained for the stage at RADA and worked with the National Theatre and RSC before becoming a television actress. She then turned to writing and made her breakthrough with the phenomenally successful TV series *Widows*. She has written over thirty international novels, all of which have been bestsellers, and is the creator of the Anna Travis, Lorraine Page and *Trial and Retribution* series. Her original script for the much-acclaimed *Prime Suspect* won awards from BAFTA, Emmy, British Broadcasting and Royal Television Society, as well as the 1993 Edgar Allan Poe Award.

Lynda is one of only three screenwriters to have been made an honorary fellow of the British Film Institute and was awarded the BAFTA Dennis Potter Best Writer Award in 2000. In 2008, she was awarded a CBE in the Queen's Birthday Honours List for services to Literature, Drama and Charity.

✉ Join the Lynda La Plante Readers' Club at
www.bit.ly/LyndaLaPlanteClub
www.lyndalaplante.com
⚏ Facebook @LyndaLaPlanteCBE
⚏ Twitter @LaPlanteLynda

For my readers

Chapter One

DI Jane Tennison arrived at her new station, hoping for a fresh start. She'd been transferred, at her own request, after she had investigated the case of the bodies found in an old air-raid shelter. She had been proud of the way she had handled the complex enquiry, but the DCI had given her little credit and she had found it impossible to continue working alongside him.

Jane had worked at three other stations, on a variety of cases, but none of them had really stretched her. After taking a month's long-overdue leave, she had been eager to find out where she would be posted. She had requested that it be closer to Bromley as the travel had been an issue on the last investigations she had worked on. One case in particular had been centred around Greenwich, which was a long drive from where she lived.

She had become rather disillusioned with her career and had even considered, albeit half-heartedly, quitting the Met. And when she had received the details of her new posting, it didn't immediately make her feel any more positive. Although it was closer to home, the station only had a very small CID section. However, on the plus side, Jane was interested in meeting her new boss, DCI Fiona Hutton. She had never worked alongside a high-ranking woman, and wondered if it would give her career the boost it needed.

Jane was now living with Eddie Myers and they were engaged to be married, although they had not yet agreed a date for the wedding, partly because they had been so focused on refurbishments to the house. Eddie's handiwork had already almost doubled the property's value, and he was now working on the front and back gardens, laying down paving and ordering trees and plants.

During her leave, Jane had enjoyed spending time with Eddie, helping him to put the finishing touches to the redecoration, though at times she had found their lack of a shared interest beyond the house a little bit worrying. But he was so caring and good-natured that she put her doubts aside. And he certainly impressed her with his work ethic. He was becoming increasingly successful as a builder and renovator, and he and his team were working non-stop.

The drive to her new station only took fifteen minutes, and Jane arrived dressed in one of her smart suits, with a white shirt and Cuban-heeled shoes. She had recently had her hair cut shorter at her sister's salon, and Pam had encouraged her to have some more highlights. She was pleased to see there was a parking bay marked 'DI Jane Tennison' on a white plaque, and she was smiling as she made her way to the modern-looking, double-glass-fronted entrance.

Inside, the reception area was small, with a pine desk, typewriter and telephone, and a row of three hard-backed chairs against one wall. The access into the station offices was situated behind the desk and had a security keypad. The door was ajar and as Jane approached, a young, red-haired, uniformed officer walked out.

'Good morning. I'm DI Jane Tennison.'

He smiled. 'Good morning, ma'am, I am Constable Peter Thompson. If you go straight down the corridor, you will see the main double doors for the CID office. I will inform DCI Hutton that you have arrived.'

The young man stepped to one side to allow Jane to pass, holding the door open and then closing it behind her.

The strip-lighting on the ceiling gave the corridor a clinical feel, not unlike a hospital, and it seemed much less atmospheric than any of the stations Jane had previously worked at. Jane hesitated, then opened the door and walked in.

It was a spacious room with a double row of empty desks with typewriters and telephones, all with decent swivel office chairs. Placed along one wall facing the desks was a large whiteboard with various scrawled felt-tipped messages. The office door to one side was closed and had a neat plaque saying 'DCI F. Hutton'. As Jane was taking in the empty room, the office door opened and a middle-aged woman in a tweed suit with a pink blouse came out carrying a thick file.

'You must be DI Jane Tennison. I'm Dora Phillips, head of the clerical staff. I think that desk by the window has been allocated to you. Right now, everyone is gathering for a briefing in the board-room. Usually, we have a meeting on the first Monday of the month which always kicks off at eight thirty so everyone can have break-fast in the canteen. However, this morning there's a lecture taking place in about ten minutes. Now, if you would like to put your coat in the closet just by the double doors, and leave your briefcase on your desk, I can take you through.'

Jane deposited her coat and briefcase and followed Miss Phillips down the corridor to the boardroom.

Jane began to feel nervous as the door closed behind her. Seated around a large table were fifteen officers, some in uniform and others in street clothes. They all turned expectantly to look at Jane. Two of the officers half-rose out of their chairs.

'Good morning,' Jane said.

One of the officers, a big, burly, balding man, pushed his chair back and stood up.

'Detective Constable William Burrows . . . you must be Detect-ive Inspector Tennison. Let me introduce you to everyone, and feel free to take the seat at the end of the table.'

Burrows went round the table making introductions and every-one smiled and raised their hands in acknowledgment. In all the years she had worked at the Met, Jane had never had an introduc-tion like it and found the formality extraordinary. It was as if they were college students.

The double doors opened and DCI Hutton made her entrance. She was wearing an immaculate suit and high-heeled shoes that accentuated her six-foot height. She had thick blonde hair, held by a tortoiseshell clip, and Jane thought she was quite a formidable presence as she moved around the table to stand by her empty chair.

'DI Tennison, I must apologise to you for not being available to welcome you and introduce you to everyone, but I am sure DC Burrows has already done that for me. I would just like to welcome you and give you a brief outline of how we usually work. We normally have a once-a-month informal morning's briefing, but today there's something a bit different.'

She drew back her chair and sat down, giving Jane a warm smile, before opening a large, initialled, leather notebook.

'Detective Paul Lawrence is due to arrive any moment to give a talk about a major breakthrough in forensic science. I felt it would be beneficial for everyone to listen and take notes.'

Jane knew Paul Lawrence well, and when a moment later he was ushered into the boardroom by Miss Phillips, she was really pleased to see him. Paul had hardly changed from when they had first worked together, when she was a probationer at Hackney, although his wavy blond hair was now thinning a little. He gave Jane a quick smile of recognition as he went to stand beside Hutton.

Paul opened a thick file, thanked DCI Hutton for the invitation, and began.

'I am sure many of you have heard of the new scientific breakthrough: DNA. DNA stands for deoxyribonucleic acid, which is a complex molecule that contains all of the information necessary to build and maintain an organism. All living things have DNA within their cells; in fact, nearly every cell in a multicellular organism possesses the full set of DNA required for that organism. Although 99.9 per cent of human DNA sequences are the same in every person, enough of the DNA is different that it is possible to distinguish one individual from another with a DNA profile. To make any test, a smear or swab has to be taken from inside the cheek or mouth. Or you can use blood, saliva, semen, vaginal lubrication and other bodily fluids, or even personal used items like hairbrushes, toothbrushes and razors, which can all have traces of DNA, as well as stored items such as banked sperm or biopsy tissues.'

Paul looked up from his notes and asked if anyone had any questions. Hutton was the first to speak.

'Do twins have the same DNA?'

'Only if they are monozygotic, which means identical. Anyone else have questions, or shall I go on to give you an example, which will hopefully help you fully understand this amazing breakthrough?'

'Please go on,' Hutton said, when no one spoke up.

Paul nodded. 'When a sample such as blood or saliva is obtained, the DNA is only a small part of what is present, so before DNA can be analysed it has to be extracted from the cells and purified.'

It was Hutton again who raised her pen to indicate she wanted to ask a question.

'Could you give us an example of a case that has recently used DNA to obtain a result?'

'Sure. As I have said, this is still a very new science but very soon it's going to become a vital tool, particularly in solving murder and rape cases. In July last year a young girl was murdered, and from the MO the officers were certain the same killer had murdered another young girl in 1983. The police already had a suspect arrested, and a sample of his DNA was compared with the DNA from blood samples recovered at both crime scenes. He was released because his genetic code did not match.'

There were frowns around the table as the officers wondered how DNA evidence had helped solve the case.

Paul waited for a moment before continuing. 'Hard to believe, but a woman in a bar overheard two men talking – one of them saying he had got away with murder because the police had arrested someone else for the crime. The man was traced and his DNA was found to match both crime-scene samples. He admitted to the murder and also pleaded guilty to previous rapes.'

The conclusion of Paul's story was met with unanimous applause, and the meeting broke for coffee, during which Paul answered more questions before continuing for another twenty minutes, focusing on how important it was to observe a strict protocol to protect DNA samples from contamination, and make sure any samples taken were transferred correctly to the laboratories.

When he finished, Jane was keen to talk to him, but he only managed a quick 'Let's catch up soon' before being ushered from the room by Miss Phillips and on to his next appointment.

DCI Hutton asked for everyone to stay and have their usual update meeting but to keep it as brief as possible. Jane opened her notebook as officers began talking about various cases. Jane was surprised that there seemed to be no murder enquiries or investigations into any other serious criminal offences, and instead most of the discussion was about petty crimes and disorderly conduct. The most serious case involved a teenage cannabis possession arrest. DCI Hutton glanced at her wristwatch, and that appeared to be the unspoken signal for the team to get to work. Notebooks were closed and chairs pushed back as Hutton gestured to DC Burrows.

'I'd like you stay, DC Burrows, and brief DI Tennison on the dispute at Clarendon Court.'

Burrows moved his chair to sit beside Jane as Hutton left the boardroom and opened a file bulging with documents.

'Right, this has been quite a lengthy investigation involving a dispute between neighbours that has been ongoing for many years, and is basically about one of them building a fence around his property and a set of gates allowing access into his garden. There were letters and all sorts of insults and lawyers getting involved, until the planning board eventually gave permission for the fence to be built, which is apparently when the dispute escalated, culminating in an incident that left one man in hospital on a life-support machine. I've spent many hours interviewing the families of both parties to try and find out what happened. I have also had a brief interview with the neighbours living opposite, but they were not at home when the incident occurred.'

After initially being disappointed that this seemed to be a case of neighbours quarrelling over a fence, Jane's interest was now piqued, especially when Burrows explained that the victim was still in a critical state and that it therefore could turn out to be a murder case, even though the alleged assailant, Mr Caplan, armed only with a garden spade, was claiming he'd acted in self-defence. She started looking through the documents.

'His wife claims that he was not in any way intent on using it; it just happened to be leaning against a wall when the two men began to argue,' Burrows explained.

Jane turned a page and tapped it with her finger.

'Is this his statement when he was brought into the station? Did Mr Caplan have any injuries consistent with being hit with an iron bar? I see he claimed that he only used the spade to protect himself, as his neighbour had an iron bar and struck him first.'

'Yes, but there was no bruising or other marks where he said he was struck, and no iron bar was recovered from the scene. So Mr Caplan looks like he's going to be facing an assault charge at the very least.'

'I'd like a map of the area,' Jane said. 'It's difficult to visualise the exact layout of the properties. And also the letters regarding the dispute.'

Burrows collected all his documents and handed them to Jane. Then he pushed his chair back and suggested they go into the CID office where a drawing was pinned up on the board.

The large room was busy and Jane put the file on her desk and went to join him in front of the board, where she saw a rather amateurish drawing in crayon showing a large square marked TARMAC.

On one side were the outlines of two substantial properties, along with drives and garages, numbered 4 and 8. On the right-hand side of the tarmac were two smaller properties numbered 10 and 7 respectively, with MARTIN BOON PROPERTY written prominently and in brackets VICTIM.

Then, opposite numbers 4 and 8, there was the most substantial property of all. This was number 12 and the owner was marked as DAVID CAPLAN.

'As you can see it's a very secluded courtyard,' Burrows explained. 'We have an estimate of the value of the properties. Numbers 4 and 8 are fairly new builds and we reckon to be worth £500,000 each, if not more, as they both have extensive back gardens. The two smaller ones, numbers 10 and 7, are more likely around £300,000 as their rear gardens are not up to much. The big property, number 12, would have been the original twelve-bedroomed manor house, with indoor swimming pool, two large gardens and a triple garage – valued at about three to four million. I would say that all the properties around it had been built when the land was sold off by the original owner's heirs. It's now owned by David Caplan. He bought it five years ago.'

Jane stifled a yawn, trying to concentrate, as Burrows tapped the number 12 with his pencil.

'This is the fence and the gates that have been the cause of all the bad feeling between them. Mr Caplan had been given planning permission to take down the fences and replace them with a high wall and a pair of electric gates, even though Boon had objected to the wall and complained to the council. Boon also claims that where the fence is now is four inches over the boundary!'

Jane chewed her bottom lip, then pointed to the tarmacked courtyard.

'Who owns that, or do they all share it?'

'They've all got right of way, but they are not allowed to park there. It's owned by number 10.'

'What? The tarmac area belongs to that small house? That doesn't make much sense.'

Burrows shrugged. 'You tell me! It's owned by Mr and Mrs Larsson, and she is a nasty piece of work; very rude and unhelpful. According to Mr Caplan, her husband has threatened his wife because she had parked outside their own double gates. She was also unpleasant when they moved in, and claimed the new double gates would not be allowed to open outwards as she owned the courtyard.'

Jane shook her head. It all sounded like a very odd situation.

'So, this woman, Mrs Larsson, has she got any involvement in the assault?'

'No, but we think that she is pulling Mr Boon's strings. He seems to have been very friendly with her and easily influenced.'

Burrows looked at his wristwatch. 'I ought to be going to the hospital. If Mr Boon dies, obviously it puts a whole new slant on the enquiry. I'll leave you to go through the file, and we'll get back together in the morning to discuss the next steps. I think Stanley should be back soon, and he'll be able to answer any queries you might have.'

Jane went to her desk. It all seemed so tedious, she had not really been paying much attention to what Burrows was saying. She decided to go and have some lunch before returning to her desk and making some notes.

It was after two when Jane returned to her desk and started wading through the contents of Burrows' file. Jane turned her head when she heard the door opening. She could hardly believe it! DI Stanley stood there, wearing a smart dark suit and black tie, his usual wild hair cut neatly, and with no moustache. He looked older, with lines etched on his face. On seeing Jane, he gave her a wide grin and walked over to her desk.

'Long time no see, Jane!'

He leaned over to give her a kiss on the cheek. She could smell the alcohol on his breath, and he looked quite flushed.

'I didn't expect to see you here!' she said, as he pulled up a chair.

'I could say the same about you! I'm just waiting out the last couple of years for my pension. And then my knee needs replacing . . . same old injury . . . so what's your excuse?'

Jane blushed. 'I haven't really got one, Stanley. I wanted to be transferred closer to home. I live in Chislehurst now.'

He rolled his eyes. 'Yeah, actually I don't live that far from here either . . . but I never thought I'd end up in this tin-pot excuse for a cop shop.'

Jane kept her voice low, moving closer to him. 'I expected we would have our own offices, even more so now I know you're here.'

''Fraid that's down to me. I've always liked to be in the thick of things. I was shown a poxy office, far end of the corridor, so I asked to have a desk here. The office is now used as a storage cupboard. It's better to be in here.'

He leaned forwards to look over the papers on her desk.

'Christ, you been put on this with Burrows. I've been doing the rounds on it, but it's just a bloody load of domestic shite . . . unless the bastard dies, of course . . . then there'll be piles of paperwork.'

'Have you been able to obtain any previous medical history?'

'Not yet. I was going to talk to his GP this morning, but it was Dexter's memorial service, and I wasn't going to miss that.'

Jane felt as if she had been punched in the stomach. She could hardly get the words out.

'A memorial service for Alan Dexter?'

Stanley nodded, his emotions clearly close to the surface.

Before Jane could say anything more, DCI Hutton entered the room and called Stanley over. He stood abruptly and hurried to join her. Jane watched Hutton place a comforting hand on Stanley's shoulder. Then Stanley went to his desk, took a file from a drawer and before Jane could say anything, walked out of the room. Hutton went into her office and Jane got up from her desk and hurried after Stanley.

The corridor was empty. Jane was not sure if he had gone to the gents' or whether he had left the station. Then she spotted young DC Thompson coming down the corridor.

'Have you seen DI Stanley?'

'He just passed me as he headed out of the station.'

'Thank you.' Jane raised her hands in a confused gesture.

'Straight down the corridor and through the car park exit, ma'am.'

Jane ran to the indicated exit, pushed the door open, and went down three steps into the rear yard of the station that was used by the patrol cars. She could see Stanley striding towards a Morris Minor and called out to him. He turned, swinging the car keys in his hand, as she joined him.

'Boss gave me the rest of the day off. I'm sober enough to drive now. Left my car here and got a taxi back from the memorial.'

'I need to ask you about Dexter,' Jane said. 'I hadn't heard anything, and didn't know about his memorial.'

Stanley pursed his lips, then opened the passenger door to toss in the file he had taken from his desk.

'What happened?' Jane asked.

'Get in, it's cold out here. There's always a nasty wind whistling through . . . The high walls act like a wind tunnel.'

Jane climbed into the passenger seat, picking up the file and putting it on her knee as Stanley went round to sit in the driving seat.

'Was it a bomb disposal incident?' Jane asked.

'No, love. Dexter sort of sidestepped from working for that unit. He was on a six-month sabbatical, or sick leave, whatever you want to call it. He got badly burned, but he was recovering well when I last saw him.'

'So what happened?'

'Well, you know what a mad keen racing driver Dexter was. He went over to France to have a private session at Le Mans. Apparently, he'd driven the Sarthe circuit there a couple of times, which is well known for being very fast. He took a sharp right corner, near the River Sarthe. There was another safer circuit he could have driven, the Bugatti, but anyway, he was on the main track driving his Porsche 917 . . . they reckoned he was doing over 120 miles per hour when he lost control. I'm just repeating what I've been told, so I don't know all the details. It was a fatal accident. A family member had his body brought back for a private funeral, then the lads got together for the memorial today. It never made it into the press. I suppose he went the way he lived . . . right on the edge.'

Jane was struggling to swallow; her mouth felt bone-dry. She didn't know what to say, and it was hard to take it all in. Stanley had talked as if he had repeated the story many times.

She took a deep breath.

'Thank you for telling me. Feeling a bit shell-shocked.'

Stanley watched Jane walk back towards the station, feeling relieved that she hadn't broken down in tears. He doubted he would have been able to handle that. He had cried for his crazy, adrenaline-fuelled and fearless friend, even though he had not been that close to him. Not many people had really got to know Dexter, as he always kept himself at a distance, but he could also turn on the charm and be a warm and charismatic man. He had been a real ladies' man and always had a different beauty hanging on his arm; in fact, there had been three ex-girlfriends at the memorial.

Stanley sighed as he saw Jane turn at the station door to look back to him. Her face was drained of colour. He wondered if Dexter had ever screwed her, but he doubted it; she didn't seem his type. He chuckled to himself, realising he didn't know what Dexter's type was; like everything about that man, it was a mystery.

He started the engine and noticed that Jane was still standing by the door. She had pressed her face to the glass panel, and he now suspected that Dexter must have had sex with her. But it didn't matter one way or the other. Now crazy Dexter was dead and buried, it was all in the past. He drove out.

Chapter Two

Jane finished reading all the statements in the file. She made copious notes, and put together a list of suggestions about how they should proceed in the morning. Burrows came to tell her that Mr Boon was still unconscious but stable, and then Jane left the station, trying to block thoughts about Dexter from her mind. She still felt very raw inside but she couldn't allow her feelings to surface until she had some time alone.

To distract herself she went food shopping on the way home. Eddie was parking his van outside the house when she drew up.

'Hi there,' he said cheerfully. 'I've just got to unload some cans of paint I need for the morning. I'll put them in the garden shed.'

Jane let herself in through the front door, went straight to the kitchen and then opened the backdoor. Eddie had built a small shed that dominated the garden, which he used for storing building supplies and garden equipment. Not that he actually did any gardening, as there wasn't much of a garden, other than a flower-bed that she tended to at weekends.

Jane hadn't been particularly enthusiastic about the shed, but Eddie claimed it would save him a lot of time by not having to go to his storage unit. There were numerous ladders stacked against it, which had been there for some time, as there were tiles on the roof that needed replacing. Jane had learned that Eddie's best intentions weren't always followed through, as he was constantly working, often even at the weekend.

From the kitchen window she could see him carrying large cans of paint down the small path at the side of the house. She started preparing dinner while Eddie made trips back and forth between the shed and his van. He appeared at the kitchen door to say that he was going to drop something off at his storage unit and would then be coming straight back.

'How long are you going to be? I've got that pork with crackling in the oven,' she said.

'Fifteen to twenty minutes . . . Is that OK?'

Before she could answer he had closed the backdoor and had disappeared. She peeled the potatoes and put them on to boil, then filled the kettle with water for the fresh broccoli. She had bought the 'meal for two' pork from Waitrose, which had separate crackling to place under the grill.

By the time she had taken a quick shower and changed into some joggers and a sweatshirt, the potatoes were almost done. She drained them and put them onto a baking tray with some olive oil and seasoning to roast them. She took out the Bisto gravy tin and put two heaped tablespoons of granules into a jug, then checked the pork.

Finally the table was laid, she had opened a bottle of red wine, and the plates were warming on top of the cooker.

Ten minutes later Jane took the pork out, placed the crisped crackling on top of it, and put the potatoes and broccoli into a serving dish. There was still no sign of Eddie. She was just about to lose her temper when she heard the front door slam. Eddie appeared at the kitchen door.

'Perfect timing!' He grinned.

She watched him cross to the sink and run the water to wash his filthy hands. He had what looked like brick dust in his hair, and his jacket was covered in it as well.

'Can you take your jacket off because you're covered in dust. I don't want you getting it over the food,' Jane said.

'Right . . . I had to haul a few things from off a tarpaulin in the yard. This all looks delicious . . . I'm starving.'

Jane got up from the table.

'I'll carve, you take your jacket into the hall, and leave it at the bottom of the stairs. And take your boots off while you're at it!'

'Right, you're the boss!'

Jane snatched up the carving knife. It really irritated her the way he constantly left a trail of dust when he got back from work, and he always forgot to remove his work clothes before tramping through the house. She served them both then sat down and took a gulp of her wine.

'Is there any apple sauce?' he asked.

Jane got up, went to the cupboard and took out a jar of Bramley's and plonked it on the table beside him. Eddie poured himself a glass of wine as she sat back down.

'Had a good day?' he asked.

'Not really. For starters, I don't have my own office . . . I suppose I could request one, but the other DI isn't bothered . . . added to that, I'm working on this tedious assault situation with two warring neighbours.'

Eddie grinned. 'Is it about boundaries?'

'Yes, one property is worth a few million and is in a private courtyard. The other property is much smaller and modern; apparently, they're rather cheap-looking houses. For some crazy reason the man accused of the assault has an obsession about people parking on a large, tarmacked area to the rear of the expensive property. He opposed planning permission for years, but it eventually came through recently, resulting in an assault which left one of them in a critical condition in hospital.'

Eddie winced. 'What was the planning permission for?'

'To have electric gates and a wall around his property.'

'So, if it's his land, what's the problem?'

'The neighbour, Mr Boon, claims that Mr Caplan cannot have a wall or gate as it is not in keeping with the other properties. He also claims that the existing fence is one inch over his property boundary and three inches over a tarmacked area in front of all the other properties, which is basically used as a car park. He's been writing abusive letters for years, so when the council at long last approved the application for Caplan to go ahead, Mr Boon went ballistic. That was according to Caplan's wife, at any rate, although Boon's wife insists he is a caring, quiet man who would never get into a confrontation. But I haven't had a conversation with any of them yet.'

Eddie crunched into some crackling. 'Blimey! I almost broke my front tooth!'

'Maybe I did it for too long under the grill, but it's good, isn't it?'

'It is, my beloved one, and you're getting to be a dab hand at the roast potatoes . . . they're really crispy.'

'That's down to your mum telling me how she does them. Anyway, this case . . . the situation is now serious because if Boon dies then it potentially becomes a murder.'

'Listen, I've seen open warfare over property lines and usually it's fences being erected that create the problems. How did he hit the bloke?'

'With a spade.'

'On the back of his head?'

'No, in the face apparently, but he went down hard. Mr Caplan swears he only picked up the spade because Mr Boon had an iron bar and was threatening him. Says he just swung the spade in self-defence.'

'Did they find the iron bar?'

'No, not yet.'

'Well, I'd say Boon just got unlucky.'

'I think part of it is jealousy. I mean, Caplan's property is huge. At one time it would have been the only manor house in the area.'

'Whereabouts is it?'

'I can't tell you; it's illegal if I do.'

'For God's sake! I might even know the place.'

'Maybe, but just forget it.'

'Fine, have it your way. Forgive me for even asking. But how come you as a detective inspector for the CID are dicking around with this kind of nonsense?'

'I am "dicking around" with it, Eddie, because it has serious consequences if the victim dies and it becomes GBH or even murder. The question is whether it's section 18 or 20.'

'All a bit domestic, though, isn't it? I'd have thought you would have been assigned something with a bit more grit.'

'Believe me, I can't wait to get something with more "grit", but right now this is all I've got.'

Eddie put his dirty plate beside the sink, then drained his wine glass.

'Well, I'm going to take a shower, then I wouldn't mind going over some of my accounts with you. Since you encouraged me to keep an invoicing diary, I think I am in better shape than ever, financially. Before, I was constantly waiting on payments.'

Jane shrugged as she cleared the table, annoyed that he had not put his dirty plate and glass in the dishwasher. After clearing everything away and switching on the dishwasher, she went into the hall and picked up his dusty jacket which he had left on the banister. His boots were lying where he had kicked them off, so she fetched an old newspaper, spread it on the floor near the front door and put his boots on top. She then went into the closet beneath the stairs and took out the hoover to clean the hall carpet. By the time she had finished tidying up it was after ten thirty.

Eddie was still in the bathroom when she went upstairs to the bedroom. She sat on the bed and opened her briefcase, checking what meetings she had the next day. Wearing boxer shorts and with his hair still wet from the shower, Eddie walked in carrying his dirty work clothes.

'Should I put these in the laundry basket in the bathroom, or downstairs?'

'Downstairs. I wash them separately because of the dust and grime. The basket is by the washing machine.'

'Right, then are we going to go over the accounts?'

'I'll be down in a minute; I'm just sorting out my schedule for tomorrow.'

Eddie walked out and Jane pursed her lips. How many times had she told him that it would be easier if he took off his work clothes downstairs and put them in the laundry basket by the washing machine? Eddie occasionally did what he was asked, but he constantly had to be reminded. Just as he had to be reminded that when he took a shower, he should put the wet towels over the towel rail, not leave them in a pile on the floor. Jane looked into the bathroom and was surprised to see the towels on the rail, although the sodden bathmat was left scrunched up on the floor.

Eddie was whistling in the kitchen when she eventually joined him. He had made two cups of coffee and had laid out his account books and invoices, along with a stack of potential job offers. Jane sat down and checked over the invoices and dates and smiled.

'This is looking good, Eddie, and the new jobs are quite substantial. Which one are you thinking of taking on?'

'Well, I have to do the estimates, but I think the biggest job is that new block of flats by the station. They want all of the interior and exterior decorated. I would have to take on extra hands to do it, but I dare say I could stall the smaller jobs. What do you think?'

'I would check how much you'd make from the three smaller ones and see what you'd earn. If it's close to the station project, then there would be no need to take on extra workers, which would mean additional wages out of the profits. I'm sure there are a lot of men out of work right now, but you are such a perfectionist, and you don't want to run yourself ragged.'

He nodded. 'I've been talking to Dad about helping me out. If he could oversee the smaller jobs while I concentrate on the station job, that would really help, but he's getting on a bit. What do you think?'

Jane sighed. It seemed that Eddie had already made up his mind and just wanted her to confirm he was doing the right thing.

'It's your decision, Eddie. As you said, your dad is getting on, but he's always handled his own business, so just talk it through with him.'

Eddie gathered all the papers and placed them in a folder with different tabs for banking, work and invoices.

'I think we might be able to get a bigger house soon,' he said. 'You could sell this one for quite a good profit after all the work that's been done on it.'

Jane sighed. 'I don't know . . . we've only just got this one finished. Are you thinking of buying a property that needs doing up again?'

'Of course, but this is your house, Jane, and I want us to have one that we share between us . . . like a family home. I would do all the renovations, and we could stay living here until it's done up, although that would obviously be quite a big investment. What do you want to do?'

Jane suddenly felt really tired. 'I don't know, Eddie. I'll need to think about it. Right now, though, I'm ready for bed.' Eddie picked up their coffee mugs and put them by the dishwasher before getting his diary up to date. By the time he headed upstairs to the bedroom, Jane was already in bed, her bedside light turned off. He switched the main bedroom lights off and climbed in beside her, leaving his bedside light on.

'You going to sleep?'

'Yes.'

Eddie switched his bedside light off and pulled the duvet up, turning towards her.

'You all right?'

'Yes, just tired.'

'No, there's something else. I can tell. Is it about not wanting to move or sell your house?'

'No, it's not that. I got some sad news today, but I can't really talk about it.'

'Why not?'

She gave a long sigh, and when he put his arm around her to draw her closer, she pushed him away.

'Not tonight, Eddie.'

'For God's sake, I don't want sex. I'm just concerned. You said you had some bad news, so tell me what it is?'

'Sad news, Eddie. There was a memorial service for someone I knew today, and I should have been there. I just feel bad that I didn't know anything about it.'

'Who?'

There was a long pause while Jane chose her words. 'Someone I cared about, but hadn't seen for some time.'

Eddie was unsure how to respond.

'He was a bomb disposal expert. His name was Alan, but everyone called him by his surname, Dexter. I worked with him a long time ago. Anyway, he was racing his Porsche in France, or using a racetrack over there, and he crashed. I can't stop thinking about it.'

Eddie made a commiserating sound, and Jane continued in the same soft, unemotional voice.

'He had this great flat that was very modern, and a flamboyant style that I had never seen before. I remember I asked about these three plaques he had on his wall. They were carved wood with gold-painted dates. He said the first date was when James Dean crashed his Porsche and died, the second was the date his brother had died in a skiing accident, but the third one had no date. I asked him why not, and he said that would be the date when he died.'

'Isn't that a bit freaky?' Eddie said, yawning.

'Yes, I suppose so, but now the date can be added.' Jane spoke through her tears but she didn't want Eddie to know that she was crying.

'Did you have a fling with him?'

Eddie leaned up on his elbow, but Jane turned away.

'I mean, was this plaque thing in his bedroom? It sounds to me like he was crazy or had some kind of death wish.'

'You don't understand . . .'

'So why don't you try telling me? You're crying, Jane. Did you have some kind of thing with this guy? Jane? Jane, look at me . . .'

He tried to turn her face towards him, but she jerked away and started sobbing in earnest. He threw off the duvet and turned on his bedside light. She curled up her knees and wouldn't look at him, hugging herself tightly.

'For Christ's sake, Jane, was this going on while you've been with me? I need to know! Were you fucking this guy while living here with me, letting me run around after you doing the house up while you were out shagging this Dexter bloke?'

'Eddie, it was a long time ago,' she said between sobs. 'I haven't seen him for years, and certainly not since I moved in here.'

'How long did it go on for?'

Jane sighed and gritted her teeth. 'For God's sake, it was not a real relationship, Eddie. He was someone I was very fond of and we just saw each other occasionally.'

'I don't believe you, Jane. Why are you crying your eyes out then?'

'Because I didn't know that he had died until today, all right?'

'If it was just someone you saw occasionally, why are you getting so angry with me for asking about him?'

'Please, just leave me alone, Eddie. I don't want to talk about it anymore.'

'Fine, I'll leave you alone. I'm going to sleep on the sofa.'

He walked out, slamming the bedroom door behind him. Jane sighed. She knew that at some point she would have to try and explain to Eddie just what Dexter had meant to her, but that brought on another spate of tears. Eventually she threw back the duvet, got out of bed, put on her dressing gown and slippers and went downstairs.

Jane poured a glass of brandy and walked into the sitting room. Eddie was on the sofa with a rug wrapped over him. She went and sat on the edge of the sofa.

'Is that for me?' he asked.

'No, it's for me. I thought I owed you an explanation . . . not that I think you really deserve one. If you must know, Alan Dexter was someone I met very early on in my career. He was with the bomb squad, and I was with him the night he had to defuse a bomb, on Good Friday, the night of the annual CID dinner. He was a real daredevil character, fearless and charismatic. I think I fell in love with him on that night, but it was more like a schoolgirl crush. To be honest, it was sort of like that all the time I knew him. It wasn't a relationship. I'm not saying that I wouldn't have wanted one because I did, but Dexter was a real womaniser and never gave the slightest indication that there would ever be anything serious between us . . .'

Jane hesitated and sipped her brandy. She had known that whenever she parted from Dexter, they might not see each other again for weeks or even months. Then there were times when he seemed to intuitively know she needed him to be with her, and those nights . . .

Eddie reached over and took the glass from her hand. 'Carry on, Jane.'

'He met someone special, and she moved in with him . . . so I never saw him again.'

Eddie drained the brandy glass and handed it back to her. He smiled. 'And then you met me!'

Jane looked away. 'I need to go back to bed and get some sleep. Why don't you stay put as I know you will be out early, so then you won't wake me up.'

She leaned over and kissed him, drawing up the blanket around him as if he were a little boy.

'Night-night.' She walked out, leaving the empty glass on the table, and hurried up the stairs to her bedroom. She snuggled down, curling up beneath the duvet, and cried for Dexter, who she knew had loved her in his own way, or the only way he had known how.

Chapter Three

Jane sat with Burrows and Stanley in the boardroom discussing how they would proceed with the investigation, given that as yet they had no statement from the victim. According to Burrows, the hospital was confident he would come out of his coma, but it might not be for a few days. Jane asked if there was any information regarding any previous medical issues that could result in a minor blow to the front of his forehead causing his present state.

'Well, I've not been given any details,' Stanley said. 'I spoke to his wife, but she was in such a state when I interviewed her that I decided to ask at the hospital. I talked to a nurse on duty. She couldn't give me any information, and the surgeon wasn't on duty so I couldn't get access to the victim's previous medical history.'

'Well, we will need to get that as soon as possible. You need to talk to his GP to confirm any other medical issues,' Jane said.

Stanley flicked through pages of statements. 'I'm doing that, gimme a break, OK? We questioned his wife about the iron bar, but like Burrows said, she was in such a state. She said she had never seen her husband with one and was certain he went over to see Mr Caplan empty-handed.'

Jane nodded. 'That differs from Mr Caplan's statement then. He said that Boon came through the garden gate waving it around, and that he warned him to get out, but he kept on heading towards him and . . . So basically, it's his word against Boon's, who as we know can't say anything! What about Mrs Caplan?'

'She claims that she was in the kitchen that overlooks the garden, and she heard Mr Boon but did not actually see the assault until her husband called her. She said she had to put their dog away as the gate was open. When she went out and saw him, she called an ambulance.'

Stanley tossed the statement down on the desk.

'I think we need another round of enquiries and a visit to the hospital to see what medical history we can get from them. If you ask me, this is all about jealousy. The Caplans' property is worth millions, and the couple are obviously minted, so Boon was probably just a bitterly envious bastard.'

Jane decided she'd go and talk to Mr and Mrs Caplan while Stanley went to have another session with Mrs Boon and the neighbours at number 10. Burrows was to go to the hospital and then join them at the properties.

Stanley could see that Jane was puffy-eyed, and he didn't want to get into emotional stuff about Dexter, so he suggested they make their own ways there, saying that if there was any new development, one of them could then return to the station.

Jane parked her car outside the double gates of the Caplans' rear garden. There was a NO PARKING sign attached to it, and the same sign was also pinned up on a smaller ivy-covered garden door. The driveway round to the courtyard was very obviously in need of repair, and there were potholes in the tarmac.

No sooner had Jane parked her car than a tall, slender man with wispy, thinning hair approached.

'You can't park there,' he snapped.

'Excuse me?'

'This is a private area; this courtyard is privately owned, and there is no parking.'

Jane locked the car. 'I am Detective Inspector Jane Tennison. I am here to speak with Mr Caplan.'

'You can't park here. Drive to the front of their property and park there. This is private land.'

Jane hesitated. The man was clearly in a tense state, his hands clenched tightly at his sides.

'And you are?'

'Edward Larsson. My wife and I live at number 10 and we own this courtyard.'

'Mr Larsson, as this is police business, I am sure that my parking here will not be a problem. So, if you will excuse me . . .'

He stepped back, his hands still clenched at his sides. Jane went to the garden door and pressed a bell. She heard a dog barking, then after a moment the latch was lifted. An attractive woman wearing jeans with high boots and a crisp white shirt stood in the gateway. Jane took out her ID.

'I'm DI Jane Tennison. I would just like a few moments of your time to answer some questions. Are you Mrs Caplan?'

'Yes, I am. Of course, do come in.' She opened the gate wider, looked past Jane, then raised an eyebrow. 'Oh, I see the Gestapo is out. Did he try and make you drive around to the front of our house?'

'Yes.'

'Beyond belief, but please do come in. Are you all right with dogs? We have a Labrador puppy and he's a bit boisterous.'

Jane followed her down a Yorkstone path, with mowed grass either side. There was a beautiful fountain and numerous olive trees in large wooden planters. To one side there was a patio with garden furniture and a large, rolled umbrella. The walls surrounding the patio were thick with ivy that was growing almost to the roof of the large three-storey house.

As Mrs Caplan opened the backdoor, a large Labrador hurtled out and ran past them into the garden. 'I'll shut him out, but he might make his way round to the rear garden. I just have to keep my eye on him in case he dives into the fishpond.'

The kitchen was enormous with a beautifully tiled floor and a long refectory table with matching period chairs and two long benches. Mrs Caplan offered Jane a coffee, but she declined and asked if Mr Caplan was at home.

'Oh, he's just gone to the post office, he'll be back any moment,' Mrs Caplan said.

Mrs Caplan led Jane to their sitting room, which was furnished with large mirrors and oil paintings crowding the walls. Through a window, Jane could see an indoor swimming pool, with sliding doors to the rear which led to the garden, where the puppy was happily chasing a ball around.

'I was told that you were in the kitchen when the incident occurred?' Jane began.

'Yes, that's correct. I was actually just in the laundry area beside the kitchen. I heard Buster barking and went out into the kitchen as my husband was calling me. I kept Buster inside and saw Mr Boon on the ground and David, my husband, shouted for me to get an ambulance. They came very quickly, thank goodness. Mr Boon's wife came into the garden screaming that she wanted to get to her husband. She was completely hysterical and I tried to calm her down, but then the ambulance arrived. Shortly afterwards the police came.'

'Did you see an iron bar, the one your husband claimed that Mr Boon was threatening him with?' Jane asked.

'No, I was asked that before. The police took the spade, I think; it was propped up by the garden shed not far from the double gates. David was distraught and just said over and over again that he was only defending himself. He had no intention of hurting Mr Boon.'

'How long have you lived here?'

'Almost eight years. We bought it two years before that, but it was in a dreadful state, so we spent that time rebuilding and refurbishing it from the roof down, so we could then put it on the market. David is in the property business, and I am an interior designer. We had hoped to sell over a year ago but this situation with the neighbours and planning permission has been going on for years.'

Jane nodded. 'As you know, I just had a bit of a run-in with your neighbour at number 10. He said I was not allowed to park in front of your gates as it was private property. That seems very strange.'

Mrs Caplan sighed. 'Yes, the Larssons are rather unpleasant, and ownership of the courtyard is a bone of contention. They use it as a car park for themselves and, though we have right of way, we are not even allowed to park in front of our own gates.'

'Did the previous owners have the same problems?'

'I really don't know. But I think they were in a difficult financial situation, and due to the run-down state of the house we got it at a very good price. We've spent a fortune on it as an investment, but with the ongoing situation re the planning permission it has just become a money pit. And now this awful situation with the Boons . . .'

Mrs Caplan was close to tears. Jane plucked a tissue from a leather-bound box on the coffee table and handed it to her.

'I'm sorry, Detective, I can't remember your name.'

'Jane Tennison. Did you keep in touch with the previous owners?'

'No, I think he was a German diplomat, but we mostly talked to her. After they left, we found the rooms infested with fleas, and there were nests of rats and mice . . . It really was unbelievable how they could have lived in such squalor. I think there was something wrong with her.'

'Unlike her husband, who just appeared to be stoned out of his head!' said a man's voice.

Jane stood up as David Caplan walked into the room. He was handsome, with dark black hair and grey sideburns, and a suntan that enhanced his blue eyes.

'This is my husband,' said Mrs Caplan as he sat down beside her. 'Would you like a coffee, darling?'

'Yes, please, Alice. I've been standing in line to post a parcel to my son in the US. There was someone in front of me who had a problem with a post office savings account that took over fifteen minutes to sort out . . . then there was something wrong with her pension.'

Mrs Caplan looked enquiringly at Jane, who nodded. 'Thank you.'

Mr Caplan waited until his wife had left the room. 'Has there been any news about Mr Boon?'

'I'm afraid not, but we have someone at the hospital checking on his progress.'

He leaned back and sighed, shaking his head. 'It's unbelievable. I am obviously aware of the repercussions if the poor man dies. As you can imagine, it's very stressful, especially for Alice.'

'I read your statement, Mr Caplan, after you were interviewed at the station.'

'David, please. To be honest, I was so shaken and confused at the time I gave my statement that I can't really recall what I said.'

'Would you mind if I recorded our conversation?'

'Not at all, not that I think I have anything else to add about what happened.'

Jane placed her tape recorder on the coffee table between them. 'What I would like you to do, Mr Caplan, is to take me through exactly what occurred from the very beginning.'

Jane pressed 'record' as he looked up to the ceiling.

'Right . . . I was out in the small back garden, checking one of the flower-beds because the dog had been digging up plants. Mr Boon pushed the gate open, and he was obviously in a rage as he was red-faced when he came towards me.'

'Can you recall what he said?'

'Yes, it was something like, "I've had enough, you are trying to move the boundary line, I can prove it, I am warning you".'

Jane nodded. 'And then what did he do?'

'He had this iron bar in his hand, and he was swinging it as he was talking, or shouting. He had made numerous verbal threats, vocally and in letters, making accusations about me lying to the council.'

'I will need to see the letters, but can you try to concentrate on exactly what Mr Boon said to you when he confronted you in the garden?'

'I'm sorry, yes. He said he had warned me about the fact my gates were over his boundary, and he was going to prove it and stop any building commencing. I had just had the planning permission granted to erect a wall and electric gates and they had no right to stop me. When I say 'they', it's the Larssons who own the courtyard, and I think they use Mr Boon for their obsession, and it truly is an obsession.'

'Please, Mr Caplan, I just need you to tell me what Mr Boon said.'

'Like I said, he was shouting that he would stop any building commencing.'

'What did you say?'

'I told him to get off my property or I would call the police.'

'That was all?'

'No, I think I swore at him. I called him a mental case, and then he came at me.'

'Just a second . . . How far away from you was Mr Boon when you swore at him?'

'He was about halfway down the path.'

'Then what happened?'

'He started to swing this iron bar at me.'

'Describe the bar?'

'It was about fourteen inches long, not very thick, and he was doing this . . .' He gestured with his right hand, making a swinging motion.

'You seem very certain it was an iron bar, not perhaps a stick?'

'Well, I suppose it might have been some kind of stick, but it looked very solid and it was black.'

'Then what happened?'

'I backed away from him and when he still kept on coming at me, I picked up a spade, to warn him to stay back.'

'Did you warn him verbally?'

'Yes, I told him to get out, but he swung the bar at me again and . . . it was not my intention to strike him with the spade . . . I was just trying to protect myself; I was trying to knock the bar out of Mr Boon's hand, I didn't mean to hit him on the head.'

'Did you strike him with the front or the back of the spade?'

'The back of the spade . . . maybe where the handle joins the spade.'

He went on to describe how Mr Boon had fallen backwards, and then his wife had come running into the garden screaming, and Alice had come out.

'I told her to call an ambulance and I put Mr Boon into the recovery position. Then Buster got out as Alice had left the kitchen door open, so he was running around the garden and Mrs Boon was screeching hysterically. She was trying to get her husband to sit up, but I told her to leave him lying down. Buster went out into the courtyard; you know he is still only a puppy and could have run from the lane into the main road, so I had to get him back, which I did, and the ambulance arrived very quickly after that.'

'Who called the police?'

'Mr Larsson, I think, but by this time I was obviously very disturbed by what had happened, and then the two officers came in to talk to me and then . . .' He sighed, shaking his head. 'I was arrested on suspicion of assault.'

'Did Mrs Boon go in the ambulance with her husband?'

'I don't think so . . . Mrs Larsson came and looked after her and then I think she drove her to the hospital later.'

Alice walked in with a tray of coffee and biscuits as Jane turned off her tape recorder.

'Sorry this took so long, but Buster went back to digging up the plants.'

'I just need to ask a few more questions,' Jane said.

Alice glanced at her husband and he held out his hand for her to sit beside him on the sofa.

'I know you have been asked about it before,' Jane said, 'but it's very important. The officers that were here the day of the incident couldn't find this iron bar.'

Jane switched the tape recorder back on.

Mr Caplan frowned. 'I went into the garden to search for it while the officers were here at the house. We couldn't find it anywhere . . . I mean, it had to have dropped from his hand when he collapsed, but . . . I even looked around the courtyard. Alice, you looked for it as well, didn't you?'

'Yes, all I can think is that perhaps the paramedics took it when they took him away on a stretcher. We told the police officers they should ask the paramedics about it.'

Jane nodded. 'I'll talk to them. There's also a possibility that one of the neighbours picked it up.' She switched off the tape recorder and put it in her bag.

'Thank you for your time,' she said, standing. 'And for the coffee. I will be in touch if I have any news regarding Mr Boon's condition. In the meantime, I suggest you get legal representation, Mr Caplan, just as a precaution.'

'I was advised to do that when I was at the station, but I found it all so ridiculous . . . but having had time to think about it, I've engaged someone – a good friend, actually – to represent me.'

Jane nodded and walked. As she approached her car, she paused to look across the tarmac at the two houses opposite. They were mock Tudor, with neat grass verges and paths leading from their front doors to the tarmac, and low wooden fences on either side. Jane then turned towards the two smaller, cheaper-looking properties. They also had garages beside their houses, and the same low fences, looking as if they needed a bit of repair. There were three cars parked, two at number 10 and one at number 7. She also noticed that some kind of trailing plant was growing along the entire length of the Caplans' old fences, with overgrown bushes beside their damaged double gates. The whole business with the tarmac was bothering her, and she decided to check into how long they had lived at Clarendon Close.

As she was getting into her car, Stanley appeared, waving.

'I wondered if I would see you . . . I came by earlier to visit Mrs Boon, but she was out so I went back to the station.' He glanced at number 7. 'Looks like she's back, if that's her car.'

'Where's yours?' Jane asked.

'Parked in front of the Caplans'. I had that nosy woman from number 10, Mrs Larsson, telling me I couldn't park there. I was not about to tell her to fuck off as she seemed so wired up, so I went to the station to do a bit of research into Land Registry . . . have you got a minute?'

'Sure, I've just come out from interviewing the Caplans.'

They got into the car.

'You know this iron bar David Caplan says Mr Boon attacked him with? I asked if it could have been a stick, and when he told me his dog had run out into the courtyard I wondered if the dog had maybe picked it up and run off with it.'

'The uniforms were pretty thorough, but I suppose if it was a stick, the dog could have dug a hole and buried it. I can get them to do another search.'

Stanley pulled out his notebook and flicked through the pages.

'I had to do a lot of farting around to get to the bottom of all of this. Anyway, it turns out the manor house and all the land around had been owned by a Mr De Wilding. This all went back over twenty-five years. He began selling off sections of land, and those two mock-Tudor houses were built after a wood was chopped down. There was a hissy fit from the council because of protected trees, but it all came to nothing, just a few slapped wrists and a couple of fines. The two houses were built, and one sold for £200,000 and the other for £350,000. Then after De Wilding died, his heirs appear to have made a lot of cash from selling more land. You following me?'

Jane nodded. 'Yes, go on.'

Stanley thumbed through his notebook. 'OK, so after the heirs sold up all the land they could, the main property was left in a dilapidated state, and it was subsequently bought by a Mr and Mrs Victor Hoffman. He was German, and they had one teenage son, Sebastian. From old building applications it appears they intended to convert the house into flats, but they ran into major hitches with the council. The next thing that happened was a fire. I looked up old press reports . . . there were hints it might have been arson but nothing was ever proved. Then it looks like the Hoffmans ran out of money, after trying to get the insurance to pay for repairs, so they sold off the courtyard to Mr Larsson.'

'How many years ago was that?'

'Ten . . . so the Larssons were already living at number 7. I haven't got the exact date when the Larssons tarmacked the entire courtyard, but it had to have been done before Mr and Mrs Caplan bought the property. They paid £220,000, which was a bargain due to the damage from the fire, and they've spent the last seven or eight years doing it up.'

'So what is the value of their property now?' Jane asked.

Stanley shrugged. 'It must be in the millions, and it would have been a great investment if it wasn't for the situation with the fence and the gates. The neighbours have blocked things for over a year, and obviously with that ferret of a woman not allowing any parking in the courtyard they would probably have to lower the asking price considerably.'

'Did you find any discrepancies in what Boon claimed about the boundaries?'

'Nope, but replacing the old fence with a brick wall and double electric gates would probably mean digging up some of the tarmac for the foundations.'

Jane sighed. From what Stanley had just told her there was a motive for Caplan to have struck Mr Boon intentionally; even more so if, like the previous owners, David and Alice Caplan were running out of money.

'Do we know anything about the Caplans' finances?'

'I'm not sure that's necessary until Caplan's charged with something. And that depends on Boon's medical history and whether he recovers.'

'Right, I don't suppose any update came in while you were at the station?'

'No, Bill was going to Boon's GP and then meeting us at the hospital. Do you want to come in and talk to Mrs Boon to see if we get anything? I won't be able to control myself if I have to interview that Larsson woman.'

'Let's do both together. I doubt there will be any need for good-cop, bad-cop routines,' Jane laughed.

Chapter Four

Ellen Boon was wearing an odd mixture of clothing that included wrinkled stockings, fluffy slippers, a worn woollen pleated skirt, a cream blouse, knitted bolero and a grey, buttoned cardigan with big saggy pockets. At first, she was hesitant about allowing Jane and Stanley into the house, and even tried to close the door on them. Jane reassured her by smiling warmly and saying that they just needed to ask her a few questions, and that they were keen to find out if there was an update on her husband's condition.

'You can sit in here. We don't use this room very often.' Mrs Boon gestured for them to follow her down the dim, dark hallway.

The small sitting room had a worn, uncared-for feel about it. Even the curtains looked unwashed, hanging on odd rings from a wooden pole across the double window. The carpet was stained and threadbare in places, and there was a faded and yellowing fur rug in front of the fireplace. Numerous watercolour landscapes hung on the walls, some framed and on hooks, while others were simply Blu-Tacked to the faded wallpaper.

Ellen Boon sat on the edge of the sofa, placing an embroidered cushion behind her back.

'So, how is Mr Boon doing?' Jane asked gently.

'He's not come round yet . . . but he's not attached to any life-support machines . . . just a few monitors.'

Jane thought Mrs Boon was probably only in her late forties, but she had a round, puffy face with eyes as faded as her furniture. Jane noticed that her hands were paint-stained and assumed she was the creator of the watercolours. She had big, square hands and thick fingers with short, dirty nails.

'Has Mr Boon ever had any previous head injuries?'

'What do you mean?' Mrs Boon said, blinking.

'Well, we need to find out if a previous injury might have contributed to his present condition. Did Mr Boon have any medical problems, mental issues or perhaps a previous fall . . . ?'

'No, he did not!' Mrs Boon snapped, leaning forwards. 'You're just trying to prove that Mr Caplan isn't responsible for what happened to my husband. Well, he was!'

Jane nodded sympathetically, hoping to calm her down. 'Did your husband go to see Mr Caplan that afternoon with the intention of confronting him about the boundary situation between their property and the courtyard?'

Ellen shook her head. 'I had no idea he was going to go over there. I was in my studio in the back garden.'

'But you went into the Caplans' garden almost immediately after the incident had occurred,' Jane said.

'Yes, because their dog was running loose around the courtyard, barking.'

'So, you saw their dog, then what did you do?' Stanley asked.

'The gate was open, and I saw Martin lying on the ground. He appeared to be unconscious. Mrs Caplan came out and called an ambulance . . . then the police . . . then I was taken to the hospital.'

'So, you didn't witness the incident?'

'No, I just told you that.'

Stanley glanced at Jane, and she continued.

'Did you see Mr Caplan's dog carrying a stick, or anything like that?'

'No, he was running over to the house opposite theirs.'

'Did you see Mr Caplan or hear what was being said?'

'No, I told you, I was in my studio, and only heard the screams and shouts.'

'Did you see an iron bar?'

'No, I did not.'

'Mr Caplan claims that your husband was threatening him with one.'

'Then he is lying. I never saw one and I have never seen one in the house.'

'Could I just see your studio, Mrs Boon, and then we will leave you in peace?'

Jane stood to indicate to Stanley she had heard enough.

They were led out of the room and down the corridor into a large kitchen. It was surprisingly modern, with a state-of-the-art fridge and freezer and a large cooker.

'You have a lovely kitchen,' Jane remarked, and looked at Stanley, who raised his eyebrows.

Mrs Boon did not respond and opened the backdoor, leading out into the garden.

The garden was small but well maintained, with numerous plants in large ceramic planters. At the end of the garden was an expensive-looking shed.

Mrs Boon swung the door open and gestured inside as she switched on the lights. It was full of picture frames and paint brushes, cutting tools and a worktop arrayed with small saws and rows of paint jars and glues.

'It's very impressive, Mrs Boon. I presume you're the artist, and that was your work in the sitting room?'

'Yes, that's right. I only took it up a few years ago, but I find it therapeutic.'

'Thank you so much,' Jane said. Stanley was already heading back up the path towards the open kitchen door, and they were both thinking the same thing: there was no way Ellen Boon could have heard the assault from her studio. She was lying.

Alice Caplan had said that when the dog got out she called the ambulance, and that Ellen was already hysterically screaming beside her husband.

They were in the kitchen about to leave when Stanley turned to Mrs Boon with a forced smile.

'You've been very helpful, Mrs Boon. But there is just one more thing I'd like to ask you.'

Mrs Boon shrugged.

'I don't quite understand why your husband was so obsessed about the planning permission being granted? You don't own the courtyard, and it doesn't appear to have anything to do with your property. Is there some kind of personal reason behind his interest?'

Mrs Boon pursed her lips but said nothing. Stanley dropped his caring facade and continued in a more forthright tone.

'I've read the letters he personally delivered to Mr Caplan, accusing him of lying regarding the damage done by various parked vehicles knocking into his gates – but what business is that of your husband's?'

'We have permission from Mr Larsson to allow five members of my painting circle to park in the courtyard every other Thursday,' Mrs Boon said. 'They are very respectable people and have never damaged any of the fencing or gates.'

'So, if Mr or Mrs Caplan wanted to drive into their property, as they have right of way, they couldn't unless the members of your painting circle moved their vehicles?'

'That never happened,' Mrs Boon said flatly.

'But was this matter a bone of contention between your husband and Mr Caplan?' Stanley persisted.

'You will have to ask Martin. I am not aware of any letters he has written, and now I would like you to leave. This is making me feel very unwell.'

Jane was already opening the door, as Stanley gave a sigh of impatience and walked past her.

Ellen Boon shut the front door firmly behind them, then went straight into the kitchen and picked up the phone, dialling quickly.

'I have had two police officers here asking me questions over and over again,' she said as soon as the phone was answered. 'I am at my wits' end because I don't know what they want me to say to them.'

She stood with the phone to her ear for a few moments, then replaced the receiver and hurried into the hall. Halfway up the stairs she looked out through a small side window and could see Jane and Stanley standing by the front door of the Larssons' property.

Stanley pressed the doorbell again.

'Her lies about not knowing what her husband was up to were pretty obvious. I think it's all down to envy. I mean, you only have to look at how dingy their house is in comparison to the Caplans'.'

'Well,' Jane said, 'it was a very expensive-looking kitchen, so they have some money. And the studio-cum-shed must have cost a fair bit.'

Edward Larsson opened the door and Jane produced her ID.

'I am Detective Inspector Jane Tennison and this is . . .'

Larsson interrupted her, nodding towards Stanley. 'Yes, we've already met. What do you want?'

'I have only recently joined the investigation, Mr Larsson, and I would like to ask you a few questions, if it's not inconvenient.'

Mr Larsson was exceptionally thin, with a pinched face, greying hair and prominent ears. He turned back and called for his wife. Stanley gave Jane a quick grimace.

'I suppose you'd better come in. My wife is cooking lunch, so it is not really that convenient. I thought I had already answered all your questions regarding poor Mr Boon's situation.'

He stood back and gestured to an open door off the hall.

Jane followed Stanley into the room There was an elegant three-piece suite of matching velvet chairs and a sofa, and a fake-coal electric fire. Two large, silver-framed, colour photographs were positioned at each end of the mantelpiece, one of a very pretty young blonde girl in pigtails, the other what looked like the same girl as a teenager.

Jane and Stanley sat side by side on the sofa. Mr Larsson hovered by the door as his wife, wearing a white cotton apron, came into the room. She glanced at Stanley with a smile.

'I think we've met before. I am Patricia Larsson.' She looked at Jane. 'And you are?'

'Detective Inspector Jane Tennison. We are sorry to interrupt your lunch preparations. I am sure we won't take up too much of your time.'

Patricia Larsson was an attractive woman with short blonde hair. She was stylishly dressed in a straight skirt with a pink blouse under the apron and seemed to be going out of her way to be pleasant.

Stanley kicked off the questioning, pulling out his notebook from his jacket pocket.

'When I interviewed your husband after the incident, he said that you were both at home, and only became aware of what had happened when you heard Mrs Boon screaming?'

'Yes. Obviously, I came out to comfort her as she was very distressed; in fact, I drove her to the hospital when the ambulance took Martin, as she doesn't drive.'

'Did you notice that Buster, the Caplans' puppy, was out?'

'No, I didn't actually see him until Mr Caplan brought him back into the garden.'

'When you were with Mrs Boon did you notice a long stick, or some kind of iron bar, close to where Mr Boon was lying?'

'I doubt I would have noticed, there was so much happening.'

'Did you see anything like that, Mr Larsson?'

'No, I was with the ambulance driver directing them into the garden.'

Jane nodded and turned to Mrs Larsson again.

'Could you take me through exactly what you did after Mr Boon was taken to hospital?'

'Well, I was comforting poor Ellen. She was wearing slippers and didn't want to go with her husband until she had changed her footwear. So I said I would drive her there as soon as she was ready. She went back into their house while I went to collect the car keys. She came out after a few moments and I drove her to the hospital. I waited some time with her in the A&E department before poor Martin was taken into intensive care. I got her a cup of tea and about an hour later I left her there and returned home.'

Jane smiled. 'Thank you.'

Stanley flicked back through the pages in his notebook then tapped a page with his pencil.

'I have looked over the Land Registry plans for this area and there doesn't appear to be any reason why Mr Boon would be so against the Caplans' application. As far as I can determine, the matter does not have any connection to his property.'

Jane noticed the way Mrs Larsson's mouth tightened as she gave her husband a sidelong look.

'I believe he was concerned about his fence bordering on their rear garden.'

'But the plans are only for a wall and electric gates,' Stanley said.

Mr Larsson frowned. 'I am not privy to his objections.'

'But you own the courtyard, isn't that correct?' Stanley persisted. He snapped his notebook shut. 'So I can only presume that you allowed or encouraged Mr Boon to object on your behalf?'

'I don't know what you mean,' Mrs Larsson said, clasping her hands together, while her husband just stood with head bowed. 'If you have nothing further to ask, then I would appreciate it if you left.'

It was obvious who was the dominant one in their marriage, Jane thought to herself.

Stanley stood up, carrying on as if he hadn't heard her. 'Can I ask what business you are in, Mr Larsson?'

'He is a retired accountant, and he helps me in my antiques business,' Mrs Larsson said quickly. 'My company buys and sells for clients worldwide. Edward, please show the officers out . . . I think we have given them enough of our time.'

Mrs Larsson walked out as her husband gestured for Jane and Stanley to leave the room. Jane stood up and waited for Stanley to pass her before stopping in front of Mr Larsson.

'I noticed in the hall you have two of Mrs Boon's landscape paintings, and you also allow her art group to park in your court-yard. You must be very good friends.'

'Well, we do encourage her artistic interests,' he said blandly.

'Very generous. How long have you owned the courtyard?' Jane asked.

Before he could answer, Mrs Larsson reappeared.

'I don't think it is any of your business, but if you must know it used to be partly gravelled and became a mudbath when it rained. We bought the land almost five years ago and paid for it to be tarmacked. We obviously had to grant right of way to all the neighbours. I also tend to the areas of garden that border the courtyard.'

'Thank you.' Jane joined Stanley who was standing by her car.

'She's a bloody witch,' he muttered.

'I agree. So they apparently bought the land ten years ago. I need to check the dates because it would have been before the Caplans purchased their property. I don't know if you noticed, but they had two of Ellen Boon's framed paintings hanging in the hall. So much for her antiques sideline; you wouldn't get ten pence for them in a car boot sale.'

Jane drove out into the narrow lane that ran from the courtyard into the main road. The lane looked as if it had been re-tarmacked in sections like a patchwork quilt. Massive fir trees surrounded the lane, along with a single ancient oak tree. Jane pulled up outside the front entrance of the Caplans' house, where Stanley's car was parked next to a dark-blue Range Rover.

'It's certainly a substantial property,' she said admiringly. There were two life-size, stone Great Danes either side of the elegant porch and the front door was like something from a castle, with heavy studs and an iron knocker.

Stanley looked at the house. 'Yes, the climbing ivy and the lattice windows make it look very nice.' Stanley opened the passenger door.

'See you back at the station. I might get a bite to eat. I'm starving. I doubt if anything else will have required our expert attention, but that's the way I prefer it, easy life, home by five thirty and feet up.'

Jane drove off, thinking about this new Stanley. He had been a great undercover officer, totally fearless and always spoiling for a fight with his superiors. Yet now he was looking forward to retiring and getting his pension.

She sighed, feeling depressed. It seemed as if her request for a transfer from the Met's West End section to a local station might not have been a wise career move after all.

Chapter Five

Just like Stanley, Jane left the station at five thirty, both having written up their reports.

Jane was surprised to find Eddie at home when she got back, as he usually worked until later in the evening. He was standing in the kitchen and when he heard Jane coming through the front door, he shouted for her to come and see something special. She put her briefcase down on the hall table, hung up her coat and went into the kitchen.

'Look what I've got!' He gestured to a black, square-shaped contraption with what looked like the handset of a telephone.

'What is it?'

'That, my darling one, is a mobile phone.'

Jane looked puzzled. 'How do you mean?'

'If you need me when I'm out at work, you can call me and I can answer it. I'll have it connected in my van, attached to the cigarette lighter.'

'Where on earth did you get it from?'

'One of my dad's clients . . . he went bankrupt and owed him for a job he'd done . . . so he gave him this.'

'Have you checked that it works?'

'Yeah, the contract had to be changed over to my name. What you do is call the centre – you can't just call me direct – give them the number and password code and they call me with your message.'

'So I can't actually speak to you on it?'

'Well, no, the receptionist will ask what the message is, and she then puts the call in to me. It means I won't lose business, and I can also get a message to you if I need to. So if, for example, I am going to be late and there's no call box or telephone close by, I ring this, and they ring you.'

'Have you tested it out?'

'My dad did. Listen, this guy was desperate and the cost of one of these is Christ only knows how much . . . there are not many of them around.'

Jane picked up the contraption and looked at Eddie.

'I don't think it's exactly all that "mobile". It's quite heavy. Can you recharge it if you're not in your van?'

Eddie hesitated, then picked up a leaflet and flicked through the pages.

'Yep, or you can use batteries I think . . . do you want to try it out?'

'From here?'

'No, I'll take it into the van, and you call the number and speak to the receptionist.'

'What do you want me to say?'

'Anything, like, would I like fish and chips for dinner and to be home by seven.'

Jane sighed, and watched him pick up the so-called mobile, before handing her a small notebook.

'That's the code and the number, just gimme a couple of minutes.'

Eddie hurried out. He was like a big kid sometimes, Jane thought with a smile. She went to put the kettle on, wondering if this strange contraption would ever catch on.

After making two mugs of tea, she went into the hall with the notebook. She dialled the long eight-digit number and waited for the connection.

'Good evening, could I please have your code.'

Jane dictated a message while Eddie sat in the van with the engine ticking over. The mobile phone buzzed loudly and Eddie picked up.

'Mr Myers, we have a message for you: "Be at home for seven thirty this evening and bring fish and chips."'

'Thank you, could you please return a message to the caller: "Jane, I'll see you at seven thirty with supper."'

The phone rang from the hall and Jane hesitated before going back to answer it.

'Hello?'

'Could you please give your code as we have a message to forward.'

After repeating the code, Jane listened as the telephonist repeated Eddie's message.

Eddie banged open the front door, beaming. 'Did you get my message?'

'Where's the fish and chips?'

He clapped his hands. 'See! It's terrific, isn't it?'

Jane looked dubious. 'I suppose so, but you have to make sure that whoever you call has the code or they won't pass on your message.'

He frowned and went into the kitchen to check through the instruction booklet.

'I think there's another code that can do away with that, I'm just learning as I go along.'

'Did you leave the phone in the van?'

'Shit, yes! But do you want to try it out again, and leave me another message?'

'No, thanks. I wouldn't mind the fish and chips, though, and mushy peas. I've put the kettle on. We're not having our usual Monday dinner with your parents, remember, as it was my first day at work.'

Eddie gave her the thumbs-up and went out, slamming the door behind him. She decided to have a quick shower and get into her pyjamas to have dinner in front of the TV. She was just getting out of the shower when the phone rang. Wrapping a towel around herself, she hurried into the bedroom to pick up the extension. The same telephonist was on the line again with a message and this time the code was not required. The message was from Eddie to say he was just leaving the fish and chip shop.

Jane closed her eyes and sighed, hoping that Eddie would not become obsessed with his new toy. She was already finding it irritating.

Chapter Six

The following morning, Jane was having breakfast in the canteen when Stanley joined her. Her dinner had weighed heavily on her stomach all night, so she was just having a cup of coffee and a slice of toast. In contrast Stanley was having a full English.

'Have you spoken to Bill?' he asked her.

'DC William Burrows?'

'Yep . . . he got some interesting information from the hospital. Apparently our victim, Mr Boon, had an aneurysm eight years ago, a burst blood vessel in the brain.'

'I imagine that could have had repercussions when he fell,' Jane mused, as Stanley reached for the tomato ketchup.

He shook the ketchup and squirted it over his sausages. 'When we asked his wife if he had any previous medical history, she denied it.'

'I think we need to speak to the surgeon at the hospital,' Jane said, 'and then trace the surgeon who treated him eight years ago.'

Jane started feeling queasy as she watched Stanley scoffing his breakfast.

He looked up. 'Why aren't you having the full English, Jane?'

'I had a big supper last night . . .'

He nodded. 'I have to say the canteen food is pretty good, not too greasy.'

'I wish I could say that about my fish and chips last night,' Jane said.

'My old lady did a nice chicken roast; don't you like cooking?'

'I quite like making a few dishes, but last night Eddie brought home a new piece of equipment his dad had got in a trade-off with someone who owed him money, and we were messing around with that.'

'CD player?'

'No, a mobile phone . . . although it's not really that mobile. It's quite big and heavy, and he had me calling him via a receptionist in his van, then he was messaging me back.'

'This new technology is all the rage, isn't it? There was a very funny sketch that Morecambe and Wise did with one of these so-called mobile phones . . . have you seen it?'

Jane shook her head.

'I wouldn't mind getting my hands on one. Unlike the public, us cops get used to using radio contact, and I don't like doing undercover work without that back-up. Nasty times.'

'Well, you're out of that work now, Stanley.'

He frowned. 'That was a bit snide.'

'Sorry, yes, it was.' She drained her coffee cup and stood up. 'See you upstairs.'

'Right, I'll just have another round of toast before I head up.'

Jane put her mug in the used-dishes bowl and left the canteen, still feeling bad about what she had said to Stanley.

It was around nine thirty when Jane was called in to see DCI Hutton. She was thumbing through Jane's report from the previous day.

'We really don't need all this detail about the residents in Clarendon Court's Land Registry history. There are always neighbours disputing boundaries, but I think you're getting bogged down in their petty squabbles. The crux of this investigation is that Mr Boon was trespassing and behaving in a threatening manner, so Mr Caplan was acting in self-defence, or Caplan assaulted him unprovoked. We need to interview Mr Boon.'

Jane felt Hutton was being unfairly critical of her report and answered without thinking. 'That's going to be difficult while he's in a coma.'

Hutton gave her a sour look. 'I don't appreciate sarcasm, Jane. I am more than aware of the situation, but from your reports neither you nor DI Stanley has managed to ascertain whether Mr Boon did actually threaten Mr Caplan with some kind of weapon.'

'I am sorry if I sounded sarcastic, ma'am. By interviewing the neighbours we have been attempting to discover why Mr Boon was constantly objecting to Mr Caplan's planning application . . .'

Hutton interrupted Jane by raising a hand and closing the file.

'Jane, I have read your report.'

'But it makes no sense. If it infringed his boundary then it would be understandable, but there's no connection. I think we need to consider that Boon has some sort of grudge against Mr Caplan.'

Hutton sighed, pushing her chair back from the desk as an indication that the meeting was at an end. She was taken aback when Jane stood abruptly.

'All we've been attempting to do is find a motive. We have also been lied to by Mr Boon's wife regarding his previous medical history.'

Hutton stood and faced Jane. She was taller by at least five inches and her face was tight with anger. She banged the file down on the desk.

'Proof of motive is not required in a criminal prosecution. I don't know how many times I have to repeat myself, DI Tennison. I have read your report, and I am aware of the latest information from the hospital regarding Mr Boon's previous medical history. I suggest that first thing this morning you get more details and discuss this with his wife.'

Jane picked up the file and gave a brief nod before leaving Hutton's office. She could not recall a time during her entire career that she had felt so humiliated. She'd had numerous confrontations with superior officers, but DCI Hutton had made her feel completely inadequate.

Stanley was standing by Jane's desk as she slapped the file down.

'Had a bit of a dressing down from the headmistress, have you?'

'You could say that,' Jane snapped.

'If it makes you feel any better, I had one earlier. We need to get over to the hospital because it may not be an easy Q&A with the specialist, what with it being privileged information. Bill has got the contact for Boon's previous brain surgery; we might be in luck as he's retired, so we won't have to go through all the red tape.'

'It's unbelievable!' Jane exclaimed. 'We could be investigating a murder! We have to know the facts and cut through all this crap about patient confidentiality.'

'You don't have to tell me, Jane, but let's not waste any more time. Let's first get over to see what Boon's condition is and then take it from there.'

They left the station together. Jane drove as Stanley had come on public transport because his wife needed his car for some event with his kids.

DC Burrows was already at the hospital, sitting in the reception area. As Jane and Stanley approached, he stood up, draining the coffee which he had brought in a flask and screwing the cap back on.

'Still no improvement,' he said. 'I mentioned to the staff nurse that you wanted to talk to the surgeon but he's in theatre until eleven. There are two doctors on rotation in the intensive care unit, so I'm not sure which one will be available to see you. DCI Hutton has given me instructions to return to the station, and she's sending a uniform to take over from me.'

'Where do we go?' Jane asked.

'Second floor. There's a small waiting area, and the ward is along a corridor. No admittance without permission, so watch out for the matron.'

Jane and Stanley took the lift up to the second floor. A young nurse stood behind a glass-fronted counter and looked up as they entered through the double doors.

Jane held up her ID and explained that they were there to discuss Mr Boon's condition and, if possible, talk to someone about his medical issues.

'Mr Boon is not allowed any visitors other than family, under supervision,' she said. 'The duty doctor, Dr Wilde, is with matron. If you want to take a seat, I can get someone to see you, but I am not permitted to leave reception unattended. Or you can go and wait in the visitors' waiting room, which is more comfortable.'

Jane and Stanley decided to wait in reception, sitting on a row of four hard-backed chairs a short distance from the counter while they watched the nurse on the phone. Two white-coated porters wheeled a stretcher stacked with boxes and supplies past them, stopping by the duty nurse. She laughed and joked with them before they headed down the corridor.

Jane was about to go and talk to the nurse again when a young man with a stethoscope and a rather crumpled white coat stopped at the desk. The nurse gestured towards Stanley and Jane and the young man came over.

'Good morning. I'm Dr Wilde. I'm afraid Mr Simoni is in theatre until at least eleven.'

'We need an update on a patient's condition . . . is there anyone that can help us as a matter of urgency?' Jane asked.

The doctor went to talk to the nurse behind the screened desk and she made a call as he leaned on the counter. After a brief conversation he came back to them, running his fingers through his unruly curly hair.

'I can take you into his office as his secretary is there.'

They followed Dr Wilde out through the double doors, and then past the lifts down another corridor. He stopped at a door with a plaque with Mr Simoni's name and an array of credentials. He knocked on the door, opened it and stood to one side as they entered.

'Well, she's obviously not here. As you can see it's fairly basic. Mr Simoni only uses the office when he's on duty here. He has his own private practice and works for two other hospitals.'

Jane held up her ID.

'I'm Detective Inspector Jane Tennison and this is DI Stanley. We are here to enquire about Mr Martin Boon's condition.'

'I'll go back to reception and see where his secretary has got to. Is that all right?'

'Thank you very much,' Jane said.

They'd been sitting waiting for over ten minutes when Stanley decided they should just go back to the station and return later in the morning.

'That young doc looked a bit frazzled to me, probably been on the go for twenty-four hours.'

He was about to open the door, when a middle-aged nurse entered, her identification badge attached to her ample bosom.

'It is quite irregular to have left you alone in Mr Simoni's office,' she said tersely. 'His secretary should have informed reception that she was not here, and Dr Wilde is needed in A&E. I'm afraid I'm going to have to ask you to leave.'

'I apologise for any inconvenience,' Jane said, trying to keep her temper in check, while looking to see the name on the nurse's identification badge.

'I am Senior Staff Nurse Collins. I am aware that you are police officers, but nevertheless . . .'

Before she could finish speaking, a very attractive young woman appeared behind her, carrying a flask and a wrapped paper plate.

'I'm back, I was just in the cafe downstairs when Dr Wilde asked me to return to the office.'

Nurse Collins pressed herself against the open door as Mr Simoni's secretary entered, wearing a tight pencil skirt and a pale-pink sweater and a pair of stilettos. She placed the flask and plate on the desk and turned to Jane and Stanley.

'I'm Janice White. Sorry, Nurse Collins, but Mr Simoni likes the fresh coffee from the cafe and a sausage roll.'

Nurse Collins pursed her lips and gave a look of disapproval. 'Rules are rules, Miss White, and in future if you leave the office unattended, please make sure it's locked.' She turned on her heel and went.

'Please, do sit down,' Miss White told them.

Stanley pulled a chair closer to the desk for Jane, fetching the other one for himself.

'That woman is the bane of my life! She's always interfering. I actually work for three of the surgeons here, who all have private practices elsewhere. So, I sort out their private appointments, but the NHS have a different booking system. There's often confusion as they constantly have a dimwit working on the front desk . . .'

Jane coughed for attention.

'I'm Detective Inspector Jane Tennison and this is Detective Inspector Stanley . . . we really need an update on a patient, Martin Boon.'

'Well, I can't help you with his medical condition, but I do have Mr Simoni's diary.'

Miss White opened the filing cabinet again to remove a large leather-bound diary.

'Right, let me have a look. Ah, here we are. I see Mr Simoni was concerned about a visitor Mr Boon had; that is who you are interested in, right?'

'Yes,' Jane snapped, beginning to lose patience.

'Mrs Boon has been a regular visitor. Sometimes when they have a coma patient, they like close relatives to be allowed to sit and talk to them and sometimes they bring in little tape recordings of favourite tunes and chat to them about their families, and . . .'

She turned over another page.

'Oh yes, this is also underlined in red . . . Mr Simoni left a note for me to pass to the staff in the ICU that he felt the presence of a Mrs Larsson was not beneficial and might actually be distressing for his patient. I think I did pass this on . . . and there's also a second reference to the same visitor. Apparently she's been in every day.'

'So is Mr Simoni suggesting that Mrs Larsson has been upsetting his patient?' Jane said.

Miss White shrugged and before Jane could ask anything else the desk phone rang. Miss White answered it and then swivelled around in her desk chair to open a filing cabinet drawer and take out another diary. She covered the mouthpiece on the receiver.

'Sorry, just have to take this; it's for the cardiologist.'

Jane leaned back in her chair and rolled her eyes. No sooner had Miss White replaced the receiver than the phone rang again. Jane looked at Stanley.

'This is a waste of time; I need to get out of here.'

Miss White raised her hand and held out the receiver.

'It's Mr Simoni. He's in the swill room, so if you want to have a quick word . . .'

Jane almost snatched the phone from her hand. She listened for a few minutes, occasionally trying to interject without success. Eventually she said 'thank you' and handed the receiver back to Miss White. She turned to Stanley.

'Mr Simoni is getting ready for his second operation of the day, but can meet us at eleven thirty and show us X-rays that he said might be of interest. He also requested that we get a warrant to avoid any breach of his code of conduct and patient confidentiality.'

She turned to thank Miss White, but the phone had already rung again and she was deep in her appointments diary.

Jane hurried along the corridor as Stanley caught up with her, then pushed open the double doors and headed towards the stairs.

'Right. You can go and get me a coffee, because we have to get back to the station so that DCI Hutton can organise verbal approval, and then we can type up the warrant form and get over to the magistrates.'

Jane turned the car around, ready to drive out as she waited for Stanley to bring her coffee. He came out a few minutes later carrying two coffees on a cardboard tray.

Jane took a sharp left out of the hospital car park while Stanley was opening one of the takeaway coffees.

'For Christ's sake, Jane, what's the matter with you? Whatever it is, don't fucking take it out on me.'

Jane didn't slow down. 'I get a bloody bollocking from DCI Hutton this morning about the delay in getting medical information . . . and now we've been in that hospital for over an hour. You didn't hear the snide way Mr Simoni spoke to me while you were busy ogling his idiot secretary. We have to get a warrant and be back at the ICU for eleven thirty.'

Jane continued to drive with her lips pursed, and neither of them spoke until they got to the station car park. Jane sat gripping the steering wheel as Stanley opened the passenger door and climbed out. He glanced back at her.

'Just chill out, Jane, for God's sake.'

'Really, is that your advice, Stanley? It's all right for you. You're just treading water here until your retirement. After all the cases I have been involved with, being assigned here at this tin-pot station and spending hours on a fucking domestic dispute between bloody neighbours, it just feels as though I'm back to square one.'

Jane got out and slammed her door, locked the car and walked towards the station entrance. By the time she had hung up her coat and sat down at her desk she had calmed down. Stanley came in and went in to see DCI Hutton.

There were three messages on Jane's desk, all asking her to call the number she recognised as Eddie's mobile. It was the last thing she needed, but nevertheless she called back and was told by the receptionist at the call centre that Mr Myers had left a message: he would be late that evening and if there was a problem, she could leave a message for him.

Jane asked for the receptionist to send a reply to Mr Myers, asking him not to call her at work unless it was an emergency.

DC Burrows approached Jane's desk, saying he had received a call from the forensic department confirming that the fingerprints on the handle of the spade matched those taken from David Caplan, but that no blood, hair or skin fibres had been detected.

Burrows returned to his desk as Jane began to type up her report.

Stanley came out of Hutton's office. 'Ready when you are, Jane,' he said, waving an envelope.

'All we need is to get it signed by a magistrate and we're done.'

She closed her files, tidied up her desk and then went to fetch her coat.

When they were in the car park, and before she started up the engine, Jane reached over to pat his arm.

'I'm sorry for being so disgruntled this morning.'

'No problem. I reckoned it might just be the time of the month – my wife's like an aggressive polecat when it's her monthly.'

'Thanks a lot, Stanley! It's not that, actually. I'm not really sure why I feel so on edge. But I wonder if it might be connected to Dexter's death. It was quite a shock, and maybe it takes time to deal with news like that; he was sort of someone who was special to me.'

'Likewise,' Stanley said, staring out of the passenger window. He didn't want to let Jane know just how much it had affected him.

Jane sighed. 'I've been transferred to various stations after that Stockwell investigation with the mummified baby, and the poor girl left starving in that hideous old air-raid shelter . . . it just keeps on feeling as if I'm being shunted around.

'I think I may have made a big mistake asking to be out here in the sticks. I may have destroyed any hope of being attached to a team handling major crimes because I know I've been accused of not being a team player. But in the past, if it hadn't been for my doggedness, we might not have got the results that we did – not that I was ever given any kudos. I worked my butt off to get my promotion, and I hated going back into uniform for a year . . .'

Stanley shrugged his shoulders, not really wanting to get into a discussion about Jane's career. He certainly wasn't going to mention the time when she had been attached to the Sweeney and had screwed up.

'I'm not like you, Stanley. I know you're just riding it out until you retire, but that is your choice.'

'You said it, Jane. Why don't you get us to the hospital. We don't want to miss our meeting with the surgeon.'

'Stanley, I'm sorry if I insulted you.' She turned on the engine.

'For Christ's sake, Jane, please just leave me out of your angst. I've taken enough risks to last me a lifetime, and now I have kids and a mortgage. I don't want to end up working undercover in some dark alley and getting my guts ripped open by some junkie kid. My wife worries herself sick every time I leave home. Satisfied? Let's just get on with the job we're assigned to do, so I can get back home for dinner with my family.'

Jane backed out of the car park and neither of them said a word as they drove to the magistrates' court.

Chapter Seven

Jane and Stanley arrived at the ICU department and approached Staff Nurse Collins, who was looking tight-lipped and irritable. She was sitting behind the nurse's counter, her oversized bosom resting on the desk as she leaned forwards.

'Mr Simoni instructed me to tell you to go to the X-ray unit on the lower-ground floor. Follow the signs in the corridor and report to the receptionist.'

The X-ray receptionist directed them to a viewing section. Dr Wilde was waiting at the open door, looking even more dishevelled than before.

'Mr Simoni had to return to his office, but he has instructed me to show you some X-rays that he prepared for you. I gather from his notes that you need to look at two frames.'

Jane and Stanley stood side by side looking at two illuminated X-ray images of a skull.

'What exactly are we looking at?' Jane asked, becoming impatient.

'Well, the one on the right was taken while Mr Boon was here, to determine if there were any contusions from his fall. You have to understand that this is not my field, but it clearly indicates . . .'

He referred to a file then looked at the screen again.

'. . . that there was no recent damage to the frontal lobe. But Mr Simoni was able to establish that there had been a previous aneurysm in two sections. A second X-ray was therefore required.'

'Do you have more information about the patient's previous operation?' Jane asked.

'I don't know, I was just going on my break when Mr Simoni collared me to come in and meet you both here.'

'How serious was the aneurysm?'

'I'm not sure, but I would say he is a very lucky man; brain bleeds can often be fatal.'

'Thank you very much. So is Mr Simoni expecting us in his office?' Stanley asked. He could see that Jane was almost at the end of her tether.

'I'll ring through and find out if he is up there,' Dr Wilde said.

'That would be appreciated.' Stanley followed Dr Wilde out into the corridor while Jane remained to have another look at the X-rays before joining him.

Heading up to the office floor in the lift, Jane glanced at her wristwatch.

'I can't believe all this farting around; he told us what time he would be available and now he's only gracing us with ten minutes.'

Just as they were exiting the lift, Miss White hurried towards them.

'Oh good, you're here! Mr Simoni is waiting. I just have to go and get his car as he has an urgent meeting at his practice.'

Stanley knocked on the office door and a deep voice barked, 'Come in.'

Jane entered first. Mr Simoni was sitting at his desk, wearing a smart pin-striped suit with a pink shirt and a red silk tie. He had half-moon glasses perched on his nose, and curly grey hair. When he stood, he was surprisingly small in stature. Jane made the introductions as Stanley proffered the envelope containing the warrant. Mr Simoni took it from him, quickly opened the envelope and without reading it passed it back.

'Good. I like to make sure everything is in order to avoid future difficulties. So I presume you have seen the X-rays. My prognosis regarding my patient is very positive. Mr Boon is currently fully functional and does not require any respiratory assistance. His heart is strong and for his age he is a reasonably fit man. We have been monitoring him closely due to the discovery of a previous medical condition that occurred some eight years ago. He was a very lucky man to have been treated so promptly when it happened. He was at a gym, felt dizzy and became sick. He was taken to the emergency clinic in King's Cross. This was a very fortunate location, and they were able to basically save his life. He was diagnosed with a double brain aneurysm, which was successfully operated on. Some patients do not fully recover mentally and physically, but Mr Boon appeared to have had no lasting problems, and until this present situation he was in very good health.'

Simoni pushed his chair back as if the meeting was over, but Jane raised her hand to indicate that she had not finished. He peered at her over his half-moon spectacles.

'Mr Simoni, we need to talk to you about the assault.'

'Well, from the X-rays we see no frontal damage to suggest that he had been struck on his forehead. I think he fell backwards because we detected some bruising at the base of his skull and the damage from his previous aneurysm is likely to have exacerbated his condition. I made the decision to place him into a coma as that is what I would describe as a healing mechanism.'

'So, you think he will very likely recover?' Stanley asked.

'I most certainly do – although one can never be totally sure. However, it is my professional opinion that a full recovery is imminent.'

'Just one more thing, Mr Simoni . . . your secretary told us that you feel Mr Boon has had an upsetting visitor . . . a Mrs Larsson? Could you tell us what she was doing?'

Simoni sighed and shook his head. 'Really, my secretary had no business telling you my personal opinions. But Mrs Larsson was intrusive and seemed insistent on visiting Mr Boon, despite being told that it was in his best interests to be kept in a calm atmosphere and that only close relatives should be allowed to enter his cubicle. She bombarded me with questions regarding Mr Boon's recovery – which seemed very irregular given that she was just a neighbour. She was also exceedingly rude to Staff Nurse Collins.

So that is why I wrote a note for Miss White to forward to the staff. Now, I think I've assisted in every way possible . . . so if you would excuse me.'

As Jane and Stanley left the hospital, they decided to give Hutton an update before talking to the Caplans. Back at the station, Hutton listened as Stanley outlined the content of their meeting with Mr Simoni.

'Did Mr Simoni give you a statement?' she asked.

'It was just an informal conversation,' Stanley told her.

'Well, we are going to need one if this goes any further. But let's cross that bridge when we know more, and hopefully when Mr Boon has recovered enough to be interviewed.'

Hutton tapped their report.

'We still need to find the weapon Caplan says Boon was threatening him with. Jane, I think you suggested that the puppy might have picked it up when he ran out of their garden? Perhaps another visit to Mr Caplan can sort this out.'

'Should we tell Mr Caplan about our meeting with the surgeon this morning?'

Hutton closed the file and handed it back to Stanley.

'I can't see why not.' She sighed. 'I sincerely hope this can be cleared up quickly so that we can get on with more pressing issues. As it is, this situation has already taken up far too much time and effort.'

To avoid confrontation with the Larssons, Jane parked beside the Range Rover at the front of the Caplans' property. They rang the bell and waited a few minutes, hearing the dog barking furiously, before Mrs Caplan opened the door, holding onto Buster's collar, who was straining to get out.

'Do come in. Sorry about Buster . . . he is really becoming a bit of a Houdini . . . he seems to be able to escape from anything.'

As soon as the front door was closed, the puppy ambled off and Mrs Caplan gestured for them to go into the drawing room. The room was beautifully furnished, with pine panels from floor to ceiling and a tasteful pair of velvet sofas.

'What a beautiful room,' Jane said, admiringly.

'Yes, it was lucky when the fire broke out that the panels weren't touched. The fire started on the second floor and spread upwards, blowing half the roof off. Most of the damage was from the water they used to put it out though. It's hard to believe what state the property was in when we bought it.'

Stanley gestured to a baby grand piano with an array of silver-framed family photographs above the closed lid.

'Do you play?' he asked, sitting on the arm of one of the elaborate sofas.

'I used to, but it really needs a good tuning. David is quite an accomplished pianist. Apparently, the previous owner's son was a musician. He used one of the bedrooms upstairs as a studio.'

She crossed to a glass-topped coffee table and picked up a large leather-bound album. She sat down on the sofa and Jane joined her.

'As you can see, the fire really damaged the upper storey above the kitchen, and the third floor.'

Alice turned one page after another, full of photographs of the charred interior. She then tapped a double page of photographs.

'This is the son's bedroom. Presumably he painted these murals, which are quite horrific . . . a lot of devils, and one wall was covered in thick, black-painted poetry. I believe he was a guitarist, so I suppose they were lyrics. He was obviously a great fan of The Doors: on one section were the words to one of their most famous songs, "The End".' She shuddered.

'Did you ever get to meet him?' Jane asked.

'No, we only had a few meetings with Victor Hoffman . . . he always seemed anxious. I don't know if my husband told you, but we came to view the property via an estate agent, and although we could see that it had great potential we were actually warned off, and advised not to consider making an offer as Mr Hoffman was bankrupt, so we continued looking around. We then found out some months later that there had been a fire, and David and I came round on the off-chance, just interested to see how much damage had been done. Anyway, David offered to do a deal and said that he would pay off Mr Hoffman's debts, and negotiated a very good price for the house.'

Alice turned more of the album pages showing the other rooms on the top floor that had been damaged. She then began to show Jane the finished interiors.

'I think Mr Hoffman's original intention was to convert the house into apartments. But I think planning permission was refused and I suppose the financers who were backing his project pulled out. Mr Hoffman did say something about an associate letting them down, and I know he and his wife then got divorced, and I believe he returned to live in Berlin.'

'What was she like, his wife?' Jane asked.

Alice closed the album and shrugged.

'She was, or had been, a very attractive woman . . . but she always seemed to me to be very nervous. I think she was maybe Italian, very long braided dark hair, she wore long floating garments, lots of silver bangles. She sort of stayed in the background when we first came here. She did come back quite a while ago, it must have been when we had started the renovations. She didn't want to come in, just asked if her son had been round because she was worried that he might not know her new address. I told her we hadn't seen him. Anyway, she gave me a card with her contact numbers and address, and I promised that if her son ever came by I would pass them on to him.'

Buster began barking furiously as the front door opened and David Caplan called out. Mrs Caplan hurried into the hall to tell him that Jane and Stanley were there, while she dragged Buster away. He walked in, removing his overcoat.

'God, I hope this isn't bad news?'

'No, just an informal catch-up, Mr Caplan,' Stanley said. 'We spoke to Mr Boon's surgeon today and it appears that he's doing well.'

'Is he out of the coma then?'

'Not yet, but his surgeon seems confident that he will make a full recovery.'

Mr Caplan smiled. 'Thank God! So, what happens now?'

'We need to wait until Mr Boon is out of the coma so we can take a statement,' Jane said, glancing at Stanley. 'However, we just want to clear up a few things; they may sound pedantic, but it is much better to have everything clarified in case he does wish to press assault charges.'

Mr Caplan's smile disappeared. 'Terrific, that still puts me under a lot of stress.'

'This stick, or iron bar,' Jane said. 'Our searches still haven't turned it up. We wondered if perhaps your puppy may have picked it up and run off into the tarmacked area with it. However, there is a big difference between a stick, Mr Caplan, and an iron bar.'

'Yes, I am aware of that; all I do know is that he held it close to his body and his hand was clenched around it. To be honest, I am unsure if I would actually describe it as an iron bar, but it definitely wasn't just a random stick . . . it was about fourteen inches long.'

'Could it have been something like a baseball bat?' Stanley asked.

'No, no, that would have been much larger.'

'So, it could have been something Buster might have picked up and run off with?'

'I suppose so, but he was not on the loose for very long. I went out into the courtyard and brought him back.'

Stanley got up and suggested to Mr Caplan that they both have a quick look over the exact area in the courtyard where he had found Buster after the incident.

Mrs Caplan returned, clutching a piece of paper. 'Are you leaving?'

'We're just going to have another look around the garden,' Jane said, 'and then we'll be on our way.'

Mrs Caplan handed Jane the piece of paper. 'I just went into David's study. I knew I had kept Mrs Hoffman's address somewhere, but whether she's still living there I don't know.'

She also showed Jane the original card Mrs Hoffman had left. It was an embossed 'Thank you' card with tiny pressed flowers.

'I think she must have made it; rather pretty, isn't it?'

'Thank you.' Jane nodded and put the note in her briefcase. She then looked over towards the piano, topped with the photographs. 'Tell me about your family,' she said with a smile.

Fifteen minutes later Stanley returned with Mr Caplan, having had no success in their search for the 'weapon'.

'Buster wouldn't have had time to bury it,' Stanley said. 'So it doesn't look like it's there.'

'Well, thank you for looking,' Jane said as they left.

Back in the car, Jane told Stanley what she'd learned from Alice Caplan.

'Alice is actually David Caplan's second wife. He was previously married to an American architect and lived in Los Angeles. They had three children, but it was a reasonably amicable divorce. I think David Caplan has a successful business, but Alice is the daughter of a wealthy landowner, and I would say she probably has more money.'

'Well, at least we know they are not hurting for money.'

Jane drove into the station car park. Both of them reckoned they could finish their reports and get off early that afternoon. Sitting at her desk typing up the details from the afternoon's visit, Jane also made a note of Mrs Hoffman's address and contact number, in case they might need, at some point, to meet with her. It seemed odd that she had not had any contact with her son since they had sold the house.

Stanley had already left the station by the time Jane finished her report and filed it. By 5.15 p.m. she was eager to get home, and it was just after 6 p.m. when she let herself in. She knew Eddie was not coming back until late, so she decided to make a toasted cheese sandwich accompanied by a glass of wine. She carried the tray up to her bedroom and watched the news, then ran a bath and washed her hair.

Jane sat in front of her dressing-table mirror, blow-drying her hair, then curled the centre section up into large rollers, with one either side of her head. She put on an old pair of pyjamas and got into bed to watch TV, plumping up the pillows so she'd still be comfortable with the rollers in. But before she could even turn the TV on, her eyes had closed and she'd fallen asleep.

Chapter Eight

Jane woke with a start, hearing the front door bang shut. She looked at her alarm clock. It was after twelve. Eddie came up the stairs and into the bedroom and gave a comical grimace.

'Sorry, I had stuff in my arms and kicked the door closed. Did I wake you?'

'Obviously! Is everything all right?' Jane turned on her bedside lamp.

'Yes. I was at my parents', as we missed having dinner there this week. Do you want a cup of tea?'

'No thanks; actually, if you're having one then I will.'

'Right, won't be long. Are you picking up radio signals with those things in your hair? I told you that Dad would know all about that Clarendon Court, didn't I?'

Before Jane could answer he had disappeared, banging his way down the stairs. She sighed, annoyed at being woken up, but also because she didn't like him discussing her work with his father. She took the rollers out and reached over to her bedside table to put them into the bag she used for her brushes and combs.

Eddie returned with two mugs of tea, handing her one and placing his on his bedside table, before getting undressed and putting on his pyjamas.

'You know, I did tell you not to mention what case I am working on, Eddie. I know it's your dad, but at the same time it's unethical.'

Eddie pulled back the duvet and got into bed beside her, then reached for his mug of tea.

'Yeah, but it's not as if he's going to blab about it to anyone. I told you that more than likely he had done work at Clarendon Court because I remember going there one time myself, a long time ago. They built two new houses, and Dad worked on them both; he also did some electrical work at the old manor house, the big property. He said that the bloke was foreign, and he had to send him three chasing invoices because he was late paying. Eventually he had to go round and bang on their door.'

'Well, he probably wouldn't recognise the house,' Jane said.

Eddie nodded. 'Apparently it was really run-down. There was a fire, and a lot of people suspected it was a bit of a torch job.'

'Yes, I was told about the fire by the new owners.'

'I bet they got it for a good price, with all that damage. I never went inside, but I remember the courtyard was a mudbath with the new properties being built alongside it; they had cement mixers and heavy digging equipment that made a real mess. I think there was quite a lot of ill-feeling going on in the neighbourhood, and Dad said the whole courtyard belonged to the big manor house, but they were doing nothing about all the potholes.'

'Well, it's all tarmacked now,' Jane said, 'and for some reason the whole driveway is owned by the people that live in number 10.'

Eddie nodded. 'Dad also told me about their daughter.'

'What about her?'

'She died ... very young. He didn't know much about it ... it was just before he stopped working there.'

'Was she ill?'

'No idea. I just know that it was all everyone was talking about. Dad said she was a pretty little thing. Next time he comes over you should ask him about it. Mum started talking about the announcement in the papers today, about Prince Andrew getting engaged. She'll be there for the wedding. She was at Charles and Diana's, standing outside Buck House for hours; she's collected all those mugs, even got one from the Coronation.'

Jane yawned as Eddie finished his tea and turned off his bedside light.

'I'm out early tomorrow. I've got someone interested in buying my flat,' he said.

'You didn't tell me. Have you got it on with an estate agent?'

'No, it's a friend of one of the guys at work who's looking for a place. Thought I might as well test the water. But if he offers me a good price, I'll take it.'

Jane wasn't sure what to say. They had not discussed the wedding plans, or that Eddie was interested in selling her house and looking for another property to move into. All he had said was they should perhaps buy something and pool their cash and look at a larger property that needed refurbishing. The thought of all the disturbance of moving and living with the dust and workmen again was not something she relished. She chewed her bottom lip, knowing this was probably the right time to bring it up, but she was just too tired. She turned her bedside light off and closed her eyes.

Eddie had left by the time Jane woke up, reaching for her alarm clock to stop it ringing. She arrived at the station early and had breakfast in the canteen. Stanley joined her with a full fry-up and three rounds of toast.

'Morning. What do you think about Prince Andrew's bride-to-be then? Apparently she has no title, but her father runs a polo stable so they can't be short of a bob or two.'

'I caught it on the news this morning; she looks very pretty,' Jane said, sipping her coffee.

'Same colour hair as my wife; well, near enough. She tints it, to be honest.'

DC Burrows was passing their table, his overflowing breakfast tray on a par with Stanley's.

'Mind if I join you?'

'Please do,' Jane said, as he plonked his tray down on their table.

'Can I ask you something . . . do you prefer to be called William or Bill?' Jane asked.

He shrugged. 'Don't mind either. So, another day of waiting. That surgeon has the power, you know. If he induced the coma he could get him out of it and save us a lot of time hanging around.'

Jane nodded. 'I was told that the Larssons' daughter died very young. Do you know anything about it?'

Both men shook their heads as they demolished their breakfasts.

'Maybe that's why they are such a pain in the arse,' Stanley said.

'Do we know exactly when the Larssons bought the courtyard?' Jane asked.

'I reckon it's in my notes somewhere,' Stanley said. 'I think the Hoffmans were so broke they sold off anything they could to make a few quid. When the Caplans bought the big house they didn't have ownership of the courtyard, which is why they had so much trouble from Mr Boon about building their bloody wall and gates.'

Jane gathered her coffee cup, saucer and plate and stood up.

'I'll see you downstairs. Bill, can you do a check on what happened to the Larssons' daughter, just out of interest?'

Stanley carried his tray to the dirty dishes stack and headed out, leaving Bill finishing his breakfast, shaking his head over what he considered a time-waste of a case that wouldn't go away.

There was a meeting in the boardroom scheduled for nine thirty, and Jane was at her desk checking over reports when Bill came to stand beside her.

'Georgina Larsson died of sepsis. Apparently, she had an abortion, but the details are very sketchy. No charges were ever brought against anybody.'

'How old was she?'

'Fifteen, almost sixteen. Rumours are that she paid cash to some back-street bastard, so it was some time before the medical issues were diagnosed and then it was too late to save her.'

'Where did you get this information from?'

'A mate of mine at the local newspaper did a bit of digging. He found out about the abortion, but his editor told him to forget it as they didn't want any legal comeback from her family.'

'Did he find out who the father was?'

'No, but she was underage, so the lid was put on it.'

'Interesting . . .' Jane said, jotting down some notes.

'It sort of makes sense why that woman is so unpleasant; her only daughter, and just a teenager.'

'We're wanted,' Stanley said from across the room, gesturing to DCI Hutton's closed office door.

DCI Hutton was sitting at her desk reading *The Times* as Jane, Stanley and Burrows trooped in. She folded the newspaper and put it down on her desk.

'Lot of news coverage of the forthcoming royal wedding . . . It'll be a nightmare for the Met. Anyway, down to business. As you know, while we wait for Martin Boon to hopefully recover, there have been no formal charges, so while there's no update on his condition we are basically at a standstill. So, I have decided, until something happens, to put this case on the back burner. I will be assigning you other, more urgent cases, but perhaps I can ask you, Jane, to keep a watchful eye on Mr Boon and if anything changes then we will return to the investigation.'

Hutton leaned back in her chair and smiled.

'Any questions?'

All three of them simply shrugged their shoulders.

'Right then, you'll be getting new case files later this morning.'

Stanley went back to his desk and Jane finished her last report and filed it. It was only to be expected, but she was still a bit annoyed, as the Boon case was starting to show signs of getting interesting.

DCI Hutton handed over their new files just after eleven. And as they flicked through them, it quickly became clear that the cases would not, by any stretch of the imagination, be challenging to investigate.

DC Burrows was standing by the incident board with a notepad checking on the case he had been assigned to oversee. There had been a spate of robberies at a local petrol station and two young teenage boys had been identified as the culprits. They had filled their car with petrol and driven off, not once but three times. Their vehicle registrations had been forwarded to the station.

Burrows approached Stanley and told him that the boys worked for a local taxi company run by one of their fathers. Two of them had suspended licences. Warrants had already been issued for their arrest, and it would be down to Burrows to bring them in for questioning.

'The report's gone to the desk sergeant; he said he's going to decide if it's a nothing deal so the uniforms can sort it.'

'Should be an eventful day then,' Stanley said, not really paying that much attention. He noticed that Jane was packing her briefcase and pushed his chair back to face her.

'You off then?'

'You got anything of interest?' she asked, joining him.

'Depends. The boss said it was appropriate to my experience, but to my knowledge I've never had any dealings with retired dog handlers. This one left the Met with his highly trained but injured canine, Hutch. It's down to me to get him to release the dog because he's become vicious.'

'You are joking?'

'Nope . . . apparently Hutch has attacked three people and we have an order for him to be removed to the dog pound; bloody dog section have asked the boss to look into it due to the old boy being ex-Met, and he's so far refused to let them into his house.'

Jane shook her head, smiling.

'So, a man with your vast experience is handed this "very dangerous" assignment, and Burrows is off to arrest three teenagers.'

'Yeah, but they're probably not threatening anyone entering their property with a shotgun.'

'What?'

'OK, maybe he's not got a shotgun but he's refusing to allow anyone to enter . . . so he needs to be talked into seeing sense. At the same time, he has to be shown some respect as he was a good officer, apparently. Anyway, what have you got? Big armed robbery?'

Jane rolled her eyes. 'I'm going to interview a care home worker who has been accused of abuse and threatening behaviour towards one of the elderly residents. Apparently officers have already questioned her and taken statements, but Hutton felt that a more experienced DI should now act on behalf of the patient.'

Stanley burst out laughing as Jane walked off, shaking her head.

Jane was still feeling tetchy as she drove to the care home in Orpington. Again, she questioned her decision to be seconded to Bromley instead of a station nearer the West End, one that would have a strong CID team and more likely to be investigating more serious crimes.

The Winston Care Home was situated in a quiet residential street. The wrought-iron gates were closed and there was an intercom set into the brick column beside it. Jane had to get out of her car to press the button. Hutton had told her that they were expecting her, but she had to wait a long time before a distorted voice answered and told her that someone would come to open the gate.

An elderly man wearing baggy trousers and a thick sweater with a green overall came and peered through.

'I'm Detective Inspector Tennison. I have an appointment,' Jane said, showing her ID.

'These gates are not in a lot of use; visitors usually go round the back. But I'll let you in – just drive right round to the entrance.'

Jane got back into her car and waited as the old boy heaved the gates open and stood waiting for her to drive past. He was wearing an old cloth cap which he tapped with a finger. Jane mouthed 'thank you' through the window as she drove down the narrow driveway.

The entrance to the large Victorian building, which at one time had probably been a grand family home, was flanked by imposing stone pillars and had a heavy mahogany door.

Before Jane could press the bell, she heard an inner door being opened, and a tall, well-built woman in a smart tweed suit swung open the right side of the front door.

'Detective Tennison, I'm sorry you weren't given proper directions; the old gates are rarely used now. We have our main entrance at the rear of the house. I'm Deidre Brandon, director of the Winston Care Home.'

Jane stepped inside.

Jane followed Miss Brandon down the corridor to a small but tidy office, with just a desk and office chair, plus two old-fashioned leather armchairs.

Jane watched as Brandon carefully selected some papers from a pile on the desk, placing them into a large manila envelope.

'We have six private suites, with ensuite bathrooms. The residents can bring in their own furniture if they prefer. The other twenty-four rooms are all located in the new annexe section, which also houses the nursing staff and medical department. We have a dining room, but if a resident wants to dine in their room, we can accommodate their wishes. However, we prefer everyone to dine together to help them make friends.'

Jane frowned. Brandon appeared to be pitching the home to her, as if she was there enquiring about residential care for an elderly relative.

'I know why you're here, of course. In actual fact, I called the station to give DCI Hutton an update on the situation, but I was told you had already left. I'm sorry if it has been a wasted journey. I was told to give you all the details so you can make out a report and the matter can be dealt with officially.'

Jane was taken aback, but remained silent as Miss Brandon opened a drawer and pulled out an open envelope.

'Firstly, let me explain the details of the accusations made by a resident against a very trusted member of my staff. The resident, Adele Sinclair, has only been with us for seven months. She was diagnosed as suffering from progressive dementia. At first she appeared to be settling in well, but within a short time she began creating a lot of disturbance. She continually insisted that a taxi was arriving to take her home and was often found in the reception area with an overnight bag packed. When she was returned to her room, she would become abusive and angry. She had a number of visits from her personal doctor, who prescribed medication to calm her down. Unfortunately, she then began to refuse to take any of her prescriptions, refused to eat, and would not allow anyone to wash her. On several occasions she managed to leave her room during the night and was found using the telephones in the staff offices.'

Jane shifted in her seat, crossing her legs. She made no attempt to interrupt as Miss Brandon continued.

'It all spiralled out of our control when Mrs Sinclair managed to contact a local press reporter and the next minute we had a journalist here, along with a photographer. By this time, she had been a resident for six months and we had to put up with a daily onslaught of dreadful behaviour. Lena Kelly was accused of being abusive and physically attacking her, apparently forcing her to have cold baths and refusing to serve her any food.'

Miss Brandon sighed and shook her head.

'Any accusations against a care home facility have to be taken seriously, and obviously legal advice was taken.'

'Surely her family could have intervened?' Jane said, becoming impatient with Miss Brandon's lengthy explanation.

'I am just coming to that. It was rather complicated. Adele Sinclair was married to Charles Sinclair, a multimillionaire investment banker. He is one of our main benefactors and his charitable donations have been, and still are, extensive. I agreed to care for his wife after he personally approached me. To be perfectly honest, perhaps I am to blame for allowing the situation to have gone on for so long, due to our relationship with Mr Sinclair.'

'That's understandable,' Jane said, relieved that at last she was being told the full story.

'Mr Sinclair obviously had to be told, and he very quickly handled the situation and confided in us about his wife's mental state before her diagnosis. He had previously hired a private nurse – well, several actually. In all, he had hired four nurses, all of whom had been physically threatened by his wife, who had to be restrained. She also made many verbal accusations against them.'

'Why were you not made aware of Mrs Sinclair's previous mental state?'

'Well, we had her medical history, but Mr Sinclair told me personally that he felt that a lot of his wife's state of mind was connected with the fact that he was divorcing her.'

'Ah,' Jane said, as Miss Brandon passed her the envelope.

'That is a copy of the letter from Mr Sinclair's lawyers. I have here all the correspondence between ourselves and the legal team we engaged, Mrs Sinclair's medical history, Miss Kelly's CV and a statement reflecting her shock at the accusations. Obviously, until we know the facts, we had to suspend her with full pay. These are copies, but if you wish to see the originals, I will of course allow you to do so.'

As Miss Brandon handed over the documents there was a light tap on the door. 'Who is it?'

'It's Miss Martinez. I am sorry to interrupt.'

The door opened and Jane saw a petite woman wearing a long, floral dress with a Victorian-style pinafore and large pockets. She had two thick, greying plaits coiled round her head, with a pencil sticking out from one of them.

'I am so sorry to interrupt you, Miss Brandon, but Mr Baker has called asking about the upright piano. He said it really needed to be tuned before his next visit.'

'Oh gosh, yes, I'm sorry, I completely forgot. Come in. I have the tuner's contact details and I meant to arrange an appointment. Detective Tennison, this is Angelica Martinez, who helps with the arts and crafts sessions, and with Mr Baker who comes in once a week and does a little musical routine.'

Miss Martinez stood shyly by the open door. Although obviously middle-aged, she had a childlike presence with her hand stuffed into her apron pocket.

'Now then, I know I had it a couple of days ago when you first asked me . . . is he bringing his pianist with him as usual?'

'Yes, Miss Brandon.'

'Ah, here it is. I'm sorry, please do call him and see if he can come and tune the piano before Mr Baker's little event.'

Miss Brandon handed over a slip of paper.

Miss Martinez smiled. 'Thank you so much. Just one more little request regarding Prince Andrew's wedding. I know it's a long way off, but I was wondering if we could perhaps start making some bunting and little flags? We can make it a special occasion like we did for Prince Charles and Lady Di's wedding.'

'As you said, it is still a long way off yet . . .'

'Yes, but it takes a long time to make these things, and the residents do enjoy doing that very much.'

'Yes, I understand. Thank you, Miss Martinez.'

Miss Brandon couldn't wait to usher the woman out and raised an eyebrow as she closed the door.

'We have a number of very kind helpers; we do try our hardest to bring the boredom level down. Now, let me bring you a cup of coffee while you take your time reading through all the correspondence.'

Jane chewed her bottom lip. The last thing she felt like doing was wading through the whole pile, but she doubted that Miss Brandon would allow the documents to be taken from her office, despite the fact that they were copies.

'Thank you. White, no sugar, please. And if I should need to take any of these documents away, would you be able to print them out for me?'

'Let me ask our lawyer. As I said earlier, we have signed a privacy agreement.'

'I'm sure I won't need to take anything, but just in case.'

Jane couldn't wait to be left alone. Once Miss Brandon had gone, she went to sit in Miss Brandon's desk chair. She tipped out the mound of correspondence, much of which was stapled together with little notes attached. She spread everything out so that she could read it all in chronological order, suspecting it was going to take her at least an hour.

Chapter Nine

Stanley had left the station an hour or so after Jane. He had been making calls to various dog-handling branches of the Met, enquiring about what happened when officers retired and took on their canine partner as a 'live at home' pet. He was surprised by just how many retiring officers took their dogs with them.

The man he was going to see, Officer Donaldson, had an exemplary record with the Met, serving for over twenty-five years. There was not one complaint or misdemeanour recorded against him. His dog, Hutch, had been with Donaldson for seven years and had been assigned to him when he was two years old.

Stanley parked his car in a narrow lane lined with small semi-detached properties on either side.

Donaldson's house clearly needed some exterior painting, and the steps leading to the front door were strewn with dead leaves, rubbish and empty milk bottles. Taped across the letterbox was a laminated card that read NO JUNK MAIL, and when Stanley pressed the doorbell it did not ring. He knocked, waited, then knocked again. There was the sound of a dog barking, so he stood for another minute, stepping back from the door to look up at the house.

The barking persisted, then stopped. He caught sight of a curtain moving and peered into the window, but couldn't see anyone. He tapped on the glass.

'Mr Donaldson? I need to have a chat with you. I'm DI Stanley, from Bromley station. Sir, could you open the door, please? I'm sure you don't want this to be passed onto uniforms coming with an arrest warrant. I just need to talk to you. There's no one else with me.'

The curtain moved again and the window opened a fraction.

'Do you want to see my ID, sir?'

Stanley took out his wallet and held his ID close to the open window. The window closed and Stanley let out a frustrated sigh, but then he heard the front door being opened.

Eric Donaldson looked worn out. He had thinning grey hair, several days of stubble and his eyes were red-rimmed. He wore frayed pyjama bottoms and slippers, with a thick knitted sweater that was unravelling at the cuffs.

'Thank you, sir.'

'Come on through, I've got the kettle on. Do you want a cuppa?'

'I certainly do. Is Hutch in there?'

'He's in his cage.'

The kitchen looked as if it had been caught in a time warp. It had old-fashioned, yellowing wallpaper, a dirty tiled floor and green-painted kitchen cabinets. There was an old fridge covered in stickers next to a greasy gas stove. The sink was stacked with dirty dishes and pans, and there were bags of dog biscuits and tinned dog food scattered over the kitchen units.

Stanley nervously glanced towards the rear of the kitchen as Hutch gave a menacing growl, peering through the mesh of his cage. He was an enormous German shepherd and his big, black-tipped ears were pointing up as his eyes shone like amber.

'My God, he's a big fella,' Stanley said, keeping his distance as he sat down at a small table with a half-eaten bowl of soggy cornflakes on it.

'Quiet! You'll get your cuppa in a minute.'

At first Stanley thought Donaldson was talking to him, but then watched as he filled a teapot and got a dog bowl out of the sink. He then rinsed two mugs out and took a carton of milk from the fridge.

'They used to deliver . . . do you want sugar?'

'No, thanks.'

Donaldson then poured some milk into the dog bowl and added some tea. He carried the bowl over to the cage, opened the latch and put it inside. Hutch immediately started slurping hungrily.

'Old routine we had, cuppa each morning before we went on duty. Now, you pour, and I'll get a biscuit.'

'No thanks, just the tea is fine,' Stanley replied.

'The biscuit's for him, not you.'

Hutch gobbled down his proferred dog biscuit, and Stanley poured the tea as Donaldson came and sat down.

'Sir, do you want to tell me about the three accusations against Hutch? I have the police reports, but I'd like to hear it from you.'

'All you need to know is that without a command from me he wouldn't make a move against anyone.'

By admitting that Hutch obeyed his commands, it meant that Donaldson had given instructions to the dog to attack. Stanley nodded, then decided on a different approach, trying to get Donaldson's confidence.

'I'm about to retire myself, you know.'

Donaldson nodded. 'Always been attached to Bromley?'

'Good God no, I've been around the houses. I did a stint with the Sweeney and worked undercover, but I have two kids and a mortgage, and to be honest I was tired out.'

'My wife left me a year before I retired,' Donaldson said. 'She'd been having an affair with a good friend of mine – it was a real kick in the teeth. To be honest, I don't know what hurt me the most, her wanting a divorce or that someone I'd worked alongside for years was a lying, two-faced bastard. She got the house, and I moved in here with my old mum. But she died a year later.'

'Did she get along with Hutch?'

'Course she did, he's a big old softy . . . and I liked the fact that he was here if I had to go out . . . she felt safe with him.'

Stanley nodded and drained his mug of tea.

'We're going to have to discuss why I'm here, sir, the destruction order on Hutch. Before I came here, I had a chat with a few stations where there are dog handlers, and I also talked to the training centre and . . .'

Donaldson kicked back his chair and Hutch stood up in his cage, startled by the noise. He pushed his nose through the mesh.

'Lie down, that's a good boy. Inspector, you should go. He's not going to be taken from me unless it's over my dead body, do you understand?'

'Hear me out, sir, please. There's good rehabilitation kennels that can take him, and there's also a charitable foundation made up of ex-dog handlers . . .'

'You got five seconds to leave my house before I let Hutch out.'

Stanley held his hands up. 'Come on, there's no need to threaten me.'

'He's all I've got, it's just him and me. All I am asking is to be left alone.'

'Mr Donaldson – Eric – if I walk out, you know there'll be repercussions. I'm here to try and find a solution so he doesn't have to be destroyed. I won't be taking Hutch, but if you would consider the rehabilitation kennels, I could talk to someone there for you. Or you could talk to them.'

Donaldson shook his head, turning to look at Hutch.

'He's old, in dog years he's in his eighties. He's got arthritis in his hips, and no bloody rehabilitation foundation would take care of him. I pay for his medication, and I don't want any charitable aid, either for him or for me.'

Stanley gritted his teeth, beginning to lose patience. He pulled out the notes he had made from his calls that morning.

'Listen to me, Eric. Look over these and talk to the people I spoke to because I think you need help.'

Donaldson picked up the papers and tore them in two. He was physically shaking as he threw them across the table. He then turned towards the cage as Hutch began to growl.

'I'm going to let him out; go on, you get out.'

Stanley stood up and backed away from the table towards the door. Donaldson picked up a dog lead and wrapped it round the knuckles on his right hand. Stanley raised his arms, moving further towards the hall as the cage was opened and Hutch started to growl, baring his teeth.

'I'm fucking out of here. You keep that dog away from me.'

Donaldson laughed as he clipped the leash onto Hutch's collar and the massive dog lurched forwards. Stanley moved down the hall and opened the front door.

The door slammed shut behind him and Stanley walked quickly back to his car. He took a while to calm himself down, angry at being subjected to such humiliation. He was also infuriated that he'd been given the task of dealing with the Donaldson situation in the first place.

Jane was not as angry as Stanley, but she still felt her trip to the care home had been a total waste of her time. She was finally replacing all the documents in the folder when there was a light knock on the door and Miss Martinez came in with a tray of coffee and biscuits.

'I'm sorry this has taken so long, but we had a delivery and Miss Brandon is arranging for one of our residents to have guests for lunch. She will be with you in a moment.'

'Thank you, but I am just about to leave.'

'Oh, well, let me go and find her for you.'

Before Jane could say there was no need, Miss Brandon appeared and Jane had to wait as she wrote a note for DCI Hutton, putting it in a sealed envelope before handing it to Jane.

'Thank you so much for your time,' she said with a smile. 'Let me walk you out.'

By the time Jane got to her car she had decided that she would go home early. There was no urgent need to make an official report as it had all apparently been sorted, and if she was questioned, she would just say that it had taken hours of her time to go through all the documents.

Not far from the care home, Jane passed a bus stop and noticed Miss Martinez waiting. Jane pulled up, lowered her window and asked if she could give her a lift. Miss Martinez bent down towards the window.

'That is very kind of you, I don't want to put you to any trouble, but I missed my usual bus as I usually only do half-mornings.'

Jane leaned across the passenger seat to open the door. Miss Martinez got into the car, thanking Jane and telling her where she needed to go, saying that she hoped it was not too far out of her way.

'I must say I was very impressed with the facilities at the care home,' Jane said, making conversation. 'Have you worked there long?'

'Yes, a few years, but just part-time because I'm not trained as a carer. I run the arts department and organise the events. We have lots of trips out from the home to the local theatre and exhibitions; we have a small coach and a driver. I think the residents really benefit from these excursions as it breaks up the monotony. We also have a very nice lady who comes in and does their hair and manicures.'

Jane continued to drive as directed, making left and right turns. Miss Martinez pointed out where she usually got off the bus.

'You could drop me here if you like. I live just along that road, by the shops.'

'It's no trouble,' Jane said. 'Tell me, how did you get on with Mrs Sinclair, the lady that caused all the problems?'

'Oh dear, she really was a difficult lady. I felt so sorry for Lena as she is such a dedicated and caring young woman. We all felt very bad for her. At one time or another we had all been subjected to Mrs Sinclair's irrational behaviour, and she was constantly making accusations about the staff. A lot of the residents suffer from dementia, but she could be really vicious and physically abusive – nothing satisfied her. We were told that she had suffered a nervous breakdown when her husband began divorce proceedings; apparently he was having a relationship with a nurse he'd hired to take care of her.'

Miss Martinez gave a little shrug of her shoulders. 'I shouldn't gossip but I think most of the staff got to hear about it, with her husband being such an important benefactor. I think Miss Brandon tolerated much more than she would have done before it all became impossible, because of who Mrs Sinclair was married to . . .'

'It must cost a considerable amount to be a resident,' Jane said, very aware that Miss Brandon hadn't mentioned the fact that their big charitable donor was having a relationship with the nurse employed to care for Mrs Sinclair.

'Oh, yes. It is very costly, and then there are all the extras. If you just pull over by the newsagent, I live in the flat above.'

Jane parked directly opposite the small row of shops. Next to the newsagent was a little alley with steps going up to the floor above. Miss Martinez got out.

'Could I offer you a coffee? I also have lovely fresh pastries made every day.'

'Thanks, that's very kind of you, but I should be getting back to work.'

Jane watched Miss Martinez wave to someone inside the newsagent and approach the alley. Jane was about to drive off when she noticed the sign above the shop: HOLLOW LANE NEWSAGENT. She frowned, trying to recall why it was familiar. She reached over to the back seat for her handbag. Tucked inside amongst various receipts was the note from Alice Caplan with Mrs Hoffman's address: Flat A, 91 Hollow Lane, Orpington.

Jane could hardly believe it. Was Miss Martinez actually Mrs Hoffman? She decided there was only one way to find out.

By the time she had crossed the road and entered the alley there was no sign of Miss Martinez. The stone steps led up to a small stone patio area in front of a blue-painted door with 'Flat A' printed in white. There was a small potted plant beside the door, and an old-fashioned bicycle leaned against the low wall surrounding the patio.

Jane rang the bell and waited only a moment before it was opened by Miss Martinez, with a look of surprise.

'I hope you don't mind, but I just had a sort of memory jolt. I was actually given your address by Alice Caplan. She and her husband live in the Old Manor House in Clarendon Court.'

Miss Martinez nodded. 'I used to live there with my husband . . . a long time ago. I am divorced now.'

'What a coincidence. Would you mind if I came in and asked you a few questions? It's nothing of any concern, it's just that I am working on an investigation involving Mr Caplan.'

'Yes, of course, do come in. I have to tell you that I only met Mrs Caplan once or twice as my husband dealt with selling the property.'

Jane was ushered into a narrow, cluttered hallway and Miss Martinez showed her into a bright, colourful lounge with easy chairs. Woven Mexican rugs covered the white-painted floor-boards and vivid oil paintings covered the walls.

'Please, do sit down and I'll make some coffee. And I brought back some fresh pastries this morning.'

'That's very kind of you, I really do appreciate you agreeing to talk to me.'

Miss Martinez laughed and shrugged her shoulders.

'To be honest, I don't have many visitors. Please make yourself comfortable.'

Jane put her handbag on the arm of one of the chairs and looked around the room. There was a hand-painted chest with rows of photographs in ornate silver frames, including a wedding photograph of Miss Martinez in a patterned, embroidered, long dress with a very tall chiselled blond-haired man in a velvet suit. She was holding the hand of a small boy who looked about six or seven years old. Engraved on the frame was: WEDDING, MEXICO CITY, 1970. There were several other photographs of the young boy at various ages, but none of the tall blond man. In one, the boy appeared to be a teenager, with shoulder-length dark hair and beautiful almond-shaped eyes. Jane thought he had a sweet and gentle smile.

Miss Martinez returned with a tray and two bone-china cups, a silver coffee pot and pastries arranged on a delicate floral-patterned plate.

'It won't be long. I make good coffee, but let me warn you it is very strong, but *so* good!'

She placed the tray down on a small, carved, Indian table and sat down.

'I was looking at your lovely photographs. Is that your son?' Jane asked.

'Yes, my husband adopted him when we married. We left Mexico to live in Berlin, then London, where Victor – my husband, now ex-husband – is living. Martinez is my maiden name.'

'I should explain why I wanted to talk to you,' Jane said. 'I'm investigating an incident involving David Caplan and a neighbour from Clarendon Court, Martin Boon.'

'I'm afraid I can't really be of much assistance to you. Victor and I lived at Clarendon Court, but I only recall meeting Mr Caplan on a few occasions. Though my husband had some arguments with Mr Boon regarding planning permission, I think. He was also not on very good terms with another neighbour, Mr Larsson.'

Jane nodded. 'It seems that the same neighbours have a similar relationship with David Caplan.'

Miss Martinez got up to pour the coffee. Jane briefly explained about the investigation, but Miss Martinez showed no reaction.

'We're waiting to find out if Mr Boon recovers, so we can get his side of things,' Jane added.

'Victor might be able to give you more information. I had so little to do with any of the neighbours, as we were going through a difficult time, both emotionally and financially. Victor bought the property with the intention of turning it into flats. It was a very large house, and we bought it for a good price as it was in a very bad state. I don't think anything had been done for thirty years or more, so the electrics and the plumbing all needed replacing. Victor had grandiose plans, but he had not taken proper legal advice about converting the property. It was sort of a last effort on his part to make us financially secure. He had previously had a number of failed business ventures, and was depending on two friends who were interested in part-financing the conversion. But when the planning applications were denied his friends pulled out.'

'I imagine that the fire must have created even more problems?'

'Yes, it was dreadful. Victor did have some insurance, but we had no alternative but to sell. By this time I had decided that I had had enough; my first husband, my son's father, died of cancer and left me a substantial legacy, but Victor mishandled it, so we ended up bankrupt.'

'Was it at this time that Victor arranged to sell the courtyard to the Larssons?'

'I believe so; he was trying to raise money and we never used the courtyard ourselves, other than for deliveries. It was really in a very bad state: it was full of potholes and when it rained it got very muddy.'

Jane noticed that for the first time Miss Martinez seemed ill at ease. She kept straightening her skirt, then plucking at the material.

'The courtyard appears to be a continuing problem area for Mr Caplan, with the same neighbours refusing to allow anyone to park their cars on it.'

'Again, I can't recall exactly when, or for how much, Victor sold the courtyard to the Larssons, but he put the house on the market shortly afterwards.'

Miss Martinez still seemed nervous. She opened a small leather box and took out a cigarette.

'Do you mind?'

Jane shook her head. Miss Martinez's hand was shaking as she lit her cigarette. She showed the silver lighter to Jane.

'My first husband owned tin mines and made many beautiful things. We lived in Monterey, a very beautiful seaside town. He was originally from Ethiopia. My son, Sebastian, looks so like him; he has the same eyes.'

Her own eyes were full of tears as she spoke.

'Victor did not really get along with my son when he became a teenager. Sebastian was a musician; he was so talented. Victor was angry because he left school at sixteen. And Sebastian knew Victor was squandering my inheritance, and ultimately his inheritance. Then . . .'

Miss Martinez went to sit back in her chair and gave deep sighs as she tried to control her tears.

'I don't really know what happened, but the Larssons' daughter would sometimes come to the house. She was infatuated with Sebastian. The truth was that many girls would dote on him. But it all ended badly. They were both underage, and she got pregnant.'

'I know their daughter died,' Jane said quietly.

'Yes, so Sebastian left. I gave him money to travel to Mexico. The house was sold, we got divorced and Victor returned to Berlin.'

'Is your son still living in Mexico?'

'I don't know. Just before we moved out from Clarendon Court, I received a postcard saying that he was living in Mexico City, but he would be coming home to see me.'

Jane looked puzzled. 'Wasn't that a long time ago?'

'Yes, I have never seen him again. I used to go to the old house just to make sure that when I changed addresses he would know where to find me. I would have gone back to Mexico, but there was always so little money. I was so afraid that if I did, he might go back to Clarendon Court, and we would miss each other.'

Jane glanced at her watch and knew it was time she left. She stood up as Miss Martinez opened a drawer of a hand-painted dresser and took out a card.

'To be honest I needed help, emotionally, because I was waiting for him to find me. I had therapy because I was very depressed, I was so desperate for my son to make contact. After I got the job at the care home and moved here, one of the staff told me about this wonderful woman. She is a medium, and she has truthfully given me real hope. Not only hope but encouragement that I am doing the right thing, and that my son will find me. I think she is a very special woman with extraordinary insights and intuition. She gave me reason to stay here, as she told me he is close.'

Miss Martinez passed the card to Jane, pressing it into her hand.

'She knew that my son was the light of my life. She told me he was close, even at the old house. So even though I am still waiting, she gives me such comfort.'

After the odd turn the conversation had taken, Jane was eager to leave. 'Thank you for talking to me, but I've already taken up too much of your time.' Opening the front door, Jane turned back to thank her again and accidentally knocked against the bicycle. She propped it back up as Miss Martinez quickly came to help her.

In the basket of the bicycle was a black bicycle pump. Miss Martinez picked it up and showed Jane that the attachment to connect the pump to the tyre needed to be replaced.

'My friend in the newsagent is trying to find me one, but it's so old I may have to buy a new one.' She smiled apologetically. 'I don't think I have been much help to you, but you know where I am if you need to contact me again.'

Jane unlocked her car, tossing her handbag onto the passenger seat. She tossed the medium's card onto the seat next to her handbag.

She suddenly remembered that it was Friday and that she would be having dinner with her parents. And more importantly, she would have the weekend off.

Chapter Ten

Eddie was late arriving home and Jane was already changed and ready to go to her parents'. He had completely forgotten the now obligatory once-a-month dinner with her parents and didn't look happy about going. But instead of being annoyed, Jane decided that if she went alone she could be home earlier than usual, as her father always had some small job he needed Eddie to deal with.

'Listen, if I take a quick shower, I'll come with you.'

'No, don't worry about it; besides, you've had a long day. I doubt very much it was as tedious as the day I've had, but you crash out and I'll see you later.'

Mrs Tennison had made a stew and apple pie. As always, she lit up when she saw Jane, while her husband was disappointed at Eddie's absence, as he had wanted help in fitting a security alarm. During dinner Jane was asked whether there had been any decision on a wedding date, and she told them that at the moment they were just focusing on selling her house and finding a bigger property.

'That seems a shame. You've only just got it all finished. Is Eddie's business doing well enough to share in the cost of buying a new place?' Jane's father asked.

'Well, because of all the work he's done, I'll get a very good price. He has a small sort of studio apartment that he wants to sell, and he's interested in looking at a property that will need fixing up.'

'So would that mean you would have to live there while the work is carried out?'

'Yes, Mum. I'm stalling a bit because it took such a long time with all the refurbishments.'

'Eddie did an excellent job,' her father said, repeating how impressed they had been when they had last visited.

'Did you read about Prince Andrew's engagement?' Jane's mother asked.

'Yes. Eddie's mum has been to all the royal weddings. I mean, she's not invited, just part of the crowd.'

Her mother shook her head. 'You wouldn't get me standing there in the rain waving a flag; better to just watch it on TV. I'll always remember Prince Charles and Lady Di's wedding, that was a really wonderful occasion. So will you be having a church wedding, one with all the trimmings?'

'I doubt it, Mum ... it'll probably be a registry office and then lunch, nothing fancy. But as I said before, we haven't even discussed a date yet.'

'I would say that Eddie's intention of getting a bigger property means you're thinking about starting a family?'

'Oh, for goodness' sake, Mum!'

'Well, dear, the longer you leave it the harder it might be. I mean, Pam had her two shortly after she was married. Theirs was a lovely ceremony, and she looked so beautiful. Her dress set Daddy and I back considerably – cost a fortune. And then there was the buffet lunch . . .'

Her father leaned over the table to pat Jane's hand.

'You mustn't worry about the expense, Jane. Whatever you decide, we'll be paying. That hotel we used for Pam was very good and quite reasonable.'

Mrs Tennison laughed. 'We've been waiting so long, I'll need to buy a new hat.'

By the time Jane felt she could leave without them being disappointed, she was exhausted. When she got home Eddie was sound asleep, so she undressed in the bathroom, changed into her nightdress and crept into bed next to him. The evening's conversation about their wedding date had irritated her, especially her mother talking about them starting a family. Jane found it difficult to even think about, but she knew she would have to sit down with Eddie and talk things through.

It was just after eight on Saturday morning when Jane woke up. She could hear the radio on downstairs blaring out pop music. Eddie appeared to be unable to do anything without the radio being turned on, and all his workmen were the same. When they had been working at the house, there were different stations playing in every room.

Jane dressed in an old tracksuit and slippers and headed downstairs. Eddie was cooking bacon, sausages and tomatoes in a frying pan. There was another pan with simmering baked beans and a smaller frying pan for the eggs. When Eddie cooked, he seemed to be able to use virtually every pan they owned.

'Morning, my darling one,' he beamed. 'I was going to bring you breakfast on a tray. Would you like some fried bread as well?'

'No, that all looks good. I'll put some bread in the toaster and set the table.'

'How were your parents?'

'Fine. As I expected, Dad had a job for you. He wants to fit a security alarm system.'

'I'll do it next time we see them. I have some good news, though!'

Eddie began to serve up the breakfast, waving a spatula at a zip-up bag.

'Take a look inside. It was a good deal. He wants most of the furniture I've got, apart from my TV, which I can set up in the bedroom.'

Jane unzipped the bag. It was full of cash, bundled up with rubber bands.

'Good God, Eddie, how much is in here?'

'Ten grand. It'll be really useful for buying equipment for work. And there's a couple of possible houses we can look at tomorrow.'

'Isn't it illegal?'

Eddie put down her plate, grinning.

'Listen, the amount of tax and VAT added on everything really pisses me off.'

'So where did he get all this cash from?'

He sat down opposite her, unscrewing the tomato ketchup.

'Like I just said, it was a really good deal. If I had put it on with an estate agent, they would have taken their cut.'

Jane took a deep breath as he tucked into his breakfast.

'You know, Eddie, I think you sometimes forget that I am a police officer. It may well be a good deal, but you are taking a bit of a risk legally.'

'Rubbish! Anyway, the less you know about it, the better. If you like any of those houses, we can call this afternoon to arrange a viewing. Two of them are up for auction and if we're interested, we'll really need to have a good look inside for any problems, wet or dry rot, roofing, brickwork, et cetera. And at the same time check out any building restrictions.'

Jane started to eat but quickly found she wasn't hungry. It felt as if Eddie was putting pressure on her when she hadn't even made a decision yet about selling her house. She physically jumped when there was suddenly a loud ringing noise. Eddie opened the bag, taking out his mobile phone.

'Hi Caroline, what's up?'

Jane listened as he ended the call and then went and used the telephone in the hall. She could only catch part of the conversation, but from his tone of voice it sounded important. After a moment he hurried back into the kitchen.

'I have to go . . . Mum needs me to take her to hospital . . . she's fallen and thinks she's broken her arm. Dad is out on a job and she can't get hold of him.'

Eddie stopped by the table, picked up some toast and forked his bacon and sausage in between the slices to make a sandwich. He then gulped down his coffee.

'I'll get over there and ring you as soon as I know what is happening. I'll take my mobile with me, so if you need me or if Dad tries to make contact I'll have it with me.'

Jane hurried after Eddie as he fetched his coat and car keys. He gave her a quick kiss before dashing out.

Jane returned to the kitchen, tipping most of his leftover breakfast, as well as her own, into the bin. She then set about washing up all the pots and pans.

It was after eleven and Jane had still not heard from Eddie. She had changed the bedsheets, run the washing machine, hoovered, dusted and also emptied the dishwasher.

The zip-up bag sat on the floor by the kitchen table. Jane opened it and picked up one of the bundles of ten-pound notes. They were all well used, and she quickly stuffed them back into the bag, not liking them even being in the house. She zipped up the bag and took it out into the hall and put it into the understairs cupboard. She then returned to the kitchen to look at the property details Eddie had left. They were cut out from various local newspapers and clipped together. There was also a leaflet with the auction dates and times, and some had been underlined in pencil.

It was almost twelve when the phone rang with a message from the mobile centre. Mr Myers was at St Mary's Hospital in the A&E department, it was nothing too serious and he would call later.

Eddie eventually called to say that his mother had broken her right wrist. They had been at the hospital virtually all day waiting for X-rays and then for her wrist to be put in a cast. His dad had returned home, but Eddie had decided to stay over as his dad needed to finish off the job on Sunday and wanted his help.

Jane made no mention of having looked over the property details. She decided to have an early night and the following morning she drove to the new car wash that had opened at her local garage. After the car had been cleaned, she did a food shop and marinated two steaks for their dinner. It was after seven when Eddie returned, and Jane had just opened a bottle of wine.

'I found this on the path outside the front door . . .' Eddie held up the medium's card with a grin. 'Do you need some help with an investigation?'

Jane recalled tossing the card onto the passenger seat of her car and assumed it fell out when she brought in the food shopping.

During dinner Eddie explained how his mother had tripped over the hoover and fallen, breaking a small bone in her right wrist. He said she was in a lot of pain but most of her distress was down to her worrying about not being able to cook or clean.

'I don't know if you knew, but Mum has a few clients she does housecleaning for, so she won't be able to do her job for a few weeks. So she was in a bit of a state.'

'I didn't know.'

'Yeah, some of her clients she's been going to for years, so she got all upset about letting them down. I stayed over as Dad's not much help around the house. I made some shepherd's pie and took some stuff out of their freezer so she doesn't have to cook for him.'

She nodded. 'I put your cash in the cupboard under the stairs, by the way.'

'Thanks. So how come you got this card from the medium? Do you believe in all that stuff?'

'No, I don't, the woman who gave it to me works at the care home I visited. She and her husband used to live in the big house in Clarendon Court before they sold it to the present owners. She's been waiting to hear from her son who left before they sold, but he's never made contact. So, she's been seeing this medium.'

'What care home?'

'Oh, it's a case I had to go and check out. It was just coincidence really, and she's now using her maiden name, so I didn't make the connection until I was having coffee with her.'

Eddie picked up his plate and took it to the sink. She liked the fact that he now actually rinsed it before placing it into the dishwasher.

'Did you have a look over the houses that are up for auction?'

'Yes, I noticed you had ringed a few of them. Will we have time to view them now?'

'Plenty of time. I think I'll just go over to my old place and get the TV and a few clothes I've still got there.'

'Tonight?'

'Yeah. Like I told you, he's buying all my furniture, so he'll be moving in tomorrow. I want to give it a bit of a clean, check out all the electric and gas meters.'

'Fine, whatever.'

'Do you want to come with me?'

'Not really. Let me clear up here, and then I'm going to wash my hair.'

Eddie left shortly afterwards, and after cleaning the pans and putting the dishwasher on, Jane went upstairs. She was annoyed at herself for not discussing her misgivings about buying another property. She got into her pyjamas and dried her hair. It was after midnight and Eddie still wasn't back, so she got into bed, turned off her bedside light and went to sleep.

The alarm jolted her awake. When she came to, she was a bit confused to see Eddie had not come home. She flopped back onto her pillow and it took a while to get herself out of bed and ready to leave for the station. There was no message on the answerphone, so she called Eddie's mobile to check if everything was all right, leaving a message with the operator. She then drove to the station.

Jane made out a report from the care home to be filed, then had a quick breakfast in the canteen before heading to the boardroom for the Monday-morning briefing. Jane noticed that Stanley was missing and that he was obviously going to be late. DCI Hutton entered the boardroom, ready for the early start, and Jane listened to updates on the various cases for half an hour, the officers keeping their details as brief as possible. There were house burglaries, domestic violence incidents and there was a drug dealer's arrest. Hutton made notes and raised a few queries, but nothing of great importance seemed to have happened over the weekend. DC Burrows reported on the arrests of the teenagers in connection with the petrol station: two had been released but the eldest one was still in a cell waiting to be interviewed later that morning.

The boardroom door banged open and Stanley marched in, waving a large manila envelope. He looked dishevelled and unshaven and barged his way between two officers, slamming the envelope down on the table in front of Hutton.

'So do you want an update on my visit to Eric Donaldson?'

Before Hutton could reply, Stanley angrily snatched up the envelope and waved it in front of her.

'The poor bastard gassed himself and his dog. I feel fucking responsible for their deaths because I walked out on him – and right now I feel that I should walk out of here.'

Hutton pushed her chair back and stood up.

'Detective Inspector Stanley, I think we need to discuss this in the privacy of my office. Thank you for your attendance, everyone.'

Hutton walked out of the boardroom as everyone else began to collect their notebooks and return to their desks with a lot of raised eyebrows and shocked expressions. Jane went straight over to Stanley, who was standing with his fists clenched at his sides.

'Shall I get you a cup of tea?'

'The poor bugger ... he needed a social worker. What was I supposed to do? Christ, Jane, he warned me that he would only let his dog go over his dead body. He wedged tea towels under the kitchen and backdoors, turned the gas rings on and lay down beside the stove.'

Jane patted his arm. In all the years she had known Stanley – and they had been through some major investigations together – she had never seen him so emotionally affected by a case. By now the boardroom had emptied and Stanley had taken out a grubby handkerchief to wipe his eyes.

'Detective Inspector Stanley?' Dora Phillips, the head of the civilian staff, who ran the typing pool, stood at the open door. 'DCI Hutton is in her office.'

Stanley looked at Jane and in a low voice said Hutton could go and fuck herself, but Jane gave him a hug and told him to calm down, saying that she would bring him in a cup of tea.

'Thank you, Miss Phillips, there is no need for you to wait.'

The door swung closed as Stanley blew his nose, then stuffed his handkerchief back into his pocket.

'I'm bloody through with this shit. I can't take any more of it. I'm going to tell her to stuff this place right up her tight arse.'

'Come on, Stanley, calm down. Just remember your pension and don't blow it. I'm feeling pretty pissed off as well. I spent the entire day at a care home supposedly checking an assault charge against one of the staff. Turned out it had all been sorted and Hutton already knew, so it was a completely wasted day.'

He shook his head. 'I'll need a bloody care home if I have to keep working here for much longer. The truth is, that dog scared the pants off me. I've never liked those big German shepherds. My kids have a crazy little dog, which is about all I can handle.'

Jane smiled. He was calming down now. She walked out of the boardroom to go to the canteen to get him a cup of tea. Stanley headed to Hutton's office.

Stanley had returned to his desk when Jane reappeared with his tea. He leaned over and said quietly that the headmistress had apologised to him.

DCI Hutton came out of her office half an hour later, gesturing for both Jane and Stanley to join her.

'I have just been told that Martin Boon has come out of his coma and has been moved from the intensive care unit into a private room. I think we should give it a couple of days before interviewing him, but we do need to get this situation sorted as soon as possible.'

Stanley waited until Hutton had returned to her office before shrugging.

'So, what does she expect us to do in the meantime?'

'How about lunch?'

They sat at a table in the corner of the canteen with lunch on their trays. Jane told Stanley about the coincidence of meeting Miss Martinez, who turned out to be Victor Hoffman's Mexican wife.

'How come she's still living here and not in Mexico?'

'It was kind of sad. Her son left for Mexico and sent her a post-card to say he would be coming home, but she never heard from him again. She said she purposely stayed close to Clarendon Court, and Mrs Caplan told me she had called there to check whether her son had made contact. In fact, it was Alice Caplan that gave me her address, but as she is now using her maiden name, I didn't make the connection. There were photographs of her son and he is really stunning. His biological father was Ethiopian and died when he was very young, but Victor Hoffman adopted him when he married Miss Martinez. She said that her son and Victor had not got along.'

'What about the sale of the courtyard to the Larssons?'

'Oh yes, I asked her about that. She said that it was her husband who organised it. Apparently, they rarely, if ever, used the courtyard and she also said it was in very poor condition.'

'So how come she's still living here? It's been years.'

Jane shrugged, sipping her coffee.

'I can only presume she is hoping her son will contact her. I mean, she can't be earning much at the care home. I was driving out and saw her waiting at the bus stop, so I offered her a lift. That's how I discovered she was previously married to Victor Hoffman, when she invited me in for a coffee. I think something went on with her son. I'm not sure about the date, but the Larssons' daughter died around about the same time as they were selling the house. They were having a relationship and she got pregnant.'

'I'd say you got a lot of info, not that it adds up to any help with our investigation . . .'

'She even gave me a card from a medium she visits in order to try to contact her son. It was funny because I tossed it onto the passenger seat in the car when I drove off without looking at it. Then Eddie found it on our doorstep because I'd brought some shopping in and must have picked it up with the bags. He asked if we were using a medium to help with our case!' She laughed.

'I used one in a really nasty murder investigation once,' Stanley said. 'She was astonishing. It freaked us all out.'

'Well, by the time she started telling me about the medium I just wanted to leave. I was in such a hurry that I knocked over her bicycle that was propped up outside her front door.'

Jane was about to finish her coffee when she put the cup down and leaned back in her chair. 'Oh my God . . .'

'What?'

Jane ran her fingers through her hair. 'It's just hit me; she was showing me how her bicycle pump was broken.'

'What are you talking about, Jane?'

'How many times have we heard David Caplan describe the weapon he says Martin Boon was carrying? He's repeated it over and over, that it was about fourteen inches long, black and shiny, and that he thought it was an iron bar.'

'But what if it was just a shiny plastic bicycle pump!' Stanley laughed.

'Exactly! Do we know if there was a bicycle in Boon's garage?'

Stanley stacked up their dirty plates, smiling and shaking his head.

'Boon's wife doesn't drive, right? So, what if she uses a bike? I'm serious, Stanley.'

'I'm going to get another cup of tea. In the meantime, go and talk to Bill Burrows. He's done a search for the weapon, along with half a dozen officers. See if they can make any connection to anything in the Boons' garage.'

Burrows was in an interview with the teenager accused of driving out of the garage without paying for petrol, so Jane had no option but to check through the records of the various searches that had taken place around the courtyard and residents' gardens. There was a reference to a search of Martin Boon's garage, but no mention of a bicycle.

Jane was waiting for Stanley, who had gone off to use his electric shaver and had combed his hair. He needed persuading to accompany her to inspect Mr Boon's garage, reluctantly jumping into the passenger seat as they headed out of the station.

'What was the medium's name?'

'What?'

'On the card Miss Martinez gave you?'

'I didn't look. Why?'

'Just making conversation. I never finished telling you about the woman we used on the murder case. Missing young kid, disappeared from outside his home. We'd had search parties out for days and all night, but nothing. He was there one minute and gone the next. Anyway, I think she rang the station . . . or someone put her in touch with us . . . it was a good few years ago.'

'So what did she do?'

'She made some drawings, insisting that the boy would be found in a wooded area with a big overhanging tree; think it was a willow tree, near water . . .'

'Go on.'

'She was right, that's where we eventually found him. But the reason I remember it was because she was so ordinary. She didn't want any money, and no press.'

'I would say that the medium the ex-Mrs Hoffman is going to is probably coining it,' Jane said. 'She told me the medium was giving her hope that her son would be coming home.'

'I doubt it would be the same woman; like I said, it was a long time ago.'

Jane drove through the main gates of Clarendon Court and parked alongside the Caplans' Range Rover. 'Just in case we get a visit from the Larssons, we'll walk round.'

The Larssons' garage was closed, but Martin Boon's car was parked in the space in front of the open garage. They skirted around the car and Jane pointed to a bicycle propped up against the far wall. It was a black, rusty, straight-handled man's bike. There was a saddle bag attached to the back of the seat. They walked in to take a closer look and Stanley bent down with a handkerchief to detach the bicycle pump that was held by two clips on the crossbar.

Stanley held it up and it was immediately obvious to both of them that this could easily be mistaken for some kind of weapon. 'Yeah, I reckon . . .' Jane made a frantic gesture and put her index finger up to her lips to indicate that they needed to be quiet.

They edged out from the garage. She pointed to the open window by the front door. They heard Mrs Boon's voice first but did not hear clearly what was being said. They then heard the strident voice of Patricia Larsson.

'You have to ask them. It's important that you know, Ellen. I mean, was he coherent when you saw him? Does he remember everything, or has he been affected mentally? What did they tell you?'

'That he was doing very well, and that he was out of ICU. I didn't get to talk to him.'

'I hope to God he's not going to cause trouble in there. We've had enough, and we have to get rid of the police. Do you understand?'

'Yes, yes, I do.'

'OK, well, get yourself together and I'll drive you there right now. The police will be questioning him – and you.'

Jane and Stanley made a quick move towards the front door just as it opened.

Mrs Larsson gave a startled look and then forced a smile.

'Good heavens!'

'Good afternoon, Mrs Larsson. We have just been told the good news that Mr Boon is no longer in a coma,' Jane said with a smile.

'Yes, that's right. I am just going to drive Ellen to see him.'

'We just wanted to know if we could be of any assistance.'

'Everything has been taken care of, thank you so much.'

Mrs Larsson hurried past them, easing the door closed behind her. Stanley was holding the bicycle pump under his coat.

'Jane, we need to do a quick exit and get this into an evidence bag, because as you well know this is illegal and if we did find anything on it, it couldn't be used as evidence.'

Jane thought for a moment.

'I'll put a note through their door to say we've removed it. I've got a bag in the car. We could also pay a visit to Mr Caplan and show it to him, but we need to be cautious. What do you think?'

'Well, we should show it to Mr Boon first, but as he's unable to be interviewed, let's extract the prints from it. It's obviously his bicycle but we need to be certain. We can come back to show it to Mr Caplan later, or in the morning.'

Driving back to the station with the pump carefully wrapped in two evidence bags, Stanley gave Jane a sidelong glance.

'Going back over what we overheard this afternoon, Mrs Larsson said something about hoping he was not going to cause any trouble, concerns about the police questioning him. She's involved in it. It sounds like she's pulling the strings. She was in the Caplans' garden so she could have replaced the pump on the bike.'

Jane drove into the station car park and leaned over to the back seat to pick up the evidence bags containing the bicycle pump.

DC Burrows was heading towards them.

'Afternoon. I hope you've had a productive day. I've had that punk kid and his smart-arsed solicitor driving me nuts. Thankfully DCI Hutton stepped in and wiped the floor with the pair of them.'

'Great. Well done.' Jane pushed past him, not wanting to waste time getting into a lengthy conversation.

'You had three calls, and I've left a note on your desk,' he called after her.

Stanley handed the bicycle pump to the forensic department, with a request for prints to be checked asap. Jane was at her desk typing up a report when Stanley joined her again.

'Forensics are out on a job, but due back shortly.'

Jane nodded. 'I'm making the report as brief as possible, but we need to make sure it's all above board so we don't get rapped over the knuckles for not getting permission. It might be crucial evidence.'

'Fine, anything urgent from the calls?'

'No, they're from Eddie's call centre passing on a message. I've told him not to contact me at work – it's about some house auction.'

'Risky business, auctions. A bloke I know bought a mews house at auction and then discovered it had no connection to gas and it would cost a fortune to get a pipeline in.'

'Well, he's in the business, so he should know what to look for. When we get a result on the bike pump, we'll need fingerprints from Martin Boon, Caplan and his wife. If you're not skiving off home yet, what about a visit to the Caplans to see how he reacts to it?'

'Er, if you don't mind, I'd like to head off. I was not in a good state last night after I learned about the suicide, and I got very drunk.'

'You go, Stanley. If I don't get a result from forensics later, I won't hang about either. Just be in early tomorrow morning.'

Chapter Eleven

Jane stopped off at the local corner shop and bought a bottle of wine before going home. The discovery of the bicycle pump had energised her and she was certain that it would prove to be vital evidence.

She was surprised to see that Eddie's van was parked outside her front door so early. She let herself in and, holding up the bottle of wine, walked into the kitchen. Eddie turned to her, looking surprised. He was sitting at the table with a bottle of whisky, and sitting opposite him was a thick-set man with slicked-back hair, wearing a dark tracksuit.

Eddie stood up and introduced Jane as his fiancée, explaining that Brian was the friend who had bought his studio flat. Brian gave Jane a cursory nod as Eddie held up his glass.

'We were just having a celebratory drink. Do you want to join us?'

'No thanks, I'll go and change. Nice to meet you, Brian.'

Jane walked out and put the bottle of wine on the hall table. She took off her coat and flipped it over the banister before going upstairs. In the bedroom was a large TV that had been in Eddie's flat. He had put it onto a coffee table from the sitting room. Although she could see that it wasn't connected, it dominated the space between the bed and the dressing table.

She took her time changing, hanging up her suit and selecting a blouse for the morning. She could hear Eddie laughing downstairs and Brian's lower tone as he opened the front door. She crossed to the window, watching as Eddie's friend walked down the path and crossed the road to get into a Jaguar saloon.

Jane moved back from the window just as Eddie barged into the room, clapping his hands.

'So, what do you think? I'll get it connected tomorrow.'

'I'd forgotten it was so large.'

He flopped down on the bed, grinning as he nodded towards the screen.

'It'll be great, and it's got a good picture. We can watch a late-night movie on it.'

'So tell me about Brian?'

'He's a property investor. I was with him last night and got too drunk to drive home, so I crashed at his place.'

'Oh, I see . . . how is your mum?'

'She's fine, the plaster cast is on but she's not in any pain. It was panic all round as she is a bit of a drama queen at times.' He swung his legs down from the bed and gave her an enquiring look.

'What's up . . . had a bad day?'

'No, good actually. But you called me at the station . . . something about an auction?'

'Oh, right, yeah. Brian was interested in a property but he got tipped off that it was a time-waster. He's going to be a real help to me when I start looking at possible buys.'

'How long have you known him?'

'He's a sort of friend of a friend, so only a few weeks.'

'What's his surname?'

Eddie cocked his head. 'What do you want to know that for?'

'No reason, just out of interest. He seems a lot older than most of your friends.'

'Mitchell. So, what do you fancy for dinner? Maybe we could order in Chinese and I can go and collect it?'

'I might just have an omelette. We've got some mushrooms that need using up.'

'Fine, I'll just go next door for a minute as I saw old Gerry this morning and he said his wife's not well. What's her name?'

'Vi, short for Violet, but I haven't seen either of them for ages.'

'OK, see you downstairs.'

It was after eight when Eddie returned. Jane had already whisked the eggs and fried the mushrooms.

'She's got the first stages of dementia apparently, but the way she looked I would say it's a lot further along. She was sitting in a big armchair with a rug wrapped around her. Poor Gerry is having to do everything for her as she's a bit dodgy in the kitchen . . . leaving the gas rings on and so on. Gerry said that when their dog Spud died it really affected her.'

'There were lots of people with dementia in the care home I visited, but I suppose it would be out of his league – it was very expensive,' Jane said.

Eddie shook his head. 'He wouldn't even consider that. If it happened to my mum or dad there is no way I'd put them in a fuckin' care home. That's such a middle-class attitude; get them out of the way or, better still, out of sight. When my grandma started to show signs she was having a tough time living on her own, that was it. We moved her straight in with us until she died.'

'I learn more about your family every day,' Jane said.

Eddie frowned. 'That was a bit sarcastic.'

'It wasn't meant to be. I've never heard you mention your grandmother before, that's all.'

'Well, I'm not likely to as she's dead. But she was with us for years.'

Jane served up their omelettes with a side salad, and Eddie opened the bottle of wine. He poured two glasses and then checked the bottle.

'This is expensive; not like our usual plonk.'

'I had a good afternoon. I can't remember if I've told you that we have been searching for a weapon in the assault case I'm working on?'

'No. Listen, talking to Gerry, he sort of mentioned that money was tight and he was thinking about maybe selling up as the place needs a lot of repairs.'

Jane shrugged and continued eating. Eddie was obviously not interested in her discovery of the bicycle pump in Martin Boon's garage.

'Anyway, it could be a good business proposition, you know; we could get it at a good price. Like I said, he's worried about his wife. I don't think she can use the stairs, so I might talk to Brian and see what he reckons it's worth.'

'Is he going to live in your flat?'

'No, he's going to rent it out. He's got a big place of his own. He was telling me about setting up a property portfolio, buying up places like Gerry's and doing a quick refurbishment and then selling them on. He reckons we can get a good price for this place; I showed him around, told him how much work I had done and how much you paid for it.'

Jane was going to take the opportunity to say that she was having second thoughts about moving when Eddie's mobile rang. He left the kitchen as she finished her dinner and put her plate on the draining-board. Eddie had only eaten half of his so she left his plate on the table. He returned and picked up his jacket from the back of his chair.

'That was Caroline. I need to go and help Brian move some stuff into the flat as he's already got a tenant . . . but it won't take long.'

'You haven't finished your dinner.'

'To be honest, I don't really like omelettes. I'll grab a burger while I'm out and I'll see you later.'

He gave her a quick kiss, drained his glass of wine and with his brick of a mobile tucked under his arm walked out. Jane threw his leftovers into the bin and stacked the dishwasher. Her original good mood had evaporated as she went upstairs to take a shower.

When Eddie eventually returned home, he woke her up stumbling around the bedroom. She looked at the bedside clock. It was after twelve and he smelled of alcohol, sitting on the edge of the bed to kick off his boots.

'Everything all right?' she asked, leaning up on her elbow and turning her bedside light on.

'Yeah, terrific . . . but I'm knackered, and I have an early start in the morning.'

'You should be more careful about driving . . . you reek of alcohol.'

'I just had a couple of beers, so don't try and lecture me,' he snapped.

'I'm not. It's just that if you're stopped you could lose your licence, and that would be a major problem as you need your van for work.'

'I am not pissed, OK?'

Jane switched off her bedside light and pulled the duvet up around her. She heard Eddie crashing around in the bathroom, and then felt him getting into bed beside her. He rubbed her shoulder affectionately.

'Sorry, officer, promise not to ever drink and drive again.'

She lay back on her pillow, looking up at the ceiling in the dark. After a while she said quietly that they really needed to have a talk, firstly about her having reservations about selling and more importantly about their relationship, but Eddie was fast asleep. He hadn't heard a word she said.

Chapter Twelve

Jane met Stanley in the canteen for breakfast. He had the forensics results on the bicycle pump: as expected, plenty of prints. They were now running the prints through records.

'Don't hold your breath, though,' Stanley said. 'Unless Boon or his wife have a police record.'

'Let's go and see what Mr Caplan makes of it, then,' Jane said, picking up her tray.

At the house, they explained what they were going to do, re-enacting the scene of the incident.

They trouped into the garden and Stanley eased the bicycle pump out from under his coat with his back to David Caplan. He turned towards him, now holding the pump up in his right hand. He stepped forwards and raised his hand, swinging the pump.

'That's it, that's exactly what I saw,' Caplan said immediately. 'I said it was black and shiny; where did you find it?'

Stanley handed it over and Caplan shook his head.

'It's a plastic bicycle pump, for God's sake.'

'It's quite light,' Stanley said. 'But you wouldn't know that unless you held it.'

Caplan handed it back. 'My God, this is definitely what I saw Martin Boon swinging at me. I mean, if I'd known it was . . .'

Stanley nodded sympathetically. 'Thank you, Mr Caplan.'

Back in the car, Stanley turned to Jane with a smile.

'You in a better mood now?'

She nodded. 'I'm really looking forward to interviewing Mr Boon. I'm certain Caplan is telling the truth. But I'd like to find out who replaced the pump on his bike; I suppose it had to have been his wife?'

'Or one of the Larssons; they were in the garden as well. It's also possible that the dog did pick it up and ran out into the courtyard with it, although there were no teeth marks.'

'Either way, it was put back on the bike. Did it have a flat tyre?'

'I'm not sure, but maybe Martin Boon was in his garage when he heard David Caplan admonishing the dog about digging up the garden.'

Jane parked in the station car park and Stanley went and put the pump back in the evidence lock-up. While typing out the report, Jane got a call from the front desk to say there was someone on the line for her. She asked for it to be put through to her desk phone without enquiring who it was, certain it was Eddie's bloody controller at his mobile call centre.

'DI Tennison,' she said, curtly, into her phone.

'Oh, I'm sorry to disturb you . . . I just wanted to ask you, er . . .'

'Who is this?'

'It's Angelica Martinez. I got your number from Miss Brandon's diary and, er . . . I hope this isn't inconvenient. I was just wondering if there was any update?'

'On what exactly?'

'Well, you said you were doing an investigation at Clarendon Court. I was at my session with Vera James, and she said . . .'

'I'm sorry, Miss Martinez, who is Vera James?'

'The medium I go to. She said that perhaps my son was there; she was confident that there was a strong possibility . . . she has never been so adamant. I did tell her about you and that the police were investigating something to do with the neighbours.'

'I am very sorry, Miss Martinez, but there is no connection to your son in my enquiries, so I can't share any details about the investigation.'

There was a long pause before Jane heard what sounded like an intake of breath, then a deep sigh.

'I see, thank you . . . I am sorry to have bothered you.'

Jane replaced the receiver, resting her hand on the cradle. Angelica Martinez had sounded so sad, and it annoyed her that this so-called medium was feeding the poor woman hope about her son turning up at Clarendon Court.

After the lunch break Jane had a meeting with DCI Hutton and explained about the discovery of the bicycle pump. Predictably, she didn't see it as a major breakthrough. 'We'll see what Mr Boon has to say. In the meantime I'd like you to supervise two probationary officers' reports and to review some other ongoing cases.' She handed over the relevant files.

Returning to her desk, Jane was told that Stanley had left the station to meet with social services, who had been involved with Eric Donaldson.

On the way home Jane stopped at the corner shop and bought some fresh bread, butter, cheese, jam and a carton of milk. She parked outside her house, and then went next door. She had to wait a few minutes before Gerry answered and then held up the plastic bag containing her purchases.

'I won't disturb you, Gerry, but Eddie said your wife wasn't well. I was doing some shopping for myself so I thought I'd buy you a few things to save you the bother.'

Gerry smiled wearily. 'That's very kind of you. I'm actually expecting someone from social services to come this evening. They help me dress her and get her ready for bed, and then they come early in the morning to get her up. She sleeps downstairs now. God bless our GP, he arranged it all for us.'

'Well, I won't disturb you. Please give Vi my best wishes.'

'I will . . . and you've got a good chap, you know He was round earlier this morning to clear my gutters . . . they've not been done for years.'

She smiled. 'Oh, that's good. Evening then, Gerry.'

Jane wanted to feel touched by Eddie going round there, but part of her was suspicious. She was irritated with herself for not running Brian Mitchell's name through records, deciding she would definitely do so in the morning.

After changing into her old tracksuit, Jane looked around the kitchen for the medium's card. She couldn't find it anywhere, even checking the bins. She then thumbed through the phone directory but there was no Vera James listed. She also looked up 'mediums', but there was no Vera James amongst the few that were advertised.

It was almost nine when Eddie arrived carrying a big bunch of roses and a pizza.

'I am sorry about last night. You were right. I was a dumb bastard for driving home pissed. I promise you I won't screw up like that again.'

Instantly she softened. Sometimes he was so sweet. She took the flowers as he kissed her. While she put them into a vase, Eddie made a pot of tea, heated plates in the oven and then sliced the pizza between them.

'Just what I needed,' Jane said as she finished hers off.

'I took Gerry a few things earlier, and he told me about the gutters. He said I'd got a good chap.'

Eddie laughed. 'Well, I've cleared some of it, but the pipes are cracking and some of the joints were broken, so it's going to take a bit of work to sort out.'

'You remember the other night when you found that card from the medium?' Jane said. 'You don't know where it is, do you?'

Eddie took their plates to the sink and moved aside the soap dispenser, then held up the card.

'I stuck it here . . . what do you want it for?'

'Oh, I got this call from the woman who gave it to me. She sounded so sad, I just wondered if this medium was conning her out of her money. I tried to find her in the phone directory but she wasn't listed.'

Eddie grinned as he passed it to her.

'Thinking of paying her a visit, are you?'

Jane glanced at the card and slipped it into her pocket.

Eddie got up.

'Where are you going?'

'To have a shower and wait for you. This is a rare night we're both home early, so don't make any excuses.'

Jane laughed and chased after him, running up the stairs behind him. They showered together before they were wrapped in each other's arms under the duvet. Jane had no thoughts of the talk she had been wanting to have; instead it felt as if they were back in love. She was naked and curled up with his arms around her, loving the way their bodies entwined when they slept.

The following morning he kissed her and whispered that it was time for him to get up and get off to work, and that he was sorry to have woken her.

Jane stayed in bed but was unable to get back to sleep. She got up and put on her dressing gown as he finished dressing and walked out of the bathroom.

'You want me to bring you up a cup of tea?'

'No, I'm going to fill up the washing machine and do a bit of housework. Are your dirty clothes in your work clothes basket?'

'No, I left a load at Mum's . . . I might be late tonight . . . love you.'

Jane leaned on the banister and watched him hurry down the stairs. He didn't look back as he left the house. She went into the bathroom to collect her tracksuit and underwear from the previous night, then picked up the laundry basket. Only then did she hesitate, realising that he had not been wearing his work clothes last night, nor had he left for work that morning in his usual old jeans and sweatshirt. She picked up his discarded shirt and underwear from the bathroom floor and stuffed them into the basket. She was about to put her jacket into the basket when she remembered the medium's card and took it out.

Vera James, Specialist Medium By Appointment Only.

There was no address on the card, just a phone number below her name. Jane returned to the bedroom to strip the bedding, putting the card on her bedside table before removing the duvet cover. It was a job she hated, but at least she used a local laundry firm to wash it all. She took out the clean bedding ready to make up the bed.

Before leaving the house, Jane checked in the understairs cupboard where she had left the bag with Eddie's money from the sale of his flat. It wasn't there. Jane went into the kitchen and opened the drawer in which Eddie kept his work file containing his receipts, plus jobs he had lined up. It wasn't there. Jane slammed the drawer shut.

The laundry was closed and she had to wait fifteen minutes before it opened at eight fifteen. Once she had dropped off the laundry, Jane drove to the station. Before looking at her desk diary and the schedules on the board, she took out the card and dialled Vera James's number. The phone rang for a while before it was answered.

'Hello?' The high-pitched voice sounded like a young girl.

'Hello, I would like to make an appointment with Vera James.'

'Hold on . . .' Jane heard the same voice shouting.

'Mum . . . Mum, it's for you . . . I'm gonna be late.'

Jane waited a moment before she heard another voice.

'Go and get in the car. Did they say who they were?'

There was another short pause, before Jane heard the woman's voice on the phone.

'Hello, can I help you?'

'Yes, I would like to make an appointment to meet Vera James, please.'

'Who am I speaking to?'

'My name is Jane Tennison.'

'This is a very inconvenient time.' She paused. 'Did someone suggest you call me?'

'Yes, they did.'

'I see. Well, I operate in the afternoons, from twelve until four. As a new client you will need to pay for an introductory session. Could you call back later to book an appointment? Thank you.'

The call was ended so Jane replaced the receiver. If that was Vera James, she thought, she didn't sound very professional. Lost in thought, she hardly noticed when Stanley came over to her desk and started a long moan about his time-wasting visit to social services the previous afternoon.

'Stanley, can you give me a break? I'm not in the mood, and I need to see what I have lined up for today.'

'Excuse me! We need to get over to the hospital to interview Mr Boon. Do you have a specific time that suits you?' he asked sarcastically.

Jane sighed. 'No, sorry, just not had a good morning. Whenever is fine with me.'

'You seem to be having quite a few of them.'

'What?'

'Nothing . . . Let's get on to the hospital.'

Jane called the hospital, then walked over to Stanley's desk.

'We might have a problem about talking to Martin Boon. Apparently, Mr Boon is scheduled for a lot of tests today before he is discharged. I'd say our best bet is to wait until he's home to question him, along with his wife.'

Stanley swivelled round in his desk chair to face her.

'Anything else?'

Jane hesitated for a moment. 'There is something, actually. Could you run a Brian Mitchell through records to see if he has any previous? He's in the property business and I'd say he's about late thirties. I'd prefer not to do it as it's sort of personal.'

'Sure . . . everything all right between you and Eddie?'

'It was last night. This morning I've been feeling uncomfortable about some things, but I could be wrong.'

Returning to her desk, Jane finished going through the probationary officers' reports before Hutton gave her another assignment.

Later in the morning Stanley was called out to investigate a possible suspicious death, and after lunch Jane called Vera James again. The phone rang for a considerable time before it was answered by the same woman she had spoken to earlier.

'Hello, I called you earlier this morning.'

'Oh right, and your name was?'

'Jane.'

'You said you were recommended, is that right?'

'Yes, by Angelica Martinez.'

'There will be an introductory session for about twenty minutes, but that will depend on whether you want further answers, and the direction and kind of comfort you need.'

'Are you available to see me this afternoon?'

'Well, you'll have to let me check my appointments diary. Can you hold on for a moment?'

Jane waited for a lot longer than a moment before she was told that if she could be there in forty-five minutes then she could be seen, but if not then it would have to be the following week.

With nothing more important to do, Jane couldn't wait to leave the station. The address she was given was in Swanley and Jane calculated that she could easily make it in time. One thing she found strange was that Vera James never mentioned her fees.

It was early afternoon and there was not much traffic. Driving around Swanley's town centre, she headed out towards a more rural area, dominated by large detached houses with neat lawns.

Jane parked behind a Volkswagen and walked up the drive. She rang the doorbell and waited. She was about to press it again when the door was opened by a middle-aged woman wearing a trouser suit with a pink blouse.

'You are a wee bit early, but do come in.'

Jane was ushered into a small sitting room containing a sofa, two matching chairs and a coffee table stacked with old magazines. The fitted floral carpet was extremely bright and the curtains were partly drawn, with a fake log fire and marble surround.

'I'm Jane Tennison.'

'How do you do, dear. I won't be a moment; I just need to get the appointments diary and the questionnaire.'

'Are you Vera James?'

'Oh no, I'm Sandra, her daughter. I handle the appointments. I have to tell you that she was not very happy about me making time for you. We had a cancellation, so I thought it would be all right. She gets very tired, so only does a few sessions a week, just for two afternoons. I won't be a moment.'

Jane sat in one of the easy chairs and flicked through one of the magazines. There was a lingering smell of fried food.

Sandra returned with a large red diary with a single sheet clipped to the front. She sat down opposite Jane, clicking a biro.

'Now, you said you were recommended?'

'Yes, by Angelica Martinez; she spoke very highly of your mother.'

'I'm sorry, what was your name again?'

'Jane Tennison.'

'Right. I probably should have mentioned the fees to you, but I was in such a hurry this morning to get my daughter to school. Right, the charge for the first session is fifteen pounds and then any further appointments are a flat rate of ten pounds. Cash is preferable and payment is due before the sessions. Now, if you could just complete the questionnaire – and obviously we keep any information completely confidential.'

Sandra passed Jane the sheet of paper and the biro.

'I won't be a moment, she knows you are here.'

The sheet had Jane's name misspelled at the top, and then spaces for her address and contact number, her age, employment, marital status and any recent bereavements. There were also questions about medical conditions and related medication.

Jane took only a minute to fill in the questionnaire. She wrote down her employment as 'Officer'. Sandra returned and took the page from her, and Jane handed her fifteen pounds in cash.

'I'll give you a receipt before you leave. I won't be a moment.'

That seemed to be her standard sentence. Jane had been taken aback at the cost; fifteen pounds seemed like a lot of money. She wondered how Angelica Martinez could afford it, but then she didn't know how often she came. Sandra returned, and ushered her towards the stairs. There was a chair-lift on the ground, and the stairs were carpeted in the same garishly patterned fitted carpet. Sandra led Jane along the landing to the end door; she knocked and then opened the door wider for Jane to enter.

'This is Jane Tennison.'

As Sandra closed the door behind her, Jane quickly took in the room. The walls were lined with photographs and framed letters, and there were numerous bookshelves. A green velvet-covered chaise longue with embroidered cushions dominated one side of the room and there was a small, carved card table with a green velour top. A small tape recorder sat on the table, along with a note-pad and pencil and Jane's completed questionnaire. There were two hard-backed chairs with velvet-covered seats. One was drawn out, and standing with her hand on the back was Vera James.

'Do come in and sit down, Jane. I'm sorry to have kept you waiting; nowadays I find it too exhausting to have quite so many sessions. To be honest with you, I was quite thankful to have a cancellation.'

She sighed and raised her eyes to the ceiling. Jane reckoned she was in her late seventies, but she was still a very striking woman, with large, ice-blue eyes highlighted by a lot of black eyeliner. Her white hair was caught up in a loose bun at the nape of her neck and tied back with a black ribbon.

Vera was wearing a cream kaftan with wide sleeves. She was rather overweight and pulled her kaftan up to ease into the chair. Jane could see that her ankles were swollen and her plump feet were squeezed into old, worn slippers.

'Now, before I start, have you ever been to a medium before?'

'No.'

'Well, I'll keep it brief. Basically, I am in contact with those from the other side. They come forwards and pass messages through me. I will make a tape recording of each session, which is included in the cost, and if at any time you find what I am passing on to you upsetting, or you wish me to stop, just say so. I am not here to make you emotionally distressed or to upset you in any way. I only try to give you comfort and perhaps a way forward.'

Vera finished her sales pitch and then checked the tape recorder, clicking the lid open and checking the tape had not been used. She had arthritic knuckles and chipped, pink-painted nails.

'I always have to check these things for myself. Sandra gets run ragged with her teenage kids. She's a single mother taking them here, there and everywhere. She brought my lunch late today . . .'

Vera delved into a pocket of the kaftan and pulled out a pair of large, blue-framed glasses with one arm broken. She didn't put them on but used them like bifocals, holding them up to her eyes to remove something from the tape.

'Right . . . I only had a quick glance at your questionnaire . . . you put as your employment "Officer". Would that be a police officer?'

Jane leaned forwards. 'Well, yes. It might seem as if I'm here under false pretences, but I wanted to explain to you in person.'

Vera inserted the tape and put her broken glasses back in her pocket. She then pulled back the cuff of her left sleeve and squinted at a large man's wristwatch.

'You have paid for twenty minutes with me, love, so whatever your reasons for coming, I suggest you try and explain as quickly as you can.'

Jane was taken aback at the way Vera's icy blue eyes suddenly stared hard at her.

'You were recommended by a lady called Angelica Martinez.'

'Listen to me, dear, if you are asking me for any personal information about Miss Martinez, you won't get it. I keep my clients' business highly confidential, just like a doctor or a priest. And if you are here officially as a police officer, then you'll need a warrant.'

'I appreciate that, and I am not here on a police matter. I am simply here because I found Angelica Martinez to be such a sweet woman, and her desperation to be reunited with her son is wretchedly sad.'

Vera pointedly looked at her wristwatch again.

'She told me you have given her hope. It was pure coincidence that I found out she had previously owned the property where I am presently investigating a case, one that has nothing to do with her and . . .'

Vera sighed, pursing her lips and closing her eyes.

'Listen to me, dear. I get the impression that you somehow think that I am – for want of a better word – "conning" her. Nothing could be further from the truth.'

Vera leaned forwards, tapping the table with her hand.

'Sometimes they do not come forwards, from which I infer that they have not gone to the other side. Angelica Martinez lives in hope because I cannot bring him forwards.'

'She believes she will find him at her old home.'

Vera shook her head and sighed.

'You have to understand that when they cross over and their spirits come to me, I see nothing physical, just . . .' She stopped and closed her eyes for moment as if deep in thought, then reached for the notepad and pencil and started writing. She seemed to be concentrating hard.

'Right now, I have an initial M, water, very young and unable to breathe, which suggests a drowning.'

Jane sat straight-backed in her chair. She felt a chill come over her.

'He is giving me a sign that he is very happy, and I think he is holding a fishing rod; he wants you to know that no one's to blame for what happened.'

Jane could not believe it. Her little brother was called Michael and he had drowned in the neighbours' pond. Her parents hardly ever talked about the tragedy, but the sense of loss had always been present growing up, even though Jane had never known him.

Vera put down her pencil.

'So, dear, does this mean anything to you? If it does, make sure you let them know he is happy and tell them not to feel guilty about what happened.'

Jane was seriously shaken. There was no way that Vera could have known about her brother. She had never even told Eddie. The truth was that she rarely, if ever, even thought about him. She wanted to ask more questions, but Vera had pushed back her chair and was leaning on the table to help herself stand.

'Before you go, I'll tell you something I have not told Angelica because I believe she has to have hope that she will find her son. I tasted blood in my mouth when Angelica first came to see me. He did not come forwards and never has, but it is the sign of death.'

Vera opened the door, calling out for Sandra as she walked out and entered the room next door. Jane was feeling quite faint as Sandra came running along the corridor.

'Oh, I'm glad you're finished. I have to collect my daughter and I need you to move your car, I'm afraid.'

She turned back and hurried down the corridor and down the stairs with her car keys in her hand. Opening the front door, she waited for Jane to pass her and then followed her out, slamming the door shut behind her.

'I hope it went well for you,' she said, getting into her car. All Jane could manage was a polite smile. She rummaged in her handbag for her car keys, and found her hands were shaking. She reversed out of the drive and Sandra followed. As she drove off, she realised Vera hadn't given her the tape. But there was no way she was going back to ask for it.

Jane drove back to the station as if on autopilot, while what Vera had told her went round and round in her head. As she drew up, Stanley was about to get into his car. He hurried over and opened her driver's door.

'Where the hell have you been?'

'You wouldn't believe it. I'm not sure I believe it myself.'

'Well, the headmistress was asking for you, so I covered and said you had gone to the hospital to get more details about Martin Boon's recovery. I've been out most of the day on this suspicious death; you won't believe what the consensus was after dicking around for hours. This old boy had a heart attack as he was having a bowl of soup; fell face-forwards and bloody drowned.'

Stanley laughed as he delved into his jacket pocket.

'I was going to drop this round to you as I'm off home. Is this the right Brian Mitchell?'

Stanley opened the folded page to show a printed copy of a mug shot.

Jane took it. 'Yes, that's him.'

'It's a few years old, there's nothing recent, but he did time for fraud; one of those bastards that sell holiday vacation homes to pensioners, then all they get is a piece of waste ground.'

She closed her eyes and Stanley leaned further into the car.

'You OK?'

'Not really, but thanks for this. I think I might head home.'

'Martin Boon was released an hour ago. Shall we call on him first thing in the morning?'

Jane nodded. 'Meet you for breakfast. Thanks again for this.' Jane waved the Brian Mitchell printout as Stanley closed the door and then gave the car roof a friendly tap.

Stanley watched her drive away. He had never been someone to get involved in other people's business, especially work colleagues, but he could tell she was troubled. He assumed the lowlife Brian Mitchell was connected to her boyfriend, which was obviously not good news. He tried to put these thoughts out of his mind as he got in his car to go and collect his daughter from her dance class.

Chapter Thirteen

Jane stopped off to do some food shopping and was pulling up in front of her house when she saw the ambulance. Gerry was standing in the garden as his wife was being wheeled out on a stretcher by two paramedics. He gave her a sad smile, before entering the ambulance behind her.

After putting the groceries away and selecting what she would cook for dinner, Jane emptied the dishwasher. As she did so, she remembered what Eddie had said that morning. She rarely, if ever, called his mother but she was getting ready to confront him about everything and she needed to be sure.

'Hi there, it's Jane, just checking how you are doing?'

'Oh, hello, dear. Well, I'm coping, but it's very hard because it's my right wrist and I can't lift anything. I even find lifting the frying pan painful. And Eddie's dad is no help, coming home expecting his dinner to be on the table.'

'Eddie said he left his washing at your place.'

'Oh no, I can't do any ironing.'

'He said it was his work clothes.'

'No, we last saw him when I was at the hospital.'

'Oh, I was just calling to say I could collect his clothes, and to see how you're coping.'

'I appreciate that, Jane, but we won't be having our usual Monday dinners for a bit, I'm afraid, not unless we get a takeaway.'

'Let's just wait and see how you're feeling. Bye for now.'

Jane replaced the receiver slowly, deep in thought, before going upstairs to shower and change. Sitting on the bed rubbing her hair dry with a towel, she thought about calling her parents. She could still not really believe what Vera had told her and wasn't sure how she would open a conversation with them about

Michael. Perhaps there would be a right time, but at the moment she was more focused on how she was going to deal with Eddie. She wanted to be ready to confront him and no roses were going to change her mind.

It was after eight and Jane had put on a cotton robe, dried her hair and even touched up her make-up. She was already on her second gin and tonic. She had been making notes on an old notepad she kept for shopping lists, similar to the way she briefed herself when about to do an interrogation.

Eddie arrived just after nine, hands held up in apology. He hung his jacket up in the hall before joining her in the kitchen.

'Have you eaten?' Jane asked.

'Yep, had a kebab, but I'll join you for a drink. Do you want a top-up?'

'No, thanks. There's beer in the fridge.'

Eddie opened the fridge and took out a beer, then opened a kitchen drawer to get a bottle opener. He flicked the bottle top into the sink and drank straight from the bottle.

'You had a good day?' Eddie asked.

'Not bad. Sit down, I want to talk to you.'

He gave her a quizzical look as he pulled out a chair and sat opposite her. She had her notepad open and tapped the page with a pencil.

'I need to ask you about a few things that have been worrying me. Clear the air.'

'Fire away, I'm all ears.'

'OK. For starters, you haven't been wearing your work clothes when you leave in the morning. I asked you about washing, and you told me you had left your clothes with your mother. Tonight, I called her to check how she is coping with her wrist and asked if I could collect your washing. But she told me you hadn't left it there. It's been days since you wore your usual work overalls.'

Eddie shrugged and took another sip of his beer.

'Why did you lie, Eddie? And if you haven't been going to any of the building sites you've been working on, what have you been doing?'

'Well, officer, I hired a couple more guys. I oversee how the jobs are going and then I meet up with Brian to check on properties that are up for probate ... On a couple of mornings and afternoons I went to auctions.'

'Why didn't you tell me, Eddie?'

'Brian's just showing me the ropes, telling me what I need to look for when bidding. I didn't mention it to you because when I showed you some properties you didn't seem that interested. Then my mum had her accident, so we missed viewing a couple of properties that I'd earmarked.'

'You know, Eddie, this is a really big decision; we've just got the house finished and, to be honest, the thought of moving into a run-down property and living there while you rip it apart with the intention of reselling it freaks me out.'

Eddie rocked back in his chair.

'Added to that, we will obviously mostly be using the money we make from selling my house. I know you've sold your flat and you are being offered a lot of work, but income-wise we would also be dependent on my wages.'

Eddie put the beer bottle down on the table. Jane found it difficult to work out what he was thinking and stared at her notepad, tapping it with the pencil.

'Right now, I cover all the utility bills, and I do most of the food shopping. My gut instinct is that perhaps now is not the time to stretch our finances. I wanted to look at the file we made for your business, but it's not in the drawer. I also checked on the cash you'd left in the understairs cupboard, but you must have taken it?'

Eddie remained sitting, looking glum, one hand resting on his empty beer bottle.

'Are you going to say anything?'

He looked away, clearly not wanting to meet her eyes.

'And there's something else. You are obviously seeing a lot of Brian Mitchell, and I have to be honest and tell you that I had a bad feeling when I met him.'

Jane flicked to the back of her notepad and took out the printout that Stanley had given to her. Unfolding it, with Mitchell's mug shot on the first page, she passed it across the table.

'You all done now, are you?' Eddie said, gruffly.

'Yes I am, but I'd like to know what you think about everything I've just said.'

'I'll tell you what I think . . . for starters, you might want to fucking calculate how much work I did on this place free of charge . . . and even before I screwed you I was cutting costs down for you as much as possible. What I hear from you tonight is that you don't trust me and you think I'm living off you and your bloody wages when I've been trying to set us up in a new house that we both own. That's what I think.'

Eddie pushed his chair back and it toppled over as he picked up the beer bottle and hurled it into the sink. The glass shattered everywhere, and Jane jerked back as he turned towards her with his fists clenched. He smirked, then shook his head when she put her hands up as if to protect herself.

Jane stayed in the kitchen as she heard him moving around the house, then going upstairs. She couldn't stop herself from shaking. It seemed an age before she heard him thumping down the stairs again. She was still feeling afraid as he appeared in the kitchen doorway carrying a big canvas bag and an armful of shirts still on their hangers.

'I'll send one of my boys to pick up the TV.'

He slammed the front door so hard she thought the frame must have been broken and then she heard him revving his van and driving off. After taking some deep breaths she fetched a dustpan and brush to sweep up the shattered glass around the sink. Tipping the shards into the waste bin, she saw the vase of roses on the side that he'd brought home the previous night. Snatching the stems out of the vase, she kicked open the bin again and shoved the roses in, heads down, with some of their petals scattering on the floor.

After checking that the front door was secure, Jane switched off the downstairs lights and went upstairs to her bedroom. The wardrobe doors were open and almost all of Eddie's clothes were gone. Jane closed the curtains and went into the bathroom to brush her teeth with a vengeance, then got into bed and turned the bedside light off. In the darkness, she let herself cry. At first she just whimpered, but then she started sobbing uncontrollably, wiping her face with the edge of the duvet.

The following morning her eyes were puffy and red-rimmed. She had to use more make-up than usual and was trying her hardest to stay calm, but when she saw the rose petals scattered on the kitchen floor it was difficult not to break down again.

The drive to the station gave her time to clear her head and get her emotions under control.

Stanley joined her in the canteen with his usual fry-up.

'Morning. You not eating anything?'

She shook her head. 'Just coffee. I'm not hungry.'

Stanley glanced at her before tucking in and then took another look at her as she sat with her head bowed.

'Bad night, huh?'

'You could say that.'

'I went to collect my daughter from her ballet class last night. I doubt she'll make a career of it, but bless her, she tries very hard; it's just that she seems to be a beat behind the other girls. You know something, I never had the time when she was tiny, left it all to the wife. I never thought I'd be sitting with all these mothers half my age watching their children trying to be cygnets. They've got a performance of *Swan Lake* coming up and I'm going to be in the front row.'

Stanley had the ability to talk non-stop and eat at the same time.

'What time are we interviewing Martin Boon?' Jane asked.

'Oh sorry, was I boring you? What I was going to say was how good it felt not to be under pressure anymore.'

'I'm sorry, Stanley, it was a bad night.'

Stanley stirred his coffee.

'Want to talk about it?'

'Not really . . . Listen, I went to that medium I told you about, the one the ex-Mrs Hoffman – now Martinez – gave me the card for. I was worried she might have been conning her out of her hard-earned cash. Anyway, she kind of freaked me out a bit, brought up something about my family, but I don't want to get into that. It was something she said about Angelica Martinez's son.'

'Sorry, what son?'

Jane told him the story, then repeated what Vera James had said to her.

'All sounds to me as if she was just trying to distract you because you reckoned she was a con artist.'

'I don't think she is, though. I did at first, but she told me things about my family there was no way she could have known about. I mean, yes, she's making money out of these people – it's fifteen quid for the first session and then ten for any follow-up appointments.'

'Bloody hell, you paid fifteen quid? There's no way you'll be able to put that against expenses.'

'I don't intend to. But con artist or not, why does she insist Angelica Martinez's son is near to the Caplans' house, or in it?'

'Sounds like bollocks to me. Meanwhile, how many sessions is that woman paying for? C'mon, she's a con artist.'

Jane shrugged. 'Maybe you're right; it was just when she said she tasted blood in her mouth . . .'

Picking up his dirty plate to take to the counter, Stanley looked at her and then smiled. 'It's a good line. It hooked you in.'

Returning to the CID office, Jane checked for any messages. There was just a typed note from DCI Hutton to please add to the board her whereabouts after she had left early yesterday afternoon.

A telling-off from the headmistress. Just what I need, Jane thought sourly.

She looked up to see Stanley was having a conversation with Burrows. Checking her watch, Jane saw that they had more than half an hour before they had to go and interview Martin Boon. Jane got her notebook out and made some quick notes before going to talk to one of the probationers.

'I have a bit of research for you to do, Meryl.'

Meryl had a bad case of acne she was obviously self-conscious about, but she eagerly pulled out her notepad.

'I've actually written down everything I want you to do for me,' Jane said. 'First up, can you find out as much as possible about a teenage boy called Sebastian Hoffman? He might also be using the name Martinez. I've given you his parents' names and previous address. I also want you to try and trace a flight to Mexico . . . the time frame is a bit stretched but see if you can track down a return flight to London. I've given you a couple of possible dates, and you might also check if missing persons have ever been contacted about him. Next there is a medium, Vera James. Here's her address and phone number. She has a daughter and two teenage grandchildren, so just see what you can dig up on her. I doubt if you will find anything in records, but do what you can.'

'Yes, ma'am, I'll get started straightaway.'

'Good, thank you.'

Arriving shortly before nine o'clock at Clarendon Court, Jane parked in the Boons' driveway behind their car. Stanley had the evidence bag with the bicycle pump inside. The door was answered by Ellen Boon.

'Sorry to inconvenience you,' Jane said. 'We'd like to speak to your husband, please.'

'He only came home from hospital yesterday and he's having his breakfast at the moment, so this is not convenient,' Mrs Boon said with a frown.

'Who is it?' Martin Boon appeared in the hallway behind his wife.

'Morning, Mr Boon,' Stanley said with a disarming smile. 'We promise not to take up too much of your time, but it is quite important.'

He nodded. 'You better come in then.'

His wife closed the door behind them as they followed him into the sitting room.

'Do you need me with you, dear?' she asked.

He didn't answer so Stanley shut the door. Martin Boon looked none the worse for his recent hospitalisation. He wore a thick, ribbed sweater over a blue shirt, cord trousers and old, worn slippers.

'I am very pleased that you have recovered from your ordeal,' Jane said, sitting in one of the cushioned chairs. Boon remained standing with his back to the fireplace.

'What do you want to talk to me about?'

'Do sit down, Mr Boon, I don't want to tire you.' Stanley gestured to the sofa.

Jane opened her notebook and flipped through a few pages before glancing towards Stanley to signal he should begin the interview.

'Could you please describe exactly what happened between you and David Caplan from the moment you entered their property? I'm sure you're aware that we have assault charges pending.'

Boon sighed. 'He could have bloody killed me.'

'You went into his garden, is that correct?'

'I heard him shouting loudly, the gate was open, so I walked in to see if anything was wrong. He was very aggressive, his dog was barking and running around and the next minute he picked up a spade and attacked me. I tried to back away but he struck me and I fell. Next thing I'm in hospital.'

'So, at no point did you threaten Mr Caplan?' Stanley said.

'No, I did not. Like I just said, because of the shouting, I went to see if there was anything wrong.'

'You said the garden gate was open?'

'Yes. I admit that I have not been on good terms with Mr Caplan. We had to put up with months of building work. The noise was a nightmare, and there were endless trucks and vans, and even a cement mixer in the courtyard. It was bad enough when the two houses were being built opposite the Caplans; no sooner were they completed than it all starts up again, and this time closer to us.'

'I believe you opposed planning permission?'

'Of course I did. Before them we had the Hoffmans trying to convert the house into flats, even had a bloody fire there. But they sold up and the next thing we have is more builders. How they got all their planning permission through for what they did inside beggars belief. Then Caplan wants to put in electric gates and a wall.'

'I can understand how frustrating it must have been for you,' Stanley said.

'I am glad you do. I mean, why do they want electric gates when they have a garage in the back lane?'

'Well . . .' Stanley wasn't sure what to say.

Boon pulled a face. 'I have the original plans for this courtyard. They're trying to build over the boundary line onto the tarmac, by at least a foot and a half.'

'You don't own the courtyard, though, do you?' Stanley said.

'The courtyard is owned by Mr and Mrs Larsson, and as a good neighbour I have acted on their behalf. Now, is there anything else you want to know because I am supposed to be resting.'

Jane held up her pencil.

'Mr Caplan says that his gate was not open, and that you entered and made threatening remarks to him.'

'I did not.'

'He also maintains that you had what he perceived to be a weapon, swinging it towards him as if you were about to strike him.'

'Rubbish.'

'Mr Caplan described the item as black and shiny, and thought it could be some kind of lead pipe?' Stanley continued.

'I don't believe this! He struck me with his spade. If you are here on his behalf you had better wait for my solicitor to be present. In fact, it's time you left.'

'Just a couple more things,' Stanley said. 'The spade was examined by forensics. They found no blood, hairs or tissue on it, and according to your specialist you had no frontal injury. However, you did have an injury that was more than probably caused by you falling backwards, and due to your previous medical condition—'

Boon slapped the arm of the sofa, his face flushed.

'I want you to leave right now!'

Stanley opened the evidence bag and took out the bicycle pump.

'I believe this belongs to you, Mr Boon?' Stanley placed it on the coffee table in front of him.

Boon leaned forwards and picked it up.

'What is this about?' he said, holding the bicycle pump in his hands.

'Detective Inspector Tennison and I removed it from your garage.'

'You had no right to do that.'

'We had every right, Mr Boon, because it fits the description Mr Caplan gave. I can understand that if you were holding it in a certain way it is possible that he could have been mistaken in believing it to be some kind of weapon.'

Before Boon could answer the door was opened by his wife. Standing behind her was Mrs Larsson.

'We think you should not be talking to these officers without your solicitor being present,' Mrs Larsson said firmly.

'I am the victim; I don't need a solicitor,' Mr Boon said.

'As you are well aware, Martin has only just been released from hospital.' Mrs Larsson stepped forwards, looking towards Mr Boon. 'Are you all right, Martin?'

Stanley got up and took the bicycle pump from him. He held it out towards both of the women.

'Did either of you, on the day of the incident involving Mr Caplan, remove this from the scene and reattach it to Mr Boon's bicycle?'

Mrs Larsson was about to answer when Ellen Boon burst into tears, covering her face with her hands.

'Yes, I did . . . it was on our path when I went in to get dressed . . . their dog must have had it and dropped it. I didn't do anything wrong.'

Stanley glanced towards Jane and nodded as he put the pump back in the evidence bag.

'Mrs Boon, I suggest that you and your husband, with or without your solicitor, come into the station to give a formal statement. I am sorry to have inconvenienced you, sir. We are aware that you're still recovering from your injury, but we will need to know if you intend to press assault charges against Mr Caplan. Thank you for your time.'

Jane walked past the two women. Mrs Boon was still in tears, but Mrs Larsson was tight-lipped with her arms folded across her chest. Stanley calmly said they would show themselves out as he followed Jane.

Driving out through the courtyard, Stanley shook his head.

'You know, I reckon it's all about money; they think they can make a packet out of David Caplan.'

Jane frowned. 'To my mind I think that if anybody should sue it's David Caplan.'

As they drove past the Caplans' house the Caplans were getting out of their Range Rover. Jane pulled over. 'I'm just going to have a quick chat with them, give them an update.'

'Maybe jumping the gun a bit?' Stanley said.

But Jane was already getting out of the car. David Caplan was opening the front door as his wife carried in a bag of shopping.

'Hello, we were just passing,' Jane said, approaching Mrs Caplan. 'Would you like to come in for a coffee?'

Buster hurled himself towards them as Mr Caplan grabbed his collar. 'Sorry, come on Buster, let's take you out.'

They all went into the kitchen as Mr Caplan opened the back-door and pushed Buster into the garden. The shredded remnants of a large kitchen roll were strewn around the kitchen floor, and Mrs Caplan put down her shopping bag and began picking up the soggy paper.

'He can reach up to the counters now,' she said, shaking her head. 'Please do sit down and I'll make some coffee.'

Jane helped clear up the mess as Mr Caplan returned to the kitchen.

'That bloody dog ... He's started getting separation anxiety when we both leave him, so we're getting a dog-trainer in.'

After his experience with Eric Donaldson, Stanley didn't want to hear any more stories of dogs and their owners. He could see Buster charging around the garden with what appeared to be a deflated football.

'We were visiting Martin Boon – you probably know he's been released from hospital. We needed to get a statement about the bicycle pump.'

'I'll be interested to know if he now admits threatening me with it,' Mr Caplan said.

'Not exactly, but his wife has admitted that she found the pump on his driveway and put it back on his bike when she was getting ready to go to the hospital. We have also asked him to come to the station to give a formal statement and to verify if he still wants to press assault charges.'

'Off the record, I wouldn't be surprised if he was after cash,' Jane said.

Mr Caplan arched his eyebrows. 'Really? Well, if anyone is going to sue, it'll be me. He has caused me huge anxiety and frustration, on top of my solicitors' fees.'

Alice carried the fresh coffee to the table with milk and sugar, and a plate of pastries.

'You know, darling, I wouldn't even bother. We have to live here . . . well, for a while at least . . . and we want to get the gates and wall completed. I'd prefer to try and get along with the neighbours before we sell.'

Mr Caplan snorted. 'There is no way I want to get along with that pompous bastard, or the interfering Larssons. I have the builders for the gates coming to see me this week.'

Jane poured the coffee and they made polite conversation for a while, then Mr Caplan excused himself to answer the phone, preferring not to use the kitchen extension.

'We have an estate agent coming to value the house. David is eager to sell,' Mrs Caplan explained.

'Do you live in the properties when you are doing all the renovations?' Jane asked.

'Not if I can help it. We didn't move in here until it was partially completed, as I like to oversee all the interior decoration. We have a small pied-à-terre in Mayfair which David uses as his office; unless he's working from here.'

Stanley drained his coffee cup, then pointedly looked at his watch.

'We should be leaving. Thank you for the coffee.'

Jane paused in the hall.

'Has Mrs Hoffman come around to see you again?' she asked.

Mrs Caplan shook her head. 'But you know, after you left, when I gave you her address, I remembered . . . I think I told you she had called in just the once . . . but I told David about her . . .'

She turned as her husband came to join them.

He nodded. 'She came by when I was here checking on the progress; it was a real building site. But my builder told me that she had made frequent visits.'

'It was a real coincidence, because I met her at the care home where she works but she was using her maiden name, so I didn't realise she was the previous owner's wife,' Jane said. 'I wondered if you could let me have a few photographs of Sebastian's bedroom, before you did all the restoration.'

Alice glanced at her husband, and he shook his head.

'Actually, I need the album for tomorrow as I show it to clients, but Alice will I am sure have some copies somewhere.'

'Oh, I do, but heaven knows where they are. I'll have a search and make sure I give them to you when I see you again.'

'Whenever it's convenient, thank you, and we'll be in touch as soon as we have a further update,' Jane said.

She hurried back to her car and Stanley gave her an impatient look as she got into the driver's seat.

'What was all that about?' Stanley said.

Jane shrugged and drove out through the courtyard.

'I reckon that medium really got to you.'

Jane sighed. 'The reason I was out of sorts this morning is that I broke up with Eddie last night. He was really pushing for us to buy a property at auction and refurbish it, but we would have to sell my house in order to finance it.'

Stanley felt for Jane, but didn't want to get into any heavy emotional stuff. 'I would say that David Caplan would be a good person to talk to about buying and selling properties. He must have got their house for a pittance and it must now be worth a fortune.'

Jane nodded. 'You're probably right.' They were both happy to leave it at that.

Back at the station, they were making out the report of their meeting with Martin Boon when DCI Hutton came out of her office.

'Just finishing the report on Martin Boon, ma'am,' Stanley said. 'I think we now need to bring him in with his wife to get a formal statement from them both. She's lied to us, and he blustered when we showed him the bicycle pump. If we put some pressure on, I'm certain he won't press the assault charge.'

'OK, get it organised. Let Mr Caplan know, as his solicitor has been pestering me.'

'Yes, ma'am. Is there anything else?'

'No. Just sort this out, please. It's taken up too much of your time, both of you.'

Hutton went back to her office and Stanley said he'd organise transport to bring Mr and Mrs Boon into the station. He would also speak to the officers who were called out to the incident to go over their reports.

Jane was happy to leave everything to Stanley as Meryl had asked to see her. They went into a small interview room as it was more private. Meryl had brought a stack of newspaper articles she thought might be of interest. It had taken her most of the day and she was still working on her notes.

First up was her research on Vera James.

'She was at one time quite well known and did sessions with audiences all over England. They were usually in small locations such as drill halls and rooms above pubs. The public paid to enter and there were various different booths, so she would be alongside tarot card readers, palmists and psychics, as well as other mediums.'

Meryl then told Jane about Vera's daughter. Sandra was divorced from her husband, who had been arrested for domestic abuse. She had two teenage children at local schools in Swanley, and they were all now living at Vera's. The house was owned by Vera but there had been problems with mortgage arrears and an eviction order had been issued three years ago. However, this appeared to have been dealt with.

'How old is Vera?' Jane asked.

'She's eighty-one and has been married twice, both ex-husbands now deceased. From what I could find out, the venue work dried up and Vera retired. She is also receiving disability allowance and her daughter is down as her carer.'

Meryl passed over the typed report she had just gone through, clipping together some newspaper articles she had copied. Next, she told Jane what she had managed to find out about Sebastian Hoffman. He had won a piano scholarship to Tiffin School in Kingston but left when he was fifteen. She had been able to contact a tutor there who had described him as an 'exceptionally talented young man', but said he was not good at socialising and had not made many friends. He was fluent in German and had been educated there, so he had traces of an accent.

'The tutor's name is George Taylor and I have noted down his phone number for you.'

'Good. Did he mention the reason that Sebastian left at fifteen?'

'No, he didn't. I've been on to the passport office and have his passport details under the name Hoffman, but it expired five years ago. I tried to find out if he left the UK for Mexico. I contacted most of the relevant airlines that have direct flights. I also made enquiries about anyone under the name Hoffman or Martinez returning to London, but as it was a few years ago they were not very productive.'

Meryl handed Jane her typed notes with Sebastian Hoffman's name printed in large letters at the top. She tapped the pages with her pen.

'I also contacted missing persons for this area and there's no record of anyone in the name of Hoffman or Martinez.'

Jane smiled. 'Well, this is great, Meryl. Thank you very much.'

'I will keep on at the airlines and let you know if I get a result. In the meantime, do you want me to mention this research to DCI Hutton?'

'No, that won't be necessary – I will deal with it. Thank you again, Meryl.'

Jane waited until she had left the room before spreading out all the newspaper cuttings. There were two pages from a newspaper on which Meryl had written in red ink, 'Full page as other news coverage may be of interest.'

The text was rather blurred, and mostly consisted of advertisements for a disco, a bring-and-buy sale at St Mary's Church Hall, a production of *Little Red Riding Hood* by the local amateur dramatic society and some Saturday afternoon puppet shows. Then there was a black-edged section: 'Local Medium Vera James, at the Swan & Bear for two nights'. Beneath the ad were quotes from satisfied clients:

'Vera has changed my life and given me comfort.' – Norma Smith

'Vera brought my beloved daughter forwards and comforted me in my grief to know she is at peace.' – Helen Masters

Jane almost shot out of her seat as the door burst open and Stanley appeared, looking agitated.

'What in God's name are you doing in here? I've been looking all over the station for you. We had Martin Boon's solicitor here – he's withdrawing any charges against David Caplan.'

'I thought we were bringing him in for an interview?'

'I'd just started to organise that when he came to the station.'

'Martin Boon was here?'

'No, his fucking solicitor. He claims Boon never wanted any charges brought against David Caplan.'

'You are joking?'

'The best part of it was that his client wished to remain on good terms with his neighbour.'

'So that's it?'

'Suppose so . . . we just have to finish up the paperwork.'

Jane sighed and started to gather up all the papers. Stanley leaned forwards to pick up the page from the newspaper.

'That medium really got to you, didn't she? Don't tell me she knew you and your boyfriend were parting company?'

'No, she did not,' Jane snapped, standing up.

Stanley tossed the article back onto the table and turned to leave.

'You fancy a drink? I'm going over to the pub.'

'Not really, I might just head off home.'

Stanley hesitated at the door, watching as she packed all the notes into her briefcase.

'OK then, I'll see you tomorrow.'

He closed the door quietly as she clicked her briefcase shut. Picking up her handbag, she stopped and sat down again, just as Stanley returned.

'I forgot to mention, the solicitor was no ordinary local bloke, but from a big firm in the city – not the same one as before . DCI Hutton asked if he would be available should we require his presence, and he said that if Mr Larsson agreed he would attend.'

'So, they're footing his bill?'

'Exactly . . . very neighbourly, because he must charge for every second. So, come and have a drink to celebrate our case purportedly closed . . . bar the paperwork.'

Jane smiled. 'Actually, I think I could do with a gin and tonic.'

Chapter Fourteen

Jane had consumed several large gin and tonics by the time she finally got a taxi home. There had been a group of officers from the station, one celebrating his birthday, so they congregated in the small snug bar while the pub was closed to regular customers. The lock-in proved to be just what Jane needed: a lot of laughs, no talk about their case and no thought about Eddie. Surprisingly, DC Burrows turned out to be an entertaining storyteller.

Getting out of the taxi, Jane could see the hall light had been left on, and her good mood instantly evaporated as she assumed Eddie was inside. She opened the door and called out but there was no response. She looked in the kitchen to see the rose petals still scattered on the floor. Heading up the stairs, she called out for him again, as the bedroom light was also on.

The TV had been taken, along with his few remaining clothes. His toothbrush and electric shaver had been taken from the bathroom. There was no note. Jane felt empty and sad.

She felt even worse the following morning as her hangover kicked in. She cleared the kitchen, made herself a cup of strong coffee and took two paracetamol. She was waiting outside for a taxi to take her to the station when an ambulance drew up, and Gerry hurried out as the two paramedics got out to open the rear doors. They lowered a stretcher seat, with Vi wrapped up in a red blanket. She gave Jane a beaming smile.

Gerry waved to her as he ushered them into the house.

'I'm glad to see Vi's home,' Jane called out.

'Small mercies . . .' Gerry said, raising his eyes as he followed them inside.

She was still waiting for her taxi when the paramedics came out, with Gerry thanking them as they returned to their ambulance. He turned to Jane as they drove off. 'Could your Eddie spare me a few minutes? I've decided to go to a dog shelter this afternoon and I need the back garden fence fixed, so it's safe.'

'I'm sorry, not sure if he's around today.'

'Never mind then. I am not going to get a puppy, we want a rescue dog, a few years old, that won't jump up on Vi, but it'll be good for her. Well, to be honest, better for me really as she's sometimes unsure who I am.'

Jane was thankful when her taxi drew up. She waved to Gerry as it pulled away. On her way to the station, she thought about what he had said, and it made her think about the Caplans' puppy, who definitely needed training. As she was dropped off at the station, Stanley was walking in. Like Jane he had been well into his cups last night so had not driven home. When she had left, he was still drinking with DC Burrows.

'Morning,' he said with a grimace. 'I don't know about you, but I have one hell of a hangover.'

'So you won't be having your usual full English?'

'I most certainly will! Always the best cure, along with a big dose of Andrews Liver Salts first thing.'

He was already in the canteen with his plate loaded when Jane sat down. She had ordered poached eggs on toast but doubted she'd be able to eat anything.

'My neighbour was outside when I was waiting for my taxi. His wife has dementia, and I thought when I saw her being taken in an ambulance the other day she might not be back, but they brought her home early this morning.'

Stanley nodded. 'What an exciting morning! And to add some even more thrilling news, they've announced that Prince Andrew and Sarah Ferguson are getting married on 23rd July. My ballet-crazy daughter saved all the newspaper articles about Princess Diana's wedding and it's the same with this one; she has even made a wedding dress for her Barbie doll.'

'I'm surprised you're even aware of the wedding,' Jane said.

'After this morning I am, because the wife only just discovered that our daughter had cut out the satin from her wedding dress. All hell broke loose!'

Jane put her half-eaten poached eggs to one side and took out two more paracetamol tablets.

'I'll have a couple. My head's killing me.' Stanley held out his hand.

She was about to leave when DCI Hutton walked past with a cup of coffee.

'Could I just have a quick word, ma'am?' Jane asked.

'Sure, here or do you want to come to my office?'

'It won't take a moment. Just wanted to check you were happy for me to update Mr Caplan. From our last conversation, he seemed intent on taking the situation further, possibly even suing Martin Boon for trespass.'

Hutton sighed. 'Well, we don't want that. What we want is for this whole mess to go away so we can get on with more important things. You'd better go then. Just don't take all morning about it.'

The Range Rover was not parked outside the house, so Jane drove round to the rear entrance, pulling up outside the double gates, but it was obvious the Caplans were not at home. She was about to leave when she saw the neighbour from the house opposite parking in their drive.

Jane walked over.

'Good morning, it's DI Jane Tennison. I was hoping to see Mr Caplan, but I don't think they're home.'

'I saw them leaving when I left,' the woman said. 'We're only on nodding terms, but I obviously know about all the problems that have been going on.'

'Can I help you with these?' Jane nodded to the bags of groceries in the boot of her car.

'That's very kind of you. I do a mammoth shop for the entire week, stock up my freezer, and it ends up being quite a load.'

Jane carried in two plastic bags from Waitrose, still trying to remember the woman's name. She had opened her front door to carry in a crate of beer and dumped it inside, then went to collect another box of tonic water.

It was a minute before Jane remembered that her name was Ida Bellamy, and her husband was Hector. They had a few businesses, including a small hardware store. Ida offered to make some coffee, if Jane wanted to wait until the Caplans returned.

Jane accepted and helped stack the groceries in the kitchen cupboards before sitting down at the kitchen table. Jane knew neither of the Bellamys had been at home when the altercation happened, so she asked Mrs Bellamy about when they'd moved into the house. 'It was exceptionally well finished and decorated to our specifications, and we had very few hiccups, just the things you expect with a new property,' Mrs Bellamy said. 'The only drawback was that the courtyard was in a really bad state; it was like a mudbath when it rained. We were told it was caused by all the building work and wouldn't be fixed until the new build next door was finished.'

'So how long did you have to wait until the property next door was finished?'

'About eight months, but the courtyard was left in an even worse state. We eventually discovered that it was part of Mr Hoffman's estate; he was the previous owner of the big mansion.'

'Did you meet with Mr and Mrs Hoffman?'

'Fleetingly, but I could tell he was not a pleasant man. I believe he and his wife were having money troubles. We had a sort of meeting with everyone to discuss how we would try and sort it out, and we were then told that Mr Larsson had been sold the courtyard. To be honest, it was all rather strange because I think it would have been better for us all to part-own it.'

'They are certainly very rude about anyone parking there,' Jane said.

Mrs Bellamy rolled her eyes. 'Oh, I know, so we keep our distance. One night my husband heard a lot of shouting and when he looked out Mr Larsson was having an argument with Mr Hoffman. Mrs Larsson was screaming and being hysterical. I think it was something connected to their daughter. Anyway, it was after that we were told the Larssons owned the courtyard.'

'Did they begin to tarmac the area straightaway?'

She nodded. 'Not long after, anyway. My husband felt the workmen were a bit on the cowboy side. They had this big open truck boiling up the tar, and they began at the far side of the drive, round to the front entrance.'

'Did you know the Hoffmans' son?'

'Not really. But he was a very handsome young man. He didn't have any curtains on his bedroom windows, and I often saw him at night, dancing. I remember he had very long dark hair.'

'Have you seen him recently?'

'No, he disappeared before his parents left, and then tragedy struck. The poor Larssons were devastated. It's awful because I can't remember their daughter's name, but she died of sepsis. She was only sixteen, poor thing. I remember it so clearly because her funeral cortège had to manoeuvre round the unfinished tarmac.'

'Have you ever seen Mrs Hoffman here, possibly around the time the big house was being worked on?'

'No, but we wouldn't have. My husband and I both leave early for work, and don't return until six or even later.'

Jane nodded. 'I should be going. Thank you for the coffee, Mrs Bellamy. Hopefully by now the Caplans are back.'

Mrs Bellamy walked Jane to the front door. She pointed out the planting Mrs Larsson had done, all around the verges.

'She put that railing up in front of the Caplans' rear garden fence. I think it's supposed to have flowering plants of some kind, but they look wilted to me. I had a visit from David Caplan asking me if either myself or my husband objected to his plans for a new wall to replace the old fence, and electric gates, and I said it would look so much better, so I had no objections and nor did our next-door neighbours.'

'It seems the only objection is from Martin Boon, then,' Jane said.

'Well, he is a very fussy man. I can't see why he would object as it doesn't have any connection to his property.'

'Thank you again,' Jane said, heading towards her car.

Mrs Larsson was standing in her drive with her arms folded, staring towards her, grim-faced. Jane ignored her.

The Range Rover was now there, so Jane quickly parked along-side it. She rang the doorbell, and instantly heard a cacophony of barking from Buster. Mrs Caplan opened the door, holding tightly onto Buster's collar as he tried to leap up at Jane.

'Sorry to disturb you. This won't take a moment, I just need to give your husband an update,' Jane said.

Buster galloped off as Mrs Caplan called for her husband. He hurried down the staircase, pausing on the landing to look down into the hall.

'Come up to my office. Has Alice offered you a coffee?'

'No, thank you,' Jane replied. 'This won't take long.'

David Caplan waited for Jane to join him on the landing before ushering her into his office. The room was lined with books, and his desk was covered in architectural drawings.

'My boss felt that you should be given the good news. We had Mr Boon's solicitor at the station and he confirmed that Mr Boon will not be pressing assault charges . . .'

Caplan leaned forwards. 'Oh, really. *He's* not pressing charges against *me*? Well, one, he entered my property without my consent; and two, he was abusive and threatened me with what I presumed was some kind of weapon. I have been put through the wringer, being told my actions to protect myself could have caused his death. And now, he just walks into the station and . . .'

Jane straightened and apologised for interrupting. 'Not personally . . . his solicitor asked to see DCI Hutton and formally withdrew any allegations of assault. He also expressed Mr Boon's sincere wishes to remain on good terms with you as his neighbour.'

Caplan shook his head in disbelief. 'Well, I have no desire to remain on good terms with him. I will be speaking to my solicitor to discuss exactly what action I can take.'

He folded his arms and Jane took it as a sign the discussion was over.

'Thank you for your time, Mr Caplan.'

Mrs Caplan walked Jane to the front door.

'Is everything all right?'

'I believe so,' Jane said. 'Hopefully I won't need to bother you again.'

'Did he tell you that we've got the clearance from the planning board to begin demolishing the old fences and to erect the new wall and the electric gates?' Mrs Caplan said.

'That's positive news,' Jane replied. 'Good to see you again.'

Jane went out to her car, knowing that it might be good news for the Caplans, but she doubted the neighbours would be very happy about it. Still, at least it would no longer be a police matter.

Chapter Fifteen

Jane spent the rest of the day catching up on paperwork. She was just leaving for home when Meryl approached, handing her a white envelope.

'Good news. I've finally tracked down Sebastian Hoffman. He did return to the UK but used his German passport, which was why they had no record of it. I have given you dates and flight details, from British Airways.'

Jane smiled. 'Thanks, that's very helpful.'

'No problem.' Meryl turned to go.

'Have a nice evening,' Jane called after her.

It was a strange feeling, letting herself into an empty house. Even though she had managed not to think about the situation all day, now it really hit home. Deep down she had expected Eddie to make contact or to try and see her. She thought about calling his parents, certain he had moved back to their flat, but what would she say? Perhaps it was best to give the situation more time.

After changing into her old tracksuit and putting on her slippers, the doorbell rang. She hesitated, partly because of what she was wearing, certain it was Eddie.

The doorbell rang again, and she called out that she was coming, but when she opened the door, it was Gerry from next door. She swallowed her disappointment and tried to look happy to see him.

'I wonder if you could do me a favour,' Gerry began. 'I need any old newspapers or cardboard boxes, because I have to shut her in while I pop down to get some groceries.'

For a moment Jane thought he was referring to his wife, but then realised he was holding the lead of a cowering dog. The animal was shaking, head bent low, tail tucked underneath a skinny body.

'This is Wilma, she's a whippet-lurcher cross and she's been very badly treated. She was brought into the refuge suffering from malnutrition and some nasty laceration on her hind legs.'

'Well, come in, let me see what I can find,' Jane said, ushering him inside.

Gerry picked up the shaking creature, and its eyes were so frightened, Jane immediately felt sorry for it. She went into the kitchen and found some old newspaper and two cardboard boxes.

Gerry went and sat on a chair by the table.

'If you have any old towels, or woollen sweaters, I'm going to make her a warm coat, but she's not quite house-trained yet.'

Jane went upstairs and found some towels that Eddie had used when he came home covered in mud and cement dust. She put two sweaters, the towels and the newspapers into one of the cardboard boxes. Gerry remained with the dog in his arms, her head hanging down over his forearm, sad eyes wide open. She was still shaking as he gently stroked her skinny body.

'How is Vi?' Jane asked.

'Oh, she's fine; to be honest, I don't think she really took it in that we have a new little soul at home.'

Jane looked at the dog. 'She seems very nervous.'

'It'll take time for her to understand nobody is going to hurt her ever again,' Gerry said.

He carried the boxes out with Wilma cowering behind him on the lead. 'Thanks for these, Jane.'

After making a fresh cup of coffee, Jane put her briefcase on the kitchen table. Taking out the file she had been compiling for her own interest on Angelica Martinez, plus the material Meryl had researched, she opened the envelope with the flight details.

Sebastian Hoffman had returned to London shortly after his parents had moved out of his old home, but after that Meryl had been unable to find any trace of him. There were no medical, dental, national insurance or employment records; it was as if he had disappeared into thin air.

Jane began to put together a chronology:

1. The Hoffmans divorced during or shortly after they sold their property to David and Alice Caplan. Their son Sebastian left to travel to Mexico.

2. Father Victor Hoffman moved back to Berlin, sells courtyard to Mr and Mrs Larsson.

3. Mother Angelica returned to her maiden name, Martinez, after leaving the property but remained in close proximity to be reunited with her son. She had received a postcard before the sale from Sebastian to say he was well and returning shortly.

4. Angelica began to visit the medium Vera James needing confirmation she would find her son. Concerned he would not be able to find her and worried something had happened to him.

5. David and Alice Caplan purchase their property but do not take up residency for nine or ten months while it was being renovated.

6. Mr and Mrs Larsson organise the tarmacking of the drive and courtyard.

7. The Larsson daughter died and funeral occurs midway through the work on the tarmac. The work did not resume until after the funeral.

8. Numerous objections to the Caplans building a wall with electric gates. Rejected, reapplied. Rejected due to opposition from Martin Boon, resulting in the alleged threatening of Mr Caplan. Martin Boon was admitted to hospital and put into an induced coma.

Jane put all the paperwork back in her briefcase. It was almost ten, but she went into the hall and called Vera James. She recognised Sandra James's voice when she answered the phone.

'Sorry to call you so late. This is Jane Tennison. I'd like to make an appointment with Vera.'

Sandra asked her to hold on. It was quite a while before she returned and said that Vera had declined her request.

'It's really important, Sandra . . .' Jane began.

'I'm afraid she has no available appointments for the foreseeable future,' Sandra said, ending the call.

Jane returned to the kitchen, deciding that she would pay an unscheduled visit to Vera, whether she liked it or not. She was about to turn the lights off in the kitchen and go to bed when she heard a high-pitched howling coming from Gerry's back garden. Unlocking the backdoor, she went outside. The security lights that Eddie had installed came on.

Jane could see the terrified dog running around Gerry's garden. She went over to the broken fence, worried that Wilma would run through the gap. Gerry came out with a blanket and bent down to pick her up.

'Sorry, she doesn't like me to leave her on her own. I'll repair the hole in the fence tomorrow. Unless Eddie is around?'

'He's not, Gerry. I'll see if there are any pieces of wood you can use in his shed tomorrow morning.'

'Oh, that's very kind of you. I'll take her in now. Silly thing, she's scared of her own shadow.'

Jane relocked her backdoor, and eventually the security lights blinked off. She turned off the kitchen and hall lights, put the chain on the front door and went to bed.

Chapter Sixteen

The following morning, before going to the station, Jane called the number she had for Angelica Martinez, but there was no answer. She then called the care home and was eventually put through to her.

'Hi, it's Jane Tennison. I was just wondering if I could have a quick chat with you, not now, but when it's convenient.'

'I'm at work until after lunch.'

'I could come and collect you.'

'Well, I have an appointment this afternoon at two, so I was going to go straight there from work.'

'This appointment, it's not with Vera James by any chance, is it?' Jane asked.

'Yes, it is!' Angelica said brightly.

'You know, after you gave me her card, I went to see her myself. I have to say I was very impressed,' Jane said. 'I could give you a lift there this afternoon, if you like.'

Angelica hesitated before replying. 'That's very kind, but it might not be permissible to bring someone. Perhaps I should ring her first.'

'Oh, don't worry about that,' Jane said quickly. 'I'm not just someone. I'm sure she won't mind.'

'Oh, OK then. I will be waiting by the main gates, just after one o'clock.'

'Great,' Jane said. 'I'll see you later.' She paused. 'Oh, one other thing. Could you let me have your ex-husband's phone number? It's just to do with some details of the property purchase, nothing to worry about.'

'Well, I'm not sure . . . we haven't been on very good terms, and I haven't spoken to him for a while.' She sounded nervous and Jane wondered if she'd pushed her luck too far.

'I understand, but it's just admin really, nothing personal.'

'I suppose that would be all right. Can I call you back? My address book's in my handbag which is in the locker room.'

'Yes, of course, I'll wait. I am at home, not the station.'

After giving her the number, Jane hung up. She was excited, but at the same time worried that gatecrashing Angelica Martinez's appointment with Vera might cause trouble for her.

Taking a shower and washing her hair, she kept the bathroom door open to enable her to hear the bedroom extension if it rang. It was another thing that Eddie had organised, and the thought made her sad for a moment. She was finishing blow-drying her hair when the phone rang. She sat down on the bed to pick up the receiver.

'Hello?'

'Is this Miss Tennison?'

'Speaking.'

'Victor Hoffman here. My ex-wife contacted me. You wished to speak to me?'

Surprised that Miss Martinez had called him, she sat up on the edge of the bed, opening a small drawer in her bedside cabinet.

'This is very kind of you. I hope it is not inconvenient.'

She grabbed a pencil and notepad from the drawer.

'Not at all. We are just one hour difference. And it is more private here at my home before I go to work.'

He had a strong German accent and sounded very formal.

'What is it that you wished to discuss with me?'

'I don't know if your ex-wife told you that I have been working on a case that involved one of your old neighbours.'

'I'm not sure. We had a very brief conversation.'

Jane found her pencil and opened the notebook. 'I can't go into details, but I need to know exactly when you sold the courtyard to Mr and Mrs Larsson.'

'It is very simple. We rarely if ever used the courtyard, and we would have had to maintain the area for the other properties' use. It required extensive resurfacing.'

'Wouldn't it have been better financially to have retained the rights to the courtyard if your intention was to sell?'

There was a pause as he took a deep breath.

'I don't feel that I should have to explain to you my reasons; as I said earlier, it would have been costly to maintain not only the courtyard but also the drive. I also had personal reasons for wanting to extricate myself from residing in England and required certain finances. So I agreed a simple cash transaction with the Larssons; and as it turned out, I sold our property quite quickly to a Mr Caplan.'

'I understand, because I am aware you were getting divorced and . . .'

'There were other issues, and I was under a great deal of pressure that involved my son.'

'Sebastian?'

'Yes, he was unfortunately having a relationship with the daughter of one of our neighbours.'

'Have you seen him recently?'

'No, I have not. We arranged for him to leave before the house was sold and he went to Mexico. I don't know what Angelica has told you, but my relationship with Sebastian had become very strained. He found the move from Germany difficult . . . he was such a talented musician but couldn't settle at the school . . .'

'Angelica seems deeply concerned about him,' Jane said.

'I know, she always has been overprotective of him, to the point of being suffocating, and I partly blamed her for the situation. The girl was underage and I was threatened that he could be arrested . . . they wanted him gone, and in truth so did I . . .'

Hoffman sighed, and Jane knew enough to stay silent.

'I simply wanted to get out of England, out from my divorce. I am presently working for my brother and in a good relationship, but at the same time I am saddened for Angelica, who remains in a kind of vacuum waiting for Sebastian to come to her. He is everything to her. He looked like her first husband and she never got over his death, but I had to try and get my life back on track.' He paused. 'I hope that answers your enquiries.'

Jane had been scribbling notes, but had still not got what she was after, and it felt as if Victor was about to end the call.

'Just one more thing. You have been very helpful, and I really appreciate your time, but I just need to clarify something. Did you agree to sell the courtyard to the Larssons because of the relationship between your son and their daughter?'

'Well, that is partly true. Fortunately, I was insured to cover the damage from the fire, but not enough to make the necessary repairs to the roof and the first floor. So I needed the money also.'

Jane remained on the phone for another five minutes. She managed to get from Hoffman the dates the transaction went through, but he refused to tell her the amount he had been paid. He also confirmed the arrangement for Sebastian to fly to Mexico.

When the phone call was over, she hurried down the stairs to the kitchen to double-check in her file. She had two further outstanding queries, underlining them in red felt-tipped pen.

Jane chose a grey cashmere sweater, and one of her best suits, and was just selecting a pair of shoes when she heard some loud hammering outside. Looking out of her bedroom window, she saw Eddie's old white van parked outside. She was in two minds whether to go out, but as her car was parked next to the van, he would know she was at home, and realised it would seem churlish of her not to go and talk to him.

Letting herself out of the backdoor, she saw the garden shed open. There was a step ladder propped up outside.

'Eddie?'

One of his workmen came out from the shed with a plank of wood.

'Morning, miss, I'm just collecting the cans of emulsion. I've already taken out a lot of gear, and he wants the ladder.'

Jane frowned. 'It would have been polite to inform me first, but carry on.'

'I just need to hammer this in place. The fence needs quite a lot of new sections, but this should sort it out for now. Bloke next door's worried about his dog getting through because it could run down the alley and onto the road.'

Jane was about to return to the house when she saw Vi. She was wearing a long flannel nightdress and had bare feet.

'Vi, where's Gerry?'

She put her hands to her ears, her face crumpled. 'The hammering. I can't stand the noise.'

Jane turned to Eddie's workman. 'Excuse me, I'm sorry I don't know your name, but can you just stop for a minute, I need to go next door.'

'It's Don . . . I'll take the ladder out and then come back.'

Jane hurried down the alley and turned into next door's front garden. The gate was open and so was their front door. She stepped inside, calling out for Gerry, but there was no reply, so she went down the hall to go into their kitchen just as he appeared.

'I'm here, I'm here, sorry about this, but Wilma got out and ran up the road. Eddie's friend said he'd help out and block the gap in the fence.'

Gerry had the runaway in his arms, and she was wearing one of Jane's old sweaters, its skinny front legs protruding from rolled-up sleeves, the rest wound around her trembling body.

'Vi's in the garden. I think the hammering frightened her.'

Wilma was thrust into Jane's arms and immediately began to whimper as Gerry hurried down the hall and into the kitchen.

'Shush . . . shush . . . it's all right.'

Gerry returned after a moment, holding Vi's hand as if she were a child. As soon as she saw Jane with Wilma she broke into a beaming smile.

'My doggy, my baby.'

Jane thought Gerry was so gentle and calm as he took his wife into the drawing room. 'You can have her with you as soon as you are in your chair and wrapped up nice and warm,' he said.

Vi was helped into a big armchair with an attached footrest, a duvet was tucked around her, and then a blanket. She held out her arms, her hands clutching, as Gerry took Wilma from Jane and lifted a flap of the blanket to tuck the dog inside beside his wife.

'Baby, baby, back,' Vi said, smiling.

'You be gentle with her, Vi, stroke her softly and she'll go to sleep.'

It was touching the way the dog snuggled close, one little paw over the edge of the blanket.

Gerry turned to Jane. 'Can I get you a cup of tea?'

'No thanks, Gerry. I've got to get to work.'

He walked with her to the front door.

'It was my fault she got out. I thought Eddie was back so I went to see if he could help with the fence, but it was Don and I left the door open.'

'He's making it escape-proof now. He stopped hammering when Vi came out, but I'll tell him to finish.'

'Very kind of you, can you give him . . .' He reached into his pocket for his wallet, but Jane quickly told him that she would take care of it, and that he should go back to be with Vi until the hammering stopped.

Don accepted two pounds from Jane and said he would only take another ten minutes to fix the board against the fence. She locked the kitchen door, annoyed that Eddie was intent on keeping his distance. After all, he had walked out on her.

Jane didn't want to go back to the station and explain that she was going to see Vera, so called in sick, explaining that she had a migraine. To kill some time before meeting with Angelica Martinez, Jane selected clothes for the dry cleaners, and then went to collect the laundry. She parked outside the care home main gates at twelve forty-five, having bought herself a takeaway coffee and a chicken roll at the bakery next door to the dry cleaners. She watched people coming and going, the gates manned by the same elderly gent. She was just finishing her roll when she saw Angelica Martinez inside the gates, waiting for them to be opened. She was wearing her hair in the same style as before, two thick braids wound round her head, but this time threaded with an emerald-green silk scarf.

Jane gave the horn a single toot and Angelica crossed the road and got in the car, giving Jane a warm smile before closing the door.

'I had a very good conversation with Victor earlier this morning,' Jane said as she pulled away.

'Yes, I thought it best that I should call him as he had so many different numbers, so he could contact you directly.'

'He was very concerned about you still being in London.'

'I know, he said I should return to Mexico, and I will sometime.'

'Do you still have family there?'

'I have a brother who runs a restaurant in Puerto Vallarta. But he did not approve of my first husband, so we have not been on good terms.'

'What about Victor?'

She let out a throaty laugh. 'No, nobody liked Victor.'

Jane glanced at her watch. They were going to be early for the two o'clock appointment, but she continued to drive towards Swanley.

'I asked Victor if he had seen Sebastian.'

'I used to call him every week until he became angry and said that he had never received any call or seen him since he left to go to Berlin. So, I stopped. I always doubted that my son would want to see him, but there was just a possibility.'

Jane drew up outside a small cafe and asked if Angelica would like a coffee, as they had fifteen minutes before her appointment.

'I'm fine, thank you. Tell me about your session with Vera.'

Jane thought for a moment. 'It was quite emotional. She talked about my brother. I hardly knew him, he was just a toddler when he died, so I rarely think about him. She told me to pass on a message to my parents.'

Angelica nodded. 'Only those who have a connection to you and have passed come forwards. When my beloved husband came through, it was an answer to my prayers. She described him wearing a white scarf around his head. When he was working on intricate silver items on his machine, he would use the scarf to protect his face from sparks. To know he was at peace . . . to know his love for me had never diminished . . .'

'So does he still come forwards?'

'Oh yes, many times. He wants to know about Sebastian.'

Jane started the car. That meant that Angelica's husband was on the other side but not Sebastian, meaning that he was alive. If she really believed in all this, then her suspicions were unfounded.

Chapter Seventeen

Drawing up to Vera James's house, Jane saw there were three cars parked in the drive. Two other cars were parked on either side on the path, so Jane had to park further along the street.

'It looks as if Vera has visitors,' Jane said.

'Yes, today is a group session. Vera takes one every month. I should have mentioned it to you.'

Jane locked the car and followed Angelica up the path, nervous about how she would be received. Sandra opened the door and did not appear to be surprised by Jane's presence. She had a cardboard box in her hand.

'It's just about to begin, so can I have your payment of five pounds? Please take your seats and remain silent unless brought forwards. It is usually only six people present but we have made this one-time concession, Miss Tennison.'

They both put their money in the box, as Sandra gestured for them to go ahead into the room.

The curtains were drawn, and the armchairs and sofa had been pushed together. Two extra hard-backed chairs had been placed behind them, along with one carver chair. The coffee table had been placed in front of the sofa, still with the outdated magazines; but now also with two large lit candles in thick glass bowls, giving off a strong flowery perfume.

Angelica recognised two middle-aged women who smiled sheepishly at her. There was a twenty-ish, plain-looking girl sitting in an armchair, a grey-haired man in a pin-striped suit in the middle of the sofa and an elderly, smartly dressed, white-haired woman was sitting in the carver chair. Jane and Angelica sat in two hard-backed chairs.

All the furniture had been pushed to one side to leave a spacious area on the other side of the drawing room. Sandra came in, leaving the door ajar. She carried a small bowl of smoking incense and a little brush of twigs held together with string. She began to sweep the brush over the bowl, filling the air with a pungent smell. Sandra left the room, leaving the door wide open, returning a moment later with a wheelchair, placing it directly in front of the chairs and then pulling a small table close to the arm of the wheelchair. She took a large notepad and pencil from the big side pocket in the wheelchair. She then hurried from the room and quickly returned with a tumbler of water which she placed on the table.

Vera entered wearing the same kaftan as before, but now her white hair was loose, reaching below her shoulders. She also had heavy make-up, her eyelashes thick with black mascara and even more black eyeliner, and her mouth shiny with red lipstick.

'Welcome everyone.' She smiled warmly as she walked slowly to the wheelchair, sitting down, then carefully spreading her kaftan around her legs. She drew the table closer and opened the notebook. She then picked up the pencil and opened the notebook to an empty page.

'I recognise some familiar faces, but as always I like to give a little introduction to my group session. I am a medium and I depend on those wishing to contact their loved ones to come forwards. I have to explain that sometimes there is a dominant spirit, and this could mean disappointment for one or two of you, but I have no preconception of who will be with us this afternoon. Understand that if anything occurs that you find distressing, just raise your hand and ask for me to stop. We are here and will comfort each other and find relief from grief, and hopefully leave with our hearts uplifted.'

Vera then scribbled on the empty page, tapping it with the pencil.

'Does anyone have a wedding ring with a small . . .'

She rubbed her index finger and thumb together.

'I think it's a gemstone . . . maybe a ruby?'

The grey-haired man lifted his hand.

'Do you wear this on a chain round your neck?' she asked.

'Yes, I do. It's a garnet stone.'

'Ah well, I have your wife with me; she passed over quite recently, is that right?'

'Yes, six months ago.'

'She wants you to know that she has no more pain, she had . . .'

'Cancer, she died of ovarian cancer.'

'Yes, but it was not diagnosed for a long time. She is indicating her stomach, and something on her head. She is indicating her hair.'

'She was afraid she would lose her hair.'

Vera made long scribbles and circles in her notebook. Then she sipped from her glass. Jane glanced over to look at what effect it was having on him. He was leaning forwards, his hands clenched together.

'You were with her when she died, holding her hand and the ring.'

'It slipped from her finger.'

'She wants you to know that it was meant to happen. She knows you always have it close to you. She is with you and she is at peace. She knew you were beside her when she passed, and wants to thank you for the loving years you had together.'

Vera turned a page, as if to indicate she was moving on, brushing the empty page with the flat of her hand and frowning. She began to make circles on the empty page while everyone waited expectantly. Eventually she looked up.

'I have a young girl, touching her heart, wearing white, white shoes, white socks, a veil, too young for a wedding . . . does the number twelve mean anything to anyone?'

The smartly dressed woman raised her hand. 'I think it's my granddaughter, she was twelve years old.'

'Ah yes, she is wearing her communion dress, but the ceremony didn't take place because she was . . .'

Vera scribbled furiously, making jagged strokes.

'I have someone else coming through beside her . . . very protective . . . she is holding her arms as if to cradle her . . . is she the mother . . . did they go together?'

'Yes, it was a car accident.'

Vera began to make very strong zig-zag strokes on the page. She was visibly perspiring, her face flushed, and she spoke rapidly.

'Dark night, not in city, country lane, very fast turning a corner, no control, car went down an incline, hidden ditch, an embankment.'

'Yes, yes it was very badly lit. They found skid marks in the mud the following morning and there was no hope.'

'You feel a great deal of guilt, but there was nothing you could do. It was not your fault. It was an accident. Your granddaughter is touching her chest, her heart showing me she wants you to know there is no blame, that her love for you is strong and they are together. She says that she liked her veil and . . .'

Vera pressed her hand to her top lip.

'She calls you by a nickname. Josie?'

'My name is Rosemary. She never called me Grandma, just Rosie.' The tears were streaming down her cheeks.

'You placed some white roses, tea roses in a coronet and the petals fell.'

'Oh God, yes I did . . . they did.'

'She wants you to know that was her, with the petals. She is always aware of you and wants you to find peace, to know she is happy.'

Jane could feel the hairs stand up on the back of her neck. It was freaky but at the same time she noticed that Vera didn't talk about the dead girl's mother, instead turning to a clean page. The grandmother was blowing her nose on a handkerchief, saying 'Thank you, thank you.' The grey-haired man leaned towards her and held her hand.

Jane was trying to calculate how long the session would go on, as the two middle-aged women and the young girl had still not had

Vera bring anyone forwards. Angelica remained listening intently and smiling, obviously used to being at these sessions.

Vera suddenly laughed softly, looking at the two women. 'Your father is with me again. He is making a motion with his hand ... like writing. Are you in the process of signing some kind of document? Oh yes, you are, because he is making strong signals that it is very important . . .'

Vera put her hands together with just the fingers touching, like a cat's-cradle game. Both the women were eagerly leaning forwards.

'He's a very dominant man, likes to know exactly what plans you have for your future. He is making funny comical gestures, birds, and a basket . . . Ah, he is advising you not to put all your eggs in one basket. I recall when he came forwards before, he was very protective of you both and wanted you to know he is guiding you at all times. Now he is stepping back; no, not quite yet, he has something else to say. What is it? Do you have a necktie with you?'

They both nodded, one opening her handbag.

'It was one of his favourite ties; when we sent all his clothes to charity, we kept one each.'

'Well, he approves. Does it have a small insignia on it?'

'Yes, it was his golf club tie.'

Vera frowned, picking up her pencil. She scribbled for a moment. 'He is stepping back now because I have someone else coming forwards who is very insistent. I have the letter S, and he is a young man. He's showing me something . . .'

Vera opened her mouth and gestured as if putting something in, then pressed her throat, making a gurgling sound. Jane straightened. Was this going to be Sebastian? But the young girl raised her hand.

'My brother was called Simon.'

'He is with me, dear; recent, wasn't it? He is very distressed because of the pain he has caused. Oh, my goodness, he is very emotional.'

'He was a heroin addict, and he had just got out of rehab and came to live with me. I have to care for my mother as she has MS, and I just couldn't be with him enough.' She broke down sobbing.

'Listen to me,' Vera said gently. 'You did everything you could for him. You gave him a home, and hoped that he was going to turn his life around. You are a very special young woman. Simon knows he had every opportunity to begin his recovery. He is deeply distressed that he let you down and wants you to know that his depression overwhelmed him, and he did not want to be a burden on you.'

The young girl was sobbing. 'I loved him so much. He was so talented and brave. He had always taken care of me when we were young because our father was a terrible alcoholic, and all I wanted was to take care of him the way he protected me.'

Vera was nodding. 'He knows you were always there for him, and he is here with me now to tell you how much he loved you and appreciated everything you did for him. He is asking you to let go of your grief and guilt, as he is now in a better place. He is at peace and wants you to know that his love for you will never fade.'

Vera was sweating as she made circles on the page, bigger and bigger rings over and over again. She stopped abruptly and took a drink. 'He left a note for you but did not take his life at your home?'

The young woman nodded through her tears. Everyone was clearly moved by her outpouring of grief. Jane had been watching Vera closely, noticing how she quickly latched onto little clues in her clients' reactions, just like an old-time professional. But after listening to the young woman whose brother had committed suicide, she was no longer so sure.

Vera wiped her perspiring top lip. 'He left you a note, like a list. He tells me he could not put into words what he felt. Did Simon have a record collection, not the big vinyl ones but the small CDs, small round ones, and they have a message for you. He chose each one and they each have a special meaning. He wants you to listen to them in the order he left them and that when you play each one, he will be beside you, listening.'

Vera closed her notebook. It was a signal the session was over, and everyone got ready to leave. Sandra opened the door, standing to one side as she ushered everyone out. As they filed past Vera, those who had been given messages from their loved ones thanked her.

As Angelica passed her, Vera reached out and took her hand. 'I'm sorry, Angelica, I became very tired, but we'll have our usual session next week, and I hope we will have Kofi coming forwards.'

'That's OK,' Angelica said with a smile. 'It was very moving this afternoon. It gives me such a wonderful spiritual energy to be present.'

Angelica turned and put her arm around the young girl, suggesting they have a cup of coffee together along with the sisters.

'Would you like to join us, Jane? We like to go over everything as it is such a wonderful experience.'

'Another time,' Jane said.

Sandra hovered at the door as Vera waved her hand dismissively. 'It's all right, Sandra, show everyone out.'

Jane remained standing by Vera, who ignored her as she collected her notebook and slipped it into the pocket of the wheelchair.

'What do you want?'

'I'm sorry I came without an appointment.'

'Angelica called to say she was bringing you. I thought it was cheeky, and I didn't like you being here; it made it harder work for me.'

'I was very impressed. Although some things I questioned.'

'Like what?'

'Well, you were so comforting about the little granddaughter, but her mother died in the accident, too. Why didn't you mention her?'

Vera laughed, shaking her head. 'You think I held back to get another session in? What do you take me for? Do you think it would be a comfort to know her daughter was drunk and caused the accident? Or is it the boy's suicide? That poor girl blamed herself because she kicked him out of her flat, and now she'll get comfort. As for the sisters, their father was a dominating bastard that drove their mother to an early grave, but they are still dependent on him. Anything else? Because I am tired out.'

'I want you to tell me about Angelica's son Sebastian.'

'Get the fuck out, Miss Tennison. You are really beginning to make me angry. I've told you more than enough. It is breaking a confidence.'

She picked up her glass and drained the last drop before placing it back on the table.

'Miss James, I know that you are making a good income from your sessions, and I doubt very much you declare it; you could be investigated for tax evasion.'

'You are a nasty piece of work, aren't you, making threats to me!'

'I am not saying I would report you, all I am asking is for you to tell me if Sebastian Martinez is alive. You said that you felt the taste of blood in your mouth, and I asked you what it meant but you refused to answer. You said he has not passed to the other side.'

Vera pursed her lips, taking deep breaths through her nose.

'I give you my word that whatever you can tell me remains with me and I will not repeat it to Angelica,' Jane said.

'Why? What do you want?'

It was Jane's turn to take a deep breath. 'I just have a gut feeling that something happened to him. I mentioned that I've been investigating an assault on the owner of the house where Miss Martinez lived with her son.'

Vera cocked her head to one side, and then took out her notebook.

'I know you suspect I am some kind of fake, but you know something, you have a side to you that is almost spiritual. You have what you said is a gut feeling and you should listen to it. I have always been able to contact the dead, and as a result I can give some kind of peace to the living.'

Jane suddenly felt like crying.

'I am so sorry, Vera, I didn't mean to insult you. I am sorry that I came here under false pretences. Please accept my sincere apologies.'

Vera looked at her, her face glistening with sweat. She gripped the arms of her wheelchair and heaved herself up to stand. Then she reached out and drew Jane into her arms.

'It's all right, dear, you will find him. He's long dead. And it had to be brutal because he cannot lie in peace.'

Sandra opened the door as Vera stepped back.

'Show her out, Sandra. I need to go and lie down.'

As Jane sat in her car, the tears that she had felt surfacing at Vera's now came with a vengeance, and suddenly she was sobbing. It was as if all her emotions about the bust-up with Eddie were flooding out. She realised she wanted to see if they could get back together. She took deep breaths to calm herself down, focusing on the last thing Vera had said. She was certain now that Sebastian Martinez had been murdered.

Chapter Eighteen

Jane did not return to the station but went straight home. She had made up her mind to talk to Eddie. She had only just taken off her coat when the doorbell rang. She assumed it was him, being stubborn enough not to use his house keys. Pulling the front door open, Jane was surprised to find Stanley on the doorstep.

'Stanley?'

'I just stopped by to check you were all right. Actually, I came by earlier, but your workman told me you'd left. When you didn't turn up at the station . . . Listen, are you going to invite me in, or leave me standing out here?'

'I'm sorry, come in.'

Stanley walked into the hall and looked around.

'Wow, this is very nice . . . I like the wallpaper.'

'Thank you. I'll make you a cup of tea.'

He followed her into the kitchen. 'Very nice, my wife would be impressed . . . all new appliances, and these tiles look good behind your sink.'

Jane put the kettle on as Stanley sat at the small table. She fetched mugs and milk and sugar as he looked at the glass-fronted cupboards. 'These are well made, makes me feel bad about never doing anything in our place. But with the kids bashing around and the dog scratching at the doors, he'd have the paint off within minutes.'

'All down to Eddie and his team. I'll show you around if you like.'

'Sure, how's the migraine?'

'Well, you caught me out; it was just an excuse.'

He grinned. 'Thought it might be. I've never known you take time out for a headache. That's why I was worried about you. Not my business, but is it all sorted with you and him?'

'Nope, but thank you for coming by because I want to talk a few things over with you.'

'Look, I'm no agony aunt, Jane. I never give advice on personal issues. But judging by the look of the place he must be a good craftsman. I bet this has put the value of your house up a few grand.'

Jane waited for the kettle to boil and took out a tin of biscuits.

'It has actually, but I didn't want to bore you with what's going on between me and Eddie. I took time out to go and visit the medium again.'

'You are joking!'

'No, I'm not. I went with Angelica Martinez; you know, the ex-Mrs Hoffman that used to live at the Caplans' house? It was a group session, and honestly I was taken aback by some of the things she came out with.'

Jane told Stanley about the way Vera used a notepad to make strange drawings, and how she brought certain people forwards. 'I was going to come into the station afterwards to talk things through with you, but now that you are here it's probably better to explain everything here rather than in the incident room.'

Jane poured their tea and Stanley ate his way through the biscuits.

'OK, I am now certain that Sebastian Martinez was murdered . . . and before you say anything, hear me out.'

He shrugged, stirring his tea, as Jane went through the whole story: the neighbours' relationships before the Caplans bought the property, the Hoffmans' financial troubles, and the sale of the courtyard to the Larssons.

'There were bad feelings between them because Sebastian got the Larssons' daughter pregnant; she was underage and the boy was packed off to Mexico. The Larssons began to tarmac the courtyard, but then their daughter died.'

Stanley held up his hand. 'Hold on, I'm trying to follow this, Jane. Did all the neighbours pay for the tarmac or just the Larssons?'

'They all chipped in, and the neighbours have right of way to gain entry to their properties.'

'But nobody can park there, right?'

'Yes, as we both know.'

'So, go on, their daughter died, then what?'

Jane poured them both another cup of tea while she explained about how the girl's funeral held up the workmen finishing the tarmac. She then opened her briefcase and took out the file on Sebastian Martinez, his return flight, and the fact that no one had seen him since his return. She finished by telling him about Vera James and her conviction that he had died violently.

'I am certain that he was murdered, Stanley, and that the Larssons and Martin Boon are involved.'

'Jesus Christ, Jane, I don't know what to say. I mean, this isn't just supposition, it's ... I don't know, it's mind-boggling. You have zero evidence, and if you try explaining to Hutton that you are basing all of this on the word of a medium, you'll be laughed out of her office.'

Jane refused to be put off. 'But what do *you* think?'

'What do I think?'

'Yes, the boy has disappeared off the face of the earth, his father has had no contact, nor his mother, but we know he returned to London ...'

Stanley shrugged. 'He's a teenager, he could be anywhere. Did she report him missing?'

'No, but I think that's because Vera never told her the truth. All she said to her was that her son is close to home.'

'Right, and she keeps on paying how much for these sessions?'

'I know what you're thinking, and it's not cheap, and I thought Vera was a fraud at first. But after this afternoon I don't think she is.'

'Look, I'm going to be honest with you. I think maybe what is going on in your personal life is sort of leading you astray. Even taking into consideration everything you've told me, I think you are wasting your time.'

'What if I'm not?' Jane persisted.

'For God's sake, Jane,' Stanley said, beginning to lose patience. 'You don't have a shred of evidence, so just forget it. If you start bringing in a bloody medium as your only reason for investigating the boy's disappearance . . .'

'Murder.'

Stanley sighed and got up from the table, taking his mug and putting it on the draining-board.

'I've got to get home. If you really want to keep digging, I suggest you contact Mispers, see if there are any unidentified bodies. Maybe the boy died after he got back to the UK, but no one knew who he was.'

Jane sat back in her chair. 'Right, well, thanks for coming by. I was hoping you'd sort of back me up.'

'Back you up? To do what, exactly?'

'I want to know more about the Larssons' daughter. I'm not sure how she died or exactly when, but if it was around the time Sebastian returned then that could be a motive. When Victor Hoffman sold the courtyard to the Larssons, he inferred it was because he needed the money, but also because he was threatened by them when they discovered Sebastian was seeing their underage daughter.'

Stanley sighed. 'I'm going home. If you want some advice, just forget about all this.'

Jane showed Stanley out, locking the front door after him. She was angry that he'd been so dismissive, but the feeling quickly faded, and she started wondering if her obsessive focus on Sebastian Martinez was just a way of not facing up to the situation with Eddie.

After a shower and getting into her pyjamas, Jane didn't bother going down to the kitchen to make herself something to eat but just got into bed. She picked up the phone and called Eddie's parents, assuming he would be there.

Eddie's mother answered.

'Hello, it's Jane, and I just wondered if Eddie was there?' Jane said in an over-cheery tone.

'Oh, hello dear, no, he's not been here for ages. I think he was helping his dad out on some big job. I can ask him if he knows where he is.'

'No, don't bother. I'll wait for him to call me. Thank you, and sorry to bother you.'

'No bother, dear. Everything all right?'

'Yes, fine, hope to see you soon,' Jane said, not wanting to get into a conversation, as it was obvious Eddie hadn't told them about their separation. She thought about calling his mobile, but to have to go through all the rigmarole of leaving messages with the receptionist, she decided not to bother. It was still only nine thirty, but she felt exhausted after the talk with Stanley, and she turned off the bedside light and settled down for an early night.

Jane woke up early the next morning, and instead of going straight to the station, she went and did a grocery shop at the local supermarket which opened at seven thirty. By the time she had bought everything and returned home to stack the fridge and freezer, she had to hurry to get to the station in time for a quick breakfast.

The canteen was almost empty as she ordered scrambled eggs and bacon with toast and coffee, and was just tucking in when Burrows appeared with a tray of coffee to take into the incident room. He stopped by Jane's table to ask if she was feeling better. She nodded, her mouth full of toast.

'I'm getting in a round as the trolley doesn't come by until eleven,' Burrows said. 'Stanley was looking for you earlier, by the way.'

'What did he want?'

'Not sure, but something's kicked off at that bloody Clarendon Court. Uniforms were called out and the boss told Stanley to get over there.'

Jane quickly finished her breakfast and hurried to the control room. No one there had any further information, so she tapped on Hutton's office door.

Hutton was checking over some documents and held up her hand for Jane to wait.

'Sorry, Jane, some of the CPS case queries get more complicated by the minute.'

'I was just told that something is going down at Clarendon Court.'

Hutton sighed. 'Yes, we had a call from Mr Caplan to say that the wretched Mr Boon appeared at his front door with maps of the Land Registry, and was demanding that work stops. Caplan refused to talk to him but he then called the police as his neighbours were stopping his builders working. It really is becoming ridiculous, with both parties demanding the police do something; and as Mr Boon is just out of hospital I would hate for this to escalate, so I asked Stanley to go over there and try to defuse the situation.'

'Should I go over there?'

'No, Jane, I would like you to check some of these documents, run over the evidence and answer the questions raised by the CPS. Oh, how's the migraine?'

'Fine, thank you.'

'Good, I used to get them, really awful cluster migraines, but thankfully – touch wood – I've been clear for years.'

Jane returned to her desk with an armful of case files and got stuck in, but it was hard to concentrate, wondering what was going on at Clarendon Court.

Stanley was standing near the Caplans' back garden. Three builders were waiting to erect the stone posts for the electric gates.

They explained that it was necessary to dig quite a substantial hole for the concrete and then insert the posts, four in all, and it meant that they would need to remove Mrs Larsson's flower pots.

The issue seemed to be that they would have to lift about five inches of tarmac where the gates were going to be, even though Mr Caplan had assured Mr Boon that they would make good the damage.

Stanley had firmly told Mr Boon to remain in his house, and Mr Caplan had also agreed that until things were settled, he would stay indoors. The uniformed officer had left and Stanley had inspected the area. It seemed absurd that even with Mr Caplan agreeing to resurface the area in question, Mr Boon was insisting that it was over the boundary lines, and therefore Mr Caplan had no right to touch it. They were now waiting for the inspector from the Land Registry to arrive before any work could begin.

As the situation appeared to be under control, Mrs Caplan had invited the workmen into the kitchen to make them a cup of tea. Stanley was offered tea or coffee, but felt that he should remain outside, ready to meet the inspector.

The Larssons came out of their house, saw Stanley, and then Mrs Larsson then went into Martin Boon's house. Mr Larsson remained standing on the path for some time, then returned to his house. Stanley got out of his car and inspected the dying plants on Mrs Larsson's railing, within inches of the Caplans' little garden gate. There was just four inches of soil for the plants to grow.

He turned round to look over the courtyard. There was a small indentation where the tarmac had stopped and then been continued. The ridge was opposite the Bellamys' property and Stanley remembered Jane telling him that when their daughter's funeral was taking place the workmen laying down the tarmac had stopped working to allow the funeral hearse and cars to enter the courtyard. So that meant that the two houses opposite, belonging to the Larssons and the Boons, were only tarmacked after the funeral.

Stanley was about to get back into his car when a young woman on a scooter came into the courtyard and rode into the Bellamys' property. He walked over as she removed her helmet and goggles. She had long, auburn, curly hair and was taking a leather bag from the pouch at the back of the scooter.

'Excuse me, do you live here?' Stanley asked. He showed her his ID.

'Oh, I don't live here, this is my parents' house. They're at work. I'm a student at Coventry University. I'm just home for a few days as it's my mother's birthday. I'm Kathleen, by the way.'

'Ah, well, Kathleen, maybe you can help me. It might sound a bit odd, but do you know when the tarmacking of the courtyard was done?'

'Yes, I remember it because of Georgina's funeral. It had been partly finished, but they stopped work because of all the cars and the hearse.'

'Did you know Georgina well?'

'Yes, we were good friends. I got to know her when we moved in. It was very sad.'

'Can you remember when exactly they finished the tarmac?'

'Oh, gosh, it was quite a while after the funeral because according to my father they were a bunch of cowboys. He complained to the Larssons because they had left our section a mess of potholes.'

'So, when they began work again, were you at home?'

'Some of the time. They did our section first, then worked their way around.'

'So was the last section tarmacked across from your house?'

'I think so. I remember they had this truck boiling the tar. It took quite some time.'

'Did you know the previous owners, Mr and Mrs Hoffman?'

'Yes, but not very well.'

'What about their son?'

'Sebastian?'

'Yes. He'd be about your age?'

'I knew him; we both did.'

'You mean Georgina?'

'Yes, he was her boyfriend.'

Stanley was eager to question Kathleen further, but then a battered Morris Minor drove into the courtyard and parked next to Stanley's car. A small, balding man in a waterproof jacket that looked two sizes too large got out and leaned into the passenger seat to take out a clipboard. Stanley knew it had to be the man from the Land Registry. He quickly thanked Kathleen for her time and hurried across the courtyard.

The man was about to ring the Caplans' garden gate bell when Stanley called out to him.

'Just a second, sir, I need to have a word with you.'

Stanley had his ID out as he approached the rather startled man. 'I'm Detective Inspector Stanley from the Met; I need a few minutes of your time before we get into this situation here. You are from the Land Registry, correct?'

'Yes, I'm Adrian Fellows. I have the documents here.' He showed his clipboard with his name at the top as an investigator employed by the council.

'Do you have a map showing the courtyard's boundaries?'

'Yes, I've researched the boundaries in question, dating back to the original owners, the De Wilding family.'

'Terrific, would you just come and sit with me in my car as I'd like to go through a few things.'

The rather confused Mr Fellows accompanied Stanley to get into the passenger seat of his car. His cheeks were flushed and his small eyes blinked rapidly.

'So, Mr Fellows, Mr Caplan was granted permission by the council to erect new gates and for them to open on to the courtyard, is that correct?'

'That's right. There was opposition from a neighbour, but as this is not a street road, with no passing traffic, permission was granted.'

'But you have been called out because there is still opposition from the same neighbour, Mr Boon?'

Mr Fellows flipped through pages of documents on his clip-board, then nodded. 'That's right.'

Stanley scratched his head, trying to get things clear in his mind.

'Can you tell me why you think Mr Boon has been opposing all of David Caplan's plans for the electric gates and his fences? They do not appear to have any logical reason; his plans do not encroach on any part of his land.'

'Well, the reality is we have to take any objections seriously.'

Stanley nodded. 'Have Mr and Mrs Larsson also made objections?'

'No, not to my knowledge.'

'Thank you for your time, sir. I'd just quickly like to show you something I noticed earlier.'

Stanley and Mr Fellows walked from the car to the double gates, and Stanley pointed out the concrete section that bordered the gates.

'Mr Caplan can't open the gates outwards because the paved stones are blocking them, so they must have always opened inwards.'

'Well, you have me there because I do not know when these paving stones were laid down.'

The conversation had to end there as Stanley saw Martin Boon walking out of his house with a sheaf of documents under his arm, just as David Caplan came out with the three builders.

It felt like a neighbourhood high noon. The nervous Mr Fellows clung tightly to his clipboard as the two neighbours approached each other, while the builders remained standing at the gate. Stanley was wondering how to keep things from getting heated when an elegant Bentley drove into the courtyard. Everyone turned as the driver drew slowly to a stop.

A man in an immaculate navy suit with a red cashmere scarf stepped out of the car, carrying a leather briefcase.

'Perfect timing,' Caplan said.

'Good afternoon, David.'

'Let me introduce you.' He turned to the others. 'This is my legal advisor, Michael Littleton. This is Detective Inspector Stanley, Martin Boon my neighbour and . . .' He glanced at Mr Fellows.

'Adrian Fellows from the Land Registry.'

Littleton gave a little nod and then shook Mr Fellows' hand, before he turned to Martin Boon.

'I don't think your presence is necessary, Mr Boon. I am here to talk to Mr Fellows about the boundaries of my client's property.'

Mr Boon puffed himself up. 'I have the plans from Her Majesty's Land Registry here, clearly indicating that Mr Caplan's proposed erection of large concrete gate posts would cross the boundary line.'

Mr Littleton shrugged. 'I would suggest that your maps are outdated, and I would also suggest that you have no legal right to oppose Mr Caplan's plans as your property is not involved. Perhaps you might suggest to Mr and Mrs Larsson that they should be present since they own the courtyard. I have certain issues with them that need to be formally addressed.'

Boon's mouth opened and shut like a drowning man and his face flushed with anger. Mr Littleton turned to David Caplan and Mr Fellows. 'Shall we go inside to view the documents?'

Mr Caplan asked the builders to wait in their truck, as he gestured for everyone to follow him into the house.

Littleton pointed to the ridge of stones outside the property's old wooden double gates.

'There used to be stables here, and part of the courtyard was cobblestones. I would say those stones are perhaps left from that period.' He then pointed to the edge of the tarmac with the toe of his highly polished shoe.

Boon remained standing, clutching his documents, as the gate was closed behind them.

Inside the house, they all sat down at the mahogany dining table. Littleton removed a stack of files from his briefcase, spreading maps and legal papers out in front of him. Buster had managed to get out of his cage and charged in, bounding around the table. Mr Fellows cringed back in his chair.

'I'm not very good with dogs, I'm afraid. I have allergies.'

Caplan grabbed Buster by his collar and led him out as Mr Fellows frantically brushed at his coat sleeves.

Littleton smiled. 'They always seem to know if you're scared of them. I have a Siamese cat that's always vicious to the one person I know who hates cats.' He then got out a calculator and placed it on the table.

'Do we wait for Mr or Mrs Larsson, or shall I just get on with it?' he asked.

Stanley looked at his watch. He'd already been there for some time, but he was also quite eager to hear the outcome – even more so when Mrs Caplan carried in a tray of pastries. 'Please help yourselves while the coffee's brewing,' she said with a smile.

Littleton waited until the coffee had been served before beginning. 'Right, I have been on quite an expedition, tracking down every single legal document pertaining to this property. I mentioned earlier there had been stables, probably taking up most of the garden, which is the bone of contention with your neighbour. There is a legally binding document from 1932 that stipulates access must be allowed, probably for carriages to be driven in and out of the courtyard.'

Littleton passed some documents over to Mr Fellows. 'The important thing to note is that at no time were the original boundaries pertaining to the stables and courtyard revoked.'

He picked up one last document, unfolding it carefully.

'Finally, here's a map Victor Hoffman found, and this is the only one that indicates the exact boundary of the property. It was drawn up in 1952. Mr Hoffman said he didn't really examine it when he sold Mr and Mrs Larsson the courtyard.'

He handed it to Mr Caplan.

'As you can see, not only do your plans not encroach on the boundary, but the truth is that Mr and Mrs Larsson encroached on your land by just over 25 inches when the tarmac was laid.'

Mr Caplan stood up, clapping his hands. 'This is good news!'

Littleton smiled. 'Well, don't celebrate quite yet. Mr Fellows will need to verify it on behalf of the council.'

Stanley chose this moment to make his excuse to leave. He was certain with the formidable Michael Littleton on board, Mr Caplan would have no further problems with Martin Boon. He was surprised that the Larssons had not made an appearance, but as usual, they seemed to be hiding behind Martin Boon.

Mr Fellows took the map from Mr Littleton and followed him out, just as the Larssons pulled into their drive. As they got out they frowned at the array of vehicles parked outside the Caplans' house. Martin Boon must have been poised, waiting for their return, as he hurried out from his house. They had a brief conversation and then Mrs Larsson strode across the courtyard.

'Are you Mr Fellows from the council? I'm Mrs Larsson.'

'Ah, yes, I was hoping to speak to you earlier. We just had a meeting regarding the boundary situation, and I am about to return to the office to verify a document.'

'You were supposed to be here earlier this afternoon. I have been waiting for a site visit for weeks.'

'Well, I had both Mr Boon and Mr Caplan asking me to be here this morning. I did suggest Mr Boon contact you to join us for the meeting with Mr Caplan's legal advisor.'

'You had no right to have any kind of meeting without my presence. Why didn't you attend, Martin?'

'I was told by whatever his name is that I had no right to be privy to their discussions.'

Mr Fellows held up his clipboard. 'Well, I can tell you the outcome of the meeting, which is that contrary to what you have been led to believe, the tarmacked courtyard is encroaching on Mr Caplan's property. He therefore has every right to commence building work. I will write to you formally to confirm the council's decision.'

Mrs Larsson was furious. 'How dare you!'

Mr Fellows got out his car keys and hurried round to the driver's side of his car, but she went after him and held onto the open door as he tried to shut it.

'Get out of your car now, do you hear me? *Get out!*'

Stanley hurried over. 'Please let go of the door, Mrs Larsson.'

She turned on him, shoving him hard in the chest, before attempting to drag Mr Fellows out. He managed to shrug her off and started the engine, but she leaned in and tried to grab the steering wheel, inadvertently scratching him on his face. Sitting in their truck, the builders were enjoying the show, one of them applauding while the others laughed.

Stanley finally managed to pull Mrs Larsson away, holding onto her as Martin Boon came to assist him; but his presence seemed to antagonise her even more.

'Get away from me, you imbecile. After all I have done for you, don't you know what this will mean? Get out of my sight!'

Fellows managed to do a U-turn in the courtyard, then drove off with a handkerchief held to his cheek. Boon tried to calm Mrs Larsson down, but she wouldn't let him touch her, jerking her arm away.

He said something to her and she slapped his face, hard, then ran across the courtyard.

'Are you all right, Mr Boon?' Stanley asked.

A dejected-looking Martin Boon stood with his hand pressed to his cheek.

He said nothing, his gaze following Mrs Larsson as her husband appeared at the front door. She ran sobbing into his arms, and he quickly drew her inside.

Stanley drove out, shaking his head. Nothing he'd just witnessed made any sense. He needed to get back to the station and talk to Jane. Maybe she was right and something else lay behind what was going on at Clarendon Court.

Chapter Nineteen

It was late afternoon by the time Jane returned to the station, after being called out to a wretched domestic situation. A young mother had reported her daughter missing. The child had eventually been found at her grandmother's, with the woman's husband, who was accusing his wife of physically mistreating her. It had taken up most of the day, as the accusations of abuse and kidnapping took time to unravel. No one wanted to press charges and the couple were eventually reunited, though Jane insisted that social services should monitor the couple.

Stanley listened impatiently, eager to recount his visit to the Caplans.

'I've been waiting to tell you, because you will not believe what happened at Clarendon Court this morning.'

Jane sighed. She had not had time to have lunch, so suggested they have a break in the canteen. They were both heading out of the incident room when Hutton opened her office door.

'Ah good, I need to have a word with both of you. I have just had David Caplan on the phone and then Michael Littleton. I don't know if you have come across him, but he is a top property lawyer. He must have cost Mr Caplan a fortune. Anyway, it appears that the situation at Clarendon Court has finally reached an amicable agreement.'

'Well, from my visit this morning . . .' Stanley began.

Hutton nodded. 'I know what happened earlier, but this after-noon they apparently came to an amicable agreement, and Mr Caplan is going to minimise the damage to the tarmac.'

'I don't understand,' Stanley said, frowning.

'Well, the crucial point is we can finally turn our attention to more important things,' Hutton said, dismissing them.

Stanley and Jane went up to the canteen. Jane laughed as Stanley described the sequence of events, with the builders applauding the whole thing.

'I have seen women fly into tempers,' Stanley said in a more serious tone, 'but Mrs Larsson was totally out of control, and all about a foot and a half of tarmac. You would have thought they were going to bulldoze her house, the way she behaved.'

'But now it's all peace and quiet,' Jane said.

Stanley snorted. 'I don't believe it. If you'd seen the way she slapped Martin Boon, it's more than an obsession with her bloody boundaries. Martin Boon was the target of her abuse. So why was he doing her bidding? There has to be something else going on apart from property boundaries and bloody tarmac.'

'I can't believe what I am hearing from you,' Jane said, shaking her head.

'Well, I'll admit this thing about Sebastian has now got to me as well, because to suddenly be told that there is no animosity between the neighbours when it has been like outright war . . . I just don't believe it.'

Jane sighed. 'Stanley, I had just finally decided to let it all go. I mean, you told me to drop it, so what's changed your opinion, apart from the rows this morning?'

'I'll explain,' Stanley said, 'but first I want you to talk to a young student called Kathleen. She's the daughter of the Bellamys that live in the house opposite the Caplans. She told me she knew both Sebastian and the Larssons' daughter Georgina. She also told me she was at her funeral.'

'When did this happen?'

'This morning, before it all kicked off. She's home for her mother's birthday, but before I could have any kind of a conversation, the little fella from the council arrived. I think you should talk to her and get some more information about Sebastian and Georgina.'

Stanley put his teacup down. 'You up for it?'

Jane shrugged her shoulders, looking at her watch.

'I suppose I could write up my report from today and then get over there. Are you going to come with me?'

'I can't. It's *Swan Lake* tonight; besides, I think you'll get more out of her by yourself.'

'What exactly do you think she can tell us?' Jane asked.

'I don't know, but I have a bad feeling about it now. I know what I said to you last night, and I meant it, but after today, I've changed my mind because things don't add up. For one, I don't believe for a second that David Caplan just suddenly agreed to play nice with the Larssons after he's paid Littleton a fortune to prove he can do what he likes because they're encroaching on *his* property.'

'Could be he just wants a quick sale of the property with no more aggravation.'

Stanley frowned, annoyed that Jane wasn't backing him up.

'All right, all right. Don't fucking bother going to see this Kathleen.'

'Maybe I want you to tell me that I was right.'

'I have told you that I changed my mind,' he snapped.

'About what exactly?'

He took a deep breath and then pushed his chair back. 'If you are right, and Sebastian Martinez is dead, I think Martin Boon is involved. And I think it has to do with Georgina Larsson. So go and talk to Kathleen to see what she knows.'

Stanley stood up. 'And if you come up with anything, you know what else we need to do?'

Jane stood up. 'You tell me!'

'Dig up the fucking tarmac.'

It was after four thirty when Jane left the station and drove to Clarendon Court. She parked her car in the Bellamys' driveway, hoping that Mr and Mrs Bellamy would not have returned from work yet. She rang the doorbell and waited. A voice called out, 'Coming,' and soon after the front door opened. Kathleen was wearing an apron, with smears of flour across her cheeks.

'Hi, I am Jane Tennison from the Metropolitan Police. I wondered if you could spare me a few moments for a chat?'

'Oh, my parents aren't in, I'm afraid. They won't be home from work until after six.'

'Kathleen, right?'

'Yes – oh God, don't tell me it's something to do with not wearing a helmet on my scooter.'

Jane smiled. 'No, it's actually nothing to be worried about. There's just something you might be able to help me with.'

'Oh, OK, then you better come in. If you don't mind talking to me in the kitchen. It's my mum's birthday cake and I have to get it finished and hidden before she comes home.'

Jane followed Kathleen inside and sat down at a large kitchen table. It looked as if she had been cooking up a storm. There were mixing bowls and packets of nuts and decorations covering every surface. A recipe book lay open and on the stove was a glass bowl heaped with melting chocolate over a pan filled with boiling water.

Kathleen opened the lid of a large plastic container and removed a three-tiered sponge with a big dip in the centre, then began covering it in chocolate icing.

'How well did you know Georgina Larsson?'

'Gosh, it's been a long time now. We weren't at the same school. I was at the comprehensive and she was at a posh private school, so it was months before we actually became friends. Why do you want to know about her?'

'Oh, it's just a query about an insurance situation. What was she like?'

'Well, she was really shy, scared stiff of her mother, who was very protective of her because she had been suffering from asthma since she was a toddler. Sometimes she was so thin and pale. I know about it now because someone at college has it, but I think she was anorexic. Anyways, she was outside in the courtyard one day with a stray cat, and that's how we first met. Like I say, she was very slim and pale-skinned with almost white-blonde hair which was always very shiny. She would hardly look you in the face, but she did have gorgeous eyes.'

'So you became friends?'

'Yes, well, one of the reasons was that I had this terrible crush on the boy that lived opposite. I used to find any reason to be out in the courtyard when he came home from school. He was always carrying a guitar or a violin and he used to tie his hair in a ponytail. Then he stopped going to school and spent all his time riding a racing bike around the place. One day he came careering into the courtyard and straight into a big puddle. I was just coming out and got soaked.'

Kathleen laughed as she spread the chocolate around the sides of the cake with a spatula.

'He was so apologetic. I asked him why he didn't go to school anymore. He told me that they wanted him to cut his hair so he walked out. I thought he was so cool.'

Kathleen looked down at her apron.

'I'm making a bloody mess of this, aren't I?'

Jane smiled. 'That was Sebastian, right?'

'Yes! Anyway, after that meeting I started going round to his house to listen to him playing music. He had this huge room and could play the piano, guitar, violin . . . anything . . . and he composed these amazing songs. He always wore high-heeled cowboy boots and leather trousers, and his shirts were thick linen, very stylish. He told me his mother brought them from Mexico. Some had lovely embroidery around the collars and cuffs.'

Kathleen threw her hands up. 'This will just have to do. I just need to put it away and clear up the mess or there won't be much of a surprise.'

Jane wanted Kathleen to tell her more, so took off her jacket and rolled up the sleeves of her shirt.

'Right, let me wash up for you.'

'God, that's really nice of you. Soon as we're finished, I'll take you to my bedroom and show you my photo album.'

'That would be really good. Let's get cracking then.'

Between them they cleaned up the kitchen in double-quick time. Kathleen stashed the cake tin in a cupboard and helped dry the dishes. 'Sebastian had such a funny way of walking . . . sort of like a dancer . . . like this . . .'

Kathleen mimicked how Sebastian bounced on tiptoes, and then laughed at how he would tease her about being so tall. When Jane asked if she had met his parents, she pulled a face.

'His mother was adorable, but his father, he was so nasty. He would shout and scream at Sebastian, and always spoke to him in German. One time there was a terrible argument because apparently his mother had cooked something after its sell-by date and he went into a rage. We used to hate it if he was at home. Sebastian told me that they were broke; his father had been a diplomat but had been fired and was living off his mother's inheritance. I knew they were in some financial difficulties because Mr Hoffman came over to see my father. I mean, he didn't even really know him. After he left, my dad said that I should steer clear of them. He had actually asked to borrow money. He said it was a good financial proposition, turning their big house into flats, but my dad said there was no way he would trust him.'

'Did they know you saw Sebastian a lot?'

'Christ no, I was only just sixteen. He was younger but appeared much older, and it was our big secret. We had a signal for when I could steal over there to be with him. He would put a candle in his bedroom window and leave the garden gate open. I mean, I was crazy about him. Dad said he was a hippy and my mother . . . well, any boy with long hair was a junkie!'

Kathleen tossed down the dishcloth, looked around the kitchen and clapped her hands.

'Right, finished. Do you want to see the photographs?'

'Yes, I really would like to, thank you.'

'No, thank *you*, that was a fast clean-up.'

Kathleen led Jane up the stairs and into a large, untidy bedroom. Clothes were strewn everywhere, including on the floor, and drawers were open with items hanging out. But she didn't seem embarrassed.

'Sebastian had the biggest bed I had ever seen,' she said. 'Really enormous, with all these wonderful Mexican rugs thrown over it, and he had painted the floorboards white. There was a grand piano and all his musical instruments everywhere. He had painted poetry on the walls and a big sunflower on the ceiling.'

As Kathleen chattered on, she got down on her hands and knees and searched beneath her bed before pulling out a cardboard box.

'Not a very good hiding place, but my mother hasn't found it so far. I've got all my letters from my last boyfriend in here, along with . . .' She stopped as she took out a stack of envelopes tied with a ribbon and put them to one side.

'So, did Sebastian have the same feelings about you?'

'Sadly, no, he didn't. I mean, he knew I was infatuated, and just liked to tease the hell out of me. Now this is my old photo album, and . . .'

She held up a blue plastic-covered photo album, bulging with loose photographs, letters and postcards.

'I haven't looked through this for years; the truth is, after Georgie died and Sebastian left for Mexico, it was as if my teenage years were suddenly all over.'

Kathleen flicked through several photographs, before holding up one. 'This is Sebastian . . . and this one . . . and this one. God, he is so gorgeous! That's me with him. He was right, I looked awful. That perm! I wanted to have curly hair like him but it turned into a God-awful frizz.'

Jane looked at the photographs. With his dusky skin and coal-black hair, Sebastian was very handsome. He also had the most incredible almond-shaped eyes.

'Wow, he is extraordinary-looking. No wonder you had a crush on him.'

'I was besotted, forever hopeful, but then he met Georgina. I have one of her somewhere.'

Kathleen riffled through the photographs like a pack of cards before she found one. She stared at the picture and sighed deeply.

'She was so fragile. It was a brilliant sunny day, and we were going to go for a walk, when Sebastian walked out into the court-yard. I introduced them. He asked if we'd like to come and hear his new song. We went in via the old, broken garden gate, and no one was at home. He got some orange juice and biscuits and we went up to his bedroom. Georgie was her usual shy self, sitting on the edge of his bed with her head bent down, and it was really extraordinary because I actually saw it happen. You know you read about things in romantic novels, but honestly it was like a sort of brilliant light came on. As he sang, she lifted up her head and then he stopped singing . . . it was as if I wasn't in the room . . . they just looked at each other.'

Kathleen passed Jane the photograph of Georgina. She was just as Kathleen had described her. Blonde silky hair, pale skin and wide, childlike blue eyes. She was very petite, wearing a denim smock dress. Kathleen took out two more photographs and passed them to Jane. One was of the three of them with their arms around each other, and another had Georgina wearing one of Sebastian's shirts. She was smiling and appeared to be a different girl to the one in the earlier photographs.

'He made her feel confident for the first time, really bringing her out of her shell. And he cared deeply about her. I was madly jealous to begin with, of course, but they were so in love. I remember one summer, he had all the windows in his room wide open because there was a huge old lilac tree outside and the perfume was incred-ible. He leaned out and picked some of the blossom and made it into a crown for her. She looked so beautiful. After that time, I hardly saw him. Weeks would go by and then he would send me a message to come out with them. I was told that the new owners cut the tree down to make room for their swimming pool, but whenever I pass or see a lilac tree it reminds me of her, that lovely delicate perfume.'

Kathleen explained how Georgina's mother had found out that she was seeing Sebastian and was furious, forbidding her to see him anymore. So they had to meet in secret. When her parents were out for the evening, he would climb up the trellis outside her bedroom. One night there was a terrible confrontation between Mrs Larsson and the Hoffmans. She accused them of allowing their son to take advantage of an underage girl and they were going to report them.'

'Is that when Sebastian's father sent him to Mexico?' Jane asked.

'I don't know, I just remember the Hoffmans were selling the house, and Sebastian went away.'

'Did Georgina stay in contact with him?'

Kathleen rubbed her eyes, and then delved into the album again.

'Georgina asked me to receive letters from Sebastian in Mexico because she was afraid her parents would find out. I agreed, of course. She then came over one evening and she was sort of glowing and very flushed. She made me swear not to tell anyone, but she was going to run away to be with him because . . . she was pregnant. She was so excited, telling me how she had done the tests and it was positive. She said that she had managed to get out and post a letter telling Sebastian that she was expecting their baby and they could run away together as soon as he got back to England.'

Jane waited as Kathleen continued to look through the stack of cards and photographs.

'A month, or maybe longer, and I hadn't seen or heard from her. The next thing I knew, she was seriously ill in hospital. I didn't even get the chance to see her. Her father came round and told my parents that Georgina had died of sepsis.'

Kathleen found a postcard. She held it close to her chest as the tears welled up.

'Sebastian had to send this to me so her parents wouldn't find it and destroy it, and I never even got to show it to her. Here, read it; it still breaks my heart.'

It was a picture of a Madonna and child. On the back, Sebastian had written, 'I will be home to be with you and our precious child and together forever my precious beloved little angel.'

Kathleen shook her head.

'Do you think Georgina had an abortion?' Jane asked.

Kathleen looked shocked. 'I don't know. I don't even know how many months pregnant she was. God, she was only fifteen years old. I mean, maybe she was just fantasising about it . . . I don't know.'

'Could I take a photograph of Sebastian? I'd give it back, obviously.'

'No, it's precious. I'm sorry, I couldn't.'

Jane stood up, not wanting Kathleen to get any more upset. She was snatching up the photographs and stuffing them back into the box.

'I'm going to go now, Kathleen, but I do need to ask you one more question. Did you see Sebastian at the funeral, or ever see him again after you received that postcard from Mexico? I know he did return to England.'

She shook her head. 'No, I never saw or heard from him again. It must have broken his heart.'

Jane headed down the stairs, with Kathleen following. She paused midway.

'You know the tarmac on the courtyard – do you recall when you saw it being finished?'

Kathleen frowned. 'No, it wasn't finished when the funeral happened, and then I got a place at Coventry, so I left home. I just needed to get away; it was all too much for me to handle.'

The house was in darkness, but the porch security lights came on as Jane got to her front door. She walked in to find an envelope just inside the front door. Taking it into the kitchen, she opened the envelope and found her house keys and a note from Eddie.

'Came by to see you as we need to talk. Will call you tomorrow. Eddie.'

Jane suddenly felt dizzy, and thought she was actually going to be sick, but after sitting at the kitchen table for a minute the feeling passed. She decided that she needed to talk to Eddie that evening. She rang his mobile number to give a message to the receptionist.

'Hello, this is Jane Tennison. Could you please give a message to Mr Eddie Myers that I am home and would he please call me. Thank you.'

'Good evening. I am afraid the message cannot be relayed to Mr Myers as he is no longer the contract holder of this number.'

'Could you please tell me who is the new contract holder?'

'I'm afraid not. It is our privacy policy.'

'It's Caroline, isn't it? I recognise your voice.'

'Er, yes, it is, and I'm sorry not to be able to help you.'

Before Jane could say another word, the line went dead, so she replaced the handset.

She made herself a hot chocolate and got ready for bed, even though it was still only ten o'clock. Sipping her drink, she tried to fathom out what Eddie was thinking. The way he had not attempted, until this evening, to make any contact didn't really feel like him. Unable to sleep, she got out of bed and went over to her dressing table. She searched one of the drawers for an old pack of Marlboro cigarettes. There was a little book of matches tucked inside. It was from an Italian restaurant they had often been to, and she suddenly felt sad. There had been so many good times, and the abrupt way it had all ended still confused her.

She found an ashtray on her dressing table and went back to bed, balancing it on her knees as she smoked. It tasted bitter and after a few puffs she stubbed it out. She physically jumped when the bedside phone rang.

'Hope it's not too late?'

'No, I'm awake, Stanley. How was *Swan Lake*?'

'You know, the cygnets don't come on all that much. I was impressed with my girl, though. I only just got home. So, tell me how it went with Kathleen?'

Jane reached for her pack of cigarettes again, and lit another one as she cupped the phone under her chin. Stanley didn't interrupt as she recalled her conversation with Kathleen, smoking the entire cigarette.

Stanley was silent for a moment. 'Well, maybe now we've got our motive. We just need to find out if Georgina had an abortion and that led to her death. Right, goodnight, Jane. See you tomorrow.'

Jane was surprised to find she'd managed to smoke three cigarettes. She drained the last of her now lukewarm hot chocolate and turned off her bedside light. She was no longer thinking about Eddie. The following morning, she and Stanley had work to do.

Chapter Twenty

Stanley was already halfway through his full English breakfast when Jane joined him. She had a bit of a dicky tummy, so only ordered toast and tea. He gestured with his knife to indicate that Burrows was within earshot at the next table, then passed over his notebook. Jane saw he had underlined access to Georgina Larsson's death certificate, hospital contacts, and how they would approach the patient privacy issues they would no doubt come across. He had also underlined a note that they should not approach the Larssons until they had more evidence.

Jane passed his notebook back to him.

'I also want to double-check the date he returned from Mexico against the date of the funeral.'

Stanley nodded. 'Why don't you start with that, and I'll do the hospital checks.'

They returned to the incident room to sort through any pressing assignments that had come in overnight. Stanley was able to pass over three interviews to DC Burrows, and then gave Jane a wink as he made his escape. Jane was unable to do the same, having some paperwork she couldn't hand over to anyone else.

Stanley had already been able to get a copy of Georgina Larsson's death certificate from the General Register Office. She had died aged fifteen at St Thomas' Hospital on 15th March, four years earlier, from sepsis. It was the same hospital where Martin Boon had been treated. As he drove to the hospital, he was hoping to find someone who had treated Georgina Larsson.

Staff Nurse Collins was sitting at the reception desk by the ICU section. Stanley showed her his ID.

'I would appreciate it if we could have a private conversation about a very serious allegation.'

She hesitated for a moment, then told him to go into the meeting room, and she would join him there as soon as she found a nurse to take over at the desk.

Stanley was thumbing through some old magazine when Nurse Collins came in, closing the door behind her.

'Thank you so much,' Stanley said. 'I really appreciate having such a senior member of staff give me their time.'

She remained standing, clasping her hands together in front of her.

'If you had a patient with sepsis, would they be admitted to this department?'

'Yes, that is correct.'

'Were you working in this department four years ago?'

'Yes, I was not made senior staff nurse until two years ago, but I was attached to this unit. Is this something about complaints or irregularities, because if so, I don't think I should be questioned without another member of staff present.'

'I assure you, Nurse Collins, this not connected to a complaint. It is a separate investigation regarding a patient called Georgina Larsson.'

'I am very sorry but I don't have any recollection of this patient. We are a very busy unit and I have dealt with hundreds of patients over that period.'

'Could you check the hospital records for me, then.'

She frowned. 'I honestly don't think I can do that without permission from the head of the department.'

'Fine, then who do I speak to? I presumed as you are the staff nurse . . .'

'Yes, I am, but there is obviously a procedure to protect patients' privacy.'

Stanley was finding it difficult to remain polite. 'I don't need to take any documents. I just need to verify some facts about her stay here.'

'I'm sorry, Inspector, but I am unable to assist you.'

Nurse Collins opened the door and Stanley followed her out. The young doctor that Stanley had met before was leaning on the desk, chatting up the pretty nurse that had taken over from Collins.

Nurse Collins shooed him away. 'Dr Wilde, I am sure you have more pressing work than flirting with Nurse Julia.'

Stanley gave him a nod of recognition as he grinned. Stanley pushed through the swing door into the corridor and Dr Wilde followed.

'She catches me every morning on my coffee break. It's beginning to be a running gag. But for all her bluster, she's a mainstay of this department.'

'How long have you worked here?'

'Me? Well, I earned my stripes here five years ago, and now I'm back, but they sort of shuffle us around different departments.'

'Were you in the ICU four years ago?'

'Christ, I might have been. Most of the time I was in A&E.'

They headed towards the stairs. 'I was asking about a patient that died of sepsis, but Nurse Collins couldn't help. I don't suppose you'd remember? Her name was Georgina Larsson.'

Dr Wilde stopped so abruptly that Stanley almost bumped into him.

'I do remember her. Very young and pretty. Brought in as an emergency. I was in the A&E department when the ambulance arrived. She had a very high fever and they had to take her straight up to the ICU. I went up with her.'

Stanley couldn't believe his luck.

'Would you like me to buy you a coffee and a sausage roll, Dr Wilde, or perhaps a chocolate doughnut?'

* * *

Jane was just about to get in her car when a Range Rover pulled up and the driver lowered his window.

'Hi. If you're leaving, do you mind if I park up in your space? I'm only going in for a few minutes.'

Jane hesitated, throwing her briefcase onto the passenger seat.

'Well, this is staff-only parking.' She then shrugged and waved her hand to say OK, possibly because he was such a handsome man.

He beamed at her. 'Thank you. Have a good day.'

She slammed her door shut. It had been a while since anyone smiled at her like that. He was just her type, too, and even looked the right age, and then she made herself laugh as she thought it would be just her luck that when he got out of the Range Rover, he would have short, bowed legs. She was driving out and waiting for the traffic to move before turning into the road when she saw him in her rear-view mirror locking the Range Rover. She sighed. He had to be way over six feet, and she even noted that he was wearing a very stylish tweed jacket.

Nathan & Markus Funeral Directors were situated in the town centre with parking available at the rear of the establishment. The narrow alley led into a small courtyard with two hearses under an open-fronted shelter. There was also a Morris Minor and a small white van, leaving just a small space for Jane to park.

Jane walked back down the alley and into the building. The interior was cramped, with a two-seater sofa and a coffee table, and a dark-green fitted carpet. On a neat desk was a telephone, a typewriter and a large black-leather diary. Jane waited. She looked over the desk to see if there was some kind of bell to press, but there was nothing. A door behind the counter was firmly closed, and just as Jane was about to call out, the shop door opened. A plump blonde woman wearing a dark-maroon suit that was rather tight around her hips, bustled in carrying a cake box and a flask.

'Oh, I am sorry, did you have an appointment?'

Jane took out her ID as the woman scuttled round the counter, opening the diary.

'I just went to get a sandwich and refill my flask.'

'I'm Detective Inspector Jane Tennison from the Metropolitan Police, and . . .'

'Just a minute, let me go and see if Colin's out the back, I'm his mother.'

'Are you Mrs Nathan?'

'Yes, it's a family business, my son runs it all now my husband passed. There's nothing in the diary, I'm afraid.'

'I just needed to ask you or your son a few questions. I am not here to organise a funeral. This is my ID.'

Jane held out her warrant card as Mrs Nathan bent down to open a drawer in the desk and take out a pair of glasses. She squinted at the card and looked up.

'Police? Is something wrong?'

Jane explained that she wanted to ask some questions about Georgina Larsson's funeral. Mrs Nathan asked Jane to wait, and she would get her son to talk to her. She disappeared through the door behind the counter and Jane could hear her calling for him. After a few moments, Mrs Nathan returned, saying her son was just taking his overalls off and washing his hands. 'Is it a loved one?' she asked.

'No, it's a police matter.' Jane sighed.

'Well, Colin will only be a moment. There's a very nice brochure for flowers if you'd like to look through it while you're waiting.'

Jane was relieved when Colin Nathan walked in. He was prematurely bald, with a small, pale, oval face. He gave Jane a polite nod, then told his mother that she could have her break.

'Sorry about the confusion. After my father died, I encouraged my mother to come in a few days a week. She's sort of still in training!' He laughed softly as he straightened his tie.

'I am not here regarding a funeral arrangement, Mr Nathan. This is a police enquiry regarding Georgina Larsson's funeral. There's nothing to be concerned about, I just need to ask you a few questions.'

'How long ago did you say?' he asked.

'Four years. The family live in Clarendon Court.'

'I will have to get the file from that year. I won't be a moment,' he said, disappearing through the door.

He was at least ten minutes before he returned carrying a large file. 'Sorry it took so long, but things are in a bit of a muddle.'

He began to flip through the pages before unclipping the hooks to lay the file flat.

'Miss Georgina Larsson, you said?'

'Yes. I have a copy of her death certificate.'

Nathan turned over another section of the file before he looked up and unhooked the relevant pages.

'We collected Miss Larsson from St Thomas' Hospital mortuary on the afternoon of 17th March. The death certificate was issued on 15th March. Her body remained at their home until the family arranged her funeral on 21st March.'

'Is that usual, for the deceased to remain at her home?'

'No, but there is always a certain amount of time before the funeral, and it's not unknown for the family to want to remain with the deceased during that period. Mrs Larsson had chosen the casket but returned here on the 19th March to discuss flowers and the hearse. They chose a very elegant white coffin with brass handles and a plaque, which we also inscribed.'

'So you delivered the coffin to their home on the 17th?'

'That's correct.'

'Do you recall the courtyard of Clarendon Court being tarmacked at the time of the funeral?'

Nathan looked surprised. 'As a matter of fact I do recall the circumstances because we had been having a lot of rain, and the driveway was, I believe, freshly tarmacked, up to the area of one of the new properties. But that still left an extensive area of the courtyard very muddy, with deep potholes.'

'The area you are referring to, would that be outside the Larssons' property and as far as the large manor house?'

'That is correct, and the reason I may sound rather pedantic about the situation is that all our vehicles are very highly maintained and polished. We had another funeral later that same day, and the vehicles required extensive cleaning and valeting.'

'Thank you. And what was the date of the funeral?'

'Twenty-first of March, at the Eltham Crematorium.'

Jane could hardly hide her surprise. 'So Georgina Larsson was cremated?'

'That is correct. Again, we liaise between the bereaved and the crematorium, but the collection of the deceased's ashes is always down to the family to arrange.'

Jane nodded. 'There is just one more thing. Do you have a photograph of the style of coffin that was chosen?'

Nathan bent down to the shelf beneath the counter, bringing up a large leather-bound volume. He turned a few laminated pages before angling the volume for Jane to see. 'You can choose the satin or velvet inlay, and the option of a frilled satin pillow.'

'It's very elegant,' Jane said. 'Especially with the brass fittings. It also seems quite large. Did Mr and Mrs Larsson come here to choose the casket?'

'I'm not sure I can recall exactly, but Mrs Larsson did come alone the first time.'

'Thank you very much. You have been very helpful.'

Nathan nodded as he replaced the volume under the counter. He then laid his hands flat on the pages from the file. 'Is there anything else?'

'Do you personally accompany the hearse?'

'Yes, I do. We are a very small company. I like to make sure everything's professionally carried out.'

'Were there many mourners at Miss Larsson's funeral?'

'Not that many, from memory. There were quite a lot of young people, her schoolfriends, I imagine, but only two mourners' cars were required.'

'Do you remember seeing a young man, rather unusual-looking, very long, dark hair. He may even have had his hair in a ponytail.'

Nathan closed the file, taking a moment before he shook his head. 'I'm afraid not.'

Jane thanked him again before leaving. She was still puzzling over the fact that the Larssons had cremated their daughter. Her own parents had buried her young brother, his gravestone a small, carved, white cross they visited on his birthday. She had always been aware of Michael, or aware that he had died tragically, but had only ever been to his grave once. Jane believed her parents never wanted their grief to affect their two daughters, but after the session with Vera James, she wondered if it was time to be more open about it.

Jane got in her car and was about to drive back to the station when she suddenly felt violently sick. She had to take several deep breaths before the nausea subsided. Still feeling unwell, she decided to go straight home. After parking outside the house, she went into her kitchen and drank a glass of water. After a cup of tea she felt better. She was jotting down all her notes from the interviews when her phone rang. It was Eddie.

'Can I come round? I'm only round the corner.'

'OK. See you in a minute then,' she said, her heart suddenly racing. She hurried upstairs to change, while checking her hair and make-up. The doorbell rang, she looked out of her bedroom window, and there he was.

Chapter Twenty-One

Eddie was wearing his usual leather jacket, but was otherwise very smartly dressed in a white shirt, washed-out jeans and cowboy boots. He was holding a bunch of roses.

He smiled. 'Hey, this was fortunate. I was just over at my dad's work site and hoped you might be home.'

'Well, I am. I just got in. Come in and I'll make you a cup of tea.'

'I'm fine. Anyway, these are for you.'

Jane took the flowers and he walked ahead of her into the kitchen.

'I was doing an interview and felt a bit sick so came home, otherwise I would have been at the station.'

'You feeling all right now?'

'Yes, I'm fine. Look, it's good to see you. Are you sure I can't get you anything?'

'No, honestly, I can't stay long.'

He eased out a chair and sat down. Jane went to the fridge. There was a half-bottle of white wine open and she hesitated, about to pour herself one but then closed the fridge door.

'OK, I'll make this brief, and maybe I should have talked it through with you a long time ago, but after that row we had it sort of brought it all to a head.'

'I think I may have said a few things that I regret now,' she said, sitting down.

'No, whatever you said was right, because the truth is, it's not been really good between us for some time. So I'll be totally honest with you: I've been seeing someone else for quite a while. At first it wasn't that serious, but now it is, and so I felt that you should know.'

'I'm not quite following,' she said, even though it was perfectly clear what he had just said.

He sighed and shook his head.

'Like I just said, it was not really serious. I saw her a few times, and then things changed.'

'Who are you talking about?' Jane said, suddenly feeling sick again.

'I've been seeing Caroline, the girl at the mobile call centre. We just started having these conversations and then we met and now . . .'

'Now what?' Jane said, her mouth dry.

'Well, we're together, and I know I should have talked this over with you days ago, but I just didn't have the bottle because part of me wasn't exactly sure what was happening. Anyway, I felt you should find out from me and not someone else.'

Jane was hardly able to take in what he was saying. She took a deep breath. 'So you were seeing this Caroline before we had that row, is that what you are telling me?'

He hesitated. 'Look, I'm sorry if I have lied to you or not been exactly honest about my whereabouts for a while, but now we're living together. I've moved into her flat until we find a place for both of us.'

'I see, well, I'm sorry because I've missed you and was hoping we could sort things out between us, but obviously that was stupid of me.'

Eddie pushed his chair back and stood up. 'Listen, I'm really sorry it's ended this way, but I want you to know I really cared about you.'

Jane couldn't think of anything to say. She remained sitting at the kitchen table as he walked round to her and kissed her cheek.

'Take care, and if you ever need any work done, you just call me.'

She nodded.

'Did you get the house keys I put through your letterbox?'

'Yes, I did, thank you.'

'OK, I'm going to go, and like I said, if you need anything you can call me at my dad's.'

Eddie walked out of the kitchen, into the hall and closed the front door behind him. Jane sat at the table, trying to come to terms with what had just happened. Eventually she got up and opened the fridge, taking out the wine and pouring herself a glass. She drank it quickly and then another glass more slowly, and then turned off the lights and went upstairs. She needed a cigarette. Sitting on the side of her bed, taking deep drags on the cigarette, she wanted to cry, knowing that was exactly what she should be doing, but for some reason she couldn't. She stubbed out her cigarette and lit another, saying out loud, 'The bloody two-faced cow.'

* * *

The following morning Jane woke with a violent headache, feeling that she hadn't really slept. The last thing she felt like doing was going into the station, but she forced herself to take a shower and get dressed and was feeling a little better by the time she got to the station. Stanley wasn't around so she couldn't tell him what she'd learned at the undertakers. Instead, she had to force herself to concentrate on the slew of cases that had come in overnight, but from the excited chatter around her it quickly became obvious that something big had gone down the previous night. According to an exhausted and still shaken DC Burrows, the police wagon and five uniformed officers had been called out to a major incident at a housing estate, and they had brought in the big guns from the armed section to be on standby.

Stanley, it turned out, had been involved in negotiations with a pair of drug dealers holding two women and a child hostage. It had been a long, tense night with Stanley placing himself in jeopardy by entering the corridor of the flats. He used all his old skills, ordering in pizza and Cokes, constantly keeping up the conversation with the hostage-takers as the estate was surrounded, ramming equipment at the ready. Finally it was Stanley who led out the terrified hostages and then returned to persuade the young and by then hysterical teenagers to give up their shotguns.

The boys were now being fingerprinted and the duty solicitor was ready for the interviews.

When Jane finally caught up with Stanley, he was heading down the corridor, on his way to the exit. He had been told to go home and get some sleep, before returning to go through the lengthy process of taking statements. Like Burrows, he was exhausted, unshaven and his eyes were red-rimmed.

'Christ, Stanley, are you OK?'

He managed a tired smile. 'Shaken and very stirred. It was a hell of a night. Hyperactive, drugged-up kids with two sawn-off shotguns, one not yet sixteen, and a stack of cocaine, a lot of it up their own nostrils. I was just going home when it went down; in fact, I was going to come over to see you.'

She put her hand on his shoulder. 'You get some rest. We can catch up later.'

'Yeah, sort of puts everything into perspective, you know, like we're wasting our time with this bloody Clarendon Court situation when there's fucking drug dealers working out of a high-rise estate and holding one of their grandmas hostage.'

'I heard it was a nightmare.'

Stanley gave one of his gruff laughs. 'Yeah, but it made me ask myself why I am sitting it out here; when that buzz kicks in there's nothing like it.'

He walked out to the car park and Jane followed. When he got to his old, battered car she couldn't resist asking him one question. 'Did you get anything useful from the hospital?'

He opened the driver's door and got in, one hand on the open door. 'Yeah, from the scruffy young Dr Wilde, you know, the bloke with the biro all over his white coat. Fill you in later. I gotta crash.'

He slammed the door shut as Jane stepped back, feeling bad that she had asked him about it. Walking down the corridor towards the incident room, she saw DCI Hutton was heading towards her with a thick file of police records.

'I was just seeing Stanley off,' Jane said. 'Is there anything I can do? It sounded like quite a night.' Hutton nodded. 'It was, and I have to say Stanley was incredible. I doubt any other officer here could have remained calm and in control in such a high-pressure situation.'

They walked together towards the incident room. Hutton stopped. 'You know, I heard such a lot about him, as an under-cover officer and with the Sweeney, that he was known to be a bit of a risk-taker. But without him last night, someone could easily have died. At one point I thought it might well be him, the way he sat on the stairs outside the flat they were threatening to shoot their way out of, eating pizza.'

The incident room was now filling with officers who had been on duty the previous night, and you could feel the charged atmosphere.

'OK, Jane, if you give me ten minutes to go through these records we've pulled up from the kids' previous arrest sheets . . . my main objective is to get one of them to talk about who was supplying them with the cocaine and shotguns . . . and then we hand it over to the drug squad.'

Hutton went into her office as Jane returned to her desk. She could hear the teams talking about Stanley and what he had accomplished, and she felt sure that Hutton was going to put him forward for a commendation. Having worked alongside him many times over the years, Jane knew it was well-deserved. At the same time, she'd felt a tinge of annoyance when Hutton had said there was no one else at the station that could have handled the situation; in her battered emotional state, it made her feel even more demoralised.

Stanley returned later that afternoon, shaved and smelling of cologne and, unusually for him, wearing quite a sharp suit. He received a cheer from everyone gathered in the incident room before Hutton called her into his office to go over the statements made by the woman and young girl the two boys had held hostage. They then went downstairs to meet the solicitors representing the boys, before interviewing them.

Jane put her head own, and by the time she'd finished her assignments it was almost five thirty. She tidied her desk, and having no more orders or pressing requests, put the hood over her typewriter. Her headache had persisted all day, and she had a pain in her right side that felt like her period was due and that no amount of paracetamol had eased. She went over to see Dora Phillips, the head of clerical staff.

'I'm taking off now, Miss Phillips. I'm not feeling very well. Think I'm getting a migraine.'

'You should maybe see if our nurse is here. You know she comes in every other day. I do hope that migraine won't mean you have any more days off.'

'I beg your pardon,' Jane snapped.

'No offence, dear, I used to have them myself. Very debilitating.'

Jane walked out, unsure whether she'd overreacted. All she wanted to do now was go home and get into bed. She wasn't feeling hungry, so as soon as she got home she got changed and was about to get into bed when the pain in her side sharpened. She took two more paracetamol and made her way slowly downstairs into the kitchen to warm up some milk, hoping it would help. She was sitting at the kitchen table and about to take the pan off the stove as the milk was boiling when the pain suddenly became excruciating. Jane buckled over, taking deep breaths. She knew this was not any kind of period pain; it had to be something more serious, maybe her appendix. Deciding not to wait for an ambulance, she put on her raincoat and made the slow walk to her car then drove herself to the A&E department at Queen Mary's Hospital in Sidcup, gritting her teeth in agony all the way. After finding a parking space, she staggered into the casualty department and was approaching the reception desk when she collapsed.

The next thing she knew, Jane was in a cubicle in the casualty department and a nurse was drawing back the curtain. She had only a vague memory of what had happened, but the pain was now even worse, and it was all she could do to stop herself crying out loud. It was almost midnight when Jane, after being examined by two doctors, was told that she needed an emergency operation.

'It's my appendix, isn't it?'

The young female doctor bent towards her and took hold of her hand.

'No, you have an ectopic pregnancy. This means the foetus is growing in one of your fallopian tubes between your ovaries and uterus. It's important we get you into surgery. We're just waiting for the surgeon.'

It was hard for Jane to take it all in as the pain made it hard to think until finally the medication she'd been given started to kick in, but by then she was exhausted. By the time the surgery went ahead it was almost four o'clock in the morning.

Waking up later in a private room, Jane slowly began to regain her senses, but she was still very confused when the matron came to check on her.

'Good morning. I'm Matron Jameson. I'm afraid I have a few forms that will need to be filled in. The duty doctor will be checking how you are feeling shortly, then later this morning the surgeon will be doing his rounds.'

Jane tried to sit up but quickly fell back against the pillows again. The matron moved round to the bedside table, opening the small door in the cabinet. 'Your handbag is in here and your clothes are in the cupboard by the door. The bathroom is directly across from your room, and if you require any assistance this morning, you have a pull cord by your bed.'

Jane could hardly take it all in. 'I need to make some calls.'

'We do have a phone that can be brought in for you to use, but we do need some particulars first. Now, we know your name is Jane Tennison, but we also require a date of birth, your doctor's details and your address, and who you wish to be contacted.'

Jane somehow managed to give the matron all the details, and then a nurse came in wheeling a blood pressure monitor. Jane was helped to sit up and ease her legs to the ground as her blood pressure was taken, and then the nurse helped her back to bed and gave her some pills.

'Antibiotics,' she explained, holding a cup of water to Jane's lips. 'And let me know if you need any pain medication.'

Jane shook her head. 'Not at the moment. Thank you.'

She closed her eyes, listening to the sounds from the ward and the chatter of nurses and patients, before trying to piece together what had occurred the previous night. She recalled parking her car and making her way painfully to the A&E reception, but then everything blurred, and her brain felt like a dead weight.

Sometime later a young doctor came and examined her, then explained what had happened. 'If the fallopian tube had burst, it could have been life-threatening, which is why we had to operate.'

Jane tried her best to make sense of it all, unable to understand how she could have had no warning signs. But perhaps the stress she had been under with the Eddie situation, and then her near obsession with the Sebastian Hoffman investigation had blinded her to how fatigued and irritable she had felt, along with the persistent headaches. She did recall feeling the pain in her side, and dismissing it as period pain. But on reflection she realised she had not had a period for more than two months.

It was close to lunchtime, and Jane had managed to go to the bathroom unaided, then had returned to lie down. She had been checked by two different nurses and had asked both if she could be brought the telephone to make important phone calls. The telephone had not been brought to her and she was beginning to get very anxious about no one being contacted at the station. Sometime after lunch the matron ushered in Mr Kenneth Halifax, her surgeon, a tall, angular-faced man wearing dark-rimmed glasses.

'Good afternoon. This must have been very stressful for you, Miss Tennison, but you are a very lucky lady. How are you feeling?'

'Fine, thank you.'

'Jolly good. Now I would like to examine you. If you have any questions, or need to know the exact procedure that took place, or have any worries or concerns, I am all ears.'

'It's actually Detective Inspector Tennison, Mr Halifax. I am a police officer. I had the doctor explain it all earlier but I am still somewhat confused.'

He pushed his glasses up the bridge of his nose with his index finger. 'My apologies, Inspector Tennison. You were brought into the theatre for an ultrasound scan by the nurse on duty. I was called in immediately. You had the possibility of a rupture occurring in your right fallopian tube. You were given general anaesthesia, and I removed the fertilised egg along with the affected fallopian tube and ovary by keyhole surgery.'

He began to examine her.

'How does that . . . I mean, will I be able to get pregnant again?' Jane asked. Mr Halifax looked at the notes on the clipboard at the end of the bed, then looked up and smiled.

'Hopefully, yes, because you still have one fallopian tube intact and an ovary in good shape.'

'How long will I need to recover?'

'That rather depends on how you feel. It is by no means major surgery; uncomfortable, yes, but it should not be too painful. It is quite a common procedure and occurs in about one in every ninety pregnancies a year. In very simple terms what occurs is that the fallopian tubes connect the ovaries to the womb. If an egg gets stuck in one of them, it won't develop into a baby and your health would be at great risk the longer it remains growing.'

Jane nodded. 'I understand.'

'A few days' rest and you should be fine, but I will leave a booklet for you, and I suggest you spend the rest of the day and night here and then consult your GP if you have any further concerns.'

After the surgeon left, Jane felt very tearful. Eventually a phone was brought in and Jane called the station and spoke to Miss Phillips. She then called her parents and asked her father to collect her the following morning, hoping it would be all right to stay with them for a few days' recuperation.

The following day, after a final examination, Jane got dressed and made ready to leave the hospital. Her father drove her home to collect everything she would need for the next few days, and then she followed him in her car back to her parents' house. She had been given some antibiotics and painkillers, plus the leaflet explaining her ectopic procedure, including a section to help with the sense of grief at losing her baby.

Her father had been his usual quiet self, obviously concerned about her but didn't ask her anything personal, and didn't mention Eddie. Jane knew that when she got home it would be a different story as her mother would no doubt want a blow-by-blow account of everything that had happened, and would be sure to bring up the fact that Eddie was not with her at the hospital.

Jane was beginning to feel very tired by the time she had unpacked her bag in the little bedroom, having managed to avoid her mother's queries until she'd got into a nightdress and dressing gown. Mrs Tennison had prepared a light supper of chicken soup with thinly sliced brown bread and a portion of cheese flan. She had carried up the tray even though Jane said she would join them in the kitchen, insisting that bed was the best place for her. She plumped up the pillows so Jane could sit up.

'So, tell me all about it,' she said.

Jane had planned to tell her parents that she'd had a burst appendix, but suddenly found she was telling her mother the truth. Mrs Tennison took a tissue out of her pocket and dabbed at her eyes, asking if it meant that Jane could never get pregnant. Jane leaned over to the bedside cabinet and handed her mother the leaflet she had been given in the hospital.

'No, it doesn't,' Jane said. 'And you can read all the details in there. Right now it's the last thing I want to think about.'

'I understand, darling, of course I do. I'll read this over with your father later. Is there anything else I can get you? Maybe a cup of tea, and I'll let Pam know you're here. She'll be worried because I called her after you rang to get Daddy to collect you from the hospital.'

'Cup of tea later would be nice,' Jane said.

Jane managed a few spoonfuls of the soup and half of the flan before she put the tray on the floor and went into the bathroom. She felt a bit woozy as she cleaned her teeth, and splashed cold water over her face before returning to bed. Mrs Tennison appeared a moment later with a cup of tea, but Jane was fast asleep.

It was almost seven when Jane woke up, having slept through the night. She still had a slight headache, so took two paracetamol. Mrs Tennison tapped on the door and brought in a cup of tea.

'How are you feeling, dear? I looked in on you last night, but you were fast asleep. Would you like a little scrambled egg and toast, or poached eggs? Whatever you want.'

'No, Mum, I'm fine. I'll just stay put for a couple of hours.'

'Whatever you feel like doing. I'll be in the kitchen if you want anything.'

A few hours later, after taking a shower, washing her hair and changing into a fresh nightdress, Jane felt well enough to join her mother in the kitchen. Mrs Tennison was peeling potatoes for a shepherd's pie, and Jane knew she was trying her hardest not to ask why Jane had come home to recuperate.

'The thing is, Eddie and I have separated. It had been sort of coming on for some time but it's final now. And it's perfectly amicable.'

'Well, your father will be disappointed as he had a few jobs lined up,' Mrs Tennison said, trying to be light-hearted about it. 'We've still got problems with the boiler and the timer isn't working properly. It seems to have a will of its own, and we never know when the hot water is coming on. My bedside light keeps flicking on and off, too, and I think we have a leak from one of the central heating panels.' She paused. 'I suppose it was his?'

'What?'

'The . . . pregnancy.'

'Of course it was, but I didn't even know I was pregnant and so I never told him. And we had already separated.' Jane took her dirty dishes to the dishwasher.

'Was it just that you were incompatible, or had you met someone else?'

Jane couldn't help laughing. 'Yes to the first query and no to the other.'

Mrs Tennison started rinsing the dishes before stacking them in the dishwasher, and Jane headed down the corridor to the spare bedroom to get dressed. She was just going in when she overheard her mother talking to her father.

'She just told me that she's separated from Eddie, so you are going to have to get the porter to find an odd-job man to fix my bedside light. I keep on thinking I am going to be electrocuted.'

'I liked him,' her father said with a sigh, 'but whatever is best for her is fine by me.'

'Well, I said I didn't think it would last, didn't I?'

'Yes, you did, but he did a hell of a good job on her house. I had another look around when I went to collect her from the hospital. I think it's probably doubled in value.'

Chapter Twenty-Two

Jane rested for two further days with her parents. She was feeling a lot better, especially since she'd managed to avoid any further conversations about Eddie. She had a follow-up appointment with Mr Halifax at the hospital on Saturday, so decided it was time to return home. She packed her suitcase and her father put it in the hall. 'You know what I'd like before I go? Maybe a little walk along the canal to feed the ducks?' she said.

'Your mother's out grocery shopping. Do you want to wait for her to come with us?'

'No, just you and me, Dad, then I'll get off home. I'll be going back to work on Monday.'

Jane had her arm hooked into her father's as they made the short walk from their block of flats down to the canal towpath.

'You know this case I have been working on . . . about a boundary dispute . . . I think I mentioned a bit about it last night.'

They reached a bench and sat down.

'Yes, what about it?' he asked.

'Well, I spent some time with a really nice woman who was looking for her son. She told me she had been seeing this medium.'

'Oh, yes.'

'Well, I went to see her and it was actually fascinating. She claims to be able to communicate with the dead, and of course I was very sceptical about it, but then when she said something to me . . .'

Mr Tennison leaned forwards as if concentrating on the ducks, while Jane tried to think how to put it into words. He opened the paper bag he'd brought with him and started tossing pieces of stale bread into the canal.

'Go on, I'm listening,' he said as several ducks swam towards them.

'She . . . brought up Michael. It was impossible for her to have known anything about him . . . but do you want to hear what she said to me?'

He didn't look at her as the ducks circled in the water with more swimming to join them.

'She said he is at peace; he is a beautiful boy and that there is no reason to feel guilty about what happened.'

Jane tried to reach for his hand, but he stood up abruptly and shook out the rest of the bread from the bag before he crumpled it into a ball and stuffed it into his pocket.

'That's not quite right, Jane, I'm afraid. There will always be guilt. He was alone in the garden, wanting me to come out. I had made him a little fishing rod, with a loop at the end of it. I had taken him to the fair, and he had stood on tiptoe with one of their rods over a paddling pool filled with water and yellow plastic ducks. I helped him scoop one up to win a prize. I filled an old dustbin lid in the garden, and we brought out a couple of plastic ducks he played with at bath time. It was a hot sunny day, and the bin had no water left. The next-door garden had a big pond. He somehow squeezed through the hedge with the two little ducks and the fishing rod . . .' He paused, trying to control his emotions. 'They found him face down in the water.'

Jane wanted to put her arms around him, but he remained staring at the canal. Then he turned and said quietly that they should go back as her mother would be worried. She walked beside him, and he eventually allowed her to slip her hand into his.

'There is guilt, Jane, always was, always will be; it is a wound in our hearts that will never heal.'

When they got back to the flat, Jane's mother was putting portions of shepherd's pie into freezer containers, to heat up when she got home. Jane didn't say anything more about Michael or what Vera James had told her.

Driving off, she saw the way they stood together, their arms entwined, and it brought tears to her eyes. They had never hinted at the wound they still felt. They had shown such love and pride in their two daughters Jane and Pam, but their beloved first-born little boy Michael occupied a part of their hearts that neither daughter could touch.

Her house felt empty. She went into the kitchen, put the shepherd's pie in the freezer, and filled the kettle to make herself a cup of tea. She was carrying her suitcase up the stairs when the phone rang. She hurried into the bedroom, tossing her case onto the bed, and reached for the phone.

'Jane? It's Fiona. I was just calling to see how you're doing.'

'Oh, it was not that much of an emergency. Grumbling appendix but very unpleasant and probably if it occurs again, I will have to have it removed.'

'Let's hope that won't happen,' Hutton said. 'In the meantime, take all the time you need to get fully fit.'

'Thank you, but I have the weekend and I will be in on Monday.'

'Well, as long as you feel fully recovered, we've certainly got our hands full here. Things have escalated, as it looks like those youngsters were mixed up in a drug gangs feud.'

'I'll be up for anything needed,' Jane said.

'Good to hear. We'll get you up to speed at the Monday-morning briefing. Until then, I hope you have a restful weekend.'

'I'll be there, and thank you, ma'am, for calling.'

Jane replaced the receiver and sat on the edge of the bed, then lay back, staring at the ceiling. There was no way she was going to tell Hutton the real reason she'd been in hospital, and she had the next two days to get her energy back. After unpacking, she couldn't face any of the shepherd's pie, so instead took a big mug of tea up to the bedroom. She left her file on Sebastian Hoffman on her dressing table, deciding that perhaps Stanley was right, she should just forget about it. She drew the bedroom curtains closed, then opened the bottle of sleeping tablets, took three, and swallowed them with half the mug of tea. After washing her face and cleaning her teeth, she pulled off the plaster on the right side of her abdomen – the only indication that she had undergone any surgery. She dabbed the area with disinfectant and put a fresh plaster on it, then returned to the bedroom. She soon felt the effects of the sleeping tablets, her eyelids heavy, and with the comforting duvet wrapping her naked body, she quickly sank into the darkness.

Saturday was a bright sunny day, and drawing back the curtains, Jane already felt refreshed. She put on a soft, grey tracksuit and white T-shirt, with a pair of cleanish trainers, planning to have her eight thirty appointment with Mr Halifax at the hospital and then go and do a grocery shop, return home and get down to giving the house a thorough clean and hoover.

Mr Halifax's appointment was in the gynaecological and maternity section of the hospital. It was situated near to the wards, but off a corridor with various examination rooms. At eight fifteen Jane was the only person waiting, having reported in at the reception desk on the ground floor.

A nurse opened Mr Halifax's door.

'Jane? Please come in.'

Mr Halifax gave Jane a noncommittal glance, as he looked over her notes from a plastic clipboard. 'How are you feeling?'

'Fine, no real pain or discomfort,' Jane said.

He nodded, indicating for Jane to lie down on the white paper-covered examination bed.

The nurse asked Jane to remove her tracksuit bottoms and drew her top up to her breasts. Mr Halifax put on a pair of surgical gloves, then eased off the plaster, gently feeling Jane's pelvic area and abdomen. He took her temperature, then asked the nurse to take her blood pressure and went back to his desk.

Fifteen minutes later Jane left the hospital. Mr Halifax had given her a letter to give to her GP, and no further prescription was necessary. He had also given her his private practice card and address in Harley Street should she wish to contact him directly.

Jane decided she would have breakfast in the little cafe she remembered Stanley had recommended, enthusing about their pastries and coffee. She ordered a cappuccino and a hot bacon and egg roll and sat at the nearest table. The young waitress was having a spot of trouble with the hot milk contraption that was frothing and gurgling.

'Morning, Cheryl. Still not got the hang of it, have you. Don't press it down so hard, just tickle the lever. I'll have my usual with three caramel lattes, one with no sugar.'

Jane recognised Dr Wilde, with his rumpled white coat and biro-stained pocket.

'Good morning,' she said pleasantly.

He turned towards her, and after a moment's confusion raised his hand, smiling.

'Hello there, I thought I'd given your inspector all the information my little grey cells could recall.'

There was a yelp from behind the counter as the frothing milk overflowed. A middle-aged woman wearing the cafe logo apron appeared and hurried towards the machine. 'Now what have you done? How many times have I told you that if you press two levers at the same time it overloads. If anyone is waiting for their orders, give them our apologies because it'll be another few minutes. Get a mop, Cheryl . . . now!'

Cheryl went off to get a mop and bucket as Jane gestured to the empty chair at her table. Dr Wilde sat down. 'You know, it was such an odd coincidence because your colleague was asking me about . . . er, name's gone.'

'Georgina Larsson?'

'Right, and last night I had another patient with sepsis. Young boy had been self-harming.'

'What exactly is sepsis?' Jane asked.

'Normally the body releases chemicals into the bloodstream that help fight an infection, but then when the body's response to these infection-fighting chemicals gets out of control, like it's out of balance, then sepsis occurs. This can then trigger a chain reaction throughout the body, resulting in a cascade of bodily changes that eventually leads to organ failure.'

'Is that what happened to Georgina Larsson?'

'Yes. She was already in shock when she was brought in. You see, any infection can trigger sepsis; it can be brought on by pneumonia, abdominal infection and so on. In her case the surgeon determined it was an abdominal infection.'

'Could she have had a miscarriage, or an abortion?'

He spread his hands.

'I was not privy to the details, I'm afraid. She was exceptionally underweight, though, and I was told only fifteen years old. It was tragic. She didn't last through the next day and her life support was withdrawn.'

'Would the coroner's report have more details?'

He shrugged. 'Possibly.'

'Well, thank you for the information.'

'My pleasure. OK . . . duty calls . . . nice to meet you again, and have a nice day.' He turned towards the counter where Cheryl finally had his order ready.

'Just one more thing. Would the young girl we've talked about be taken to the hospital mortuary, or would her parents be allowed to take her home?'

'I'm not sure, but it would have to have a coroner's report and all the legal stuff, then be held in the mortuary for collection . . . sorry, need to get these delivered, goodbye!'

Jane opened her handbag and took out a pen. She sipped her cappuccino, then began making a list on the back of her receipt. First, she wrote 'mortuary', then 'crematorium', 'tarmac company', and finally 'photographs', underlined.

It took her some time to find it, but the hospital's mortuary building was a short distance from the main hospital. It was a plain, square, brick building with a large chimney. A sign saying NO ADMITTANCE UNLESS AUTHORISED was framed on the double entry doors. She knocked on the doors with no result, until eventually an overweight man wearing a green uniform opened them.

'DI Tennison. I need to speak to someone who could answer some questions relating to a police enquiry,' she said, holding up her ID.

'That has to be me, then,' he said with a frown. 'It's the weekend so we only have two members of staff on duty. My name's Chris Morgan.'

He led her into a spartan office with a desk and a chair, and a row of grey steel cabinets along the wall.

'Thank you,' Jane said, perching on the edge of the desk while he sat down in the only chair. 'First, could you talk me through what happens when a deceased patient from the hospital is brought to the mortuary?'

'Certainly. They'd be brought in in tagged body bags, and put straight in a chilled drawer. There's usually a fast turnaround due to having limited space.'

'So, the body would not be kept here for a lengthy period?'

'Usually they are removed pretty quickly by the funeral directors.'

'Are relatives allowed in here when the body is removed?'

'Very rarely. They have usually had time to be with their loved ones while still in the hospital, and that can sometimes be a couple of days. Again, it's down to space; beds are always needed.'

'Can I test your memory, Chris?' Jane asked. 'I'm going back about four years, four and a half, maybe.' He laughed wryly.

'That's asking a lot. You'd be surprised how many we have coming and going. And I doubt it'll still be in the records.'

'I want to know about a fifteen-year-old girl called Georgina Larsson. She would have been brought in from the ICU department on 15th March, 1982.'

He paused. 'You're not going to believe this, but I do remember. Not her name, but the date, because 15th March was my mother's birthday. I mean, she'd been gone a few years, but there was something else that makes me remember it. They bring them down here on a gurney, right, and the porter wheels it over into the chill section, and usually two of us lift and place it on the drawer, right? Anyway, the reason I remember it is because I am always affected when it's a child, you know? The bag was so light I asked if it was a little one, but the porter told me she was a teenager. She weighed hardly anything and he lifted her into the drawer himself.'

Jane looked thoughtful for a moment. 'That's really helpful, Mr Morgan. Thank you for your time.'

The next on her list was the Eltham Crematorium, and it was almost eleven o'clock before she got there. She had to wait some time as there had been a service earlier, and a few mourners were still examining the array of wreaths and flowers in the garden area at the rear of the church. It was almost eleven thirty before a man called Gordon Sands took her inside the small chapel.

They sat in one of the chapel pews and Jane explained that her questions were of a general nature and the enquiry didn't relate to this crematorium specifically.

Sands nodded, then straightened a prayer book on the shelf of the pew.

'Is it possible, Mr Sands, that in a cremation service, two bodies could have been place in the coffin, if one of them was very light?'

He shook his head firmly. 'Oh, no.'

'Is it usual practice to check inside a coffin before it is cremated?'

'The funeral directors might well. I have never been required to do so.'

'So would that mean it is possible?'

He grimaced. 'On many occasions I have been asked if it's permissible to place items of particular meaning in the coffin with the deceased, such as jewellery, books, letters and soft toys.'

'So, on these occasions, did you check what was in the coffin before the cremation?'

'No, I did not. But I think that's beside the point; the thing is, if two bodies had been place in the coffin, the extra weight of the ashes would be quite noticeable.'

'How much would the ashes normally weigh?'

'Well, it varies of course, but something around four pounds.'

Jane nodded. 'I see. Well, thank you for your help.'

Mr Sands stood up, then gestured for her to leave the chapel. She could feel his eyes on her as she walked out.

After doing a big grocery shop, she returned home, filling up her freezer and preparing a salad for her lunch. She was going to wait until two o'clock to call Angelica Martinez as she remembered that she worked half days. She needed to persuade her to provide a photograph of her son. The original idea about giving the house a good clean had gone out the window.

Jane was just rinsing her salad bowl and coffee mug when she heard hammering from the back garden. She looked out of the kitchen window and then dodged back as she could see Eddie's father working on Gerry's fence, removing the makeshift bits of wood that had been fixed up by one of Eddie's boys. She hesitated, then thought he might have seen her at the window, so went out into the garden.

'Hi there . . . I heard the hammering and saw you . . . just wondered how you are.'

He looked rather embarrassed. 'Sorry if it's disturbing you. Eddie asked me to come over to make this more secure. Their little dog squeezed through and did a bit of a runner.'

'Oh, you are not disturbing me at all, and it's very kind of you. How is Lynette? I suppose by now her wrist must be out of plaster.'

'She's fine, had it off a few days ago. So how are you keeping?'

'Oh, I'm fine too. Give Eddie my best when you see him.'

She was about to return to her kitchen when she stopped in her tracks. 'Can I ask you something. It's about a case I'm working on. You remember the time you worked at Clarendon Court?'

He was rolling some hard twine around a fence post, nodding but not looking at her.

'I'd like to know which company laid the tarmac on the courtyard.'

'Funny you should ask me that, but I was doing a job over in Orpington last week, and I saw their wagon. Well, it's an old, converted lorry they use to boil up the tar. I mean, I'm not slagging them off, but I would have to call them a bunch of cowboys. They go round knocking on doors for business, and the reason I remembered them was they'd done a job on two old-age pensioners' bungalow, just to tarmac their drive, and hit 'em for a few hundred quid. I made a note to be certain not to ever use them.'

Jane frowned. 'They sound very dodgy. You wouldn't have their details, would you?'

He dug into the back pocket of his dungarees and took out a notebook. He thumbed through it.

'Patrick Kelly and Sons, out of St Mary Cray in Orpington. They didn't have a phone number on their lorry but if you try making contact with them, you be careful. Like I said, they're a rough outfit.'

'Thanks.' Jane smiled and turned back towards the house.

'Sorry it didn't work out with you and Eddie,' he said. 'He's a good lad really.'

'I'm sorry too. Thank you again for the information.'

In the kitchen, Jane thumbed through the phone book but couldn't find Patrick Kelly and Sons.

Jane rang Angelica Martinez again and she agreed to see her at three o'clock. Jane used the time before seeing her to go to an arts and crafts shop. She bought some thick coloured pens and a big sheet of white cardboard as well as a smaller black sheet and some thin red ribbon. It was a little after three when she parked up outside Angelica's flat.

Angelica welcomed her in with a smile, but Jane sensed a new reserve.

'I really won't take up any of your time,' Jane said. 'But it would be really useful to have a photograph of Sebastian.'

Angelica frowned. 'What for?'

'We're still looking into his whereabouts,' Jane explained.

Angelica signalled for Jane to follow her out of the small sitting room, passing her bedroom and opening the door to a little box room beside the bathroom.

Angelica stood back for Jane to enter. 'This room is for Sebastian when he returns,' she said. The small room had a single bed, a dressing table and a wardrobe. The walls were covered in photographs of Sebastian as a child, in Germany, in school uniform and then as the young teenager. Jane was taken aback, looking from one photograph to the next. She then moved closer to one wall.

'When did you take these?'

'Just before he left for Mexico.'

The photographs were of Sebastian with Georgina Larsson, the pair laughing with their arms wrapped around each other.

'She was so sweet, so gentle, and they adored each other,' Angelica said sadly. 'I know her parents accused him of being perverted, which is a horrible accusation. I didn't know how young she was, but he was just a child himself.'

'May I have one of the photographs of Sebastian?' Jane asked.

Angelica went over to the small single bed and pulled out a drawer beneath it.

'I have many copies, so choose which ones you would like to take.'

Jane sat on the bed and selected two of the teenage Sebastian, and then one of him with Georgina Larsson. She was easing them out of the plastic folder when she saw another photograph.

'What is this one?'

'Oh, I took that when I was waiting for him to come home. I used to walk around the courtyard, but then Mrs Larsson told me I was not allowed to be on their property.'

The black and white photograph was of the lorry laying the tarmac, and beside it a white van. Clearly printed on the side in thick black letters was 'Kelly and Sons' with their phone number.

Jane jotted down the number in her notebook. 'Can I just clarify that after Sebastian left for Mexico, your husband sold the courtyard to the Larssons, and the house was sold around the same time?'

'Yes, but in all honesty, Victor was under such pressure as they threatened to have Sebastian arrested. He not only sold the house at a huge loss because of the fire, he virtually gave them the courtyard as we needed to get it fixed, but we had no money.'

Jane thanked Angelica for the photographs, promising she would contact her as soon as she had any news of Sebastian. She had caught the haunted look in Angelica's eyes, and felt bad, because by now Jane truly believed her son was never coming home.

Returning to the house, Jane called the number for Kelly and Sons but it appeared to be disconnected. She called the operator to ask if there was another number for them but there didn't seem to be. She tried to track them down through other companies advertising the same type of business, such as tarmac, roof repairs, paving stones or garden maintenance, but no one could recall Kelly and Sons.

As a last resort, Jane called David Caplan, and he couldn't wait to tell her that they had a second buyer interested in the house. 'Hopefully Alice and I will be leaving soon. The gates and wall are almost finished and look really good. That wretched woman Mrs Larsson virtually spent all her time watching their every move.'

'That's great news. I was just calling to check something: when the posts for your new gates were installed, did you need to replace any of the tarmac?'

'Yes, as a matter of fact we did.'

'Was it the same company that originally tarmacked the courtyard?'

'I believe so. I offered to pay them, but Mrs Larsson insisted that she settle it. They seemed a bit aggressive towards her, to be honest, but I wasn't going to get involved.'

'Do you have their contact details?'

'I do, just in case I needed them for any other project, but they were a scruffy lot, so I doubt I ever would.'

Mr Caplan asked her to hold on while he went up to his office and he would put the call through from there. She could hear Buster barking at full throttle and a doorbell ringing before he came back on the line. 'Right, apparently they were Kelly and Sons, but the card they gave me had that crossed out and replaced with 'Patrick McGregor, Orpington . . .'

Jane jotted down the name and phone number, thanking Mr Caplan again and hoping the sale of their house went through. As soon as she hung up, she dialled the new number. It rang five times before it was answered. The young girl's voice sounded bored as Jane asked if she could speak to Mr McGregor.

'He's out on a job. He might be back after six.'

'My name is Jane Tennison, I would really like to talk . . .'

The phone went dead.

Chapter Twenty-Three

Jane worked the rest of the afternoon on her board, cutting and pasting the photographs and dates and the links between them. But the final piece was missing: the last link in the chain of events. She had a sandwich and coffee at six and at six fifteen called McGregor's number again. This time it rang for even longer, and eventually she replaced the receiver. She was also starting to feel very tired, and although she had no discomfort from her surgery, she changed the dressing and went to have a lie down.

It was almost ten when she finally woke up, furious with herself. Now she'd missed McGregor again and it was too late for her to drive over to Orpington.

Making herself a hot chocolate in the kitchen, she looked out to see Gerry standing by his new fence. It was a good, neat job and would keep Wilma safe. She thought it was nice that Eddie had organised it, but she knew he had asked his dad to do the work so he wouldn't have to see her. She cupped the hot mug of chocolate in her hands. She'd been so engrossed in her work that she had hardly thought about him. Now she contemplated how he would have reacted if she had told him about the pregnancy. The fact that she'd been unaware of it herself until the emergency meant that she had never considered how she would have felt about being pregnant.

She was still thinking about it when she got into bed. If Eddie was already having this affair, with the voice at the end of the bloody mobile phone, then what had happened was for the best. She certainly had no intention of ever telling him about it. She had to admit that there was a sense of relief it was over between them, and she had to move on. She set the alarm for six, had a cigarette and took two sleeping tablets, drained her hot chocolate and crashed out.

The next morning, Jane was up before the alarm rang. She had breakfast and double-checked her board before calling McGregor. This time it was picked up after two rings, and a gravel-voiced man answered.

'Yes?'

'Mr McGregor?'

'That's me.'

'My name is Jane Tennison. I called yesterday but you were working. I apologise for calling this early on a Sunday, but I really need to have a conversation with you.'

There was the sound of a deep, hacking, phlegmy cough that went on for some time before his rasping voice gasped out, 'What do you want?'

'Firstly, to let you know this is not about anything criminal regarding your company; it's just a personal enquiry connected to an investigation.'

'You police, are you?'

'Yes, sir, I am a detective inspector with the Metropolitan Police, but as I said it is a personal enquiry.'

'Piss off.'

'Please. I will pay you for your time, in cash. I can come to you, or meet you at any location you suggest.'

There was another round of coughing and Jane was certain he was going to cut the call off. 'Fifty quid, you can have fifteen minutes, and me nephew comes with me.'

'Agreed, where do you want to meet me?'

'Nag's Head, corner by Bishop's Road, twelve o'clock.'

Jane was buzzing. She had a shower, washed her hair, then dressed in a clean light-grey tracksuit with a white polo shirt. She would have to go to the nearest cash point to withdraw the cash, and she still had to check the exact location of the pub, though she knew it was a rough area. For a moment, she contemplated calling Stanley to be her back-up, before deciding to leave him to his weekend.

Just as she was leaving, her phone rang. She hesitated, then snatched it up in case it was important.

It was her sister Pam.

'Listen, you just caught me running out of the door. Can I call you back?'

There was no way Jane wanted to get into a lengthy conversation with her sister, who she knew would have been talking to their mother.

'I was thinking of popping over to see you this afternoon,' Pam said. 'I think we've got a lot of catching up to do.'

'Oh, what time? Only I am just going out for lunch.'

'Say four o'clock-ish, and do you want your hair done? Mum said you might be feeling a bit below par. I'll not bring anyone else, just me. The boys are playing a football match not far from you, so is four all right?'

'That will be great. See you then . . . got to go . . . bye . . . love to everyone.'

Jane sighed; having Pam round was the last thing she wanted. She'd be in for a grilling about Eddie and the operation. She slammed the front door behind her, hurrying to her car.

Jane arrived at the Nag's Head with the cash in her handbag just before twelve. It was a real old-fashioned boozer and judging from all the cars parked outside, it was already filling up. Jane found a seat in the snug bar with a good view of the rest of the pub and ordered a half pint of lager. Most of the drinkers were men, though a few had wives and children sitting outside with packets of crisps and lemonades.

It was already twelve fifteen, and Jane was starting to think McGregor might not show, when she spotted two burly men walking in. One grey-haired man in a black T-shirt with a leather jacket over his shoulders, and behind him a younger man with tattoos and a muscular frame, jet-black oiled hair and sideburns over a stubbled chin. They glanced around the main pub and then came and stood in the archway to the snug bar.

Jane raised her hand, and then quickly lowered it as they moved back to the main bar. She thought she'd been mistaken but then the two men reappeared with pints in their hands and made their way to her table.

'I'm Jane Tennison,' she said.

Both stared at her before the grey-haired one sat in the chair at her table and the other younger man gestured to another table and removed a spare chair.

'Are you Mr McGregor?' Jane asked.

The grey-haired man nodded, then gestured to his companion.

'And this is my nephew.'

'I had a hard time tracking you down as your company used to go under a different name.'

'What do you want?' McGregor asked, while looking around the bar.

'It's connected with the work that you did, or maybe someone else at your company did, at Clarendon Court.'

He gave a noncommittal shrug without answering so Jane continued. 'As I said to you on the phone this is just a personal enquiry; it has nothing to do with any complaint against you. Did you lay the tarmac at Clarendon Court about four years ago? I know you have recently done a small job there and a Mrs Larsson, I believe, paid for the work.'

The two men showed no reaction and continued to glance around the bar, almost as if she wasn't there. She started to feel slightly threatened by their attitude but carried on.

'I believe you worked there about four years ago, perhaps you didn't do the work personally, but it was to tarmac the entire drive and courtyard. There was a funeral. The deceased was taken from Mrs Larsson's property and the work was stopped to allow the hearse and the mourners to go past.'

'I was on that, but he wasn't,' McGregor said, nodding to his nephew.

'Can you describe the condition of the courtyard when you were told to halt the work?'

'Listen, we were told to stop and that we'd be contacted as soon as it was all right to finish the job. It was nothing to do with us that we never finished what we was paid to do on time.'

'I know that,' Jane said quickly. 'I just need to know what condition the remainder of the courtyard was in after you were told to stop work.'

McGregor drained his pint and handed it to his nephew for a refill.

'You know, it was a very tough job because we come across big cobblestones under all the mud. It was full of potholes, too, and great ridges like ditches.'

His nephew returned with a fresh pint, and one for himself, and he sat down.

Jane sipped her drink, finding the nephew sitting too close for comfort, his knees almost touching hers. She eased a fraction away. 'OK, can you tell me how long it was after the funeral that work recommenced?'

McGregor puffed out his cheeks, wiping the froth from his mouth with the back of his hand.

'Maybe couple of days or so, but we'd started on another job so one of the guys couldn't do it. The woman who owned the courtyard, she was a right pain in the arse. We had to put up the cones to stop anyone using the courtyard while we finished it.'

'Why do you want to know all this?' his nephew asked, leaning in close.

McGregor picked up a dirty, stained beermat from the table, searched in his pocket and brought out a stubby pencil.

'Right, this is the courtyard. We did the main area in the centre, then worked our way over to the new properties, and lastly in front of her house and her neighbours, working our way to the area where we just done the filling in around the gate posts. That's all I can tell you.'

'Thank you. And when you did this work, can you describe the state of the ground close to the owner's property and the other area you finished doing recently?'

McGregor drained his pint and put the glass down on the table. 'Listen, I don't know what you're fucking asking me all this for, but all I know is we lost money on that fucking deal. It was a lot of aggravation and we was then just a small company and had to hire extra men to do it.'

His nephew leaned forwards. 'Is it you're after him for it being a cash deal, is that what this is about? You agreed fifty quid, so put that down on the table.'

Jane could feel him edging even closer, and her heart rate was climbing, so she clenched her hands and swallowed. 'All right, I'll come clean, but only if you move away from me. You are making me feel uncomfortable.'

'Am I?' he sneered, and then his right hand grabbed her knee beneath the table.

'Get your hand off me!' she snarled. 'I mean it.'

McGregor pushed his nephew in the shoulder then leaned forwards.

'I'm listening, sweetheart.'

'OK, we had a tip-off. He might just be lying because we've arrested him, but he's not identified who was with him. He claims that they stashed some very valuable silver on the night after the funeral. He said the courtyard was full of big potholes and he buried a Georgian silver tea service, and some valuable jewellery he'd nicked from the big house.'

McGregor let out a hoarse laugh, shaking his head. Jane licked her lips as her mouth felt bone-dry. 'When you returned to do the tarmac, he never got the opportunity to reclaim it. So, you tell me: would it have been easy to bury that big a haul?'

Again, McGregor seemed to find it funny, shaking his head.

'Why didn't you just tell us straightaway; bit devious, aren't you, love?'

'I didn't want you to think that I believed you were involved.'

McGregor drew the beermat closer, licked the lead of the pencil, then jabbed it in two places, before turning the mat around for Jane to see.

'Right, there was two areas, we had to use sacks full of chips to fill them up. So, before the tarmac could cover them, we had a big iron roller to flatten them. I would say that'd be where your swag could have been hidden because it looked like it had been dug up.'

Jane nodded. 'One more thing, just to be certain. These two areas: had you filled them in when you stopped work?'

'To be honest with you, I can't remember. I mean they was the biggest, maybe for the funeral they'd been filled in. Whoever done it wouldn't have had access to our iron roller. We also have a heavy-duty plunger to flatten out the ground.'

Jane picked up her handbag and stood up abruptly. She already had her car keys hidden in her clenched fist. 'Thank you very much, and if you accompany me to the car park I'll give you the money. I would also appreciate it if you kept this to yourselves.'

McGregor pushed his chair back and gave another of his guttural laughs.

Jane had to squeeze past his nephew, who was draining his pint. She felt uneasy as the big man's hand rested in the small of her back as they walked out of the snug bar, through the main bar and out to the car park.

By the time Jane had opened her driver's door, McGregor's nephew had joined him, and they both stood watching her. Leaning over to the glove compartment, she took out the envelope and put it into his outstretched hand. She had the ignition key in, reaching out to close the car door as McGregor checked the cash, but his nephew still had one hand on the top of the door.

'Just a word of warning, guys. After your information we'll be over at the courtyard, so I wouldn't try getting there before us.' She laughed uneasily, and then relaxed a little as McGregor's nephew started to close the driver's door.

'Is there any reward?' he asked, grinning.

'I'll let you know.'

McGregor pushed his nephew aside, leaning in towards her.

'If you have to dig it up, let them know we'd be the best men for the job.'

He shut the door, stepping back as Jane turned on the ignition and reversed out of the parking slot. He gave her an all-clear gesture to drive out. Jane raised her hand to wave her thanks, relief washing over her that she'd managed to get away from the pair of them unscathed.

Now she just had to hope the rest of her plan would work.

Chapter Twenty-Four

Jane pasted her new information onto her board, and then sat back to see if she had missed anything out. Satisfied, she carefully rolled it up into a long cardboard tube, then put a packet of Blu-Tack, Sellotape and drawing pins into a box. The photographs she put into a hard-backed envelope. She placed everything on the small hall table, along with her briefcase, ready for when she left in the morning.

After taking a shower she put her clothes into a laundry basket, realising she had been perspiring a lot during her meeting with the McGregors.

Pam arrived just before four o'clock, carrying a pastry box and a bottle of wine. She had put on weight since Jane had last seen her, and after removing her coat, quickly wagged her finger at her.

'Don't say it! I know, I've put on about six pounds, so the pastries are for you, but I'll have a glass of wine. You look as if you've lost weight though. My God, has your hair grown! I think we should get cracking on the tint and cut – I don't want to have to leave mid-way to collect the boys. Good – you're in your dressing gown so we can get started right away.'

As usual, Pam hardly drew breath, but Jane knew it was partly embarrassment because she'd asked herself round. She continued talking non-stop while she looked around the kitchen and then followed Jane up the stairs, loudly admiring the wallpaper even though she'd been given a tour months before.

They went into the bathroom and Pam took out all her equipment from a large plastic bag, while Jane sat on a stool with a plastic cape around her shoulders. Mixing up the tint in a tin bowl, Pam peered at the colour on the box and swore. 'Shit, I've brought the wrong one. It'll be slightly blonder, but you know, your hair looks as if it could do with a bit of a lift. How much will you want off?'

'Not a lot . . . you cut it quite recently . . . maybe just an inch and a half.'

Pam focused on brushing in the tint, separating the strands with bright pink hair grips, but it didn't take her long to ask what had happened with Eddie.

'Mum told me you'd parted company. That's so sad, he seemed a really nice bloke. And after the brilliant job he did on the house. It must be worth a packet.'

'Yes, he was special, but you know, we sort of just grew out of each other.'

'So, it was all amicable, was it?'

'Yes. I miss him, obviously.'

'So how did he feel about the pregnancy?'

'To be honest, Pam, we'd already separated, and I didn't even know I was pregnant. I thought it was my appendix. I was lucky to get to the hospital in time as it could have been really serious if it had been left any longer.'

'So can you still get pregnant?'

'Yes. Are you sure this tint is not going to make it too blonde? It's a bit Diana Dors on the box.'

'No, it'll be fine, it's not that much lighter. So how are you coping with it at work?'

'I've just had a few days off; it's not as if it was major surgery, and I've said it was a grumbling appendix so I don't get asked too many questions. I'm going back tomorrow. Ow, this is stinging a bit, Pam.'

'OK, I'll not leave it on too long, then after a wash I'll cut it – you've got lots of split ends, you know.'

'OK. So how is everything with you?'

'Same as usual. Could do with more work on the carpentry side, but the salon is doing very well. I've actually hired a new colourist as it's never been my forte. He's very camp, always has me in stitches, and the clients love him.'

'How are the boys?'

Pam rolled her eyes. 'Teenagers, so a nightmare. I'm living with two massive hoarders. I never even clean their bedrooms now, just let the junk pile up, and you know, their ruddy sneakers cost a fortune as their feet seem to grow so fast.'

Pam kept up a running commentary about her two sons as she washed Jane's hair over the bathtub using the attached shower spray. She used a lot of perfumed conditioner, then two rinses before wrapping her hair in a white bath towel. Pam stood behind her as Jane sat on the stool facing the mirror in front of the wash basin rubbing her wet hair dry, ready to begin the cut.

'We have a lot of clients wanting to go red like Fergie now, you know.'

'Who?'

'Sarah Ferguson, the girl marrying Prince Andrew. She's got lovely natural curly auburn hair.' Pam removed the towels.

'Good God, Pam, it's very blonde! Maybe I should just have had highlights.'

'Rubbish! But if you like, next time come into the salon and I'll get Clive to do highlights and maybe take it down a tone or two.'

Pam combed out the wet hair, and then parted it down the centre to begin cutting. It was more than Jane wanted, but she worked so fast it was all over before Jane could stop her.

'It'll just have a light curl, and I'll blow-dry it so it'll get some body. I think the colour is really nice.'

They went into the bedroom and Pam plugged in her hairdryer while Jane sat at her dressing table. Five minutes later, Pam stood back to admire her work.

'There! You look fantastic, Jane. I don't care what you say, going that bit blonder really suits you.'

Jane smiled and nodded. She knew she would have to flatten the bouffant and it was too blonde, but she wasn't going to say anything.

They went into the kitchen, had a glass of wine and, despite saying she wouldn't, Pam managed to eat two chocolate eclairs, her excuse being she didn't want to drink and drive and it would soak up the alcohol.

After making sure she'd collected all her equipment, Pam pulled Jane into a hug. 'You know, we should do this more often. I've not even asked about how you are doing at work. I mean, are you investigating any big murders or serious crimes?'

'No, it's mostly a bit boring, nothing very serious.'

'Well, they will be very impressed with your glamorous new hairstyle. Anybody there fanciable?'

Jane laughed. 'No, nobody. Give everyone my love.'

She opened the door. Pam turned on the doorstep, suddenly serious. 'I was really worried about you, you know. But I wanted to tell you I know someone who had an ectopic pregnancy, and that she went on to have two kids, just in case you were worried.'

Jane smiled. 'Well, let's hope I can find someone else to have them with. As Mum would say, sooner rather than later!' Watching her sister hurry off towards her ancient Volvo estate, Jane suddenly felt quite emotional. They did care about each other, but they were so different. She hadn't told Pam about her disappointment being at Bromley station, her sadness about the way she had split from Eddie or what she really felt about the non-pregnancy, let alone her session with Vera James. She felt very alone.

Locking the front door and turning to head up the stairs, she paused to check everything she had put out for the following morning. She laid a hand on the envelope of photographs and then caught her reflection in the mirror above the table.

'Bloody hell, Pam, it really is too blonde.'

Chapter Twenty-Five

The next morning Jane dressed in one of her sharpest suits. She was at the station before eight, setting up her work on a movable whiteboard. She then wheeled it to the back of the boardroom and draped a green sheet over it. She was just leaving when two uniforms came in to arrange the chairs for the morning's briefing.

'Just leave that where it is, please,' Jane said as she walked out. She headed up to the canteen and was embarrassed to have all the canteen ladies admire her hair, although she had to admit the attention was nice.

Stanley arrived just as she was finishing her poached egg and toast. 'Sorry I haven't been in contact. Miss Phillips told me you were recuperating at your parents' place. Did they take it out?'

'It was just grumbling, Stanley, so I've still got it, for the moment anyway.'

'Yeah, I had mine out years ago. Can I get you another cup of coffee?'

'No thanks, I'm just about to go and check what's on my desk.'

He started to walk off, then turned back to look at her. 'Have you done something different to your hair? Blonder? Very glamorous.'

'Thank you.'

Jane left the canteen and went into the incident room. She checked her desk for any urgent memos or reports she needed to review, but there was nothing. She then looked over the incident room crime reports in the crime binder and then checked the office message book for any messages for her, noting how much work had been recorded for the time she had been absent. Clearly the hostage incident had taken up a lot of their time, but the drug squad were now handling the investigation.

Miss Phillips announced that the morning briefing was about to start and everyone needed to attend. The young, uniformed officers were quick to leave their desks, along with the probationers, and Jane followed behind. DCI Hutton swept in and sat down.

'Right, let's get started.'

For twenty minutes, Hutton went through the latest developments in the drug gang case, with Stanley being tasked with bringing in the grandmother who'd been one of the hostages for questioning: she was now suspected of allowing her flat to be used to stash the drugs.

Hutton checked her watch and closed her notebook.

'Unless anyone has anything further, I'm going to cut the meeting short.'

Jane stood up. 'There's something I'd like to bring to your attention, ma'am.'

Hutton frowned as Jane walked around the table to the back of the room, then wheeled her board round to the front.

'Please don't tell me this is connected to the assault at Clarendon Court,' Hutton said curtly.

'No, not exactly,' Jane said, 'but there is a connection.'

'So can I release anyone here that has not been involved in that enquiry?' Hutton asked.

'Yes, what is important is that you are made aware of my information.'

Officers started filing out, leaving plain clothes and detectives along with DI Stanley. Jane uncovered her board.

Hutton angled her chair to face the board. 'All right, Jane, you have our attention.'

Jane pointed to the board with a chopstick. 'Firstly, you can see my drawing of the courtyard. We have the two houses facing Mr Caplan's property, and these two at the side belonging to Martin Boon and the Larssons. The entire black area covering the courtyard is where the tarmac was laid.'

Jane next used her chopstick to point out the photograph of Georgina Larsson.

'This is the young teenage daughter of Mr and Mrs Larsson. Next is the photograph of Sebastian Martinez. He is the teenage son of Angelica Martinez, who was Victor Hoffman's wife.' Jane knew she had to cut to the chase, as she could feel Hutton's impatience mounting. She quickened her pace as she explained the Hoffmans' financial situation and how the Larssons came to own the courtyard.

'Her parents discovered that fifteen-year-old Georgina was having a relationship with Sebastian. They threatened to have him arrested for sexually abusing their underage daughter. As a result, Sebastian was sent off to Mexico. Shortly afterwards, Hoffman sold the courtyard to the Larssons. The Hoffmans subsequently sold the property to the Caplans and Mr Hoffman returned to live in Berlin. Sebastian's mother remained in the area, hoping to see her son as he had written to say he was coming home.'

Hutton sighed and looked at her watch. Jane knew she had to get her attention in the next minute or she was going to walk out.

'Georgina Larsson was heartbroken, but then discovered she was pregnant. Not allowed to contact or receive any letters from Sebastian, she used her friend who lived in this house to receive his letters and cards. This young girl is called Kathleen and knew that Georgina was pregnant. She also received a postcard from Sebastian to say he was on his way home. Georgina never saw the card because on 14th March four years ago, she was diagnosed with abdominal sepsis, rushed to St Thomas' Hospital and died on 15th March. It is possible she'd had an illegal abortion or a miscarriage.'

Jane now slowly withdrew the black section on the board depicting the tarmac.

'This tarmac was not laid until after the Larssons had organised their daughter's funeral. The workmen, they were ordered to stop work to allow the hearse and funeral cars to drive in and out of the courtyard. By this time the courtyard was in a very bad state.'

Stanley sighed, clearly fed up with hearing about the courtyard. Hutton had started drumming her fingers on the table.

Jane knew she had to get a reaction from them. 'I believe that Sebastian Martinez did return to see Georgina, but not a single witness has seen or heard from him. Sebastian disappeared off the face of the earth. I believe he was murdered, and I am certain he's buried in that bloody courtyard. I just know it. Those two crosses mark where I think he could have been . . .'

Hutton leaned back in her chair and muttered quietly, 'Oh, Christ.'

'What about the medium, Jane, you going to bring that up?' Stanley said.

As Hutton turned towards him with a questioning expression, Stanley put both hands in the air.

'I'm not saying anything, just that the boy's mother has been visiting one all this time, hoping she can tell her where he is.'

Hutton pushed back her chair and snatched up her notebook. 'I think Inspector Tennison has given us all a very entertaining session which I need to discuss with her. In the meantime, we have some more serious cases that require our immediate attention. That's it, everyone.'

'Entertaining!' Jane snapped angrily.

Hutton glared at her. 'Jane, I want you in my office in ten minutes. Thank you for your time, everyone.'

Hutton walked out. A few officers gathered around Jane's board, looking at the photographs, clearly trying to show they were interested. Jane went up to Stanley and leaned in close.

'Fuck you, Stanley.'

She walked out and hurried to the ladies' where she splashed cold water on her face. As she dragged on the roller towel to dry her face, she smudged her eye make-up, making her look owlish.

She sat on one of the toilets, still trying to calm herself down, then after a few minutes returned to the boardroom, collected her handbag and walked outside to the car park. She opened a new packet of cigarettes and sat on a low wall smoking one after another.

Jane could feel the tension when she returned to her desk, with everyone avoiding eye contact. Stanley's desk was empty, and after a few moments she decided to go into the boardroom and collect her board and all the photographs and documents. As she was passing Hutton's office, the door opened and Miss Phillips walked out. She indicated for Jane to go in, standing to one side and holding the door open.

DCI Hutton was signing documents.

'Give me two minutes.' She flicked through the pages before stacking them like a pack of cards and handing them to Miss Phillips, who'd remained hovering at her desk. 'I want these delivered this afternoon.' Miss Phillips left, closing the door behind her.

'Right, we need to have a talk about your performance this morning. You really seem to have a thing about burial sites, don't you? First uncovering the coffin with the body of a nun, then the newborn child found in an air-raid shelter.'

Jane pursed her lips at the mention of these previous cases, wanting to interrupt but maintaining her control.

Hutton picked up a silver letter opener. 'So now we have yet another Inspector Tennison investigation into a possible burial beneath a residential estate's courtyard. I gathered from your presentation this morning that it is entirely based on your suspicions rather than any actual evidence, and clearly you have become emotionally involved.' She put the letter opener down and her voice softened. 'Look, Jane, I can see you've put a lot of work into this, but still all you've got is speculation. It's simply not enough.'

Jane swallowed. 'I believe if we were able to obtain thermal imaging from the courtyard, it would prove that this is more than just speculation.'

Hutton shook her head. 'I don't know what planet you're on, Jane, but we do not have thermal imaging equipment at our disposal at the Met and are very unlikely to have access to it for many years. Nor would I, at this stage, agree to it being brought in, even if we did have it. You have no witnesses to a crime, in fact no evidence whatsoever that this young man is dead. He has never been reported missing. He may have returned from Mexico to the UK, but he could easily have travelled abroad to God knows where. I honestly think you are dramatising the situation like some sort of Romeo and Juliet story. I am advising you very seriously to shelve this enquiry, which, I should add, you have been pursuing without my permission.'

Jane felt battered, but wasn't going to give up.

'Nobody has seen or heard from him, ma'am. His mother has waited years for him, afraid to leave the area in case he can't find her. Then we have the Larssons not allowing anyone to park in the courtyard and using Martin Boon to assault David Caplan so he wouldn't dig it up.'

'Jane, I am fully aware of that situation.'

'So why would they do all that unless they were involved in Sebastian Martinez's death?'

Hutton took a deep breath, running a finger up and down the paper knife as if she would dearly like to stab it into her desk. She carefully placed the knife down and clasped her hands together.

'You have no evidence the young man is dead. I wasn't going to bring this up because I was hoping you would listen to reason. But I am aware that some of your so-called information has come from a medium . . .'

Before she could finish, Jane stood up angrily and leaned against Hutton's desk.

'I suppose Inspector Stanley has been telling you stories . . .'

'*Sit down*! Sit down, Jane, before you say something that you will regret. Whether or not I believe in mediums is neither here nor there, but you have to realise that if it was ever to get out that you based your suspicions on the words of a medium . . .'

Jane bowed her head, and then took a deep breath. She spoke very quietly.

'She said she had the taste of blood in her mouth. Sebastian was murdered.'

Hutton slowly pushed back her desk chair. 'Wise up, Jane. Don't make me take disciplinary action. We have a lot of work on right now, and I will need you to oversee the forthcoming trials.'

Jane felt there was nothing more she could say. Hutton had made it obvious the meeting was over and just wanted her out of her office. She nodded as she walked out, closing the door firmly behind her.

Not wanting to talk to anyone in the incident room, Jane went to the boardroom to pack up everything she had brought that morning. She turned as DC Burrows tapped lightly before entering and then stood looking slightly embarrassed.

'Did you want something?' she asked curtly.

'Not really. I just wanted to tell you that I believe you. I don't know how you intend taking it further, but I wish I had spoken up.'

She sighed. 'Well, thank you for that, Bill, but it's finished. I have strict instructions to discontinue the investigation.'

He nodded, hesitating a moment before walking out. By the time Jane had loaded everything into the boot of her car, she had calmed down, but felt completely defeated. She had not seen Stanley, and wasn't sure she could face him. It was obvious he'd had words with DCI Hutton about Vera James before Jane's presentation. But why? Not so long ago, he'd been all for ripping up the tarmac to see if Sebastian's body was there.

Jane returned to the incident room and began the laborious task of checking through statements and legal documents attached to the forthcoming trials of the boys involved in the drug bust. Instead of going to the canteen for lunch, she drove herself to the nearest

McDonald's drive-thru and ate her cheeseburger and chips in her car. When she got back to the station car park, a white Range Rover was parked in her space. She was about to get out and confront the driver when the same handsome man came running towards her. He bent down to her window.

'My apologies. I'm leaving straightaway.'

Jane watched as he backed out and then waved as he drove out of the car park. She keyed into the staff entrance door and went down the corridor towards the cloakrooms as she could smell burger and chips on her fingers. Glancing in the mirror, she was yet again taken aback by how blonde her hair was. She noticed she still had dark rings beneath her eyes where she had washed her face earlier.

After washing her face again with the awful soap from the dispenser, she rubbed it dry with the roller towel, and then combed her hair furiously as if it might tone down the colour. Returning to the incident room, she got back down to her paperwork, determined not to give Hutton any further reason to complain about her.

Chapter Twenty-Six

It was coming up to lunchtime when the desk sergeant called through to ask Jane if she would take a call from Alice Caplan.

'We've accepted an offer on the house,' she told her.

'That's great. Congratulations,' Jane said, trying to sound enthusiastic.

'The thing is, it's all happening rather quickly, so I've been sorting things out, deciding what to take and what to leave, and I found a load of photographs of Sebastian Hoffman's bedroom which must have been taken for the 'before and after' album. I wondered if you were still interested in seeing them.'

Jane was out of the office within moments of ending the call. She felt bad, knowing that the discovery of a body buried near their property might put an end to the sale of their house, but she also knew she couldn't let it lie.

Alice Caplan opened the front door with a smile, and Jane handed her a bunch of flowers she'd bought from a nearby petrol station.

'Oh, that's so sweet of you. Come in, it'll be a good excuse for me to stop working. I am collecting bundles of things to give to the charity shops.'

Mrs Caplan led Jane through into the kitchen and made a pot of coffee. Buster could be heard barking somewhere in the background.

'The photographs are in that big manila envelope on the table.'

Jane opened the envelope and emptied out a pile of photographs, all of Sebastian's bedroom, taken from different angles.

'The fireplace had lovely pine designs from the twenties, but it had so many coats of awful paint over it, it took forever to clean it up.'

Alice put Jane's coffee down on the table as Jane leafed through the photographs.

Jane took the photographs she wanted and put them into her briefcase, then put the others back into the envelope. She was eager to finish her coffee and leave, but felt she ought to make conversation for a few minutes.

'The house is certainly looking amazing now. You've obviously put in a tremendous amount of work. And you clearly know what you're doing when it comes to interior decoration.'

Mrs Caplan laughed. 'Well, it was sometimes hard work persuading David not to cut corners. He has such a temper, and can fly into absolute rages about my overspending!'

Jane smiled as she finished her coffee, but at the same time she took a mental note of what Mrs Caplan had just let slip. They had appeared to be the perfect couple, and she'd seen no hint of David Caplan's temper.

'I hope all goes well with the sale, and thank you again. I've taken the photographs I need, but I will of course return them.'

'Oh, don't bother, they were just extras. All the good ones are in the album.'

Mrs Caplan walked Jane to the front door and was still standing there, smiling and waving, as Jane drove out. So much for the perfect couple, Jane thought.

Instead of driving back to the station, Jane returned home. She took out the photographs and laid them out on the kitchen table. Now that she looked at them closely, they were actually quite disturbing, with the words THIS IS THE END MY BEAUTIFUL FRIEND scrawled over and over again in thick, black letters on the walls. There were images of tombstones, death's heads, devil faces in dark red, skeleton faces with hideous female lips. But what really had Jane's heart racing was the wax doll lying on the floor by the big double bed. It was dressed in a suit with a collar and tie and had a noose around its neck. Next to it was a naked blonde-haired doll with what looked like splashes of red paint on its chest and stomach.

Jane felt a chill as she gathered up the photographs. Had Sebastian been some sort of devil-worshipper? Had he been involved in aborting Georgina's baby?

She grabbed the envelope and got back in her car, knowing exactly who she needed to talk to to find out what it all meant.

Jane parked behind Sandra's VW, hurried up the path and rang the doorbell.

'I need a consultation with Vera. It's very urgent,' Jane told Sandra when she opened the door.

'You can't. She's resting,' Sandra said with a frown.

'I just need to show her some photographs. It's really important, Sandra. Please,' Jane persisted.

'Wait here,' Sandra said, closing the door.

Ten minutes later, Jane was about to press the bell again when the door opened.

'She can give you ten minutes, and then you will have to leave,' Sandra told her.

Jane was ushered into the hallway and up to Vera's room. She knocked on the door. Vera was wearing the same kaftan and had a tray of food on her card table. She glanced towards Jane as she wiped her mouth with a napkin.

'This was awful, some takeaway which I can't eat, noodles swamped in some sweet sauce. I don't know where she orders this rubbish from.'

Vera bent down and placed her tray of food beside her as she gestured for Jane to sit.

'I've got a session tonight and I can't tire myself out, so you'll have to be quick. I don't think you have any idea what these sessions take out of me.'

Jane opened the envelope of photographs and laid them out. Vera seemed completely uninterested.

'What do you want me to do with these?'

'Explain what they mean. They're from Sebastian Martinez's bedroom.'

'Lovey, I am a medium, not a fortune-teller. What do you want me to do?'

'I am just very concerned. It all looks like some kind of devil worship. They freaked me out.'

'Oh, these are from Angelica's son? Let me get my glasses and have a proper look.'

Jane waited as Vera put on her glasses and selected one photograph after another, peering at each intently before putting them down. She then placed a couple to one side and looked at Jane.

'Well, I recognise all the Jim Morrison lyrics. I was quite a fan of his many moons ago. The poor bloke was an addict, but he could write poetry. Sebastian was obviously a fan, and some of the other writing is Sebastian spelled backwards. Then there are all the skulls, which I think are to do with the Mexican Day of the Dead – it's like a big holiday celebrating the dead.' She paused. 'Are you wearing a flowery perfume?'

Jane shook her head. 'No.'

'Odd smell, can't say what, maybe lilac.'

Vera tapped a photograph with her finger. 'This skull, he's made it with eggshells. I know Angelica is from Mexico and her first husband died, so that skull would be a sort of celebration of his passing. Sebastian might have been taken to a celebration as a child, or his mother encouraged him to remember his father in this way. You'd have to ask her. They all dance and dress up as skeletons and some are in devils' capes and masks. It's nothing to do with Satanism. I just think this boy is Mexican and has embraced the memory of his father.'

'What about the dolls?'

'Well, I'd say he hated his adoptive father and wanted him out of his life, dead or alive. I know his mother loathed the man, so she might have encouraged it.'

'What about the other doll, the girl covered in blood?'

Vera shrugged. 'I don't think he meant her any harm. This is just a tormented teenager in love. You know, not all of the writing was done by the same person. Some of it's much smaller and neater.'

Vera brought the photograph close to her face as she held onto her glasses. Licking her lips, she read aloud.

'"Thou lovest me", and the next line . . .'

She squinted, peering through her broken glasses.

'"Too much, as I loved thee, we were not made,
To torture thus each other, though it were
The deadliest sin to love as we have loved."'

Vera put the photograph down.

'Byron, and don't think I'm a literary genius: it's written underneath, and in even smaller writing is another name, Georg . . . I can't see.'

'Georgina,' Jane said quietly.

Vera gathered up the photographs, putting them in a neat pile before handing them back to Jane.

'I am not going to charge you for this session, love. Truth be told, I feel sorry for you because I haven't given you what you wanted to hear, which I think was me telling you that this boy was dangerous and evil, when in reality he was just a screwed-up teenager who was sent packing by a man he detested, his stepfather, after whatever love he found with that young girl was taken away from him. I've heard enough about him from Angelica to know he was abusive and never accepted the poor kid.'

Jane was taken aback when Vera leaned across the table and grabbed hold of her hand.

'You have to let this go, love, you are taking more interest than is good for you, I can feel it. If you don't let it go it will consume you, because you're trying to distract yourself from what is happening in your own life. Go home, and please don't bother me again, dear, because I can't help you.'

Jane could feel herself getting emotional. 'I am here because of what you told me, that you could taste blood.'

Vera shook her head. 'Oh, for God's sake, I've said a lot of things that maybe I shouldn't have, and you have taken them literally.'

'But you said you were certain he was dead.'

Vera grabbed the edge of the card table to push herself up. She glared angrily at Jane. 'I will not be a part of this obsession of yours, and I refuse to have any further meetings with you. So don't try and see me again. I mean it, love, let this go and sort yourself out.'

Jane didn't say another word. She put the envelope in her briefcase and walked out, passing Sandra by the front door. She gave her a ten-pound note, then hurried to her car, eager to get home.

Sandra walked in and held up the ten-pound note.

Vera frowned. 'Should have charged her a hell of a lot more than that, and from now on, Sandra, you never let that woman back in here again.' She sank back in her chair, the taste of blood filling her mouth. 'And don't you ever order from that Chinese takeaway again. I feel sick to my stomach.'

On the way home, Jane had clenched the steering wheel so tightly her knuckles were white, and she was so pent up and angry she dropped her door keys before she could unlock the front door, kicking it hard to slam behind her. She went into the kitchen and took a bottle of vodka from the fridge, pouring a large measure into a glass before gulping it down. She then hurled the glass into the sink, where it shattered. She had never felt such rage, banging her way up the stairs and then kicking open her bedroom door. Furious with Vera and her dismissal of the photographs, she stood staring at her reflection in her dressing-table mirror. The marks left on the carpet from where Eddie had fixed up his TV made her want to scream.

She took a deep breath and then did just that, letting out a howl which kept on and on as she looked at herself. Eventually she flopped onto her bed, emptied of emotion. First, she went over in her mind how she had mismanaged the situation with Eddie, how she would have really liked to face him out, even slap him for his betrayal and lies. Then she thought how much she would like to confront that tweeting-voiced Caroline: she had certainly moved fast. She closed her eyes, making herself face the truth that it had stopped working between them some time ago; she had not wanted to sell her house and if she was honest with herself, she had been hesitant about marrying him. She sat up, looking around the bedroom.

Standing by the open doors of her wardrobe, looking at the few empty hangers where his clothes had been, she swished her clothes along the rail. It was as if he had never lived there – but he had, and she had been pregnant with his child. For the first time, Jane allowed herself to really accept the loss, and she cried for a while, a different emotion to her tears of anger because the truth was it had been in many ways a relief.

Sitting on the edge of the bed, she wondered how Eddie would have reacted if she had told him. She shook her head, trying to fathom how she could have been so blind to what was happening. She had spent more time thinking about Angelica's missing son than what was going on right under her nose. She thought about how many hours she had spent on the ridiculous situation with the warring neighbours, and how she had been wrong about the Caplans as being the perfect couple. At no time had she even considered that David Caplan was guilty, but now after Alice had said her husband had a short fuse and a nasty temper, she thought it was perfectly possible he had swung that spade with the intention of harming Martin Boon.

Jane forced herself to accept that she had become dangerously obsessed with Angelica Martinez and her missing son, that perhaps DCI Hutton was right. She questioned the way her theories had come to dominate her every waking hour, and accepted that it was to avoid facing the reality of her failing relationship with Eddie.

Vera had told her to let it go, and now she had let all her emotions out and was calm again, she decided that was exactly what she was going to do. She undressed, preparing to take a shower, and thought about calling Eddie, not to have a showdown, but an adult conversation.

She laughed suddenly, surprising herself.

'Maybe I'll ask him to lay down a new carpet!'

Chapter Twenty-Seven

Jane had ordered a Chinese takeaway and was opening the cartons in the kitchen in her pyjamas. She had cleared away the shards of glass in the sink and found a half-bottle of Chablis open in the fridge. It tasted as if the cap had been unscrewed for some time, but she poured herself a glass anyway. As she munched some prawn crackers she heard high-pitched barking and Gerry calling for Wilma.

The barking eventually stopped and Jane tucked into her sweet and sour chicken and fried rice. It was very sweet, and after eating only a small portion, she tipped the remainder into the bin.

The barking started up again as she was about to leave the kitchen, and this time she could hear Gerry shouting '*Drop it!*' Jane opened the backdoor and walked over. Wilma was hurtling around their garden like a miniature greyhound, with a woollen sock in her mouth, circling the small patch of lawn as if it was a running track. Gerry was doing his best to catch her, but she was too quick for him. Seeing Jane, Gerry turned and grinned.

'It's one of my best pure wool socks!'

Wilma, having briefly lost Gerry's attention, dropped the sock and padded towards Jane. Panting, her tongue hanging out, she stood on her hind legs, her sharp nose just level with the top of the fence and her tiny front paws on the edge.

'Well, aren't you looking fit and healthy?' Jane said, stroking her soft ears.

Gerry grabbed the sock. 'She's a right little minx. If I don't get my newspaper in the morning before she does, she's shredded it. Vi's back to knitting again . . . little coats for our baby girl.'

Jane smiled. 'That's good. Please give her my love.'

'Oh, I will. To be honest with you, it's like the before and after. Wilma's given her a new lease of life. She's often still unsure who I am, but she loves our little girl.'

Gerry and Wilma went back into their house. Jane locked the front and back doors and was heading up the stairs when she stopped midway, close to the print she had straightened that morning. It might have been Gerry saying 'before and after' that triggered the memory, but Martin Boon's wife's wishy-washy watercolour paintings, the ones in their awful drawing room, were of gardens. And she had been surprised to see that the Larssons also had two; in fact, she recalled mentioning it to Mrs Larsson.

Turning on her bedroom lights, she sat on the edge of her bed. The Larssons' were watercolour paintings of the courtyard before and after the tarmac had been laid. Jane tried hard to recall if one also showed the potholes. She remembered it was a strange yellowish-orange colour and showed a broken fence. She hit the wall with the flat of her hand. 'Stop it, just bloody stop this right now.'

But hard as she tried to stop it, Jane's mind followed its own train of thought: she recalled the impressive kitchen and the exceptionally well-built garden shed Mrs Boon used for working on her paintings. She was getting money from somewhere. Could it be that Martin Boon was blackmailing the Larssons?

Unable to sleep, she went downstairs to the kitchen, taking her pack of cigarettes from her handbag, then fetching the small bottle of brandy and pouring herself a good measure. She took a mouthful and coughed as it hit the back of her throat. She lit her cigarette from the gas stove and put the packet back in her handbag and found the beermat. She inhaled deeply, leaving the cigarette in her mouth as she held the stained beermat with the scribbled drawing made by McGregor. Did the cross mark the spot where he thought the stolen items she'd made up could have been buried? She couldn't remember.

Finishing her brandy and lighting another cigarette from the butt of the old one, she left the beermat on the kitchen table. She was cleaning her teeth in the bathroom, ready to go back to bed, when the phone rang.

'Jane? This is DCI Hutton.'

'Oh, good evening, I'm sorry I skived off a bit early, but my mind's a lot clearer for having had a bit of a break.'

'It's not about that. I'm on my way to Clarendon Court. We got a 999 call from Mr Bellamy, owner of one of the new builds. It appears two thugs were digging up the courtyard and all hell's broken loose. When the squad car and uniform got there, they'd already done a runner, and I'm not surprised after what they dug up.'

The ground felt as if it was shifting beneath Jane's feet, and she had to gasp for breath. 'What . . . ?'

'See for yourself, Jane. Just get over there.'

Wearing an old tracksuit, Jane chewed gum furiously as she drove, hoping it would mask the smell of alcohol when she got to the site. At eleven thirty the streets were almost empty. Driving into Clarendon Court, she parked up behind several squad cars, an ambulance, and officers' personal vehicles. A forensic tent had been erected on the courtyard inside a large area cordoned off with yellow crime-scene tape. The Caplans had the yellow tape crossed over their new electric gate.

Jane went to the forensic wagon to get a protective suit, over-shoes, mask and gloves. She had seen Stanley's car and presumed he would be inside the tent. By the time she was suited and booted, more uniformed officers had been brought in to keep curious onlookers at bay. Mrs Bellamy was standing outside her front door wearing a dressing gown and slippers, offering to make tea and coffee. Jane found DC Burrows, who had interviewed Mr Bellamy, and listened as he repeated the gist. He had described the smallish digger driven by one of the men. The machine had been brought into the area on a low-loader truck. As he waited for the police, he saw the two men had been bent over something and had then put the machine back onto the loader and driven out, damaging one of the fences in their haste. He was unsure if they had made off because the police sirens could be heard.

Jane entered the forensic tent. One forensic officer was kneeling over the hole. They were taking great care checking through the rubble, collecting samples and bagging them. Placed to one side was what looked like an old sack, partly open at one end and wrapped with duct tape. It looked as if it had been tied with a cord, which was placed beside it. There was a slash down the side of the sack, and Jane could see long strands of dark hair clogged with soil. Stanley ducked inside the tent.

'Have you had a look inside the sack? I've not let anybody touch it; the blokes must have had heart failure when they tried to open it. They used a knife to slit the duct tape, saw the hair and freaked out, driving off just before the first patrol car got here. We might get lucky if Mr Bellamy is correct and it was a digger. He thought it might have been one called Priestman, so we can run some checks on any local firm using one. That's an expensive piece of machinery, so shouldn't be too hard to trace.'

Jane didn't answer. She bent down and eased back the sacking with a pencil and looked inside. Despite the fact that it was partly bound with duct tape, there was no doubt it was a human head in an advanced state of decay. She stood up as a forensics officer carrying a large plastic container and evidence bag walked into the tent.

'What are you going to do with it?' Stanley asked.

'Take it to the mortuary for examination,' he said. 'We can't touch it here.'

Jane watched as they put the sack into the evidence bag and then placed it in the plastic container. DC Burrows looked in, asking if anyone wanted a tea or coffee because Mrs Bellamy was offering to bring over a tray.

'I'll have a tea,' Stanley said.

Jane shook her head. 'Not for me. I think I need some air.' She walked out and Burrows followed.

'What about the other neighbours?' She gestured over to the Larssons' house.

'They got home from the theatre after the police had arrived. Martin Boon apparently tried to get close to where the action was, but the uniforms told him to go back indoors.'

Stanley joined them. 'They're bringing in more officers to check the surrounding area for body parts. Hutton will be here soon – this is going to be a long-drawn-out night. You sure you don't want a cup of tea, Jane?'

'No. I'll have to bite my tongue from saying I effing told you so if I see her, so I'm going to go to the mortuary.'

'They won't be doing anything tonight,' Stanley said. 'You'll have to wait until the morning to even begin to identify her.'

'It's not female. It's Sebastian Martinez. He had long dark hair, Stanley, and I may be wrong, but I doubt they will find any further body parts.'

Stanley stared at her for a moment, then turned away as a uniformed officer carrying a tray with mugs of tea and coffee approached. While he helped himself to a mug of tea, spooning in sugar, Jane walked to her car. She was driving out of the courtyard just as DCI Hutton's car was turning in.

Jane decided that Stanley was probably right, and nothing could be accomplished at the mortuary until early morning. She went home, wanting to get some sleep, ready to watch the experts examining the head.

Lighting a cigarette in her kitchen, she picked up the beermat, tapping it on the edge of the table. She knew she had to square things with McGregor, and even though it was nearly two o'clock she went out and drove to the nearest telephone kiosk. His number rang for a long time before it was answered, and she put in the coins.

'Mr McGregor, this is Jane Tennison.'

'What?'

'You need to pay very careful attention to what I am going to say.'

'What?' he said again.

'Where were you tonight, between the hours of nine o'clock and ten?'

'I don't fucking believe this. Are you crazy?'

'No, it is imperative that you be honest with me. You could be arrested on a very serious charge, so I am calling you to make sure you are aware of what can happen within a few hours.'

She could hear his rasping, phlegmy breath. Eventually it dawned on him that she was serious.

'I was in the pub celebrating me sister-in-law's birthday.'

'Was your nephew with you?'

'Yes, he organised the male stripper. You satisfied?'

'You have witnesses for both of you being at the pub between nine and ten tonight?'

'Yes. Got home at midnight. What's this about?'

'Did you or your nephew – even though I warned you not to – tell anyone about our meeting regarding the tarmac?'

He coughed and cleared his throat but didn't answer, so she continued.

'I told you that there would be a police presence there, if you attempted to recover the stolen property.'

'I don't understand.'

'Two men attempted to dig up a section of the tarmac you laid at Clarendon Court.'

'OK . . .'

'So did you or your nephew tip someone off that there might be valuables stashed under the tarmac?'

'No.'

'Think about it, it's very serious.'

'I swear before God I never done. I mean, he gets drunk, he might have mentioned it, but I'll slap him around if he did.'

'Your alibis are very important because human remains were found in the exact location you described and marked on the beer-mat you gave me. So, I am warning you that you could be detained and questioned about a murder. Two men used a small portable digger described by a witness as a Priestman mini-digger.'

'Jesus Christ.'

'Do you own one of those?'

'No, I mean we sometimes hire in something for different jobs, you know.'

'So, you do not have this machine, or have had one stolen?'

'No, we just do tarmac jobs. I mean, I might have hired one at some time. I get a lot of gear stolen, you know, cos I have to hire a few alkies or ex-cons. I'm always reporting gear being nicked but I can't afford insurance nowadays.'

She could still hear his heavy breathing but remained silent.

'Have the blokes been arrested?'

'Not as yet. They managed to drive out before the police arrived.'

McGregor had another heavy coughing fit.

'I am going to hang up now, Mr McGregor. Let me remind you of how serious it could be if you are involved in any way. I cannot protect you and will deny not only having this call but ever having met you or your nephew.'

'I understand, thank you.'

'Goodnight.'

She took a deep breath as she replaced the receiver.

Jane drove home, knowing tomorrow was going to be a full-on day, more than likely followed by an all-nighter. She checked over all her notes, photographs and drawings that she had pinned up in the boardroom, then returned them to the boot of her car.

Lying in bed in the dark, she knew there was no point in trying to sleep.

Chapter Twenty-Eight

Jane was at the mortuary early the next morning, hoping that it would be one of the pathologists she had worked with previously, but by eight fifteen there was no sign of anyone at all. She had eaten a toasted crumpet at the nearest cafe, and was now sitting impatiently in one of the anterooms with a takeaway coffee and the morning paper. Just before nine she heard sounds of movement from the corridor, but it was only a cleaner starting to wash down the floors.

At nine fifteen Jane left the anteroom to go to the reception area. Finally there was someone behind the desk, but there was still no pathologist signed in, so Jane went to the nearest call box to ring the station. The desk duty sergeant put her through to DC Burrows.

'Where are you? Hutton's been trying to get hold of you all morning.'

'I am at the mortuary waiting for the pathologist to get here. As soon as they can give me some indication of the victim's identity, I will return to process the information.'

'We already had a call from them.'

'What?'

'Apparently it is going to take some time removing the duct tape from around the skull, so they are waiting for a mobile X-ray wagon.'

'Where is the mobile X-ray wagon?'

'I don't know.'

'Who is the pathologist?'

'Er, I think it was Mr . . . er . . . Chadra.'

'Thank you. Please pass on the message that I will be back at the station as soon as I've talked to the pathologist.'

Jane went to the reception desk but there was no one on duty. She exited the mortuary and walked past the car park into the gated yard where the ambulances would be parking up to bring in the bodies. The double gates were closed, and a sign said STAFF ONLY. She tried to open them, but they were stiff with rust. Suddenly a uniformed driver appeared on the other side of the gates and started pushing them open.

She showed him her ID. 'Is that the mobile X-ray unit?' she asked, nodding towards a large white van with blacked-out windows.

'Yes, ma'am, we are just off to our next location.'

Jane hurried over to the passenger door where a white-coated woman was checking over papers on a clipboard. Jane rapped on the window, holding up her ID.

'Excuse me. I am here regarding the head. I was told it might be with you.'

The woman lowered the window. 'We had to make a re-route as the pathologist was insistent that it had to be X-rayed before he could begin a post-mortem.'

'So where is it now?'

'They took it back into the mortuary.'

Jane stood back as they drove out of the yard, then hurried back to the mortuary. At the end of the corridor she saw a young, white-coated assistant with a face mask tucked under his chin standing outside the double entry doors. He was taking deep breaths through his nose and exhaling through his mouth.

'I am DI Jane Tennison. I'm here for the post-mortem of the head.'

'It's just started.'

She made as if to enter but he quickly grabbed her am. 'You can't go in without being gowned and masked. Get a nose clip if they have one available. I nearly threw up. The stench is horrific.'

'Who's doing the PM?'

'Aiden Chadra. Go down the corridor, fourth door on your right. There should be someone there who can give you what you'll need.'

As Jane hurried off, he fixed a nose clip and pulled up his mask before re-entering the mortuary.

Inside the mortuary, Aiden Chadra, wearing full protective clothing, and with a paper drawstring hat over his pale-blue turban, was examining the sacking the head was found in using a twelve-inch, stainless-steel prod with a slightly scooped end. His methodical probing finished, he gestured to the assistant Jane had seen earlier to place it in a plastic container. He then concentrated on the thick cord that had been used to tie the sack. This was then placed in a second plastic container.

He pulled down the microphone positioned above his head. His soft voice sounded muffled as he spoke through the white mask over his nose and mouth, noting items of interest for the forensics team. Jane entered and stood by the closing door. Chadra turned to acknowledge her with a nod. His dark eyes were unwelcoming as he rubbed his hands together in their tight surgical gloves.

'Detective Tennison, please come and stand to my left. I believe this young man warned you about the putrefaction, which is very pungent. I was informed that this victim has possibly been buried for some time.'

Jane nodded. 'Four years.'

'The X-rays show an intact skull, with no peripheral damage from when the sack was opened.'

He drew a larger plastic container towards him, revealing the head, bound with duct tape. Chadra pointed. 'In my opinion, unravelling the tape would be almost impossible as the sticky side has bonded with the tissue and now forms a hard shell. I'm going to begin where we have a four-inch sliced opening. You can see it's revealing long strands of black hair, by this time no longer attached to the skull but stuck firmly to the glue of the tape. There is an abundance of the same dark hair inside the shell as seen on the X-ray. The opening also released the stench and brown fluid that is still oozing out, and I'm afraid it'll get more pungent as I continue. The tape is also wrapped tightly around the stem of the neck, severed around the third vertebra. I do not see signs of congealed blood around the stem; what we have are thick, dark-brown stains from the disintegration of brain matter, skin and tissues. We might get more insight when I cut through the tape.'

Mr Chadra drew to his side a tray of instruments, including surgical knives and scissors. He picked out a lethal-looking blade. Although he was speaking towards the microphone, he spoke very quietly.

'Right, as our victim is face down, and because we already have a slit, I am simply going to gently begin to cut around the skull to hopefully remove the duct tape in two sections.'

Jane watched as Chadra began to slowly slice through the tough outer layer. He gestured for his assistant to use a pair of large tweezers to ease out more strands of hair as he proceeded. She noticed how small his hands were. Suddenly the stench became almost overpowering as thick fluids oozed out and Chadra paused as his assistant used a small jet spray to remove them, then went back to work, slicing through the hardened tape.

'Right, we now have the tape cut into two halves, and I will need you to help me in easing off the first section that encased the back of the skull.'

Together they slowly eased off one section, still clogged with decayed matter and hair, and placed it on a clean white sheet. Then he turned the skull over to reveal the second section. They could now see what remained of the head. There were no visible features. The slit of the mouth was tightly closed. Chadra used a spatula to ease it open to reveal the teeth.

'Ah, you should be able to compare with dental records; the teeth are in good condition and are not from an adult, but perhaps a young person.'

'Would DNA help identify the victim?'

'That procedure is still very much in its infancy, Detective, and I doubt with the putrefaction it would not be satisfactory, but perhaps an expert might be able to advise.'

Mr Chadra next examined the stub of the neck and concluded that decapitation had been accomplished by severing at the third vertebra. 'I will need more time to give a proper evaluation of the instrument used, but it had a serrated edge, like a saw.'

For the first time he glanced towards Jane. She was trying to keep her breathing steady, as she had felt like throwing up several times already.

'Do you want to ask me anything, Detective?'

'Can you tell me if it's male or female?'

'Not yet. I will arrange for a forensic odontologist to examine the teeth and do comparisons with any dental records you recover, so that might help us.'

'Thank you.'

Chadra nodded.

'Detective, come here, please.'

Jane moved to his side as he stepped away from the two halves of hardened tape he had removed from the skull. The section he had moved last was placed face down on the paper, and he had now turned it over.

'Look. Extraordinary . . .' he said softly.

She gasped. Imprinted into the shell of the duct tape was a face.

'As the victim's head had been bound so tightly, the facial features were imprinted on the tape before decay and putrefaction occurred, in effect making a perfect death mask,' he said.

Although Jane had only seen photographs of Sebastian Martinez, the high cheekbones and the widely spaced eyes made her certain.

'We will get a plaster cast made as soon as I have completed my tests,' Chadra said. 'It should give you a clear impression of the victim's face.'

Jane wanted to thank him again, but she had to get out. As soon as she was out of the room, she ran to the nearest ladies' toilets and threw up. She splashed her face with cold water until the nausea subsided, then hurried out into the fresh air.

Chapter Twenty-Nine

The incident room was full, with a buzz of anticipation. The chatter subsided when Jane walked in, heading towards her desk. She hung her jacket over the back of her chair and put her briefcase down, trying to steady her nerves.

DCI Hutton came out of her office and looked over.

'Can I have a word, Jane?'

Jane picked up her notebook and entered Hutton's office. As she closed the door, Hutton was speaking quietly into the phone. She nodded for Jane to stand by her desk.

'Yes, everything is fine. I'll call you later. Bye, darling.'

'I just got here from the mortuary and was about to write up my report,' Jane told her.

'Give me a quick update.'

Jane explained about the death mask.

Hutton's eyes widened. 'Wow, that's interesting. Any positive identification?'

'Not one I could be a hundred per cent about, but we will get a dental test done as soon as possible.'

Hutton leaned forwards in her chair. 'I think I owe you an apology. It may have been a coincidence that the tarmac was illegally dug up, but it nevertheless proves without doubt that your intuition was correct. I have decided that you will be the SIO and take over control of the ongoing investigation and . . .' Hutton smiled. 'I hope you still have that board you brought in. It should now be displayed in the main incident room.'

Jane tried not to grin. 'It's in the boot of my car, ma'am.'

'Good. That's all, apart from a second apology from me. Good work.'

'Thank you, ma'am.'

Jane hurried out to the car park and quickly took out everything she needed.

By the time she had returned to the incident room the word was out, and she received a round of applause from the assembled officers, who then helped her set up her board and arrange all the material. Standing in front of her handiwork, she gave a brief report of what had happened at the mortuary. SOCO had already handed in some photographs from the courtyard, including pictures of the head, and DC Burrows now pinned them up on the board.

'We'll see what the death mask tells us, but I'm also making enquiries about getting a facial reconstruction from the skull, though that may take months and be very costly. I have also asked about DNA testing, and I will ask Paul Lawrence to assist if possible.'

Jane picked up a black marker pen, moving to the second board that had been brought in to stand alongside hers. 'Right, I am going to list priority actions. First, ask Sebastian Martinez's mother for his dental records.'

Burrows raised his hand. 'Is it him?'

'We won't know for certain until we get a dental match. Next I want warrants issued to search the Larssons' and the Boons' properties. The items we're looking for will be two watercolour paintings in the Larssons' hallway. I also want the two similar paintings removed from Martin Boon's drawing room. Also, there would have been a lot of blood, so a diligent examination of carpets and bathrooms by forensic teams will be required. And, of course, we're still looking for the body. It could have been buried at either property. The decapitation was done with a serrated blade, probably some kind of saw, so we need to look for that. I doubt we'll find any clothing, but there might be luggage or possibly a musical instrument, maybe a guitar. It seems likely that Sebastian Martinez arrived from Mexico and went straight to see Georgina Larsson, so he would have had everything with him.'

She paused while the officers made notes.

'We don't have enough evidence to make any arrests, but until we do, we will need to maintain round-the-clock surveillance on the Larssons and the Boons.'

Jane couldn't think of anything further to add. 'Any questions?'

DC Burrows raised his hand.

'What about the men with the digger? Why did they pick that exact spot? They must have known the head was there. Shouldn't we be tracing them as an urgent priority?'

Jane nodded. 'I have obviously thought about that. During the installation of Mr Caplan's electric gates, there had been a spate of burglaries in the area. It is quite possible that some of the stolen property could have been buried while the work was going on, but then couldn't be retrieved when the tarmacking was finished. So, to answer your question, I think it unlikely that the men with the digger had anything to do with the death, and identifying them should be put on the back burner while we focus on more important avenues of investigation.'

By the time the room had settled, and Jane had allocated everyone their duties, it was lunchtime. She had decided that she would be the one to interview Angelica Martinez. She knew that she finished work at the care home at two, so hurried into the canteen to get a quick sandwich and coffee.

Returning to the incident room after giving herself a once-over in the ladies', combing her hair and retouching her make-up, she found it was almost empty as most of the officers were having lunch. Just a few probationary officers were still around. As she crossed to her desk to collect her bag, DI Stanley turned from the board.

'Congratulations. This all looks very impressive.'

'Thank you.'

'I just got back from court.'

'I hope it was productive.'

'Very.'

'Good. I'm going to interview Angelica Martinez now.'

'Is it her son?'

'I think so, so I thought I should be the one to talk to her.'

Stanley nodded. 'I've got another couple of days in court, and then I would appreciate being on your team.'

She hesitated for a moment, tempted to tell him where he could go. 'Fine. I would appreciate your input.' She walked out.

Stanley remained standing by the board, carefully looking over the extraordinary work that Jane had done. He paused by the section concerning the digger. He had spoken to Mr Bellamy and taken his statement. Now DC Burrows had added the update, confirming that they had not yet traced the two men who had dug up the head. Also noted was DI Tennison's suggestion to check out recent house burglaries.

Stanley shook his head. Something didn't sound right. He smiled. He knew how to bait a hook to catch a fish. He had played that game many times. Taking another look over the board, he realised she had learned to play the game too, perhaps even better than him. DI Tennison was now a force to be reckoned with. But it could be a dangerous game. She might well need some protection.

Chapter Thirty

Angelica Martinez was coming out of the bakery in the row of shops below her flat. Jane had parked across the street, having already been to the care home. When she did not see her exit at two o'clock, she had called from a phone booth and was told she had already left. Now she was waiting to have a conversation that she knew was going to cause Angelica terrible distress.

She locked the car and headed across the street as Angelica started up the staircase leading to her flat. 'Miss Martinez,' Jane called out.

Angelica turned with a warm smile. 'Oh, this is good timing. I have fresh pastries. Do come up.'

Jane followed her and stood back as she unlocked her front door. The bicycle was still chained up outside against the wall. Angelica ushered Jane into her sitting room, saying she would put the kettle on, but then stopped, looking perplexed.

'You seem serious. Have you any news for me?'

Jane nodded. 'Yes, I do. Please come and sit down. We can perhaps have tea later.'

Angelica put her bag of pastries on the arm of a chair.

Jane took a deep breath. 'I am sorry to tell you, but we have discovered remains that may be Sebastian's.'

Angelica gasped, but then seemed to steady herself. 'But you are not certain?'

'Not until we have Sebastian's dental records to determine if we have a match.'

'I will need to see him.'

'I am afraid that is not possible, not until we have confirmation. Do you have Sebastian's dental records?'

'No, I don't have them. He never went to a dentist in England. My husband did take him to have a brace fitted in Berlin when he was very young. It was a plastic thing but he hardly ever used it and then lost it.' She laughed lightly, shaking her head. 'I think he lost it on purpose because he hated it.'

'Would you mind if I contacted your husband?'

'No, no, please do, or do you want me to call him now for you?'

Jane stood up. 'That won't be necessary. I have his contact numbers.'

'No tea or pastry? I can put the kettle on.'

'Thank you, but I really should go.'

'Yes, but what happens if you cannot get my son's dental records? What else can you do? Because you are not sure that you have found my son, are you?'

Angelica started pacing the room, clasping her hands together.

'You have to tell me where you found him. I have to know. You cannot expect me to understand what you mean by his "remains". What do you know?'

Jane kept her voice calm and controlled as she reached out to take Angelica's hands, holding them tightly.

'Angelica, listen to me. Try and stay calm. We have the remains of someone. We think it is a young adult; we do not know if it is male or female. We will only be able to tell by getting a forensic dentist to examine the teeth, and if we can have Sebastian's dental records, we will be able to confirm if it is your son or not. It's possible we may also be able to do DNA tests.'

Angelica looked perplexed, but Jane decided not to try and explain it to her. She recalled from Paul Lawrence's lecture that she would need samples of Angelica's hair and saliva but at this moment it did not seem appropriate to ask. Angelica cupped her hands under her chin. 'I'm sorry, my heart is breaking, but I appreciate that you have taken the time to be here and not sent someone else. I will pray and ask God to be sure my son is still safe.'

Jane gave Angelica a hug, but as they parted, she saw a look of such anguish in her eyes that she felt a painful guilt. She was certain they had found the remains of her beloved son but was unable to be honest with her.

'I'll call you as soon as I know anything,' Jane said. 'Is there anyone you can ask to be with you?'

'No, I will go and see Vera for comfort. She has always been there for me.'

Jane sat in her car, letting her emotions settle. She felt she had done the right thing, even if she had not been truthful. How could she tell Angelica that her son had been decapitated?

When Jane got back to the station, she found that the searches of the Larsson and Boon properties were already underway, with officers from the station accompanied by four forensic officers, while DCI Hutton had dealt with complaints from various lawyers.

Having come back empty-handed from Angelica Martinez, Jane placed a call to Victor Hoffman. He didn't pick up so she left a message to call her back urgently. Jane went over to the board to check what new information had been gathered and Stanley joined her.

'I made some progress on tracing the digger. I was just going to mark it up on the board.'

'Really?'

'I called Mrs Caplan, and she found some papers on her husband's desk. She found a cash receipt for a Mr McGregor, who did the new tarmacking.'

'That's good. Have you contacted him?'

'Yep, he also laid the original tarmac in the courtyard. But his business ran into difficulties, so he started a new company with his nephew.'

Stanley watched her closely, but she gave no sign of being nervous.

'The digger in question was never used by his team as they required a bigger model, but he reckoned a few of his competitors may have had access to a similar machine. If he found anyone that might be in the frame, he'd tip us off.'

'Good. Anything else?'

'Yeah, just to be sure, I checked out McGregor and his nephew's whereabouts on the night in question, and they were both at a party with a shedload of witnesses. So personally, I think we don't waste any more time trying to track these blokes down. They'll be long gone, and I would say the digger has probably gone walkabout by now as well, after what they uncovered. You never know, though, we might get lucky and McGregor tips us off.'

'Well, thanks for all that. I appreciate you sorting it out.'

Stanley gave her one of his hooded smiles, but she just nodded in return, giving nothing away, even though she knew he was covering for her. It felt good to know he had her back. Her desk phone rang, and she hurried over to answer it.

Mr Hoffman was as abrasive as ever, and at first refused to discuss his son's dental history. To get him to be more cooperative, Jane was forced to tell him about the discovery of the head. He quickly became emotional and agreed to look in some old diaries as he could not recall the dentist's name.

As the day went on, Jane waited for reports from the searches, but the news was disappointing. The teams had found no items of clothing that might have belonged to Sebastian, and no luggage or shoes. The search of Martin Boon's property had proved a little more productive, as he seemed to have been a keen mountaineer and rock climber in his younger days, and they found some small axes and lengths of rope. They also found some sacking in his garden shed for protecting plants in the winter.

The forensic teams were still working, but by the end of the first day they had found no bloodstains or blood spatter, even though they had been diligent examining bathroom tiles and pulling back carpets to examine old floorboards. The following day they would begin to search both rear garden patios.

It was almost six when a call came in from Mr Chadra to say he had completed his report. He apologised for the delay, but he had been waiting on a forensic expert to examine the edge of the bone where the head had been severed. He sounded very pleased with himself when he announced he was now certain a very unusual Gigli saw had been used.

Jane was surprised that she had never heard of it.

'It was widely used for amputation in the First World War and even at times in the Second,' he explained. 'It is basically a small chain with two handles or rings at either end. The action of drawing it from side to side cuts quickly and strongly, which you need for amputations.'

'That's very interesting,' Jane said.

'I'm also arranging for a plaster cast of the face to be made, from the impressions on the duct tape. I'll contact you as soon as it is completed. I must say it has been a fascinating and unusual post-mortem, and an imprint of the victim's face is something quite unique in my experience – although as far as identification is concerned it would still not be as reliable as a facial reconstruction.'

'I understand,' Jane said. 'Thank you again.' She pushed her chair back and called over to Stanley, who was just getting his coat out of the cupboard.

'Have you ever heard of a Gigli saw? I just had the pathologist on the phone, and he was certain that is what was used to sever the head.'

'Never heard of it. Is it unusual?'

Jane repeated Chadra's description, and Stanley suggested they ask one of the forensic officers who were in the boardroom. 'They've got a load of evidence to be bagged up and stored for the night, so they might have found one, you never know.'

Jane was about to leave with Stanley when her desk phone rang. Reception had a Victor Hoffman calling. Jane asked for him to be put through straightaway, telling Stanley to go ahead into the boardroom.

'Mr Hoffman, thank you for calling.'

'I am afraid it is not good news; the dental surgery has been closed for over two years, and I have been unable to trace his address.'

'Thank you for trying, but can you give me his name?'

'It is a very common name, but he was Mr Felix Schneider. He was, as I recall, quite elderly.'

'Thank you very much. I will obviously contact you if I have any further news.'

Hoffman hung up and Jane tried to think how she could trace Felix Schneider. Standing up, she asked the room if there was anyone who spoke German.

Meryl the young probationer raised her hand.

'Great, can you come over to my desk? I need you to do a trace for me on a dentist who had a practice in Berlin, possibly retired or may even be deceased. His name is Felix Schneider. See what you can do tonight, and tomorrow morning we'll contact London's Interpol office, who can help us with contacts in Germany.'

Meryl sat down at Jane's desk, opening her notebook. 'If I trace him, do you want me to explain why we need to speak to him?'

'Just say it is with regard to a patient named Sebastian Hoffman. Stress that it is very important. I'll talk to him.'

Jane went into the boardroom. Two forensic officers were making out labels and bagging items for storage. The entire table was covered with stacks of photo albums, clothing, string and coils of rope, along with bits of sacking and numerous tools removed from Martin Boon's garden shed, including a small, wooden-handled axe. The four paintings she had requested were placed in a line, one behind the other. Jane pulled on a pair of protective gloves as she examined the paintings. She held up her hand.

'These two were removed from the Larssons' property, correct?'

'Yes, ma'am, the top two are from Martin Boon's drawing room,' one of the officers said.

Jane gently turned the first painting over. Under the glass the painting was glued to a piece of cardboard. It had no date or signature. She turned the other paintings over to check the back, and they seemed very similar – as if prepared by the same person. In the bottom right-hand corners of the paintings were the initials EB, who had to be Martin Boon's wife Ellen.

Stanley walked in. Jane had been concentrating so hard she physically jumped.

'Sorry, I've been on the blower. After a few enquiries about this saw, I got in touch with a retired pathologist who is going to fax over some pictures. Like Chadra said, it was mostly used by surgeons in the First World War, but is still used for some operations because it is very fast. Because it's compact, it's also often used by mountaineers and hikers to slice through wood to make fires. You can get one that – when it's coiled together – is no bigger than a wallet. They can still be bought from stores that sell camping gear. And Martin Boon was into camping or climbing when he was younger,' Stanley said.

They moved down the table to examine the items brought in from Martin Boon's house. Numerous tools and an old, mouldy rucksack had already been examined and tagged by the officers.

'I don't suppose you guys found any rolls of duct tape?'

Stanley was just about to pull on surgical gloves when DC Burrows walked in with some faxed photographs showing different types of Gigli saw. Taking the pages, Stanley first showed them to Jane and then held them out for the two officers to look at.

'See anything that resembles one of these?'

'No, sir, and no duct tape,' one of them replied. 'But we are back searching tomorrow. We did find some old magazines in the pocket of the rucksack; they are bagged at the end of the table. We ran a test for blood traces but it came up negative. They are old trekking journals and mountaineering circulars. Judging by the state of them, I doubt the rucksack's been used for years.'

Jane nodded. 'Thank you. Stanley, can you just look over these paintings with me? I won't say anything until you've finished.'

The two forensic officers continued working.

'You want any tea or coffee brought in?' Burrows asked.

Jane checked her watch. 'I think you two guys can get off, as you're on duty tomorrow. We'll finish up here and lock up. What about you, Stanley?'

'Canteen will be closed now. I'm not leaving.'

'Surveillance teams have just switched over, so is it OK if I take off?' Burrows asked, hovering by the door as the two forensic officers gratefully departed. They had been on call from six that morning.

'You go on home, Bill. It's been a long day,' Jane said.

Stanley, who had now drawn on surgical gloves, finished examining the last painting. As the door closed behind Burrows, Stanley gestured to the first painting. 'Right, the first two I remember were hanging in Martin Boon's drawing room, and from the initials at the bottom corner they were done by his wife Ellen. They appear to be rather amateurish watercolours of the courtyard before any tarmacking was done. So, you have a cracked paved area, some plants growing in and around the Caplans' old fences, and sections of their rose trees in their front garden. The second one shows more damage to the Caplans' gates and sections of his fence broken. I presume these were done when the Hoffmans owned the property and clearly show neglect of the plants and the damaged courtyard, with bits of old cobblestones visible.'

Jane nodded as Stanley then gestured to the two paintings removed from the Larssons'. 'I remember you remarked on these two being even more amateurish, which meant they were out of kilter with their quality decor, am I right so far?'

'Yes, go on.'

'Well, what we now have is still the same damaged gates and fences, and no flowers along the edges of the gates, just a dirt-filled ditch, and the dark-grey colour covering most of the courtyard. I presume this has to be the artist's impression of the tarmac. I'm assuming the last painting was done around the same time, as it's virtually identical, the same dark grey for the tarmac, but now she's added two areas painted in a different sandy colour, one larger than the other.'

Stanley puffed out his cheeks, pointing to the larger pothole. 'That's where the head was buried. I don't understand, is it a reminder of the location? So they know exactly where it is, if you needed to dig it up?'

'If you're right, then why hang the bloody thing on their wall?'

Stanley rubbed his chin. 'Maybe it's a threat, even blackmail. Whatever it is, it suggests that they are all in on it; that both couples knew what was buried under the courtyard.'

Jane nodded. 'The question is, then, which of them committed the murder? I'm putting Martin Boon in the frame because of the way he has behaved. Now we know why he was adamant about not allowing the Caplans to erect their new wall and gates. He had to have known what could be found; the painting clearly shows that the head was buried just a short distance from the proposed work.'

'Yeah, but what about the hysterics from Mrs Larsson about anyone parking in the courtyard? They are all in on it, Jane. But right now we still don't know for sure who the victim was. It's all supposition, even with the paintings.'

She nodded, moving down the table to examine some of the items brought from both suspects' properties. She first opened the clear evidence bag containing the magazines removed from the rucksack, flicking through them and noting that they dated from 1979.

Stanley was searching the pockets of the rucksack. It smelled of mould and mildew. He withdrew a sticky strip of melted cough sweets. The tin foil had stuck to his gloved fingers. He shook his hand to get it off and then swore as it fell onto the floor. Bending down to retrieve it, he saw beneath the table was a big plastic container full of musical instruments, and a black guitar case.

'What you doing?' Jane said, looking down at Stanley. He was kneeling to draw out the instruments that had all been tagged as belonging to Martin Boon.

'Looks like Mr Boon's a bit of an amateur musician. With this lot he could have a full orchestra; there's a mandolin, flutes, a squeeze box, a little saxophone, two flutes . . .'

Stanley reached further under the table to pull out the guitar case. He lifted it up and put it on the table.

Jane edged over beside him. The case looked cheap, the surface worn and in places peeling away. It had two clasps, both rusted. Stanley carefully turned it over to check for any labels. He could see patches with a residue of glue, suggesting they'd been removed.

'OK, let's open it up,' he said.

Jane's heart was pounding. If the guitar belonged to Sebastian Martinez, it would be the most incriminating piece of evidence they had discovered. Easing open the lid of the case, she saw the royal-blue velvet lining was torn, hanging in frayed edges. The guitar itself was covered in dust but it looked to be in perfect condition, with all the strings intact.

'Should I take it out?' Stanley asked. So far he had not touched it.

'I think we wait for fingerprints, then we get Angelica Martinez to identify it,' Jane said.

'I agree, because if this has been left in the case for however many years, I doubt the strings would still be as taut as they look, so we might get the murderer's prints as well as the victim's.'

'We have no prints for Sebastian Martinez,' Jane said. 'But I can see if his mother has anything of his. We will also need sets of prints from the Boons and the Larssons.'

'You have been so certain for a long time, Jane. I've had my doubts, but you never budged. I respect that. However, we have to consider the possibility it might not be him. We could still find the rest of the body. Tomorrow the team will be checking out both back gardens, digging up their paved patios.'

Jane felt exhausted, too tired to really take on board what Stanley had said. There was nothing more to be done until tomorrow. She asked him to lock the boardroom to protect all the evidence and then left.

Walking along the corridor, Jane felt a black cloud of depression coming down like a dead weight. She went into the ladies' room, taking deep breaths as she leaned against the cold edge of the sink.

She splashed cold water onto her face and pulled down the towel to pat it dry. Even if the guitar had belonged to Sebastian, there could be any number of reasons why it was found with Martin Boon's collection of musical instruments. In a fit of temper, she pulled the roller towel down so harshly it almost came off the wall.

When she entered the incident room, most of the desks were empty. She paused in the doorway. Meryl was framed in a pool of light from an Anglepoise lamp, talking quietly on the phone in fluent German. Jane felt guilty, having completely forgotten about her. She must have been working since she left her at six o'clock.

'Meryl?'

She turned towards Jane with a smile as she replaced the receiver. 'I was just going to come and find you. I've traced Felix Schneider but I'm afraid he died two years ago.'

Jane sighed. For a moment she had thought there might be some positive news. She perched on the edge of the desk, which was littered with torn pages and lists of names and phone numbers.

'But after a long round of calls, I found Mr Schneider's daughter Erica. She is no longer using that surname as she is married and has her own dental practice. She was very helpful because she took over many of her father's patients.'

Meryl thumbed through her notebook.

'At first I didn't think I would get a result, because we are looking at more than four years ago; in fact, it was even more than that, but as soon as I mentioned the name Hoffman . . .'

Jane closed her eyes. 'Meryl, please tell me it's good news.'

'Yes, because when she took over the patients from her father's surgery, there were a number of outstanding accounts, and one of the largest was for Sebastian Hoffman's brace and retainer, along with Victor Hoffman's outstanding bill for a root canal and a gold cap for a molar.'

'Meryl, I am having palpitations. Does she have X-rays?'

'Yes. She didn't retain the plaster cast for her files, but she has the X-rays and accounts owing in her filing cabinet at her practice. I'm going to call first thing in the morning to arrange collection – I just wasn't sure how to go about getting them sent over.'

Jane got up and wrapped her arms around Meryl. 'Brilliant! You are a genius. Give me the details and I will organise the collection and get them on the first flight over to the UK.'

By the time Jane had everything she needed, her depression had lifted. Now we'll see if it really is you, Sebastian, she thought to herself.

Chapter Thirty-One

The alarm woke Jane at five thirty. She had slept deeply from the moment her head hit the pillow. Arriving at the station at seven, she had made an urgent call to Miss Phillips on her home number, to organise the delivery of the X-rays from Berlin on the first flight. Miss Phillips was clearly not happy to be woken, but took down the details and said she would get on it. Jane told her to contact Meryl if there were any language problems.

After a quick breakfast in the canteen, Jane checked over the reports from the previous evening's surveillance teams. There had been no visitors to either property and no one had left. But the forensic teams had already arrived to first begin the search of the Larssons' rear garden and patio, and to then move on to the Boons' paved back garden. The forensic tent remained in position as two other teams were still checking the area. Jane had also suggested it remain in situ so the officers could have coffee or tea inside rather than impose on the various property owners' generosity. She also liked the fact that it must appear threatening to the suspects who were under surveillance.

Stanley had already ordered the fingerprints to be taken from the guitar case and the guitar, as well as photographs. He had also arranged to have photographs taken of the four watercolour paintings. All these items were marked urgent. The sections of rope removed from Martin Boon's shed, along with the hemp sacking, had all been delivered to the laboratory to be tested alongside the hemp sack the head had been in. Jane also asked a favour, calling her CSI friend Paul Lawrence to see if he could oversee the tests.

'Glad to do it,' he said. 'I also got a call from the pathologist, about doing DNA tests on the victim's remains. He explained the condition, and I said I would see what I could do, but it might take some time. I would also require a DNA sample from a relative.'

'I could easily get a swab from his mother,' Jane said. 'But we have his dental records coming in, so hopefully we will be able to make an identification in the morning.'

DCI Hutton had asked Jane for a press release, as a local reporter had already contacted the station. Jane firmly said it would be premature to release the news about the discovery of the head, but they could say they were investigating a recent spate of burglaries.

Hutton agreed. She had also approved the cost of a courier from Berlin, and arranged a police car to take possession of the package at Heathrow and deliver the package to the forensic odontologist. Mr Chadra was also on standby.

The teams working on both rear gardens had by mid-morning found no evidence of a burial. However, they were now lifting sections of the patio in the Larssons'. It was heavy work, removing the paving stones one by one and replacing them after testing the soil beneath.

DC Burrows reported the disappointing news back to Jane as she stood by the incident board marking up the progress of the investigation. By now she had been given the news that the X-rays had arrived from Berlin and were with the forensic odontologist who was examining the teeth. She had been pacing back and forth as the calls came in, and everyone in the incident room was equally on edge. Every time the door opened, heads turned expectantly.

The guitar and case had been tested for fingerprints. They had discovered two clear sets on both the instrument and the case. Stanley also had the photographs of the guitar and case for Jane to show Angelica Martinez. Jane chewed her lip. 'I should be the one to show her these, but there is so much coming in. I'm waiting on the dental X-rays, and the sacking is being tested at the lab.'

'Do you want me to go and show them to her?' Stanley asked.

Jane looked at her watch. It was already one thirty.

'Better still, why don't we send a car and bring her in?' he suggested.

'OK, but use the quiet room.' Jane hurried to her desk and checked through her notebook to give Stanley the address of the care home. She looked over to Meryl.

'Meryl, can you give me a minute?'

DC Burrows opened the door and raised a hand.

'Gov, they want you out at the courtyard. I've got a car on standby.'

Jane grabbed her bag and jacket off the back of her chair and hurried out. By the time they reached the car park, the patrol car was drawing up. Stanley came hurtling out after them.

'They just radioed in from Clarendon Court. They've dug up something under the paving stones at the Larssons' place.'

The blue light went on as the patrol car drove out. When they pulled up and they drove in through the courtyard, Martin Boon was standing with arms folded outside his front door. As Jane got out of the car, he started shouting abuse. Stanley promptly crossed over to warn him to go indoors and remain there.

'It's disgusting. I'm going to complain to my MP. You have no right to keep that tent up. We are being treated as prisoners and I want an explanation.'

Eventually Mr Boon turned on his heel and went back into his house, slamming the front door behind him. Stanley then had to contend with Mr Larsson, who was equally angry, demanding that whoever was in charge should explain it all to his wife. She was refusing to allow any further invasions of their property.

Stanley persuaded him to go indoors, then followed Jane into the forensics tent. A forensics officer was waiting, wearing work overalls and Wellington boots from digging up the Larssons' patio.

'Right, what's going on?' Jane asked.

'The woman went crazy. She just threw herself at me. I had to call for back-up. They are refusing to allow us to continue.'

'What did you find?'

'It's still there. I mean, there was nothing to indicate to us exactly what it was, so we backed off, but Grant is still there.'

Jane shook her head and turned to Stanley. Considering what they were investigating, the behaviour of both the Larssons and Mr Boon was ridiculous. None of them appeared to have understood the seriousness of the police investigation. It was as if they were in total denial.

'They're certainly putting on a good performance,' Stanley said.

'OK, let's go and see what they've found,' Jane said as they walked out of the tent. They had to ease past the car parked in the driveway, using a small gate that led into the Larssons' rear garden. At the rear of the house was a paved patio. Wicker chairs and a glass-topped table had been removed and stacked to one side. The patio had already been worked on, with a row of square paving stones propped against a low wall, and beyond that was a small square of immaculate grass edged with flowering plants and rose bushes.

As Jane and Stanley approached Grant, the forensic officer, Mrs Larsson came to stand by the open French doors. She looked distressed, her face red and blotchy. She was holding a wad of tissues which she waved at them. 'They can't take it; I refuse to allow them to take it. I know the law. I want them off my property.'

'Would you please go inside, Mrs Larsson,' Jane said, as politely as she could.

'No, I will not. You cannot allow them to take it. *Get out! I want you all out!*'

Stanley stepped in front of Jane as it looked as if Mrs Larsson was about to lash out, and then Mr Larsson appeared behind his wife.

'Take your wife inside, Mr Larsson. We have warrants to search your premises which you have been made aware of, so please, let's just do this quietly. Take her inside now.'

She struggled for a moment and then burst into tears, sobbing inconsolably as her husband gently drew her inside and closed the patio doors.

'It's Grant, isn't it?' Jane asked.

'Yes, ma'am. We had only just lifted the paving stone, and were starting to dig beneath, when she came out screaming blue murder. Some kind of metal object is just visible.'

Jane and Stanley could see a small section of what looked like a brass container. Jane gave him the nod to keep using a small, pointed trowel to dig around and loosen the earth. He gradually cleared enough to use his gloved hands to ease it further out.

'My God, it's a bloody urn,' Stanley said.

Jane crouched down as Grant wiped the earth away.

'I think it must contain her daughter's ashes. Just put it to one side for a minute,' Jane said as she straightened up.

'So this is why she was so hysterical,' Stanley said.

'But there was no cross, or indication something like this was buried,' Grant said apologetically.

'You weren't to know,' Jane said. 'Have you uncovered anything else?'

'No, we checked all along the adjoining wall. The flower-beds are not deep enough to bury anything substantial, and we've not checked over the grass, but there doesn't appear to be any uneven sections so we just started on the patio.'

Jane turned to look back towards the French windows. A wooden trellis covered most of the wall at the back of the property. Thick ivy had threaded itself between the trellis, apart from a centre section; the wood in this area was a slightly different colour, and the ivy not as dense.

'What do you want to do about the urn?' Stanley asked, taking Jane aside.

'I need to go into their house. I think the best move would be for you to go to their front door and apologise for the distress. Hand the urn over and let Grant carry on here, specifically on the patio sections closest to the house.'

Stanley picked up the urn, seeing Jane heading to the French windows.

'You just going to walk in?'

'Why not? We have a search warrant, and I want to check something out.'

Stanley carried the urn, leaving the way he and Jane had come in, easing past the parked car before going to the front door. He rang the bell and waited. Mr Larsson opened the door, his face taught with anger, as his wife came to stand behind him.

'I understand how upsetting this must be for you,' Stanley said, 'and obviously we regret what has occurred, but you must be aware we are investigating a serious crime and to date you have not been very cooperative.'

Mrs Larsson moved forwards as if to challenge him, but her husband blocked her with his arm. 'We have had no option, Detective, but to be subjected to what feels like harassment, and we have never been told why we have been virtual prisoners in our own home. We cannot help but be aware of the officers' presence, day and night. Plus we have had personal items removed, our home searched . . . so this was the last straw . . .'

Jane could hear their conversation as she walked quietly up the stairs, pausing a moment to get her bearings before heading towards what she calculated must be the bedroom overlooking the patio. She eased open the door and stepped inside. The bedroom was tastefully decorated, with pale-blue ribboned wallpaper perfectly matching the ice-blue paintwork. Muslin curtains framed the window overlooking the patio below.

The carpet seemed new as she left her footprints in the pile, crossing first to the window and then back alongside the little bed. On the dressing table was a silver-backed mirror and brushes, and embroidered on a white satin cloth was the name Georgina. The only item that seemed out of place was a small leather-bound volume of Byron's poetry. Opening the flyleaf, in small, neat handwriting, Jane saw Georgina's name. She sniffed and held the book closer. It had a faint smell of flowers. The drawers were empty, and the wardrobe had only a row of satin coat hangers inside. It was as if it had never been occupied, a sterile room without a single photograph or picture, but from the book of Byron's poems Jane now knew that it was definitely Georgina who wrote on Sebastian's bedroom wall.

Heading back downstairs, not caring if they found out she had been in their daughter's bedroom, Jane walked towards the front door. She paused, seeing the kitchen door was open. The Larssons had their backs turned as they emptied the contents of the urn into the pedal bin.

Jane hurried out to Stanley who was standing by the patrol car, with the uniformed driver waiting. Stanley opened the passenger door, got into the seat beside the driver as Jane got in the back, then he leaned over the seat towards her. She was physically shaking.

'Are you all right?'

'I will be. I just have to get back to the station.'

'On our way,' he said, gesturing to the driver. He was wise enough not to ask her what the matter was, as he watched the way she fought to gain control, her hands clenched tightly together. Whatever she had seen at the Larssons', he would have to wait to find out; right now, she was like a dangerous, coiled spring, with a dark, angry expression. Not until they drove into the station did he turn around to face her, but she already had the passenger door open. He watched her straightening up, back in control, striding ahead of him. By the time he caught up with her she had already punched in the code to open the security entrance. As the door closed behind him, he saw her disappearing down the corridor.

DC Burrows met Stanley as he was about to enter the incident room, carrying the guitar in its case. 'What was the emergency at the Larssons' place?'

'Forensics dug up the urn with their daughter's ashes.'

'Shit. She just told me to bring this to the quiet room. Miss Martinez is with Meryl, been here for fifteen minutes. She told me to wait outside the room until she could take it from me.'

'We get anything on the dental match?'

'Not yet.'

'What about Paul Lawrence at the lab?'

'Nothing yet. I'd better give her this. Is she all right? She looked a bit uptight.'

Stanley nodded, not wanting to be drawn into a discussion. She didn't just look uptight, he thought. She was furious.

Chapter Thirty-Two

Angelica was sitting in a low-backed tweed armchair. Two others, one in orange and another in mustard, were placed around a coffee table. A two-seater sofa in the same green fabric was against a wall with two square, covered tables either side. The fitted carpet and subdued lighting gave the small room, as was intended, an informal peacefulness.

Meryl had brought in a tray with a teapot, milk, sugar and a plate of biscuits. She poured Angelica a mug of tea, and then one for herself. Meryl had found it hard making conversation, both in the patrol car and now in the quiet room. She had not been told any details, so couldn't tell Angelica why she was being brought to the station, only that DI Tennison had requested her presence but had been called away on an urgent matter.

To Meryl's surprise, Angelica smiled. 'She is very nice. We have met a few times, first at the care home. It was a coincidence because I used to live in Clarendon Court, the big old manor house, with my then husband and my son. Long time ago. She was working on a case there, about the neighbours.'

Meryl nodded, sipping her tea. 'How odd.'

'We went to a medium together.'

'Really?'

'Have you ever been to a medium?'

'No, I haven't. I suppose I'm a bit sceptical of palm-reading and fortune-tellers and that sort of thing.'

Angelica shook her head. 'No, no, mediums do not read your palms. They are able to converse with the dead. Those loved ones who have crossed over to the other side, they come forwards. Where are you from?'

'Me? Oh, Nottingham originally, but I live here now.'

'I am from Mexico, and we have each year a wonderful festival of the dead, where we dress up with flowers and skeleton masks, and have dances and music to celebrate the dead.'

There was a light tap on the door and Jane entered. Meryl immediately stood up, but then sat down again as Jane gestured for her to stay.

'Angelica, I am so sorry to keep you waiting, but I had an urgent situation that required my attention. I would have tried to come to see you rather than have you brought here, but time is of the essence and I needed to see you as soon as possible.'

Jane drew the orange chair closer. Angelica sat back, twisting one of her bangles around her wrist. 'It's not good, is it?'

'No, it isn't. We recently discovered a guitar in a case. I want you to look at it and see if you recognise it. Can you do that for me?'

'You think it is Sebastian's?'

'I don't know, Angelica. Can I show it to you?'

'Yes, of course.'

Jane got up and opened the door. Burrows passed her the guitar case then handed her a pair of latex gloves.

'Anything come in?' she asked quietly.

'Not yet, ma'am.'

She nodded and closed the door. Turning towards Angelica, she carried the case to the coffee table as Meryl moved the tray to one side.

'I will need you to wear these, please.'

Jane knew instantly that Angelica recognised the case. She eased the surgical gloves on, then stared at the case for a moment before gently patting it.

'This belonged to my first husband. It used to have stickers over it from his travels. We never removed them. But it is the same.'

'Can you open it, please?' Jane asked quietly.

'Yes, of course.'

The sound of the clasps clicking open felt loud in the room as Angelica gently lifted the lid of the case to reveal the guitar.

'You can take it out,' Jane said.

'Thank you.'

It was painful to watch the way she gently lifted the guitar and held it away from her for a moment before drawing it close.

'It is called a Gibson guitar, like the one Elvis Presley had. It was his pride and joy. He took it everywhere, and I remember him being worried that they might not allow him to take it on the plane when he went to Mexico. If you have it here, it means he did come back, I was right.'

'Angelica, are you sure this is Sebastian's guitar?'

'Of course. You see the little scuffed area by the first string? That was made when he was a little boy. He cried because he believed he had broken it, too young to understand that you can replace them.'

She slowly turned the guitar over, brushing her gloved hand over a hardly detectable scratch. 'That scratch was from a buckle on his belt.'

Angelica carefully replaced the guitar in the case, then eased the lid closed, clicking down the clasps. Jane was trying to think what to say that could be of comfort, but before she could speak, Angelica looked directly at her, tears in her eyes.

'Vera had the taste of blood in her mouth. What more do you have to tell me? Because I think you know where he is.'

Jane stood up, unable to control her emotion as she picked up the guitar case.

'Forgive me, Angelica, but I am unable to give you any further details right now. You have my promise that I will tell you everything as soon as I can. I will organise a car and Meryl will go home with you. Thank you for agreeing to come.'

She walked out. Burrows was standing just outside the room. 'I didn't know whether to interrupt, but you have a call waiting. It's Paul Lawrence from Lambeth.'

Jane passed him the guitar case. 'Get that back into the property lock-up and arrange a car for Miss Martinez to go home.'

She hurried into the incident room, where everyone was poised, waiting. Stanley was standing by her desk, the phone in his hand. She almost snatched it from him.

'Hello Paul, it's Jane.'

She eased past Stanley to sit at her desk, gathering her notebook and pen. She remained expressionless, making one note after another, before thanking him and asking for the official report to be delivered. She then slowly replaced the phone, knowing she had everyone's attention.

'We have a match on the hemp sacking the head was wrapped in. It was cut from the roll removed from Martin Boon's property.'

There was a loud gasp, but she held up her hand.

'I'm not finished. We also have a match from a reel of cord removed from Martin Boon's property with the cord tied around the sack.'

Stanley had returned to his desk, and he now gestured to her. 'Line two, urgent line two.'

Jane pressed her second line, and this time she wasn't able to hide her emotion as she listened to the one call she had been hoping and waiting for. When she replaced the receiver, she raised both arms above her head.

'We have a match on the dental records. Our victim is Sebastian Martinez.'

Stanley and Jane hurried to give DCI Hutton the news.

'How do you want to work this, Jane?'

'I want to arrest both Mr and Mrs Larsson and Mr and Mrs Boon on suspicion of murder. I want them kept in separate cells. I think my first interrogation will be with Ellen Boon as I think she will break faster than the others.'

'How much time do you need to prepare?' Hutton asked.

'I'm ready, ma'am. I would like DI Stanley to work alongside me.'

Hutton glanced at her watch. 'Right, it's now four fifteen. Let me get the warrant organised and maybe, Jane, you should take a quick break.'

Jane and Stanley left together. He squeezed her elbow. 'Thanks. Why don't I arrange a tray of sandwiches, and you and I can have a session before the shit hits the fan.'

'Great, just need to check something with Meryl.'

'I think she took Angelica Martinez home.'

'Right, I promised I would let her know as soon as I had more information. Well, I have it now, but I don't think I can tell her over the phone. I want to be with her when she discovers the truth.'

'Thank God you didn't have a scene like you had with Mrs Larsson over finding her daughter's ashes.'

Jane shook her head. 'That woman is evil. She had no grief left, just a twisted need to protect herself.'

'I'll go and order the sandwiches. Tea or coffee?'

'Coffee, and get a flask. I need to check something out, so I won't be long.'

Jane went into the incident room and found DC Burrows. She went to her desk and took out her notebook, quickly running over her notes of the meeting with Kathleen Bellamy.

'Bill, can you radio the forensics team at the Larssons' and tell them to check the patio at the centre of the trellis, where the ivy is not as thickly grown? Also, to check the garden furniture they have stacked to one side.'

'Yes, ma'am.'

Hutton came out of her office and asked Jane for a quick chat. 'The arrest warrants are finalised, but I need a couple of lines to feed that local journalist. He's been tipped off about the forensics tent and the searches of the properties in Clarendon Court.'

Jane pursed her lips. 'He's a real pain in the butt. I just don't want any photographers around when we pick them all up.

Let's just say that police enquiries are still ongoing due to the continued spate of robberies. Maybe just add something about the hostage situation we had. That should send him off in the wrong direction.'

Hutton reached for the phone as Jane paused at the door.

'Maybe give him a hint that when we do have more to say, he will be the first to know; try and get him onside.'

Jane closed the door quietly behind her as she returned to her desk to select the files she would need for the interviews.

* * *

Meryl sat beside Angelica in the patrol car, wondering whether she should try to make conversation or if that would just make things worse. The rain had started as soon as they had driven out of the station, and it was now pelting down, making Meryl think of Angelica's unstoppable tears. All she could hear was the rain and the sound of the windscreen wipers, until she became aware that Angelica was humming very softly a repetitive tune while staring out of the window. Meryl caught the driver's eyes in the mirror as he listened too. Then softly, barely audible against the sound of the rain, Angelica began to sing: 'Love me tender, love me true, all my dreams fulfilled.'

The patrol car drew up outside Angelica's flat by the row of shops. She turned and touched Meryl's hand. 'My son used to sing that to me. Thank you for accompanying me home.'

The driver did not have time to get out and open the passenger door, as Angelica was already stepping out and hurrying towards the steps leading to her flat. The radio crackled, with a request for their ETA back at the station, and he told them they were on their way. As the patrol car pulled out, Meryl looked back to see Angelica standing in the downpour, the rain mingling with her tears.

'That was Elvis Presley, wasn't it?' the driver asked as he put on the siren.

'I don't know, but it sounded like a love song,' she said sadly.

She leaned back in the seat as he put on speed, overtaking the rush-hour traffic. His patrol car was needed for the arrests.

Chapter Thirty-Three

Jane and Stanley had worked together for over an hour. She seemed to have been gathering detailed information for weeks, and he found it difficult to absorb it all, even though she had done a good job of laying it all out on the board with photographs and graphic links. They were interrupted by Burrows, who had brought in the final documents from the post-mortem.

Jane flicked through the report, then stopped and tapped one of the pages. 'See what he says about the indentation at the base of Sebastian's skull. He reckons severe trauma would have resulted from some sharp-edged instrument. He can't say what it was, but the blow would have rendered Sebastian unconscious, even though his long, thick hair would have blunted some of its force. He also confirmed that the neck was severed by a small Gigli saw, leaving tiny, jagged scars on the vertebra.'

She handed the report to Stanley, who read through the rest, then flicked through a stack of photographs that had been attached. 'Look, here's a photograph of the plaster cast,' he said. 'And here's a memo saying a facial reconstruction is underway.'

The sound of the sirens indicated the return of the patrol cars, and Stanley went over to the window overlooking the station yard. The rain was still pouring down.

'Here they come, first out is Martin Boon. Did you tell them to bring his wife in separately?'

'Yes, same with the Larssons, and they are to be taken to the cells and not allowed to speak to each other.'

'We've only got four cells. That means we've got a full house.'

'OK, first up is Ellen Boon, interview room one. I just need to take a bathroom break, then let's go.'

She put all her files in order and gathered them up. 'I'll see you in five minutes.'

The sirens wailed again and Stanley went back to the window to see Mrs Larsson being brought out of the patrol car by two uniformed officers. Her face was taut with anger as she shrugged away one officer's arm, but he insisted, and she struggled for a brief moment before being led out of sight. Stanley was about to turn away when the next patrol car drove in, bringing her husband. He had to stoop down to get out, but unlike his wife he kept his head bowed, waiting to be taken into the station, his arms held stiffly at his sides. Stanley waited, and last to arrive was the patrol car with one female uniformed officer seated beside Mrs Boon. She was wearing a hooded raincoat, and she slowly walked with the officer into the station.

Stanley made his way down to the cells. The duty sergeant told him that the Larssons had already requested a phone call, as was their right. Stanley told him to take each of them out separately to make the calls and to get another officer to remain in earshot of their cells.

Jane washed her face, combed her hair and then powdered her cheeks with a light foundation before applying lip gloss. Licking her index finger, she ran it over each eyebrow before she was satisfied. After checking her blouse was properly buttoned and smoothing out her skirt, she slipped on her jacket, and stood staring at her reflection for a moment, before picking up her stack of files.

Interview room one was on the first floor, with two smaller rooms on either side. DC Burrows was standing outside as she approached. 'There's water and tissues, ma'am. Stanley is already waiting. The Larssons have both made separate calls to their solicitor, so there will be some delay before they arrive.'

'What about Martin Boon?'

'He made his call, but it seems that whoever he contacted told him that he would be unable to represent him as well as his wife. I suggested we get one of the legal-aid guys we use but he declined and said his wife would not require representation.' He shrugged his shoulders. 'He didn't try to speak to her, but then shouted for her to not answer any questions until he's talked to his solicitor. I already told the duty sergeant to have an officer outside the cells to see if they try and pass any messages to each other.'

Jane nodded. 'Well, Boon's probably relying on the fact that a wife can't give evidence against her spouse.'

'Do you want me to bring her up now?'

'Yes please, and did you forward my instructions to the forensics team at the courtyard?'

'Yes, ma'am, radioed them in immediately I was asked.'

'One more thing, Bill, can you check out for me the value of the guitar? I know it looks very worn but it's a Gibson and I'm not sure if that means anything, but check with Boosey and Hawkes – they're a top musical instrument maker. Hopefully, they might still be open.'

As he walked off down the corridor, Jane took a deep breath and then entered the interview room. Although the largest at the station, it was not like any of the interview rooms in the older stations she had worked in. The usual insipid green and faded yellowish paint and functional furniture had been discarded, and replaced with fresh cream tones, good lighting and comfortable chairs.

Stanley stood up as she walked in. She put her files down on the table, and selected one of the pair of chairs along one wall, moving it nearer to the table. Stanley sat in the other, to the side and slightly behind. The only other chair was facing them across the table. Plastic cups and a water jug sat next to a box of tissues.

'You familiar with the recorder and everything?' she asked.

'Yes, been using it recently,' he said.

'Good, I don't want to be bothered. As soon as she's brought in, you do the honours and read her her rights, but keep it low-key;

she's going to be very nervous as her husband already warned her to keep her mouth shut, but as soon as she is relaxed, I'll up the tension.'

Stanley nodded. 'No solicitor?'

'No, said she didn't want one, so we're good to go.'

There was a firm knock on the door, and a female uniformed officer led Ellen Boon in. She was wearing a pleated grey skirt, a white blouse and a knitted cardigan, partly buttoned. Jane waited until she was seated and Stanley had switched on the recorder.

'I am Detective Inspector Jane Tennison, and this is Inspector Stanley. We will be conducting the interview.'

Stanley read her her rights.

'Mrs Boon,' Jane began. 'I think you are aware that two of your watercolour paintings were removed from your property, and we also have two further paintings that belonged to Mr and Mrs Larsson. They are signed EB, so we assume that you were the artist, is that correct?'

'Yes, I am just an amateur,' she said, looking slightly bemused.

'They show the Clarendon Court courtyard at various times, so you can see how the courtyard used to look before the two new properties were built. The old fenced area of what is now the Caplans' property had considerable foliage and plants. I also believe at one time there had been stables, and the courtyard originally would have been cobblestones, as you have depicted. Is that correct?'

'Yes, where the new houses are now used to be a wooded area, and when the buildings started, they created so much damage, with cranes and cement mixers and huge trucks. Mr and Mrs Hoffman used to own the big house and they never repaired any of the fences or gates, and they left the plants to rot, and no matter how many times we complained about the condition of the courtyard they never did any repairs. It was quite hazardous, especially in winter.'

Jane nodded. 'You very clearly show in your paintings the state it had been left in. It must have been very frustrating as your property borders the courtyard.'

'Yes, and I think perhaps our house and next door might have been originally built for the staff, in the old days when the stables were in use. There used to be an area for the carriages, but that was a long time before we lived there.'

'So, it must have been a relief when Mr Larsson bought the courtyard from Mr Hoffman.'

'Yes it was, because at last something was going to be done about the terribly uneven driveway.'

'You are referring to the tarmac being laid?'

'Yes, everyone was very relieved. We couldn't afford to do it all – it was very costly.'

'So, the paintings belonging to Mr Larsson are of the work commencing?'

For the first time, Ellen Boon looked wary. Jane smiled encouragingly, and she nodded.

'Were they a sort of thank-you gift, to show your appreciation of the work going ahead in the courtyard?'

Ellen nodded again but had the same uneasy reaction. 'Er . . . yes, that's right.'

'One interested me because you clearly show how part of the tarmacking was already completed, but then it appears to have been stopped, is that correct?'

'Yes, it was because their daughter Georgina Larsson had tragically died.'

'Do you know what she died of?'

'She had been ill for some time. They had always been so concerned about her as she was very frail.'

Jane opened a file and pulled out the photograph she had been given by Kathleen. She passed it across the table.

'This is Georgina, isn't it?'

Ellen Boon looked at the photograph sadly. 'Yes, such a pretty child. It was devastating.'

'In the painting you gave to the Larssons, clearly showing the unfinished tarmacking, was that painted before the funeral? Or after?'

'I don't remember.'

'You don't remember? Let me describe it to you. Your painting shows two large potholes, the largest one being only a matter of feet from the Hoffman property's broken-down fence. The small pothole is about six feet further away but directly in line with the deeper one. You also clearly show the darker area where the tarmac had been left unfinished, so I would suggest that you must have completed this watercolour before the funeral.'

Ellen chewed her lip. 'Maybe I did.'

'It feels as if you painted it to show what the courtyard looked like before the tarmacking was completed, as a sort of reminder, so you would remember exactly where these potholes were located.'

Mrs Boon didn't say anything. Jane was not getting the response she wanted, so she changed tack, withdrawing the second photograph given to her by Angelica Martinez. She placed it on the table in front of Ellen.

'Do you recognise this young man?'

Ellen stared at the photograph. 'I'm not sure.'

'This is Sebastian Hoffman. He began to use his mother's name, Martinez, after his parents divorced. Surely you must recognise him? He used to ride his bike in the courtyard. Let me show you another photograph.'

Again, Jane slid out a photograph from her file, pushing it with one finger across the table, face upwards. Ellen Boon was beginning to get anxious, blinking rapidly as she stared at the photograph.

'For the benefit of the tape recording Mrs Boon is shaking her head.'

Stanley poured a beaker of water, passing it to Ellen Boon. Her hand was shaking as she sipped, and she then used both hands to put it down on the table.

'Along with your paintings,' Jane continued, 'we also removed from your garden shed lengths of string and rope, plus some hemp sacking material. This shed is where you work on your watercolours, isn't it?'

'Yes.'

'And your husband also uses it for storing gardening equipment, and things to do with his hobbies?'

'Yes.'

'What are his hobbies?'

'Well, he kept his camping equipment in there at one time, but that's not really a hobby anymore.'

'Does anyone else ever have access to this hut?'

'No.'

'No gardener?'

'Oh no, we couldn't afford one; it is just used by my husband and myself.'

'It looks to be a recent purchase?'

'No, we have been using it for three or four years.'

'Does that also mean that your very modern kitchen and, I would say, costly extension, were installed at the same time?'

'Not exactly. It required a lot of planning permission. It was two or three years ago.'

'We also removed various musical instruments from a bedroom, including a guitar in an old guitar case. This was found inside a cupboard. Do you recall where it came from?'

'No, but it would belong to my husband. He has musical evenings.'

'You are both retired, and you said earlier you didn't have the finances to pay for the tarmacking. I have recently had a lot of refurbishing done to my home, so I am very aware of what it would cost to build an extension. You have a washing machine, fridge, deep freeze, microwave, an impressive oven – so how did you pay for it all, including the shed?'

'Savings.'

'Savings ... but you didn't have the finances to pay for the tarmacking.'

Ellen Boon frowned. 'My husband arranged everything.'

'What about the Larssons? They seem quite an affluent couple, and I have to say they were certainly very concerned about your husband after the incident with Mr Caplan. Mrs Larsson also drove you back and forth to the hospital.'

'I don't drive, I never passed my test. Could I have some more water, please?'

'Yes, of course.'

Stanley refilled Ellen's beaker and passed it back. She was now visibly shaking, and her face was shining with perspiration. Stanley felt Jane was really stretching the interview out. They needed to accelerate things. As if Jane had read his mind, she selected a large black and white photograph from the post-mortem, keeping it face down.

'Did you ever use silver duct tape?'

'No.'

'I mentioned earlier, Ellen, the items removed from your hut: some hemp sacking and rope.'

She shrugged. 'They made a list, I know that.'

'Do you know what was found underneath the tarmac?'

'Er ... no.'

'I find that rather hard to believe. You must have heard what it was, and strangely enough in the exact location you have carefully painted.'

Jane turned over the photograph of the head wrapped in the hemp sacking and tied with rope. Ellen sat back in her chair, taking short, sharp breaths.

'Please look at the photograph, Mrs Boon, and tell me if you have ever seen this before.'

'*No!*' Her voice sounded strangled.

'We have been able to match this sacking, and the rope, with the items removed from your property. Do you still maintain that you have never seen it before?'

'No, no, no, I swear I haven't, I don't know what it is.'

'Can you please look at this fax sheet, Ellen, and tell me if you know what it is?'

Jane passed her one of the pictures of a Gigli saw, tapping it with her finger, as Ellen Boon blinked rapidly again.

'I'm not sure, unless it is for cutting branches?'

'So you have seen one like this before?'

'I'm not sure, maybe when there was a storm, and we had a tree fall in the garden.'

'So did you see your husband ever using a saw like this?'

'I don't know . . . I don't understand why you are asking me these questions . . . I mean, he used to go camping and had lots of useful things in his rucksack.'

Stanley kept his eyes on Ellen Boon as she started to look very agitated, her chest heaving as she gasped for breath. He was worried that as the pressure mounted, she might be unable to continue. Jane needed to speed things up.

'Inside the sack, Ellen, was Sebastian Hoffman's head, and his neck had been severed by a saw like the one I just asked you about.'

Jane quickly withdrew the second large photograph. This showed the head with the duct tape wrapping. It had been placed in an upright position to clearly show the features beneath. Ellen's reaction was extraordinary, her eyes flicking from side to side as if trying to block out the image in the photograph. Her voice seemed distorted and was hardly audible.

'I saw that, I . . . only saw that.'

'Can you please repeat that?' Jane asked.

Ellen Boon began shaking her head back and forth, her mouth twisted in a childlike grimace. Jane slapped the table with the flat of her hand. 'Tell me where you saw this, Mrs Boon!'

Between awful wrenching sobs, her body bent forwards as she rocked back and forth, she said, 'In the kitchen . . . in the kitchen.'

'What did you see?' Jane insisted.

'That, I saw that . . . thing, on the side by the draining-board.'

Jane turned to Stanley, indicating that he should terminate the interview, as she collected the photographs and replaced them in her file.

Stanley noted the time and reminded Mrs Boon that she was still under caution. 'You will now be returned to your cell.'

He had to help her get to her feet, and she clung onto his arm as he guided her to the door, rapping it hard to alert the officer outside, and then escorting her out.

The door was still ajar, and DC Burrows gave a light knock before entering.

Jane looked up. 'I think I will need more coffee and another round of sandwiches, but first get someone in here with a mop, bucket and disinfectant.'

Burrows glanced down to where Ellen Boon had been sitting. There was a pool of urine beneath her chair.

'I contacted that musical instrument place. Apparently an early Gibson, if it's a J200, could be worth quite a lot of money. Collectors really value them.'

Jane nodded. 'Anything from the Larssons' garden?'

'Not tonight, but they'll be back in the morning.'

'Terrific, I'll be at my desk. Next up I want Martin Boon brought in.'

'We're still waiting on his solicitor. Likewise the Larssons.'

Jane pursed her lips in irritation. She walked out into the corridor, almost bumping into Stanley, who was eating a Mars bar.

'Martin Boon's solicitor has just arrived, so they're being taken into interview room two. I asked the divisional surgeon to be on standby to check over his wife. She was in a pretty bad state. I reckon, if you are up for it, we go again in about half an hour.'

'I am up for it, Stanley. I'm going to walk outside for a bit of fresh air and I need a cigarette.'

'Yes, ma'am,' Stanley said, crunching up the wrapper.

Burrows looked after her and then turned to Stanley. 'How did it go with Ellen Boon?'

'Let's say DI Tennison covered a hell of a lot of ground, very tough on her, but she got a result in the end. Lucky she didn't have a solicitor chipping in, though.'

Stanley went off to the gents' as Burrows headed back to the incident room. He was actually quite shaken by how Jane had conducted the interview with Ellen Boon, going easy at first and then really putting pressure on her at the end. He took his electric shaver out of his pocket, running it over his stubble. He knew this was Jane's show, but at the same time it was imperative to make sure she didn't cross the line.

Meryl appeared through the double doors at the end of the corridor carrying a mop and bucket. 'Evening, Meryl, no cleaners around tonight then?' Stanley said, grinning.

'Not until the morning. I've been asked to wash down interview room one, and switch a chair.'

'How did it go with Miss Martinez?'

'She is such a sweet, gentle woman. I think she knew the truth as soon as she saw her son's guitar.'

Stanley nodded and gave her a sympathetic smile as he headed on down the corridor.

Jane was standing at her desk eating a sandwich and spooning sugar into a mug of coffee. He came over to help himself to a sandwich.

'I didn't think you took sugar?'

'I don't, but I needed a bit of an energy kick. I see you've smartened up and had a shave.'

She sipped her coffee as he wolfed down another sandwich. 'We using the same technique – softly, softly, catchee monkey?'

'No, I think we need to go straight for the jugular this time. We've got enough from Ellen to put him right in the shit. Who's his solicitor?'

'He's a local guy, Colin Chester. He was busy around one of the kids we arrested on the drug bust. You know something, going by Ellen Boon's reaction, I don't think she really knew what had been done to our victim, but what I also got, and I could be wrong, I don't think the decapitation occurred in their house, which meant Boon brought the head into their kitchen.'

'Maybe, but what we really need to find out is the exact time frame from when Sebastian was murdered, to the funeral, and when the re-tarmacking commenced.'

Stanley frowned. 'Not quite following you.'

'When was the head buried, Stanley? That's what I need to know.'

She began checking through her files, making sure the photographs had been replaced in the same order. Closing the file, she stood up.

'Time to go.'

Chapter Thirty-Four

Stanley and Jane returned to interview room one, which now smelled of disinfectant. As soon as they had seated themselves, there was a tap on the door and Burrows ushered in Martin Boon, followed by Colin Chester. The solicitor had a flushed complexion and small features and wore what remained of his hair in an unflattering comb-over. But his unprepossessing appearance belied a steely manner as he acknowledged Stanley with a nod.

Martin Boon sat beside him without expression.

'Good evening, Mr Chester, I am Detective Inspector Jane Tennison. I believe you know Detective Inspector Stanley.'

Stanley waited a beat as Colin Chester placed his leather-bound notebook and his pen in front of him, then switched on the tape recorder. He stated the date, time and location before repeating the caution.

'Mr Boon,' Jane began, 'this interview relates to the discovery of a human head, which was uncovered in a section of the Clarendon Court courtyard. We have been able to identify the victim as Sebastian Hoffman, who at one time resided in the large property bordering on the courtyard and close to your home.'

Jane removed the post-mortem photograph showing the head in the hemp bag. She placed it between the two men, and continued in the same relaxed manner.

'Mr Boon, have you ever seen what is depicted in the photograph before? For the benefit of the tape I am describing the bag holding the victim's severed head.'

Boon remained expressionless. 'No comment.'

'Forensic tests match the material, a rough woven hemp fabric, and the rope seen in that photograph in front of you, to items removed from your property.'

Boon clasped his hands together tightly, glancing at his brief, before leaning forwards.

'No comment.'

Jane already had the second photograph ready.

'This is a photograph of the victim's head, wrapped tightly in silver duct tape. Do you recall ever seeing this?'

'No comment.'

It was Colin Chester who appeared shocked for a moment, quickly regaining his composure, as Jane next withdrew the folded fax sheets and laid them out.

'Mr Martin, are you able to identify these items?'

There was a pause as both Martin Boon and his brief looked at the pictures. 'No comment.'

'For the benefit of the tape, I have just shown Mr Boon pictures of various-sized Gigli saws. The pathologist's report concluded that the head was severed, at the third vertebra, by a small Gigli saw like this one.'

Jane placed the last fax sheet down.

'No comment.'

Stanley cracked his knuckles impatiently. Jane was getting nowhere. But she remained calm, taking a sip of water. Colin Chester raised his hand, but she ignored him.

'Detective Inspector Tennison, I don't see where this line of enquiry . . .'

'Mr Chester,' Jane interrupted, 'I'm questioning your client about the brutal murder of a sixteen-year-old neighbour, and so far his only answer has been "no comment". If he had nothing to do with it, why doesn't he say so?'

Stanley could see Martin Boon starting to sweat. He wiped his face with the back of his hand.

'Mr Boon, even if you didn't murder Sebastian Hoffman, the evidence suggests that you unlawfully disposed of a corpse with intent to protect the person or persons who did. You have to realise that your refusal to answer any questions, even when confronted with incriminating evidence, makes you appear even more guilty.'

Jane rocked back in her chair, then suddenly leaned forwards.

'We also found on your property a guitar and a guitar case that belonged to Sebastian Hoffman. Could you please explain how you came to have them?'

'No comment.'

'I presume that along with the victim's head, you were instructed to get rid of it. Unless, of course, you murdered him yourself.'

Colin Chester spoke up. 'That accusation is entirely unwarranted. Unless you . . .'

'Mr Chester, if your client refuses to answer my questions, what other conclusion can I come to? So, I am asking you again, Mr Boon, how did you come to have Sebastian Hoffman's guitar in your home?'

Martin Boon paused, licking his lips. 'No comment.'

Jane tapped the table with her pencil.

'I'd suggest that you intended to dispose of the guitar as evidence of Sebastian Hoffman's murder, but as an amateur musician, you were aware of its value and couldn't bear to part with it. Your wife has already told us that your finances are somewhat restricted.'

'Is that a question or a statement, Inspector Tennison?' Mr Chester said tetchily.

Jane snapped back at him. 'All right, I'll make it clear. During the past four years your client has had an expensive kitchen extension built, along with a substantial shed, and has repaved the access to it. How did he pay for all this, if he had no money?'

Mr Chester leaned close to Boon and whispered quietly.

Jane raised her voice. 'It's a very simple question, Mr Boon. We know that you couldn't afford to pay for the tarmacking of the courtyard, so where did the money come from?'

Jane jotted down a note and passed it to Stanley. Martin Boon plucked a tissue from the box to wipe his face.

Stanley glanced at Jane and then at Martin Boon.

'I can see you are becoming very agitated, Mr Boon, and under-standably so. You must realise that on the evidence we have already gathered, you could be charged with the murder of Sebastian Hoffman, and your wife with being an accessory.' He turned to Chester. 'I suggest that you advise your client that it would be in his best interest to stop protecting whoever has been manipulating him.'

Boon took a drink of water, his head bowed.

Stanley sighed. 'Look, Martin, I think you are a decent man, and would not want your wife to suffer, but the only way you can help her is to tell us who killed Sebastian Hoffman.'

Boon kept his head bowed, swallowing hard.

'Tell us the truth, Martin, get it over with.'

They waited for him to say 'No comment.' Instead, he started crying.

* * *

An hour later, Stanley and Jane returned to the incident room. There were only two officers left on the night shift manning the phones. It was now after midnight, and they were both exhausted but elated. They decided that they would call it a night, and inter-view the Larssons first thing in the morning. Before leaving, they stood side by side for a moment, looking over the incident board, as Jane added the new information.

After breaking down, Martin Boon told them that he had received a panicked call from Edward Larsson on the night of 16th March. He was in a terrible state as their daughter had been taken to hospital the day before and had died shortly after being admit-ted. They had returned home and found Sebastian Martinez trying to climb into their daughter's bedroom. He had fallen and they claimed he had broken his neck. They blamed him for Georgina's death, as she had miscarried his baby.

Patricia Larsson had persuaded Martin to help them, promising to pay him twenty-five thousand pounds in cash. He had shown them how to use his Gigli saw but denied he had played any part in dismembering the body. Edward Larsson brought round the head bound in duct tape along with Sebastian's clothes, rucksack and guitar. He was promised another five thousand pounds if he got rid of everything, but he did not know what they had done with the torso. He had wrapped the head in the hemp sacking and hid it in the garage, then taken the clothes and rucksack to the Princess Alice charity shop. He decided to bury the head in the courtyard, enlarging one of the potholes. He intended to move it at a later date, but then the Larssons ordered the tarmac to be completed.

Jane stood back, checking over their additions to the board, neither of them believing everything Boon had said. But they did now have a clear time frame for Sebastian's death. He was dead the day after Georgina Larsson's death. That was 16th March. Martin Boon claimed he had buried the head on 18th March, and the funeral took place three days later.

Stanley watched Jane underline the dates, and then draw an arrow to the date Sebastian Martinez arrived in the UK. She tapped the board with the felt-tipped pen.

'I think Martin Boon had to have threatened the Larssons, so they coughed up the cash, but he then was caught in a catch-22. Forget that crap about accidental death; they killed him. And now we know why there was so much at stake if that tarmac was dug up by the Caplans.'

'Unless the boy's torso is under the tarmac as well,' Stanley said.

Jane shook her head. 'I don't think it is. Right, I don't know about you, but I need to go home.'

'Fancy a quick drink first?' Stanley asked. 'I've got a bottle of Scotch in my desk drawer. Maybe we could decide how we're going to work it tomorrow. I think I played a blinder after your note, if

I do say so myself, so if you need me to step up to the plate again, just say.'

She laughed, crossing to her desk to collect her jacket. 'You're a class act, Stanley. But I've had it. See you in the morning.'

As the incident door closed behind her, he had already opened his bottle of Scotch. He took a heavy slug and felt the warmth as it went down. They had certainly taken a major step forwards, but there was still a way to go. He took another swig, then put the cap back on the bottle and returned it to the drawer. He knew she would not be satisfied with a verdict of 'accidental death', and reckoned tomorrow she would be going for the jugular.

DC Burrows walked in, looking exhausted. 'Still here?'

'Just about to go home, what about you?'

'Yeah, I reckon our guests are sorted for the night, thank God.'

'How was Martin Boon when he was returned to the cells?'

'Hutton told us to make sure he was fit, so we had the divisional surgeon check him out. He seemed pretty shaken, was ranting and raving a bit. He was given a couple of paracetamol and a hot chocolate, and when I last checked him, he was snoring his head off.'

'What about the Larssons?'

'She's a piece of work, still making a fuss, but he's pretty subdued.'

'What was Boon shouting about?'

'Something about it being "all over", pretty garbled really, and his wife has been crying a lot.'

Stanley sighed, exhaustion suddenly hitting him as he shrugged himself into his coat. 'I'm off. G'night, Bill.'

He left as Burrows went to the incident board to check the night's progress. He saw the arrow Jane had drawn, linking the date of 16th March to Sebastian Martinez in London. The photograph pinned above it showed a strikingly handsome young teenager, and Burrows was taken aback at how emotional it made him feel. 'Dear God, what a terrible thing they did to you,' he murmured.

Chapter Thirty-Five

Stanley drove into Clarendon Court at eight o'clock, heading round the drive and into the courtyard. The forensic tent was still in position, but much of the yellow crime-scene tape had been removed. A white forensics van was parked up, and to his astonishment next to it he saw Jane's car.

There was no one inside the tent, just empty takeaway food cartons and dirty coffee mugs. Knowing that both the Boons and the Larssons were in the cells at the station, he headed towards the Larssons' house, easing past their parked car, and entering the garden via the gate. Two officers wearing protective clothing, gloves and masks were examining a large bamboo and wicker garden table.

In a wheelbarrow was a section of the wooden trellis, with a pile of cut-down ivy.

'Good morning, Stanley.'

Jane was leaning out of the bedroom window.

'You coming down?'

She closed the window. He turned and watched the two forensics officers carefully dismantling the table. 'That glass looks new,' he said.

'That's what we thought,' one of them said. They began to ease the glass out carefully, afraid it might shatter as it was a very tight fit. Eventually they were able to lift it clear and then carried it to where they had laid out some flattened cardboard. On their knees they began carefully examining the edges, using test sticks with bulbous cotton ends to take samples.

Jane appeared, carrying her jacket and briefcase. 'I think the window frames have been repainted, not recently, but they don't match the other bedroom. Mind you, the entire bedroom has been redecorated along with new carpet and wallpaper.'

'We are pushing it a bit being here, especially inside the house,' Stanley cautioned.

'We still have the warrants, and I've not removed anything. We have these two guys as witnesses.' The forensics officers straightened up, placing two sticks into a tube for analysis.

'What about the trellis?' she asked.

As the officers returned to the table, now minus its glass, they gestured to the stacked section of trellis.

'Definitely a newer addition, nailed onto the old, and in a few places secured with cable wires,' one of them said. 'Take a look at the brickwork underneath. In four places you can see quite deep indentations.'

Stanley and Jane looked where he was pointing.

'Would you say they could have been made by someone climbing up?' Jane asked.

He nodded. 'Yes, and from the shape of the indentations, it looks like they had pointed shoes of some sort.'

Jane turned to Stanley. 'Sebastian Martinez wore cowboy boots with pointed toes.'

The officer turned his attention back to the table. 'Inspector, I'm finding a lot of tiny shards of glass, caught between the bamboo, just fragments, but they could be from the previous glass top as the one we just examined doesn't have so much as a scratch.'

He teased out small bits of hardened Blu-Tack with a thin wooden spatula. 'These were probably used when they fitted the new glass top. Hang on, the bamboo legs have open tops.' He probed the bamboo tube with an evidence stick. When he drew it out, the tip was discoloured. He put it in a plastic container full of a clear chemical and shook it up. He held the result up to the light.

'Yep, it's blood,' he said.

Stanley and Jane waited as all the hollow legs of the table were similarly tested, each with the same result.

'Blood must have dripped down and congealed,' Stanley said.

'We need to verify that it's human blood, and then see if we can match it to the DNA samples taken from the head,' Jane said.

'Right,' Stanley agreed. He nodded to the forensics officers. 'And in the meantime, keep looking for more evidence. My guess is there was a massive blood pool when Sebastian Martinez was decapitated. Even after four years, that could show up in the soil.'

Jane and Stanley left them to get on with it, and drove back to the station. As soon as they arrived, Stanley went straight to the incident board to add the new information, before heading up to the canteen.

Jane was already there, carrying her tray of scrambled eggs and bacon, two rounds of toast and a large mug of coffee to a table. Stanley went and got his usual full English and joined her.

'I can't believe I'm so hungry after what we've just seen,' she said.

He shrugged, dipping a piece of toast into his egg yolk.

They finished their breakfast in silence. At ten fifteen they were ready in interview room one. Jane was checking through her files, making sure every item was tagged for easy access during the interview.

'So do you think the rest of Sebastian's body is buried in the Larssons' garden?' Stanley asked. 'We've already dug up most of it, and Martin Boon's.'

'No, I don't think we'll find it there,' she said.

'Then where?' he asked. But before she could answer, there was a knock on the door and DC Burrows looked in.

'We have Edward Larsson's solicitor here but not his wife's. Do you want them brought in?'

'Yes, wheel them in. Do we know him?'

'It's a her,' Burrows said. 'Anita Conrad.'

Burrows closed the door quietly behind him as Jane glanced at Stanley.

'You know her?'

'Nope.' There was a rap on the door. 'I guess we're about to find out what she's made of.'

Burrows ushered in Edward Larsson, followed by Miss Conrad.

Jane nodded to her as she sat down. 'Good morning, Miss Conrad. I am Detective Inspector Tennison, and this is Detective Inspector Stanley.'

'Good morning.' Anita Conrad looked to be in her late thirties and was smartly dressed in a navy-blue suit with a frill-necked white shirt. Her auburn hair was scraped back from her slightly puffy-cheeked face into a neat bun. She placed a notebook on the table and signalled that she was ready to begin.

Stanley switched on the tape recorder and went through the usual preliminaries, finishing up with a caution.

'You do not have to say anything. But it may harm your defence if you do not mention when questioned something that you later rely on in court. Anything you do say may be given in evidence.'

Jane took a good look at Edward Larsson while Stanley was speaking. He looked drawn and pale, his eyes red-rimmed.

'What business are you in, Mr Larsson?' Jane began.

'I have a company importing goods from Sweden,' he said. 'Home furnishings, domestic appliances, that sort of thing.'

'So you are Swedish?'

'Yes, but I moved to England many years ago. It was originally my father's company.'

'And it's successful?'

'Yes, I now employ four staff full-time.'

'Do you have a warehouse?'

'Yes.'

'So, when these items are shipped to your warehouse, are they already boxed up, ready to be delivered?'

'That depends on the item. The smaller items of kitchen equipment require separating to be re-boxed for deliveries. And the glassware.'

'When you re-box items, what do you use to secure the lids?'

'We use various kinds of tape.'

'When you say we, does your wife also assist in repackaging the small items?'

'Yes, to begin with, until I was able to employ workers for the deliveries and boxing.'

'And what kind of tape do you use, Mr Larsson?'

He turned to Miss Conrad and gave her a quizzical look.

'These questions are absurd. What possible relevance can that have?' she said, frowning.

Jane leaned forwards, ignoring her. 'I mean, is it narrow like Sellotape or more substantial?'

Larsson folded his arms. 'We use strong, wide tape. But I have not been involved in that area for many years.'

'But would you agree that you were proficient at one time, before being successful, so you had experience in taping parcels?'

'Yes, I suppose so,' he said in an exasperated tone.

'What is the name of the tape you use?'

'It's silver duct tape.'

Jane pulled a photograph from her file and placed it on the table.

'Look at the photograph, please, Mr Larsson.'

He glanced at it quickly then immediately started shaking. He seemed unable to speak.

'For the benefit of the tape, I am showing Mr Larsson the photograph of the severed head wrapped in silver duct tape and discovered buried under the tarmac at Clarendon Court.'

'I don't know what that is,' he managed to say, finally.

'Let me clarify that for you, Mr Larsson. We have identified the victim as Sebastian Hoffman, and my point, Miss Conrad, is that it was expertly wrapped with duct tape. So I am suggesting . . .'

Miss Conrad interrupted. 'I need to speak privately to my client.'

'I am simply asking him a direct question, Miss Conrad.' Jane turned to Larsson. 'Did you wrap Sebastian Hoffman's head in duct tape?'

Larsson was shaking his head. Underneath the table his legs were trembling.

'It is not the way you think, I have to explain the reasons, it was a terrible, heartbreaking time . . . my beloved daughter was dying. There was no hope left . . . I was out of my mind.'

Jane put the photograph back in the file. 'Tell me about your daughter.'

Larsson seemed relieved he no longer had to look at the photograph. And Jane's gentle tone of voice seemed to calm him down. Clearly he wanted to talk about his daughter, not Sebastian. It was like floodgates opening.

'She was so very beautiful, but she had always been very frail, asthma dogged her early years, and then she began to starve herself, and then self-harming . . . We were at our wits' end. She was only fifteen years old and it seemed like her life was over. Then, like a miracle, she began to get better, put on weight. She wanted strawberries and ice cream all the time! She went back to school and suddenly I believed she had a future. Then my wife discovered that Georgina was spending hours with the Hoffman boy, and lying to us about it. One day we went to an outdoor concert that was rained off. We came back early and found him in her bedroom. They were both naked.'

He grabbed a tissue, wiping his face.

'Was this when you warned the Hoffmans about their son?' Jane asked.

'She was only fifteen years old, for God's sake! Of course I warned them. I told them that they had to send him away, or I would call the police . . . I would have him arrested.'

'Sebastian was also underage, wasn't he?'

'That was not the way he looked. Anyway, they agreed. They sent him abroad.'

'Was it at this time they sold you the rights to the courtyard?'

'What? The courtyard? Yes, it was around this time, I believe.'

'I suppose you were able to get it for a good price, considering the circumstances?'

'They needed money, they wanted to sell the house. I would have done anything to make sure he was not able to see my daughter.'

'So, your purchase helped the Hoffmans send their son to Mexico, and shortly afterwards they sold their property?'

'Yes, I can't remember how long the sale took. After the fire the house was boarded up for some time, and then the Caplans did extensive rebuilding which went on for many months.'

Miss Conrad sighed theatrically. 'I fail to see the relevance of this line of questioning.'

Jane smiled icily. 'Hopefully it will become clear if you will allow me to continue. Mr Larsson, did you begin to tarmac the courtyard after the Hoffmans had moved out?'

'Yes, shortly after, it was early March when work began, that would be on the main driveway to the properties.'

'So, when exactly did you discover your daughter was pregnant?'

Larsson swallowed several times before he was able to answer.

'Around about the same time, but we didn't realise that she was pregnant at first, because she began to starve herself again. She would eat, but then make herself vomit. You have to understand what it was like, watching what she was doing to herself. We didn't think it could be morning sickness, but when it continued and she was still not eating, my wife made her take a pregnancy test.'

'How did she react to being told she was pregnant?'

'She tried to run away, went over to a neighbour, they had a daughter older than Georgina, but they had been friends. We brought her back, she didn't resist, just stayed in her bedroom and then probably due to her starving herself she miscarried, locked in the bathroom screaming at us, blaming us for losing the baby.' He wiped his face again.

'You were certain the baby was Sebastian's?'

'Yes, of course, there could have been no one else, she was screaming his name to help her. We eventually broke the lock on the bathroom door and took her back to bed.'

'How far gone was she?' Stanley asked.

'I am not exactly sure, about four or five weeks.'

'So, was it small enough to flush down the toilet, or did you do something else with the foetus?'

Larsson closed his eyes and started shaking his head, as if trying to get an unbearable image out of his mind.

Miss Conrad slapped the table with her palm. 'My client's daughter tragically died over four years ago. I find this reference to a very tragic incident totally abhorrent.'

Jane looked down, appearing to be interested in her notes and letting Stanley maintain the pressure on Larsson.

'It's all about the sequence of events,' he said. 'That's what we need to establish.' He looked directly at Larsson, who avoided making eye contact. 'So what happened to the foetus?'

Larsson took a series of deep breaths. 'Yes, my wife flushed it down the toilet.'

'Did you call a doctor to examine your daughter and make sure she was all right?'

'No, she became very calm and went to bed.'

'According to medical reports, your daughter did not attend hospital until 14th March, is that correct?'

'Yes.'

'So, you discovered the pregnancy in early March, and then subsequently had the miscarriage about a week later, or would you say longer?'

'About a week, I suppose, yes.'

'And when did Georgina start to get sick?'

'It . . . began with a temperature, I think it was the tenth or eleventh when the fever took hold, and no matter what my wife did, we couldn't get it down.'

'Did you call a doctor?'

He hung his head. 'No.'

'Why not?'

'She had been pregnant and she was only fifteen years old. We wanted to protect her.'

'So, on 14th March what happened?'

'During the night a vivid rash had appeared over her body, and the fever was awful. We called for an ambulance. She was taken to the A&E department. My wife went with her, and I followed in my car, but by the time I arrived she had been taken into intensive care. We were told she had gone into septic shock and was very seriously ill. We stayed at the hospital, hoping and praying until early morning.'

'That would now be 15th March?'

'Yes, my wife was exhausted. She had been caring for Georgina day and night. She was still in her dressing gown. I persuaded her to go home, take a shower and then come straight back.'

'What time did your wife leave the hospital?'

'It was about eleven.'

'And what time did she return?'

Head bowed, tears in his eyes, Larsson seemed unable to continue. Miss Conrad offered him a beaker of water, but he shook his head. Stanley scribbled a note on his pad and passed it to Jane. There was one word underlined: 'Manslaughter?'

Jane shook her head and whispered to him: 'Not enough.'

Larsson's face was very flushed, and he was beginning to sweat profusely.

'Do you need to take a break, Mr Larsson?' Jane asked gently.

He shook his head. Stanley waited a moment, then continued his questioning. 'So what time did your wife return to the hospital to be with your daughter?'

'I think we should take a break,' Miss Conrad said firmly.

Larsson shook his head slowly. 'No, it's all right. I remember it was in the afternoon sometime.'

Beneath the table Jane gently touched Stanley's knee, then withdrew a photograph from the file and passed it face down across the table. After a pause, she turned it up.

'Do you recognise this person, Mr Larsson?' Jane asked quietly.

He winced. 'Yes, it's Sebastian Hoffman.'

'Can you tell me when you last saw him?'

Larsson opened his mouth to speak, but then seemed to stop himself.

'We have evidence to show that Sebastian arrived in England that same day, on the morning of 15th March. Did you see him at any time during that day?'

'No, I did not.'

'What time did you and your wife return home from the hospital?'

Larsson licked his lips. His legs started shaking again.

'I don't remember, I can't remember, I was in a dreadful state . . . it was all such a terrible time.'

'Let me help you remember, Mr Larsson. Your neighbour Mr Boon recalled you waking him up very late that night and asking him to return to your house.'

Larsson started sobbing. After a while he wiped his eyes, then looked up at Jane. 'I . . . found Sebastian's body. He'd tried to climb the trellis up to our daughter's bedroom. He must have fallen and landed on the table. The glass was shattered. It had . . . cut his throat. His head was . . . I asked Martin to help me get rid of it. That's how it ended up under the courtyard.'

He hunched over, wrapping his thin, bony arms around himself and beginning to rock backwards and forwards in his chair.

'Why didn't you call the police?' Stanley asked.

'I . . . I thought we'd be accused of killing him. It was an accident but . . .'

'What did you do with the rest of his body?'

'I . . . I . . .' Larsson started convulsing, his chair scraping against the floor.

Miss Conrad held onto his arm. 'My client . . .' she began, looking at Jane with a panicked expression.

Jane quickly got up and opened the door. Moments later DC Burrows and two uniformed officers came in and helped Larsson out of the room, followed by Miss Conrad.

The interview was over.

Ten minutes later, Stanley and Jane were sitting in DCI Hutton's office, giving her a debrief.

'Do you believe him, that it was an accident?' Hutton asked.

Jane shook her head. 'He never mentioned his wife. There's something he's not telling us. He's definitely covering for her. And we can't be sure that it was the fall that killed him. The pathologist didn't find any glass fragments embedded in the skull and we know he wasn't decapitated on impact because we know his head was subsequently severed with a Gigli saw.'

'Whatever happened,' Stanley said, 'there would have been a massive amount of blood. We did discover a certain amount this morning in the hollow bamboo table legs.'

'We're certain it's blood?' Hutton asked.

Stanley nodded. 'They put a drop of phenolphthalein reagent on the swab, waited a couple of seconds and added a drop of hydrogen peroxide. It turned pink instantly, so it's confirmed as blood.'

Hutton nodded. 'That could mean he actually did die from the fall. And after four years we may not find any more blood traces.'

Jane glanced at her watch. She wanted time to confer with Stanley before they brought up Mrs Larsson to be interviewed. She drained her coffee cup and stood up.

Hutton nodded. 'Well done. And come and see me as soon as you're finished with Mrs Larsson.'

As they walked out of the office and into the incident room, Stanley was shaking his head grumpily. 'I'm starving. I need something to eat.'

Jane nodded. 'We've got time to order a sandwich and have a half hour together before the interview.' As they left the incident room, Jane saw the handsome man from the car park. He gave a nod to Stanley.

'This is Detective Chief Superintendent Ralph James, DI Jane Tennison,' Stanley said.

'Nice to meet you properly, DI Tennison,' he said with another warm smile, before entering the incident room.

Jane looked after him. 'What's he doing here?'

'Didn't you know? He's married to Hutton. He's a good guy, actually. Runs the Met's drug squad.'

Jane nodded. 'That explains it. I've seen him around a few times. They make a handsome couple.'

They carried on down the corridor.

'Talking of which, are you back with your builder chap?' Stanley asked.

The double doors swung closed behind them. 'No, it didn't work out. I'm on my own again, Stanley.'

Chapter Thirty-Six

Jane put her empty plate onto the tray. The soggy tuna sandwiches and ham rolls with wet lettuce had been disgusting, but that hadn't put Stanley off scoffing two of each. More importantly, they had gone through the files and discussed how they were going to approach the interview with Mrs Larsson. It was two o'clock and they had asked for her to be brought in at two fifteen, so they both took a bathroom break. Jane washed her face and hands and tidied her hair, but didn't bother about her make-up. She needed something to calm her nerves, so quickly went out into the car park for a cigarette.

Sitting on a low wall, inhaling deeply, she mulled over the key questions she wanted answered. They now had a time frame and a motive, but they still had to prove Sebastian had been murdered.

Jane smoked her cigarette down to the filter, dropping it onto the ground before stubbing it out with the toe of her shoe. She thought about the pointed shoe marks on the brickwork. Looking down at the cigarette butt, she turned to face the wall she had been sitting on. She was wearing a pair of court shoes with small Cuban heels and slightly pointed toes. Jane had been quick to point out to Stanley that she recalled Kathleen describing Sebastian's cowboy boots. She lifted her right foot and dragged it downwards against the worn red bricks. She then bent forwards, both hands leaning against the top of the wall and gave a sharp kick, once, twice. She stood back with her arms folded, staring at her handiwork. The two marks from her kicks were clear, but could you prove it was a particular type of shoe that had made them?

DC Burrows called out to her from the staff entrance, and she snatched up her bag and hurried towards him. 'They're bringing her from the cells any minute, and she's a piece of work, I can tell you.'

'Thanks, Bill. Stanley all set up, is he?'

'Raring to go, ma'am. He was just finishing a call before going to the interview room.'

She passed him as he held the door open for her, letting it slam shut behind her.

'Taking your temper out on the wall, were you?'

'What?'

'I saw you having a kick at it. Letting off steam?'

'Something like that.'

'I'll bring her up then, ma'am. By the way, she's got a solicitor from London, a sharpshooter called Ewan Thomas. The QC at his chambers is notorious.'

She gave Stanley a brief nod as she entered interview room one. He was sitting in his usual seat. Her files and notebook were on the table in front of her empty chair.

'Got a bit of info for you,' Stanley said. 'I've been making numerous calls trying to trace that young Dr Wilde, but I finally got him. I asked him if he could recall what time Mrs Larsson returned to the hospital. You got me a bit fixated about our timeline.'

'Don't keep me in suspense, what did he say?'

'Not a hundred per cent sure, but he thinks Mrs Larsson came back in the evening, around ten.'

'OK, thanks.' Jane put her jacket over the back of her chair, then started looking over her files one last time.

'Bill came out to the yard to find me, saw me kicking the wall, asked me if I was letting off steam. I was actually doing a comparison with those marks on the wall at the Larssons'.'

'And?'

She shrugged. 'Let's just say it was inconclusive. And we don't even know if Sebastian was wearing cowboy boots since we haven't traced any of his clothes. Bill also mentioned that we've got another solicitor and he's a bit of a sharpshooter, or perhaps he said sharp-suited. Ewan Thomas – have you come across him?'

'No. Are you going to take the lead?'

'Yes, you do the usual, and . . .' She was interrupted by a knock on the door. DC Burrows ushered in a distinguished-looking man, wearing a tailored pin-striped suit. He looked to be around fifty, with thick, iron-grey hair, bushy eyebrows and a deep tan. His dark-maroon tie had an emblem with two gold golf clubs.

'Good afternoon. I am Ewan Thomas, representing Mrs Larsson.' He waited for Mrs Larsson to sit opposite Stanley, making sure she was comfortable before he placed his briefcase beside his own chair.

Jane nodded. 'This is Detective Inspector Stanley, and I am Detective Inspector Tennison.'

He frowned. 'I would have preferred to have more time with my client, but as there have been no charges, I hope we can resolve this matter quickly.' He spoke quietly but in a steely, aristocratic tone.

Stanley switched on the tape, repeating his name and Jane's before the time and location, then read the police caution. Patricia Larsson sat straight-backed, with her hands folded in her lap. She had obviously made an effort with her hair and make-up, and was wearing a white silk blouse and a matching jacket with velvet trim.

Jane waited a moment, letting the tension build to upset Mrs Larsson's poise. 'I'd like to question you about the discovery of a severed head buried under the courtyard at Clarendon Court. It has been identified as belonging to Sebastian Hoffman, aged sixteen. Forensic examination has confirmed that the burial took place just over four years ago.'

Jane pulled out the photograph of Sebastian, sliding it forwards across the table.

'Do you recognise the young man in the photograph, Mrs Larsson?'

'Yes, I do.'

'Could you tell us his name, please?'

'Sebastian Hoffman.'

'How well did you know him?'

'His parents owned one of the properties in the courtyard.'

'What kind of relationship did you have with Sebastian?'

'I did not have a relationship with him, but we purchased the courtyard from his father, Victor Hoffman.'

'You may not have had a relationship with Sebastian, but your daughter did, didn't she?' Jane said.

'I think you're being deliberately offensive, DI Tennison,' Thomas said with a look of distaste.

'Mr Thomas, I have to tell you that Mrs Larsson's husband has already told us that their daughter was pregnant with Sebastian's child, and that she then had a miscarriage.'

Thomas turned to Mrs Larsson, who nodded.

'My daughter died of sepsis shortly after she miscarried. After the post-mortem and the coroner's report, I was told that it could have been the result of a retained placenta after the miscarriage.'

She sat back, her mouth tight, and gave Jane a disdainful look. Mr Thomas patted her arm gently.

'When did you last see Sebastian?' Jane asked.

'I did not see him after we discovered that he was sexually abusing our daughter. We were obviously distraught on discovering his relationship with Georgina, who was only fifteen years old. His parents then sent him to Mexico.'

'I believe you and your husband assisted the Hoffmans financially to send Sebastian to Mexico, is that correct?'

'I presume the money my husband paid them for the courtyard helped finance their son's departure.'

'Do you still maintain that you did not see Sebastian after he left?'

'Yes.'

'Shortly after the courtyard was purchased, you and your husband had the entire area tarmacked. The Hoffmans' property was also boarded up ready for the new buyers to begin refurbishing. This would be early March four years ago. Is that correct?'

'Yes.'

'You subsequently discovered your daughter was pregnant, is that correct?'

'Yes.'

'Do you still maintain that you did not see or have any contact with Sebastian after that?'

Mr Thomas leaned forwards. 'Mrs Larsson has clearly stated that she has not seen this young man since he left England to live in Mexico. I am finding your line of questioning not only repetitive but unfathomable.'

'I have proof that Sebastian didn't stay in Mexico but travelled back to England after receiving a letter from your daughter. He also sent a postcard, not to your address but to a friend of your daughter, Kathleen Bellamy, a close neighbour in Clarendon Court. I may appear to ask repetitive questions, Mr Thomas, but that is because I know Mrs Larsson is lying.'

'Do you have a witness who can verify my client met with this young man?'

'I doubt under the circumstances anyone would have seen their interaction. Let me move on then. Can you tell me the date your daughter was taken into hospital?'

Mrs Larsson shook her head as if exasperated.

'The evening of 14th March.'

'Your daughter had been suffering from a high fever after the miscarriage. Despite your best efforts, the fever got worse, but it was not until a rash . . .'

Mrs Larsson interrupted. 'I knew exactly what I had to do to bring down the fever. I had cared for my daughter her entire life. She had asthma attacks and eating disorders, and I cared for her the whole time. I resent your inference that I did anything wrong.'

'You were protecting her from any scandal, weren't you?' Jane said. 'Or were you more concerned with protecting yourself, trying to stop anyone discovering she had miscarried at fifteen years old?'

Mr Thomas spread his hands. 'I am sorry, Detective Inspector Tennison, but this is uncalled-for harassment of my client. After suffering the loss of her only daughter, this line of questioning is quite unacceptable.'

Jane paid him no attention. Instead she flicked open her notebook and continued. 'So, you called an ambulance on the evening of 14th March, and were then informed how seriously ill she was.'

'Yes, she was taken into intensive care immediately.'

'I believe you spent the night at the hospital, with your husband, is that correct?'

'Yes, it was a terrible time, very distressing, but we still hoped she would recover.'

'You had left your home wearing a dressing gown and slippers, obviously in haste to be with your daughter in the ambulance.'

'Yes, that is true, I held her hand all the way. My husband followed the ambulance in our car.'

Jane turned over a page, then looked up. 'The following morning, even with your daughter in intensive care, you were encouraged by your husband to return home. I have the time as around eleven o'clock, is that correct?'

'Well, as you said, I had just rushed out to the hospital, still in my dressing gown and slippers and I hadn't eaten, being up day and night with Georgina. My husband persuaded me to take the car and go home to get dressed.'

'What time did you return to the hospital?'

Stanley had been watching her closely. Up to now her manner had been confident, even arrogant, but now she looked towards Thomas as if wanting him to interject on her behalf. He gave her a blank look, as if to say he could see nothing to object to in the question.

'Could you please answer the question, Mrs Larsson? Your daughter was in intensive care, so you must have been eager to return as soon as possible. You left the hospital at eleven to shower and change your clothes, and it was no more than a twenty-minute drive. What time did you return to the hospital?'

'Later that afternoon.'

'How much later?'

Thomas finally found something to object to. 'This aggressive questioning is becoming too much. Mrs Larsson has already explained that she returned home to change her clothes, as she had been at the hospital all night, and then returned to see her daughter as soon as possible.'

'I have a statement from a witness that in fact Mrs Larsson did not return to the hospital until later that evening, at ten o'clock. Which means, discounting the time driving back and forth, she was absent for nine hours.'

'My daughter died that night!' Mrs Larsson snapped.

'I am aware of that, but could you please explain what occurred during those nine hours.'

Mr Thomas turned towards Mrs Larsson, who was plucking a tissue from the box on the table. He obviously expected her to reply.

'Was Sebastian Hoffman at your property that night, Mrs Larsson?'

He was about to interject when Mrs Larsson began speaking.

'Yes, he was.'

Jane tried to keep her expression neutral and her voice calm. 'Go on.'

'I had changed and showered before going into my daughter's bedroom to take a clean nightdress for her, and the window was open. I went to close it and was stunned when I saw he was about to climb in. I suppose he had to be equally shocked because as I approached, he clawed at the windowsill, then fell backwards. I screamed, then saw him crashing below into the table on the patio. By the time I had run down the stairs and out into the garden, he was lying covered in shards of glass. He had blood coming out of his mouth and his neck was broken. There was nothing I could do. It was an accident.' She paused, looking at Jane. 'There you have it.'

Jane tapped her file with a pencil. 'So, you returned home, showered and got changed, when this accident occurred. But that leaves hours before you returned to the hospital, so did you call an ambulance, a doctor . . . ?'

'No, I did not. I was obviously already in a very distressed state, and this felt as if it was tipping me over the edge. I became panic-stricken because at that moment I didn't know what to do. I did stem the bleeding with a towel, but a piece of glass had cut his neck wide open. There was no pulse. He was dead.'

Jane nodded to Stanley to take over. He jotted down a note before speaking. 'Mrs Larsson, you first said Sebastian's neck was broken and then a moment later . . .' he ran his pencil down the page and looked back to her, '. . . you said a piece of glass had cut his neck open.'

'If that is what I said, that's what I remember.'

'Could you just indicate to me where you saw the cut to his neck, a cut severe enough to almost decapitate him?'

She half turned in her chair to face the wall beside her, drew back her hair and then touched the side of her neck.

'Mrs Larsson, you are indicating that the cut was high up, almost under the jaw line, is that correct?'

'No, lower down, and his head was at an angle. I also never said it decapitated him, you said that. I said it was a very deep cut.'

'Thank you. So, after this accident happened, you eventually returned to the hospital. Did you tell your husband about finding Sebastian?'

'No, because when I arrived he was very distressed. Our daughter's condition had worsened and we were told there was little hope of her recovering. We were together when she died later that night. There was nothing we could do.'

'So you left Sebastian Hoffman's body where he had fallen?'

'Yes, I had covered him with a blanket.'

'How did your husband react when he was confronted by the dead boy?'

'He was like myself, as I said earlier, already very distressed, in fact he was hysterical. He demanded that I stay in my bedroom until he had decided what to do.'

'Like call the police?' Stanley said sharply.

'No, no, we talked about that but we both felt it would be ... unhelpful.'

'Unhelpful? A sixteen-year-old boy was dead,' Stanley said sharply.

Mrs Larsson glared at him. 'He was the reason my daughter was dead. We had attempted to avoid any scandal as she was only fifteen years old. We could have been accused of taking revenge. There were no witnesses to what happened. We thought we would be arrested.' She turned to Mr Thomas again.

He nodded and turned to Jane. 'Do we need to continue, DI Tennison? My client has admitted being present at the unfortunate accident.'

Jane gave him a small, frosty smile.

'Mrs Larsson still needs to account for the considerable period of time between when she claims the accident occurred and when she returned to the hospital. First, I want to show you a photograph of how the severed head was found.' She pushed the photograph across the table. 'You can see hemp sacking wrapped around the head and tied with thin rope. We have confirmation that the cloth and rope belonged to Mrs Larsson's neighbour, Mr Martin Boon. He has admitted to wrapping the victim's head and burying it in Clarendon Court's courtyard, which, as you are aware, belongs to Mr and Mrs Larsson.'

Thomas was about to interrupt but she held up her hand. 'Please let me finish, because I want you to look at the next photograph of Sebastian Hoffman's severed head. As you can see it is tightly wrapped with silver duct tape.'

He stared at the photograph, not shocked but obviously perplexed. Again, as he was about to interject, Jane forestalled him by turning over the third photograph.

'The third photograph shows the skull and the remains of the victim's neck. After forensic testing it was determined that decapitation had been executed with a saw, at the third vertebra, leaving tiny cut marks to the bone. You just demonstrated, Mrs Larsson, that the glass had cut Mr Hoffman's neck higher up, "cut wide open" as you put it. But as you can see from the photograph, that could not have been correct, as there is no damage to the vertebrae that remained intact. However, we do have a fourth photograph showing clear evidence that blunt force was applied to the lower base of the skull.'

Mr Thomas looked unimpressed. 'I think Mrs Larsson has clearly stated that the young man fell from the open bedroom window, so surely it is very likely that the blunt-force damage would have occurred when he landed on the table.'

'And considering what state I was in at the time, asking me to remember exactly where I saw the cut to the neck is ridiculous.'

Having regained her confidence, she gave Jane a tight-lipped smile.

Jane stacked the photographs like a pack of cards.

'What time did you return from the hospital with your husband?'

'Oh, my goodness, here we go again, how many times do I have to repeat that my daughter had just died, and both my husband and I were grief-stricken.'

'Mr Boon has told us that your husband contacted him that same night and was, as you described, in a distraught state. However, that was because he was asking him to assist in the dismemberment of Sebastian Hoffman's body.'

'That is not true, that is a lie.'

'But, Mrs Larsson, you stated that your husband told you to go to bed, that he would take care of the situation. So were you present when Mr Boon came round that night?'

'No . . . no, I was not.'

'Martin Boon even described the kind of saw that was used, a Gigli saw.'

'I don't know what you are talking about.'

Jane had the faxed pages ready, showing the various types of Gigli saw. She passed them over to Mrs Larsson, who pushed them back across the table without looking at them.

'It is a saw that was used for amputations in both world wars,' Jane explained. 'It's still used by some surgeons today. It is also used by campers for cutting wood.'

'Is this saw in your possession, Inspector Tennison?' Thomas asked bluntly.

'It has not yet been recovered. Mr Boon said that later that same evening, Edward Larsson came to see him again. After he was offered a substantial amount of money, he agreed to bury the head, and it was left in his kitchen. Mrs Ellen Boon admitted to seeing it in the same location, their kitchen. He also stated that he cut some hemp sacking to put the head in and tied it with rope. He then kept the head in his garden shed until he was given twenty-five thousand pounds in cash.'

'Inspector Tennison,' Thomas began, 'everything you have just described involved Edward Larsson and their neighbour, Mr Boon, but cannot be connected to Mrs Larsson as she was not present.'

'She still needs to explain what she was doing during the time between when she left the hospital and when she returned.'

'What are you inferring occurred?' he asked.

'Before her husband's business became successful, Mrs Larsson assisted in wrapping items to be forwarded to buyers, and she was therefore adept at using duct tape. Martin Boon could not identify the victim because his head was already bound with duct tape. If you recall from the photograph, it had to have taken considerable time, the tape being wound around so many times that when the pathologist attempted to cut through the tape it had formed a quarter-inch-thick shell.'

'Inspector Tennison, may I ask if you found any fingerprints on this duct tape?'

'No, we did not.'

'Then I'm afraid all you have is supposition.'

'But if I am correct, then Sebastian Hoffman was still alive when your client found him, and was suffocated.'

Thomas pushed back in his chair, shaking his head. He was about to say something derogatory when Stanley took over. He pointed at Mrs Larsson. 'I think you were so enraged on seeing Sebastian at your daughter's bedroom window, you pushed him, and kept on pushing until he lost his footing and fell.'

'This is preposterous, do you have a single witness to back that up? Mrs Larsson clearly stated how shocked she was on seeing this boy, who was obviously as shocked as her when caught breaking in. Both you and Detective Inspector Tennison are constantly directing unproven, unsubstantiated accusations against my client, who has to my mind been completely honest about how the accident occurred and at a time when her only child was dying.'

Patricia Larsson dabbed at her tearless eyes, and Jane found herself wanting to reach over and slap her. Stanley was becoming equally frustrated. Jane sipped her beaker of water, getting her thoughts in order before continuing. She took more photographs from her file.

'Mrs Larsson, before your daughter's funeral, the men working on the courtyard were instructed to stop as the hearse and other vehicles would have damaged the freshly laid tarmac. This left an area in front of the two newly built houses, your property, Mrs Larsson, and Mr Boon's. In this area there were two potholes, one considerably larger than the other.'

Jane passed a photograph of the courtyard across the table, showing the potholes and the discovery of the sacking bag.

'You can clearly see the burial site, inside the taped-off crime scene.'

'Are we to presume this is also the location of the victim's torso?' Thomas asked.

Jane held up a hand for him to wait until she had finished.

'I am sorry if this upsets you, Mrs Larsson, but do you recall your daughter's weight when she died?'

Mrs Larsson looked at her blankly. 'No.'

'Georgina was four feet eight inches tall, and when she was examined at the post-mortem, her frame was described as skeletonised, weighing just three stone ten pounds.'

Stanley was listening intently. Jane had made no reference to this when they had worked through the files. Jane removed further photographs as she continued.

'The attendant at the hospital mortuary also remarked on the light weight of the deceased, saying he assumed it was a small child. Surely at some point, Mrs Larsson, you were made aware of your daughter's weight, were perhaps even questioned about it?'

'I have already explained about my daughter's condition, how she had been suffering from an eating disorder for many years. This was exacerbated by discovering she was pregnant, and then suffering a miscarriage. I have had many years of heartbreak. Perhaps you are not aware of just what lengths the young sufferers of this condition go to, to avoid detection.'

'I am sure it must have been very difficult,' Jane said. 'I believe you chose a casket for your daughter's remains, when she was collected from the mortuary immediately after the coroner's report was finalised. The casket was then brought to your home on 19th March, while the funeral arrangements were being finalised. The same company returned to collect the casket on 21st March.'

'That's correct.'

'So your daughter's coffin was at your home for three days and nights before the funeral.'

Mrs Larsson took a tissue from the box, making a show of dabbing her eyes, as if hardly able to deal with the memory. Stanley glanced at Jane. She had never mentioned the casket, let alone showed him any photographs of it. He was also watching Mr Thomas, who was looking at Jane, then at the photographs she had withdrawn from the file but had not yet turned over. He appeared to be trying to assess what was next in store. You and me both, thought Stanley.

Jane slowly turned over three large photographs of the coffin. One had the measurements added in felt-tipped pen; one was a side view, showing the heavy brass handles and clasps. The last showed the casket open with its white satin interior.

'Is this the casket you chose, Mrs Larsson?'

'Yes, I believe it could be.'

'You would agree that the casket is exceptionally large, considering the deceased was only four feet eight inches tall and weighed less than four stone.'

Mr Thomas pushed his chair back. 'I fail to see what this has to do with the death of Sebastian Hoffman. This whole interview is becoming a farce.'

'Just bear with me a little longer, Mr Thomas,' Jane said in a calm voice. She turned to Mrs Larsson. 'Did you love your daughter, Mrs Larsson?'

Mrs Larsson flushed. 'How dare you even ask me that! I have had enough. I am not prepared to remain here another moment. I expect you, Mr Thomas, to put an end to this immediately, to have the audacity to ask me why I chose to bury my beloved daughter in the finest . . .' She snatched at the photograph and waved it in front of Jane.

For the first time Jane raised her voice. 'You didn't bury her, Mrs Larsson; you had her cremated. And I believe you chose this specific coffin because it was large enough to contain the torso of Sebastian Hoffman as well as the remains of your daughter.'

Mrs Larsson pushed her chair back and stood up, throwing the photograph down. 'That is a lie, that is all lies!'

'Sit down, Mrs Larsson,' Stanley said firmly.

'No, I will not, I am leaving, I am not listening to any more lies.'

She then put both hands on the table leaning forwards towards Jane. 'Do you think that I would bury my beloved daughter with the bastard I blame for her death? He raped a fifteen-year-old child!'

Jane remained unfazed. 'You didn't bury her; you had her cremated. No grave, no memorial. Sit down, please, Mrs Larsson.'

Mr Thomas reached out to take Mrs Larsson's arm, but she jerked his hand free before sitting down.

He took a moment to compose himself. 'Detective Tennison, I am requesting that this interview should be suspended. That last accusation beggars belief, made with no evidence whatsoever. I was also made aware before this interview began that my client had been subjected to an horrific, emotionally distressing intrusion when forensics officers dug up her daughter's urn. You are now adding insult to injury.'

Stanley decided to try and calm the situation.

'I apologise again, as I did when I was present when this regrettable incident occurred.'

Jane calmly collected the photographs scattered over the table and placed them back in the file.

Mrs Larsson was now completely back in control. 'It felt as if they had abused my simple need to be near to my daughter. It was incredibly traumatic.'

'Of course,' Thomas murmured. This time his comforting pat was accepted and she touched his hand.

'Thank you. Please let this be an end. I really don't think I can cope with any further questions.'

Jane closed her file. 'Just one more, Mrs Larsson. What did you do with the contents of the urn?'

'What do you think I did with them? I am waiting until I can find a suitable place for her to rest in peace.'

'I doubt the bin would be that suitable a place, Mrs Larsson.'

It was as if a blast of ice-cold air had just hit the room. Mrs Larsson became rigid, her hands curled into fists as she spat out in a fury, 'Just what exactly do you mean by that?'

'It's the truth, though, isn't it, Mrs Larsson? You and your husband were so intent on emptying the contents of the urn into the trash bin in your kitchen, you didn't notice there was a witness. I believe the only reason you didn't also put Sebastian's head in the coffin is because it would have added too much extra weight.'

Mrs Larsson glared at her. 'You liar, you have lied and tortured me because that is not true. This so-called witness has to be lying because I did not do that.'

'I am the witness, Mrs Larsson. I saw you both emptying the urn into the trash bin in your kitchen. I believe you were both afraid the contents might be examined because you had put Sebastian Hoffman's torso into the casket that also held the remains of your daughter.'

Mrs Larsson's scream was so loud that the interview door was opened a fraction by the uniformed officer outside. The terrible screeching sound continued as the hysterical woman launched herself across the table in an attempt to grab hold of Jane. She was held back by Ewan Thomas, who was struck and scratched across his face. She was kicking and screaming abuse, trying to overturn the table. Stanley quickly rushed round to help restrain her, but then as suddenly as she had started, she gave up, lifting both her wrists out in front of her. A shocked Ewan Thomas pressed a tissue to the deep scratch on his face as Stanley took out his handcuffs. Mrs Larsson was gasping for breath, slowly calming down, with a blank expression on her face. For the first time she was no longer putting on the act of a grieving mother, an act she had perfected over the years. As the pretence and bravado dissipated, it left a woman finally caught by her lies.

'She won in the end, they burned together,' she said bitterly. 'Apart from his head, of course. That fool Martin Boon blackmailed my husband, then brought all this crashing down because of where he buried it.'

Jane stood up. 'Mr Thomas, I must inform you that Patricia Larsson will be charged with the murder of Sebastian Hoffman.'

* * *

It was another two hours before Jane and Stanley were able to return to the incident room. Between them they prepared the charges for Martin Boon, his wife and Edward Larsson. They were just waiting for confirmation of the time they would be taken to the magistrates' court the following morning. By now they were both utterly exhausted.

'You certainly pulled a rabbit out of the hat with all the stuff about the ashes and the casket,' Stanley said with a grin. 'Might not be so easy to prove it all at trial, though,' he added.

Jane shrugged. 'We'll be ready for it.'

'One question, though. If she was smart enough to use the large coffin, why dismember the body?'

'The weight of the head, Stanley. It might have just been enough to make somebody suspicious. You know, if Martin Boon hadn't been so anxious, and with time against him because of the tarmac being finished, we would never have even begun the investigation.'

'Right, they almost got away with it, if not for you. Oh yes, and there was that stroke of luck with that digger . . .'

She raised an eyebrow as she picked up her briefcase. 'I would advise we make no reference to that as we never caught the burglars. Do you mind giving Hutton the details? I need to take off. There's something I need to do before this hits the press. I'll be in first thing in the morning.'

Chapter Thirty-Seven

Jane parked outside Angelica's flat, hoping that she was in. She knew Hutton would be giving a press statement that evening and wanted to talk to Angelica first. She headed up the stone staircase and was just approaching the flat when the door swung open. 'Oh, hello,' Angelica said with a smile. 'I was just leaving for a session with Vera.'

'I'll give you a lift,' Jane said, 'but first I need to have a talk. Can we go inside?'

Angelica hesitated. 'Vera would not appreciate me being late. It's her evening group session.'

'I won't be long, I promise,' Jane said, ushering Angelica back into her flat.

Angelica took off her coat, folding it over her arm and sitting on the edge of a chair as Jane sat opposite. Jane took a deep breath, almost afraid to meet Angelica's eyes.

'I have confirmation that Sebastian died four years ago. He did return to England. He went straight to visit Georgina Larsson who was very sick and had been taken to hospital. He tried to see her by climbing up to her bedroom window but tragically fell to his death.' She was not going to mention that they believed Sebastian was pushed by Mrs Larsson. 'I am deeply sorry, and I promise you that as soon as it is possible, I will return his guitar to you and answer any further questions you may have about the circumstances of Sebastian's death. I have made a list of people for you to contact and will ensure that you are supported. And if you need to talk to me I will of course always be available.'

After Patricia Larsson's lies and deceit, acting the part of a grief-stricken mother, Angelica's quiet acceptance was heart-wrenching. She took a moment before she was able to speak.

'Thank you for coming to see me.' She gave Jane a sad, sweet smile. 'I think I knew when you showed me his guitar.' She paused. 'Now I do need to be with Vera.'

'Yes, of course.'

They left together. Jane held her hand as they went down the stairs, then helped her into the passenger seat. She remained silent during the drive, but when Jane drew into Vera's driveway she asked if she would come inside with her. Already exhausted from the long day, it was the last thing Jane wanted to do, but she could not refuse.

Vera's daughter was in her usual position in the hallway. She told them the session had already begun, but opened her purse to accept the money from Jane. She then asked them to wait while she went to the door, inching it open, whispered something to Vera, and then gestured for them to come in.

'Go in and sit at the back.'

Jane recognised three of the people from her previous session. Vera hooked a finger for Jane to come close.

'You've got a bloody nerve. One word out of place and you are out of here.'

She had her usual heavy make-up, eyes ringed with black kohl and her cheeks rouged, with deep-red lipstick. Her hair was loose to her shoulders but with a butterfly clip to one side. She was wearing the same kaftan. She started talking to the two elderly sisters, describing a small dachshund that had been a family pet. The sisters were nodding and becoming tearful.

'Your father's suggesting you should think about getting a puppy,' Vera said.

The room felt very stuffy, and Jane was struggling to keep her eyes open. Vera moved on to the elderly gentleman seated in front of Jane. His daughter had come forwards, and Vera spent some time explaining that he had been a constant support during her fatal illness.

Jane straightened her back, wondering how long the evening was going to continue, when Vera suddenly stopped. She appeared unsettled, gulping from her water glass that Jane knew probably contained straight gin. Vera began scribbling in her notebook, making frantic circles and then screwing up her face before she looked up.

'I have someone coming forwards ... I hear singing, I don't know this song ... ah, yes, I can hear clearer now, love me tender, love me true, all my dreams fulfilled ... he's stepping forwards and is with me now, his name begins with an S.'

Angelica stood up. 'It's my son. It's Sebastian.'

Vera was sweating. She coughed, and her tongue protruded, as if she tasted something unpleasant. She took another long drink from her glass.

'Yes, I have Sebastian with me, he has crossed over, and oh, wait, he has someone with him. She's tiny, he's very protective towards her, she has a sweet perfume, the smell of flowers, that's strange, is it lilac? He's stepping back ... no, wait. He's showing me a beating heart.'

Angelica smiled. 'Sebastian ...'

Vera made a strange gesture with her hand, touching around her head, frowning, then took a deep breath. She put both hands to her face as if she was pressing something down inside her.

'He wants you to know he is at peace now. He loves you. He's stepping back again.'

Everyone knew that when Vera said 'stepping back' their visitation was over, and they should not ask for more information. It was also obvious to everyone that Vera was exhausted, her face glistening with perspiration, and she was eager for the session to end. Her daughter opened the door to usher everyone out. They thanked Vera on the way, but she was not reacting very much, just nodding and smiling. Angelica and Jane were the last to leave the room. Angelica touched Vera's hand, thanking her tearfully, and Vera gently lifted her hand to kiss it.

'He's crossed over now, dear. I don't know who the little creature was he brought with him, but he'll come again soon. He'll be
able to come back now and not be so shy.'

'Thank you so much, my prayers have been answered.'

Angelica went out, and Jane was about to follow when Vera
heaved herself up out of her chair.

'I'm getting too old nowadays, it takes it out of me, I'm feeling poorly all the time. I tasted blood in my mouth again, which
means that poor boy was murdered. You take it easy, love. You got
something inside you that makes you very brave, but you watch
it doesn't destroy you. Now you know he's free, and that's down
to you.'

Jane nodded. 'Goodnight, Vera, take care.'

Angelica was not outside the house, and Jane presumed she had
gone off with other people from the session as she had the previous time they had been there. She was relieved, not wanting to talk
about what she had just witnessed. On the drive home she went
over it all in her mind. Part of her wanted to believe that Vera was
able to talk to the dead. But the sceptical part of her suspected it
was all clever manipulation. Did it really matter? she wondered.
She had seen the joy in Angelica's face when Vera had said Sebastian was at peace.

The following morning Jane was first up to the canteen and had
breakfast before going into the incident room. There was a large box
on her desk wrapped in brown paper with an envelope attached.
Opening the envelope, she found a note from Paul Lawrence:

*We have the original here at the lab, and we made two further
casts. You may want to retain this for your investigation.*

Jane carefully opened the box, putting the lid to one side. The white
plaster cast was wrapped in fine tissue paper. Gently easing the cast
out, then removing the last layer of tissue, she placed it on her desk.

Jane was so lost in thought, she didn't notice Stanley walking up to her desk. She physically jumped when he leaned forwards.

'Is this Sebastian?'

'Yes, this is Sebastian.'

'Dear God, I didn't realise how young he was.'

They looked at Sebastian together, then carefully repacked the case. It would be taken to the lock-up alongside all the other items they would require as evidence for the forthcoming trials. Jane wondered if Angelica would want it, along with the guitar. She thought perhaps when the time came she would ask her, but at the present moment they had more pressing issues to deal with.

The forensic teams had completed their search at the Larssons' property and the tent, along with all their equipment, had been removed. The dug-up area of the tarmac had been resurfaced.

Months later, the Caplans moved to Florida and the new owners of the property moved in with their four children. There had been a point when the sale almost didn't go through due to the gruesome publicity, but the situation had been dealt with, presumably by reducing the price.

It took many months to prepare for the trials, and much of the work involved Jane. Due to her diligence and relentless focus, the prosecution team felt confident in going for a murder verdict against Patricia Larsson. Working tirelessly, Jane rarely thought about her private life – or the fact she didn't really have one. The time when she thought about Eddie or what their future might have held was long past. Her neat and tidy house had begun to feel unlived in. The enormous pressure of work leading up to the trials meant she had made only a couple of visits to her parents at weekends, and although they asked about the case, since it had been headline news, she told them as little as possible.

Shortly before the trial dates were confirmed, Jane took a Saturday off to buy a new wardrobe of smart suits, blouses and, instead of her usual Cuban-heeled court shoes, an expensive pair of black stilettos. She was now wearing one of her new purchases on the last Monday before the trials were due to start. DCI Hutton had left a note on her desk asking Jane to see her as soon as she came into the station.

Jane was surprised when her husband opened the door.

'You've met my husband, I think,' Hutton said.

'Superintendent,' Jane nodded.

'Nice to see you again,' he smiled.

He really was a very handsome man, and she almost blushed as he excused himself and left the office.

'Sit down, please,' Hutton said. 'I want to talk to you now, because when the trials get underway you will be extremely busy and I wouldn't want you distracted. Firstly, I want to tell you something very private, which for the moment I want kept that way.' She paused. 'I am pregnant, which is the reason my husband has been seen popping in frequently, to check that I am not overdoing it.'

Jane couldn't help feeling envious. Not only did she have the most handsome husband, but she was pregnant.

'I have had two miscarriages,' Hutton went on, 'and he . . . well, both of us . . . were concerned it might happen again, but so far, touch wood, I'm fine. I do intend to continue working for as long as possible, but that is not the reason I've asked to see you. I have been so impressed with your professional ability, and I am recommending you for promotion. I also feel that you would be the right person to take over this station. There is a possibility I will return after maternity leave, but that is a long way ahead. Jane, I think you have a huge career ahead of you, and I count myself lucky to have you here at the station.'

Jane was so taken aback she didn't know what to say. 'Thank you, ma'am. I . . . I wish you good health and all the best for the baby. I promise I won't mention it to anyone.' She grinned. 'But I might not be able to say the same about my promotion.'

Returning to the incident room, she found it difficult to stop smiling, she was so proud of what Hutton had said about her. As she passed Stanley, he swivelled round in his desk chair.

'My, my, you look happy. Get laid last night, did you?'

'Chance would be a fine thing, Stanley.' She gave him a twirl. 'What do you think of the outfit? I'm testing it out before my court appearances.'

'You look like a million dollars,' he said with a grin. 'We're going to knock them dead, Jane.'

Drawing out her desk chair, she was still smiling as she picked up a pen, opening a blank page of her notebook. She wrote in block capitals DETECTIVE CHIEF INSPECTOR JANE TENNISON.

It looked good.

Acknowledgements

I would like to thank Nigel Stoneman and Tory Macdonald, the team I work with at La Plante Global.

All the forensic scientists and members of the Met Police who help with my research. I could not write without their valuable input.

Cass Sutherland for his valuable advice on police procedures and forensics.

The entire team at my publisher, Bonnier Books UK, who work together to have my books edited, marketed, publicised and sold. A special thank you to Kate Parkin, Ben Willis, Bill Massey and Isabella Boyne for their great editorial advice and guidance.

Blake Brooks, who has introduced me to the world of social media, and Holly Milnes for her support with this – my Facebook Live sessions have been so much fun. Nikki Mander who manages my PR and makes it so easy and enjoyable.

The audio team, Jon Watt, Laura Makela and Chelsea Graham for bringing my entire backlist to a new audience in audiobooks and creating brilliant new audiobooks, too. Thanks also for giving me my first podcast series, *Listening to the Dead*, which can be downloaded globally.

Allen and Unwin in Australia and Jonathan Ball in South Africa – thank you for doing such fantastic work with my books.

All the reviewers, journalists, bloggers and broadcasters who interview me, write reviews and promote my books. Thank you for your time and work.

ENTER THE WORLD OF

Lynda La Plante

ALL THE LATEST NEWS FROM
THE QUEEN OF CRIME DRAMA

DISCOVER THE THRILLING TRUE
STORIES BEHIND THE BOOKS

ENJOY EXCLUSIVE CONTENT
AND OPPORTUNITIES

JOIN THE READERS' CLUB TODAY AT
WWW.LYNDALAPLANTE.COM

Dear Reader,

Thank you very much for picking up *Taste of Blood*, the ninth book in the Tennison series. I hope you enjoyed reading the book as much as I enjoyed writing it.

In the book, Jane has been stationed back in Bromley, and she begins to fear she's made a big mistake. Yes, it's closer to her home, but she's now wondering if any serious crimes are ever committed in this small Kentish town. Especially since the first case she's assigned to involves nothing more dramatic than an altercation between neighbours over a disputed property boundary. But Jane senses something more sinister – buried secrets these neighbours will do anything to protect. Why was Martin Boon so adamant that David Caplan shouldn't install a new set of gates when they wouldn't encroach on his own property? Of course, Jane decides to dig deeper, and soon uncovers a shocking crime. I loved writing *Taste of Blood* and I hope you love reading it! It will certainly make you look at your own neighbours a little differently . . .

If you enjoyed *Taste of Blood*, then please do keep an eye out for news about the next book in the series, which will be coming soon. In the meantime, later this year sees the reissue of the second book in my Trial and Retribution series, *Alibi*, which I am very excited to share more news about soon.

The first four books in the Jack Warr series – *Buried*, *Judas Horse*, *Vanished* and *Pure Evil* – are available now. And if you want to catch up with the Tennison series, the first eight novels – *Tennison*, *Hidden Killers*, *Good Friday*, *Murder Mile*, *The Dirty Dozen*, *Blunt Force*, *Unholy Murder* and *Dark Rooms* – are all available to buy in paperback, ebook and audio. I've been so pleased by the response I've had from the many readers who have been curious about the beginnings of Jane's police career. It's been great fun for me to explore how she became the woman we know in middle and later life from the *Prime Suspect* series. It's been a pleasure to revisit the Trial and Retribution series after its television success and I am thrilled to return to it in print – the first book in the series is available to buy now.

If you would like more information on what I'm working on, about the Jane Tennison thriller series or the new series featuring Jack Warr, you can visit **www.bit.ly/LyndaLaPlanteClub** where you can join my Readers' Club. It only takes a few moments to sign up, there are no catches or costs and new members will automatically receive an exclusive message from me. Zaffre will keep your data private and confidential, and it will never be passed on to a third party. We won't spam you with loads of emails, just get in touch now and again with news about my books, and you can unsubscribe any time you want. And if you would like to get involved in a wider conversation about my books, please do review *Taste of Blood* on Amazon, on GoodReads, on any other e-store, on your own blog and social media accounts, or talk about it with friends, family or reader groups! Sharing your thoughts helps other readers, and I always enjoy hearing about what people experience from my writing.

With many thanks again for reading *Taste of Blood*, and I hope you'll return for the next in the series.

With my very best wishes,

Lynda